Icarus

He was a mortal with aspirations.

One thing we must remember is this:

All

Mortals

Fall

Eventually.

BURN WITH ME

GODS OF HAZELWOOD: ICARUS 1

LUCY SMOKE

CONTENTS

In loving memory of my grandfather.
My number one supporter.

I loved you as
        Icarus loved
        The sun—

Too close,
        Too much.

— David Jones, *Icarus in Love*

INTRODUCTION

Icarus was no God. He was a mortal with aspirations. A genius. A perfect specimen who desired to attain that which was out of his reach. So he labored day and night. Under the hot sun and the frigid moon. Until his creation was complete, and then, only then, when he and his father made their escape from Crete, was the truth realized.

Three things became impossibly clear to him in the end:

One. Wings were not meant for man.

Two. Scars lasted forever.

And three. No one could reach the sun ... at least ... not without getting burned.

PROLOGUE: RORI

I t's *empty*. The hallway. The living room. My fucking bedroom. The whole house is empty. I'm standing in the center of it all, holding what is now apparently a useless set of keys and my cell phone, when the front door bangs open, followed by the telltale sound of my mother's heels clicking across the wood floor. Something insidious awakens in my gut. A curdling sense of dread that only seems to revive when she returns from wherever the hell she's been for the last several months.

"Oh good, you're here," she says as she breezes past me.

Where the fuck could she be going? is my immediate first thought. She looks like she's dressed for a goddamn gala in a long black tank dress with a slit almost all the way up her thigh. The only things making it seem even remotely casual are the big floppy black hat, the shades, and the gray shawl over her shoulders. A shawl ... in the May heat. But I know it's because she's afraid of getting sunburned; tanning ages a person, and even in her early forties, she looks closer to a twenty-five-year-old than someone who has an eighteen-year-old daughter.

"Hurry up and double-check to make sure the movers didn't leave anything behind," she calls over her shoulder as she reaches the kitchen, and I find myself drifting after her, needing answers. *'What the fuck?'* seems to be more than a question I keep asking myself; it's my new motto.

"The movers?" I repeat. "Why did we have movers? Where's our stuff? Are we going somewhere?"

My mother pulls down her shades, tossing them to the granite countertop as she reaches into the fridge and pulls out a bottled water. Over her shoulder, I note that a single case of it is all that's left. *Am I in the Twilight Zone or something?* When I left for the last day of my senior year this morning, everything had seemed normal—and by normal, I mean my mother hadn't been home in weeks, and I'd received no phone call or messages saying when she'd be coming back. To us, *that* was normal.

This is not.

"Yes, we're going somewhere," my mother says. Ignoring my first two questions, she sets her bottled water on the counter and then thrusts her left hand in my face. It takes me a moment to realize that she's trying to shove the giant diamond sitting on her ring finger toward my eyes as if I could miss the damn thing, especially now that it's front and center to my vision.

"What did you do?" The words come from my throat like glass shards being pulled from a wound. Dizziness assails me. My stomach sinks, and then, as if she doesn't hear the horror in my voice, she says the words I've always come to hate.

"I got married!"

This is not happening. My mother pulls her hand

back, the sound of her heels clicking across the floor as she moves away.

"Now, hurry up and check the house. We're flying out to California in a few hours."

"California?" My voice sounds like it's coming from miles away, but one thing I do know is that her voice doesn't get any quieter—it remains the same steady volume, which must mean that I'm following behind her even though I can no longer feel my legs. "Why are you going to California?"

I know why I would—I'm *supposed* to go to California. In two months, to be precise. Because in two months, I'll be joining my brother at Hazelwood University, one of the premiere colleges in the world, exclusive to the upper echelon. But she was never supposed to go. She was supposed to stay here.

My mother's face comes into view again and I blink, catching sight of the open front door, and realize we're at the entrance again. She laughs and reaches forward, tucking a flyaway hair behind my ear. It's one of her rare maternal quirks. "Oh, sweetie," she says, "because we're moving there. Damien's businesses are based there—he's so amazing, oh! I just can't wait for you to meet him. And isn't it great that he's based in California? You and I will be able to spend more time together even though you'll be going to college. It'll be like nothing has changed."

With that, she pats my cheek, turns around, and disappears out the front door again, like she didn't just barge back into my life like a whirlwind tornado and wreck all of my carefully laid plans. Plans that I've had in place for months—months that she's been MIA, off doing whatever it is she does when she gets a bug up her ass and wants to go travel and play tourist or meet up with a friend in Tokyo. She's never given a fuck that she has two kids. The second she deemed us old enough to no longer need nannies, we've been on our own, and for the last three years—ever since my brother went off to college, it's just been me.

But this ... this is a game changer. I know how she is. Every time she does this—every single fucking time she gets married—she suddenly transforms into this big family-minded woman who wants nothing more than to shove her latest conquest down my throat.

After the handsy producer who thought fifteen-year-old stepdaughters were fair game, my brother put his foot down. He beat him to a pulp and has refused to meet another since. This is my turn. This is *not* happening, and if I have to dredge up the past and remind her why, I will.

1

ISAAC

Alcohol swims through my veins, wreaking havoc wherever it goes. Its destructiveness fogs over my mind. And for the first time in forever, it's enough to numb the pain—though just barely.

"Don't you think you've had enough?" Paris asks, arching his brow, the light glinting off his piercing with the movement. It's not like him to be so fucking prudish at a party. Why he's gotta choose tonight of all nights to be responsible is beyond me.

I don't even bother with a response. Instead, I just let the bottle in my hand go flying in the direction of his head. The responding inhale of breath and the shattering of glass against the backyard patio a split second later are the first part of my reward.

The second part is the dark curse that spits from his lips. "Are you fucking serious?" I hear him say. "I know you're in a shit mood, but you're lucky I don't knock your dumb ass out for that."

Shit mood is putting it lightly. Rather than getting drunk off my ass and taking my fury out on my best friend, I'd rather find my shitstain of a father and wrap my hands around his neck until he's long gone from this godforsaken world.

The sound of footsteps on the stone walkway of the garden estate echoes up the hedges into the secret alcove, and a looming dark figure appears. "What is he doing now?" Shepherd's deep baritone reaches my ears, but his question makes me snort.

My head rolls back on my shoulders, and I realize that I've closed my eyes, so I open them and look up into Paris' angry blue gaze as he bends over the top of my chair, looking ready to follow through on his threat.

"He's being a fucking dick," Paris snaps, answering the question and glaring me down all in the same instant.

Another snort escapes my lips. "What?" I ask, the image of him wavering in my vision. "You want me to say 'I'm sorry?'" I shake my head. Sober me might have. Drunk me, however? Drunk me is a fucking asshole that just wants to lob another fucking bottle at someone's head.

Paris continues to glare down at me. "If you're gonna be like this, why don't you crash here or find your own ride home?" he asks. "Because I'm two seconds from being done with you tonight."

"No, let's just take him home." Shep's words get my ass moving.

Pushing myself up from the lounge chair, I waver on my feet before regaining my balance. "Fuck no," I argue. "I'm gonna go back to the house and get laid."

"Yeah?" Paris looks me over as he crosses his arms over his chest. "You really think that's gonna happen, whiskey dick?"

"Fuck you!" I throw out the curse, but I don't mean it.

I know I'm just talking through my ass. He's right—with the amount of alcohol I've consumed, there's no doubt I won't be able to get it up for shit tonight. Fact is, I don't even want to get laid. I just don't want to go home. Not when I know that fucker is there.

Paris sighs and lowers his arms before moving towards me. "Come on, Isaac," he says. "Let's just go back for the night. We'll even crash on your floor if you want."

Shep moves in to my right and grabs an arm, lifting it over his shoulder. He doesn't say anything to Paris' offer, but I know he'll do it. I lower my head and inhale. Fuck, I really don't want to go back. I don't want to do this shit.

"Isaac?" Paris repeats my name.

"*Shit.*" I hiss the word through gritted teeth. "Fine." I don't know if the two of them are relieved or what, but the second they get my drunken approval, Shep and Paris practically whip my ass out of the garden and start up the steps making our way around the big mansion towards the parking lot.

Before I know it, I'm being pushed into the backseat of Shep's Hummer. The engine roars to life and the sound of the two front doors snapping shut reaches my ears. I lay down long ways on the backseat, one foot propped at the edge and the other flat on the floorboards. I throw one arm over my eyes to block out the street lights as they pass over my face with every passing mile.

I'm so quiet, Paris must assume I've fallen asleep because after several minutes go by, I hear the creak of leather on his side of the vehicle before he starts talking in a low tone. "He's real upset about the wedding shit," he says. "He hasn't gotten this drunk in a while."

My teeth grind together at the mention of it. "It

doesn't help that Damien's back for the time being," Shep grunts from the driver's side.

Paris' seat creaks again. "What do you think he's going to do?"

"Isaac or Damien?" Shep prompts.

"Fuck, I don't know," Paris replies. "Isaac?"

"Don't know."

"And Damien?"

"Don't know," Shep repeats. A man of few words— he's my damn favorite right now. I wish Paris would shut the fuck up. I can feel myself sobering up, and it's not a good feeling. The more time that passes, the clearer my head gets. The more I remember what's waiting for me through the doors of the Icari estate.

Paris and Shep grow quiet for the rest of the drive and after a while, I feel the familiar slow of the car as we come to a stop in front of the gates of my childhood home. Shep's window rolls down and he leans out, inputting the code he's known for years. There's a pause as he waits for the gates to slide open and then we're on the move again.

I don't sit up until the car comes to a complete stop and Shep turns off the engine. "You good?" Paris glances back at me as I turn and look up at the three-story mansion I've both revered and hated for fucking years.

Although it's well past midnight, there are lights on. Of course there are. For a man like Damien Icari, business never sleeps and neither does he.

"Yeah." I deadpan. "I'm just peachy." Then, before Paris can ask another stupid question, I slide to the edge of the seat and open my door. "Let's go."

The three of us make our way to the front door and head into the house. Already, my father's men are hard at work—it's like that shit never stops in this house.

Two months, I think. Two months and I'll be free—relatively speaking anyway. At the very least, I'll be able to escape to Hazelwood University with Paris and Shep.

"Isaac." I freeze at the bottom of the staircase leading up to my room, and at my side, both of my friends do the same. Slowly, I pivot back to face the man that called my name.

My father steps out of his office dressed in a three-piece pinstripe suit. It's so cliché it almost makes me laugh. A fucking modern mobster hiding behind his businesses is still just a mobster.

"Come." That's all he has to say and I'm no longer even somewhat intoxicated. It's like he sucks all of it right out of me. I'm stone cold sober.

I inhale sharply and shoot a look at Paris and Shep. "Go on ahead," I tell them. "I'll be up in a minute."

Loyal friends that they are—and knowing what they do—they each glance between my father and me, silently asking … but I just shake my head. No doubt, all he wants to do is remind me to behave myself when his new wife arrives tomorrow.

I turn down the hallway and follow my father back into his office. The door shuts behind me and I feel like I'm being locked in a prison cell. My father waits until he circles his desk and takes his seat before speaking.

"There has been a change of plans," he states, reaching into the right-side drawer of his desk and withdrawing a small metal box. He pops it and withdraws an uncut cigar. My eyebrows lift slightly. Of all things, I didn't expect this.

I rock back on my feet, feeling my mood slowly shift. Slowly improving. "Has she rethought the marriage?" I can't help but ask.

My father's gaze shoots to me, a glare of warning in its depths. "*She. Has. Not.*" The vehemence in his words leads me to believe otherwise, but I keep my mouth shut as he snips the end of his cigar, puts it between his lips, and lights it. Smoke curls up from the flaring red end as he shakes the match and the flame goes out.

"Her daughter, on the other hand, is not as accepting of the union," he continues. "She's apparently refusing to come and Emilia is attempting to persuade her."

Smart girl.

"Then she won't be arriving tomorrow?" I ask.

"No." One word and yet it holds all of the obvious irritation he's barely restraining. "I've spent months seducing Emilia Summers, and she will be my wife," he goes on after a moment. "This is merely a setback. From what I understand, she's not close with her son. He hasn't spoken to her in three years. I hadn't considered that her daughter's opinion would mean that much to her."

"Of course not," I say with a nod. Just as much as my opinion matters to him—which would be not at fucking all.

"There is some good news, however." My father inhales another puff of his cigar and leans back in his chair. "The girl will be attending Hazelwood next fall."

The slow snake of dread crawls up my throat. My mind runs a million miles per minute, trying to piece together the meaning behind his words before he says them.

"In two months' time," he continues, "Emilia's daughter will be a student at Hazelwood. My relationship with her mother is of the utmost importance in the coming year, Isaac. I'll need someone to watch her." He lowers his head. "Very carefully."

My jaw unhinges and drops. "You're joking."

Dark brows lower over his eyes and my back straightens automatically. Fear is always something my father has been a master at invoking. Even now, grown as I am, it's an effort just to keep my gaze level with his. "She's nobody," I say quickly, bypassing the earlier comment. "A spoiled socialite probably attending Hazelwood with the thought of finding a husband of the same class. There's no need to watch her."

"That is not for you to decide, *Son*." I swallow reflexively when he ashes his cigar into a crystal tray on the side of his desk. "If I say you are to watch her, then that means you do it. You do not question my judgment here."

My teeth grind into each other, my jaw locking tight as I withhold the slew of curses that threaten to spill forward. "When?" is all I manage to get out after several seconds of utter silence.

"At the start of the semester," he answers. "You will move into a location I have provided. You will live with Emilia Summers' daughter. You will watch her and you will report back to me. With Emilia staying with her over the summer at some resort in Macau, I'll have to push back the honeymoon, but it won't matter."

A thought fills my mind, and though I don't want to make this meeting any longer than it has to be, I can't stop the question from coming forward. "You've planned the Summers' Industry takeover," I begin. "Why do you think it's necessary for me to watch the daughter? What could she possibly do to stop it now?"

My father watches me with a careful gaze. Thankfully, though, it's not angry. He ashes his cigar once more and then sets it within the tray before leaning forward and steepling his hands together to rest his chin upon them.

"I do not like wild cards, Isaac," he states. "Emilia was predictable until now. She's left her daughter alone for months at a time, with little more than maids and cooks to look after her. It could be cold feet. It could also be her daughter's influence. I want to know. A businessman must plan for every contingency, my son, and above all—never let a woman control you. They always manage to become great weaknesses when you care. Remember that, and make sure you keep an eye on her."

"Yes, Sir." Saying the words is the start of my dismissal. I turn and head back into the hallway. Once I'm out of his presence, my body takes on a mind of its own. My hands clench into fists and my upper lip curls back from my teeth. All of the expressions I couldn't reveal in his presence come to the forefront.

Businessman? Fucking right. Damien Icari is no businessman. On paper he may be a genius—an inventor, the CEO of one of the fastest growing conglomerates in the world. Few know of its illusion, and I am one of them.

Emilia Summers is a fucking idiot for not seeing what a conniving bastard my father is. No woman in her right mind would marry Damien Icari if they knew what he really is—what our family really is.

Insidious.

Deviant.

Criminal.

And she just walked right into his trap.

2

RORI

2 months later…

I hate going to places like *Cornelia's* where the dress code is *rich-casual*. They make my skin feel itchy. Anything less than designer will have the maître d' turning up his nose and telling you that there's a lovely fast food restaurant just down the road a few miles that would be more appropriate. But here I am, stuffed like a Thanksgiving turkey into a Tory Burch dress borrowed from my mother's extensive closet when I'd rather be in a pair of ripped jeans and Converse moving into Hazelwood's dorms with my best friends.

Why? Because I've put it off as long as I could, and now that school is starting next week, I've run out of excuses to avoid meeting her new husband.

"Oh, there he is!" My mother squeals and abandons me. Before said maître d' can stop her, she runs through the restaurant like an unrestrained child. I'd use the opportunity to escape if I thought I could get away with it. Instead, I just check my phone for the hundredth time in the last ten minutes. Still no response. He must be driving. Hopefully, that means he's almost here.

Regretfully, I force myself to trail after my mother to where two men stand side by side. She fawns over the taller, older one of the two, going onto her already-heeled toes to kiss him. I can feel the bile threatening to shoot up my throat. Her lack of attention, however, gives me a moment to analyze the two of them myself.

Damien Icari is a man of massive size—a wide frame covered in a pin-striped suit with a silver tie at his throat and the shadow of a beard covering the lower half of his face. He pours all of his attention into my mother, his lips stretching into what looks like an ill-used smile. Anyone looking on would probably sigh with jealousy at how much attention he pays her, but even from the distance I'm at, it feels disingenuous. I shift my attention from him to the man at his side.

The second I do, however, something hits me deep in the chest. It's not a physical blow, but something far more powerful. My gaze connects with his and lightning shoots through me. He's just as tall as Damien, though not as broad, with cool-toned icy eyes that give him the appearance of visceral awareness as well as boredom. How that's possible, I'm not sure. Still, I'm struck by a feeling of uncertainty, of being watched—like a mouse before a blue-eyed snake. I don't like it at all.

"You must be the famous Aurora I've heard so much about." Damien's deep baritone makes me jump ever so slightly, and he moves forward, offering his hand. Even though I already don't like the man, I appreciate the distraction.

I stare down at his open palm for a moment before reluctantly taking it. "I prefer Rori."

The corners of his eyes crinkle as his smile widens. "It's nice to finally be introduced, Aurora." I scowl as he ignores my words and says my full name. I knew there was going to be a reason I didn't like him, I just didn't expect it to happen so quickly. I was quite ready to just be the asshole who simply hated her mother's new husband simply because he was just another in a long line of men that had come before. "This is my son, Isaac." Damien Icari releases my hand and gestures to the man that gave me that uncertain feeling.

My attention returns to the snake. Unlike his father, Isaac Icari has the look of a sun-kissed God rather than something from the underworld. Where his father's hair has both the color and shine of ink and is slicked straight back, Isaac's hair is golden with several various shades of blond and brown littered throughout the strands. It curls over his forehead in an almost casual shaggy sort of way. If my brother let his hair grow out at the sides, I have no doubt it'd look similar. Still ... despite the warmth of his features, his eyes are a frost-covered wasteland. More so than I've ever seen before.

It makes me curious and curiosity is dangerous, especially in situations like this.

Isaac leans down and holds out his hand. "It's nice to meet you." *Lie.* He smiles, but it's sharp at the edges.

I don't take his hand, and instead, leave it hanging in the air. *I don't want to be here. Fuck this shit. I want out.*

As if sensing my internal dialogue, my mother shoots me a warning glare. I release a pent-up sigh and reluctantly hold my hand out. He takes it, but instead of shaking it and letting it go as I expect, he holds it just long enough to be uncomfortable and my eyes jerk up to meet his once again.

"I look forward to our time together," he says coolly, holding my attention captive.

My lips part in surprise. There's no mistaking his words. The way he says them almost makes it sound like he's threatening me, letting me know not to get too comfortable.

"Likewise," I reply, adding an edge to my own tone. A warning. I don't know what he expects from me, but if he thinks I'm like my mother—he's in for a rude awakening, and I intend to make sure he knows that.

The second he releases me, I drop my hand and rub it against the fabric of my dress as if to wipe off the residual essence of him. I don't like the way he continues to watch me—like a lion watching prey.

Where the fuck is Marcus?

Thankfully, that thought seems to make him materialize out of thin air because no sooner have I asked myself that question than my phone buzzes against my hip inside of the dangling black Hermés purse I'm carrying. A true smile crosses my lips.

"Shall we sit?" my mother asks, moving to the table.

"We're waiting for one more person," I announce with a smile, reaching into my bag and pulling out my phone just to be sure, but I don't even have an opportunity to check the message because he's already here.

And it's so fucking worth it to see my mother's face blanch a split second before she whips around and hisses my way. "Aurora Dawn Summers," she growls, "you invited *him?*"

With a tight smile, I tilt my head to the side and slide my phone back into my purse with a shrug. "He is your son, Mom," I state. "Don't you want him to meet your new *husband?*" Without waiting for an answer, I turn to the man in question. "I hope you don't mind, but my brother will be joining us." I make it clear from my tone that I truly could not give a shit less if he minds. It's too late now, anyway.

Damien's face morphs into a careful mask of affability, the kind I've seen dozens of times before. Every man she marries has one—the face they all wear when they're being polite, but inside, they probably want to do something that would ruin their sparkling reputation.

That's right, I silently tell him. *Keep that mask on, buddy. We'll see just how long you can last.*

"I thought we talked about this," my mother says in a horrified whisper, panicking. "I wanted to wait until after —Marcus! Sweetheart!" She cuts herself off mid-tirade and plasters on a bright smile, moving quicker than her words as she abandons her new man in favor of greeting my brother.

Marcus frowns at her approach but doesn't immediately throw our mother off, instead returning her hug with a small pat. "Mom," he says cordially.

"It's *so* good to see you," she gushes before shooting me another scathing glare. "I wish I would've known you were coming."

Marcus looks my way with amusement, and I shrug noncommittally. He shakes his head, one corner of his mouth twitching as he pushes her back. "Wouldn't miss it," he says. "Have you already ordered?"

"No, of course not." I bite my lip to keep from laughing as my mother, in a rare moment of awkwardness, takes a step back, away from my brother, and glances from the table to Marcus as if she's trying to think of the best way to approach the new situation before her while also keeping up the facade of a loving, caring mother in front of her new man.

Checkmate, Mom, I think snidely. *You want to throw me into this? Well, I'm not coming alone.* I've always got the big guns on speed dial, and even though I don't particularly like to ask my brother for favors, he's got my back. And for something like this, I fucking needed it.

Damien takes this as his opportunity and slides a hand around my mother's waist as he reaches out, holding out his other hand for Marcus to take. "It's wonderful to meet Emilia's son," he begins. "I'm Damien."

"Yes," Marcus returns the handshake with a hard look. "So, I've heard." That's it. No other comment. No other polite greeting. This is going to be the longest lunch in history, but thank fuck, I'm not facing it alone.

I snort a little to myself as I leave the group to take my seat. If I try to off myself with the restaurant's butter knife, there will be at least one person at the meeting who might try to stop me. Funny ... but it doesn't make me want to do it any less, though.

Thirty minutes into the lunch and I'm ready to blow my brains out all over the eggshell tablecloth and fine china. I'm intimately aware of the underlying tension around the table, slowly but surely rising toward the surface.

"So, Marcus, what's your major?" Damien is doing his damnedest to appear as wholesome as my mother apparently thinks he is. I'm thankful, too, that I asked Marcus to come because now the new husband is putting the brunt of his questions on the luncheon's unexpected guest.

"International business," Marcus replies as he reaches forward and takes a sip from his glass.

"How interesting; my son is in the same department," Damien replies.

Isaac says nothing. Neither do Marcus nor I, for that matter.

"Wouldn't it be wonderful if you two became friends?" Mom says, her voice tight with hope. "After all, we're a family now."

My eyeball twitches. *Family? Yeah, right.* Fat chance of that happening. *Does she really think that another attempt at shoving strangers together and getting them to play nice will make this family of hers come to life?* My stomach churns as I stare down at the remains of the fancy chicken alfredo and it blurs in front of my vision. I drop my fork onto my plate and sit back, waiting for this horrible luncheon to end.

"Of course we are, darling," Damien replies, though with each passing minute, his expression becomes tighter and tighter. Almost like he expected a different outcome and is now pissed that things aren't playing out the way he predicted.

A slow smile curves my lips.

Good. I hope he realizes just how futile this whole thing is. It'll end that much quicker once he does.

Silence descends upon the table—the only sound coming from the still-clinking forks between the men and my mother's glass as she finishes off what has to be her third Chardonnay in the last half hour. She's left the wino and lush labels far behind and has quickly ushered her way straight into manic alcoholism.

Damien sets his fork and knife down on either side of his plate, drawing my attention as he sits up straight and turns his gaze to me. Oh no. Something sinister crawls up my throat. His responding smile is almost ... knowing. As if he's well aware that I don't like or trust him, and he thinks there's nothing I can do about it.

"Actually, the reason I wanted your mother to ask you here today," he begins, reaching over to take her hand, "is that I wanted to give you a gift."

Alarms sound in my mind. Warning signals. Bright, flashing neon lights. All of it urging me to get up and find a fucking exit. My back stiffens and I cut a look to Marcus out of the corner of my eyes. He's watching Damien like a careful tiger, curious, but cautious.

"I'm sure she'll love it," my mother gushes, and if my mother thinks that, then I can guarantee I won't.

"What is it?" I ask.

Damien reaches into the inner pocket of his suit coat and pulls out an envelope. *Money.* I almost lose control of myself and roll my eyes. I feel my brother soften at my side. I don't want Damien Icari's money as I'm sure it's nothing but a way to try and ingratiate himself to me, but when he holds it out, I take it nonetheless. Maybe I can pass it off to his son or just leave it on the table for the waitress. If it's just cash, though, it's certainly something I can forget.

Doesn't matter if it's a hundred or a couple of thousand in this envelope. Anything he gives me probably has strings attached and I don't do strings. *Ever.*

"Open it," he insists when I go to place it under my napkin.

I blink when something jingles inside of it—something that definitely isn't paper—and confusion takes over. I feel every eye at the table on me as I slip my thumbnail into one sealed edge and rip it open. The slight weight inside slides down into my palm the second I turn the envelope and a pair of what looks like house keys as well as an elevator keycard slip into my waiting hand.

I stare down at the offering, thoroughly perplexed. "Uhhhh ... thanks?"

"Isn't it wonderful!" my mother exclaims. "Now you can be near us."

"Near ... you?" I repeat.

"It's the key to your own penthouse suite at Hotel Theós, one of my businesses. Well, virtually your own place," Damien says. "Your mother and I will be on the top floor after we get back from the honeymoon, but Isaac is rarely home and—"

I hold my hand up, interrupting him. "Wait, hold on a second," I snap. "What the hell are you talking about?" A dark look falls over his face, but I ignore it in favor of turning to my mother. I couldn't care less if he doesn't like being cut off.

"It's a key," my mother says stupidly, as if I can't fucking see what's right in front of me.

"Yes, I see that," I say through gritted teeth. "But what the hell makes you think I want to move in with you? Or with..." I turn towards Damien's son and find him staring back at me in that unnerving way of his. A shiver chases down my spine at the frosty look he gives me as if he's daring me to continue. Does he think I won't? I clench my fingers around the key and card for a moment—letting the metal and plastic bite into my skin before I force my palm open and drop it back onto the table. It clatters loudly. "No."

"Aurora." My mother's tone is horrified. "Take the key and say thank you. You're embarrassing me."

I don't fucking care. "I have a dorm room at Hazelwood," I snap back.

"Not anymore," Damien says coolly.

My head turns towards him, slowly and in jerky movements. "*Excuse. Me?*"

"I've taken the liberty of canceling your dorm accommodations," he replies, picking up his knife and fork once more before slicing into his steak. "Don't worry, though. You'll be provided for—"

"No."

At first, I think I'm the one who said it. After all, I'm practically screaming the word in my head. When Damien freezes, however, and looks up—he doesn't look at me and I realize it wasn't. Marcus levels a glare across the table, reaching out as he lets his fingers grip the edge. Something crosses between them for a moment. A battle of wills? I'm not sure. Whatever the case, though, when it ends, it's clear who's the winner.

Marcus stands and reaches for me. "We're leaving, Rori. Mother?" Mom jumps in her seat and looks up at him with wide eyes. I look away as I stand. I don't want to see it again—see her reach for her husband—a virtual stranger—rather than get up and follow her own flesh and blood. I've watched it happen far too many times and it never gets any easier.

Somehow, though, instead of finding a place in the far-off distance of the restaurant, my gaze finds Isaac's. There's neither triumph nor pity in his expression. If anything, I see an absence of both as well as an absence of *any* kind of emotion that might make more sense to a guy whose father is paying more attention to his wife's children than his own.

He tips his head down, staring at me through his blond curls and suddenly I'm struck with an image of him covered in blood. It's leaking down the side of his face, over his porcelain skin, sliding into the whites of his eyes. Somehow, I can't imagine him closing them though. He strikes me as the type to lock onto a target the second he's got it in his sights, regardless of the world around him. And right now, that target is me.

I don't hear anything else my brother says. I'm so focused on Isaac Icari that I don't even realize I'm being dragged away until I nearly stumble and go down in a heap, only saved from faceplanting on the marbled floor of *Cornelia's* by my brother's hand on my arm.

"Keep walking, Rori," he says. "Don't look back."

I suck in a breath. Those were the same words he told me the last time she got married. That night we ended up in the hospital with more faceless nurses I can only vaguely recall and Aunt Carmen. I pull my arm from his grasp and move forward, my legs eating up the distance between me and the exit.

I'm not the same as I was three years ago. I'm stronger now. Independent. Maybe I called my brother here for backup, for emotional support, but I don't need him to hold me up or drag me out. Not when I can walk away on my own two feet. Hopefully for the last time as our mother chooses someone—anyone—other than us—other than *me*.

3
ISAAC

"What do you know about Marcus Summers?" My question is aimed at Paris since he's the one who knows everything about every-fucking-one at Hazelwood.

Surprisingly, however, it's not Paris who answers, but Shepherd. "I know he's not to be fucked with," he says.

My brows shoot up. "What makes you say that?"

Shep rolls his shoulders back, leans down over the pool table in the game room of my hotel-suite apartment, and lines up his shot. He waits until he's hit the cue ball and sunk another three balls, barely scraping by the fourth and ending his turn before he responds. Paris shoots us a look but steps up to take his place while Shep and I both move back to talk.

"Marcus Summers is a man with dangerous friends," is all he adds.

Irritation slithers through me and I grip my pool stick tightly, thumping the bottom against the floor once before shooting a look his way. "Care to elaborate?" I prompt.

Shep's lips press together and he eyes the table as

Paris leans over and lines up his shot. If I didn't know any better, I'd say he was ignoring me. But I know better; he has to focus on something mundane when he's thinking. The longer the silence stretches, though, the tighter my muscles grow. Winding and winding until one mere flick might shatter the tension until finally...

"Marcus Summers isn't from the West Coast," Shep states.

I frown, waiting, but when he doesn't immediately follow up with anything else, I blow out a frustrated breath. "What does that have to do with anything?"

Paris finishes up his shot and turns towards us. "It means he likely went to school on the East Coast," he answers for him. "And who do we know that runs the East Coast?" He arches a single brow, and I could punch myself for being so stupid. Of course.

"Eastpoint." The mere word has both Shep and Paris tensing, but Paris nods, nonetheless.

"He might've chosen to come to Hazelwood, but he's got strong ties to Eastpoint," Shep states. "Whatever you have going on with him, you need to be careful."

Fuck. If only I had that choice.

A groan rumbles up my chest and I bend until my forehead nearly presses into the chalky top of my pool stick. After a beat, I stand up and move into place, shooting and scratching in under a minute like an idiot. My head's so full of fucking shit, I can't even concentrate on a simple game of pool.

Neither Paris nor Shep say a word as I toss my stick into the holder to the side and take a step back, crossing my arms as my mind whirls.

"Why'd you want to know, anyway?" Paris asks.

If it were anyone else, I'd ignore the question, but

these two are as deep into my father's world as I am—we're one and the same. Their fathers are just as monstrous in their own right as mine is. It's how we became friends—birds of the bloody feathers flock together and all that shit.

"It's not me that has anything going on with Summers," I say. "It's my father."

Paris' jaw drops. Shep freezes where he's bent over the pool table and slowly, inexplicably minutely, he stands without making a shot before turning to meet my gaze. Their reactions do not offer confidence, and I know without having to go into detail that they understand the situation.

"The new wife?" Paris asks, proving me right.

I nod.

"Fuck." The curse is hissed out between Shep's lips, surprising me.

"My intel says he hasn't spoken to his mother in three years," I say. "But he showed up to the meeting we had the other day. His sister called him."

"Are they close?" Paris demands.

I shrug. "Close enough for him to come to her rescue."

"And the plan to have her move in?" he continues.

I shake my head. "Not happening." It burns my father's fucking ass that someone else is going over him. He is not a man that likes to be out of control. I should be thankful for Marcus' intervention, but after seeing Aurora Summers, I can't help but feel like he's going to be more of a thorn in my side than anything else. If not him, then *she* certainly will be.

Aurora Summers is nothing like I originally expected. There's a thread of steel beneath the beautiful exterior and also something else. Something intricately ...

damaged. Sure, most pretty rich girls have their own demons. They aren't exempt from the scars our society leaves as a result of their gender.

She's different, though. Instead of covering it with designer handbags and an elitist mindset, she seems more salt of the Earth type. It was clear by her fidgeting that she'd been uncomfortable in the expensive dress she'd worn to lunch. Or perhaps it'd just been the situation. I can't blame her for that if that's the case. She also hadn't seemed too keen on her mother's new beau. My lips twitch in amusement at the reminder of her sour-looking expression the entire way through the painful ordeal. It had only changed when her brother showed up.

Yet still, the shadows in her eyes remained even when clouded by relief.

It makes me want to find the wound she's trying so clearly to camouflage and dig my fingers into its bloody surface and see what kind of demons she's hiding beneath her skin.

"What's the plan now, then?" Paris asks.

If only I had an answer. I roll my head back on my shoulders, closing my eyes as I try to work through my options. I could just do as my father says and keep an eye on the girl—she's attending Hazelwood, so that shouldn't be too difficult. It wouldn't be hard to plant someone close to her or take advantage of the ones already in her circle. Regardless of whatever else I do, I plan to have someone watching her at all times. But if I just follow my father's orders then that would mean giving up my own agenda, and I have no intention of letting him dictate my life for much longer.

Opening my eyes, I blow out a breath and move across the room until I hit the wet bar at the edge. I yank down a glass and uncap the decanter sitting on the counter, pouring a healthy dose of whiskey into the cup before I grip the counter with two fists.

"I want the fucker out of the way," I say. It's my primary motive for this whole fucking thing. I want my father to fucking pay for what he's done. For the last several years. For my mother. And for forcing me, his fucking heir, to run after him like a dog to its master.

The question is, though, am I acting too fast? Is it too soon?

Almost as soon as I ask that, I know the answer—no, it's not too soon. In fact, I'm running behind schedule, trying to catch up with the information that's coming in from all sides. I need Marcus and Aurora Summers out of the way before my father manages to make things solid with their mother's connections.

There's always the chance that the marriage could fall apart before my father gets what he wants, but then there's always the chance that it won't, and those are the chances I can't afford. Not in this.

"This marriage can't fucking last," I snap, making my split-second decision. Grabbing the glass, I turn and face my friends, my brothers, and my comrades. "Even if it means earning the wrath of Marcus Summers, before the semester is over, I want Emilia Summers out of the picture—and if I have to drive her daughter to the brink to get it done, I will."

No matter that she's got eyes like fresh-turned graves and hair like burning sunshine. I tip the glass back and swallow it all in one gulp. Expensive whiskey burns down the throat just like cheap whiskey and leaves me feeling just as determined.

Paris and Shep exchange a silent look before they meet my gaze. "God help you, man," Paris says.

"But we're here," Shep finishes. "Whatever you need. You've got it."

For the first time since this conversation started, the tension finally drains away from me. I knew they were solid. I knew they would have my back, but having it said so openly is a relief that they can't even begin to understand.

"Just one question, though," Paris says.

"What?" I set my glass back on the bar.

He pushes a hand up his forehead and into the red-brown curls that hang into his face. "How are you going to break her?"

I let my eyes level on his before moving to Shep's and back. The words, when they leave my throat, feel like a vow and a curse all at once.

"I'll do whatever I have to," I tell them. "I'm going to make Aurora Summers wish she'd never come here."

And perhaps when she's as far gone as a human can be, maybe then ... I'll let her see the truth of it all. I'm not a good man. I may only be breaking her to save her, but at the end of the day, it's not about altruism. No, because I know I'll enjoy it.

4

RORI

I drop into my seat at one of the tables in front of *BeanBerry*, the campus coffee shop, across from my best friend, Selene, and her cousin, Helen—my new roommates. It's already been a hell of a week, and it's only Tuesday. Thankfully, though, I've got my dorm situation at Hazelwood all figured out once more.

"He really tried to force you to live with his son?" Selene asks not for the first time today. It's like she can't believe it. I get it—it's a crazy situation.

"Y*up.*" I pop the end of the word as I swirl my straw around the opening of my Frappuccino. *Dick,* I think snidely.

"Damn." Selene shakes her head. "Good thing Marcus showed up." I frown at that, but she's not wrong. It *was* a good idea to call Marcus, but that, too, has come with consequences. As if reminding me of them, my phone buzzes in my pocket. I pull it out and read the text.

I'm stopping by your dorm later. Be there.

No thanks. No please. Just "be there" as if I'm

someone to be ordered around. I love my brother, but he can be such a commanding douchebag sometimes. I grimace but don't send a reply. I already know I'll meet up with him. Whatever Marcus has to say can be dealt with later. Right now, I just want to sit back and enjoy my victory over Damien and Isaac Icari, as well as my very first taste of freedom.

I mean, yeah, even though my mom is more than a little flighty and I never knew when she'd come barging back into my life, I'd still technically lived with her. There was always the constant threat that she'd be there, fucking up all of my carefully laid plans through high school with her expectations and random selfish desires to try and make the family she's never been able to hold together with the various men that parade in and out of her life. This is different. This is me on my own. This is true freedom.

"Marcus is in overprotective brother mode," I confess.

Selene tips her head to the side and holds the top of her latte cup with two fingers. "What is he doing?" she inquires.

I blow out a breath. "It's not what he's doing," I confess. "It's what he *will* do that worries me."

"What will he do?" she presses.

My eyes slide to Hel, but her face is completely focused on her phone, her fingers flying over the screen at lightning speed. I slowly let my eyes rove over her face, dark skin, even darker hair, and big eyes. She's completely absorbed in whatever she's doing. They're complete opposites—from how they look to how they act. I shake my head in amusement before I return my attention back to Selene.

"Marcus has been on Hazelwood's campus for three years already," I point out. "He's got this place locked down. When we were in high school together—just that one year was unbearable. No one would fucking touch me, much less go out with me."

"Are you looking to date?" she asks.

I shrug. "I'm looking to expand my horizons. The last time I had sex was ... ugh, too fucking long ago." I roll my eyes and put the straw to my lips, sucking back a mouthful of chocolaty goodness. I don't even taste the coffee. Just the way I like it.

"And you think you're gonna be blue balled while your brother's around," Selene sums up.

"Pretty much," I say mournfully, setting down my nearly empty cup. "Thankfully, though, he said he's got a friend and his girlfriend coming into town soon, so he'll probably skip the first week of classes to spend time with them. They don't get to see each other much."

"Do they go to another school?" she asks.

"Yeah." I flick the tip of my straw with my finger distractedly. "And Mom is going on her long-awaited honeymoon with the current step-dick."

"Then you should take this opportunity!" Selene jumps forward, startling me. Her hands slap against the table and even Hel jerks her head up from her phone, frowning at the two of us.

"Opportunity?" I repeat.

Selene's white-blonde hair flies around her face as she bobs her head excitedly. "Yes!" she squeals. "There's a party at the end of next week at one of the houses off campus. It's a Gods and Goddesses party."

"A Gods and Goddesses party?" I feel like a parrot

just repeating every major line she says. "What the hell is that?"

Selene's pale blue eyes focus on me with intensity and I know that no matter what my feelings towards this Gods and Goddesses party are—we're going. She's got that determined look. I glance at Hel, who seems to recognize it too. She sighs and shakes her head my way as if to say 'it's too late now. We're goners.'

"It's a party the students put on a couple of times a year," Selene begins. "Once at the beginning of the year and another at the end. It's like a welcome back and goodbye thing. Everyone dresses up as a God or Goddess and wears a mask."

"A mask?" I scrunch up my face. "What's with that? Halloween isn't even for another few weeks."

Selene rolls her eyes. "It's part of the dramatics," she says. "It's just to blow off steam. You don't actually have to wear a mask if you don't want to, but most people do."

"Rich kids are obsessed with masks," Hel points out.

I turn my attention her way. "What do you mean?"

She sets her phone face down on the table and finally picks up her cup. "The amount of masquerades and masked events they have is overwhelming. Selene says it's because of the dramatics, but not everyone is like that."

Hel would know—she's far more down to earth and less familiar with the expense of the elite. She's only related to Selene by marriage and though they get along and are friends, Hel's mom was actually a flight attendant before she married Selene's uncle. Having money is not something she's used to—even years later.

My lips twitch. "Alright, tell us then," I offer when it's clear she's got something to say. "Why do you think rich people are obsessed with masks?"

Hel lifts her head and over the rim of her coffee cup, her dark eyes meet mine with a laser focus. "People who want to wear masks probably actually want to take them off." I frown at that, but before I can ask what she means, she keeps talking. "Rich kids are constantly wearing masks. Not physical ones, but ones that hide who they really are." My lips part, but she doesn't stop there. "Rich kids are under constant watch—"

Selene scoffs. "The paparazzi aren't—"

"I'm not talking about something as arbitrary as the paparazzi," Hel says, cutting her off without hesitation. "I'm talking about *everyone* else."

I stiffen, already suspecting where she's going with this. Me. I'm included in everyone else, and I don't want to hear her thoughts on my own masking. "Got it," I say before she can continue. I turn my attention back to focus squarely on Selene again. Subject change needed immediately.

"How do you know so much about this party anyway?"

Selene bites her lip and shifts until she's sitting back in her chair once more. "I just met someone who told me a little about it."

"And would this someone be a guy?" I prompt, forcing myself to smile tauntingly. I can feel Hel's gaze on the side of my face, but I don't say a word, and thankfully, she doesn't force her way back in. It's one thing I sometimes hate and sometimes love about her—she picks up on shit fast.

Cue another eye roll from Selene, and a frustrated grunt as she crosses her arms. "So, are we going or not?" she asks, ignoring my question.

"Do we have a choice?" I ask.

She grins. "Not at all."

"I do," Hel announces, sipping her coffee.

Selene smirks her way. "No, you don't. You're going even if that means I have to stuff you in a dress myself and drag you down the street."

Hel's quiet, "Damn it," has both Selene and I laughing our asses off.

Yeah, being at Hazelwood with these two is definitely better than being stuffed into a cold penthouse with Isaac Icari.

A sinister feeling creeps up my spine and even if I wanted to, I can't stop myself from looking back. I jerk as a pair of familiar blue eyes meet mine. *Fuck.* Cold washes over me.

It's as if I've conjured the man, himself, with nothing more than the power of my thoughts. I don't know why I'm so surprised. I knew he would be at Hazelwood, but I just never really expected to run into him—and certainly not this soon. He's sitting across the open greenery against a tall fountain with two guys, one of whom has a girl under his arm and a collection of piercings in so many places—his brow, his lip, all up and down his ears—that it's a wonder he's not a walking poster child for needles. The other, however, has a phone in hand and is completely attached to the screen, his face half hidden by the fall of dark hair against his cheekbones.

Unlike his posse, though, Isaac is completely focused on me—his gaze zeroed in and almost ... haunting. I want to turn away, to show him that I'm not aware of him, but it's too late now and I find that I can't.

So, what do I do? I stare back like a fucking crazy person. I match his intensity with as much of my own as I can muster and glare his way. I don't know what this is—

intimidation tactics or something else—and I don't care. I don't fucking bow, and showing vulnerability is not something I've been taught. Not after years of my mother's manipulations.

His lips twitch in amusement and he leans over, his mouth opening as he says something to his friends. Though I can't hear it, I know it's about me because, in the next second, the two guys he's with follow his gaze and their eyes lock on me as well.

Fuckity Fuck.

Thankfully, I'm saved by the sound of Hel's chair scraping back against the stones beneath our feet. The sharp noise jerks me out of whatever trance Isaac Icari put me in, and I pivot back to see her and Selene gathering their shit.

Selene gives me an odd look. "We're heading back to start picking out our costumes for the party," she says. "You coming?"

"Yeah." I quickly grab my now-empty cup and move with them to throw it away in the nearby trash.

Almost as if I have to know if he's still watching me, I casually look back over my shoulder once more as we pass the front of the coffee shop and head back towards the dorms. I pause slightly, though, when I see he's gone and so are the other two. The only one remaining is the girl—who's now surrounded by two other girls as she pouts. Her face scrunches up as she appears to be distressingly ranting to them. Guess she got dropped. Poor girl. Then again, maybe she was saved. Who can say?

Something tells me that this won't be the last time I see him, and for some reason that makes a feeling of dread bloom in my stomach.

"Damn it," I mutter as I force my legs to hurry to

catch up to Hel and Selene, who are making their way down the campus steps.

Whatever Isaac Icari thinks he's doing looking at me like that—if it's a challenge or something else—I can't let it get to me. I'm not a toy for him to play with, and I'm certainly not as easy as my mother was.

5

RORI

Hel, Selene, and I are walking up the front steps of Rozenfeld Dorm when my phone buzzes against my side again. I pause as they reach the doors, but before I can answer it, a familiar voice calls out.

"Rori!" The phone stops buzzing and I turn as Marcus jogs up to me.

"Hey—oomph!" I gasp when he enfolds me in a massive hug and my eyes widen in confusion. We've always been close, but he doesn't do public displays of affection. When he leans down and his jovial voice dips into one of seriousness—I understand what he's doing.

"We need to talk," he whispers. "Alone."

I force a smile onto my face and hug him back quickly. When he releases me, I turn back to Selene and Hel. "Hey, I'll catch up with you guys later. I'm going to go hang with my brother real quick."

Selene smiles and waves me off, but Hel seems to catch on, watching me with a curiosity that I know—thankfully—she won't push on me later. She was right about rich kids and their masks. Even if Selene can't admit it to herself, I can.

Once the two of them are gone, I turn back to Marcus and frown. "Come on," he says, grabbing my hand and pulling me after him.

"What's with the spy treatment?" I ask, not really expecting an answer. And just as predicted, he doesn't say a word. He keeps utterly silent until we reach the parking lot behind the dorm and I spot his truck a few spaces down in the front row. He releases my arm and pops open the passenger-side door for me.

"Let's go, kid."

I roll my eyes. "Not sure if you've realized it yet or not," I say snidely, "but I'm not a kid anymore."

He leans down as I settle into the seat and drops an arm over the top of the doorway. "You'll always be a kid to me, brat. Buckle up."

Douche. But I do as he says after he shuts the door, and watch him as he circles around the front of the vehicle. As soon as he's in the truck and the engine has started, I attack. "Okay, can you tell me what's up now?" I demand.

"Needed to get you alone to talk about what happened at the luncheon," he states.

My lips twist and I frown at him. "Uh, yeah, dumbo, I was fucking there. I know what happened." Marcus shoots me a look but doesn't respond immediately. I blow out a breath. "Okay, fine, enlighten me."

"We're meeting some friends of mine," he says instead.

"I thought you wanted me alone to talk about this?" I remind him.

"I do, but Dean's got more information than I do on this Damien guy, so I want to talk to him, too."

I lean back into my seat and cross my arms. "And you think he won't mind you bringing your *kid*-sister along for the ride?" I can't help the bitterness in my tone when I say the word 'kid.' That's all I've ever been to him. A child he needs to look after and protect. My nails bite into my forearms as the reminder that I'm the reason he and Mom don't speak anymore hits me hard in the guilt department.

Marcus' gaze burns into the side of my face, but I keep my eyes glued to the windshield. After a beat of silence, he sighs. "I'm thinking about transferring soon."

Shock races through my system and I whirl around to gape at him. "Transferring?" I repeat. "You only have one year left! What's the point!"

He focuses his attention on the road ahead of him. "There are friends who need me on the East Coast."

"You're talking about them, aren't you?" I demand. "Is that who we're meeting? Is Dean from Eastpoint?"

"Don't worry about it," he says, and I'm not so blind that I don't notice he's deflecting.

"Funny that you tell me not to worry about it when you know that's all I'll do," I grumble.

"I needed to talk to you alone—and with Dean—because of my transfer. I'm leaving soon and I think it's better if you come with me to this meeting. You need to know just as much about Damien Icari as I do, if not more. It would benefit you to be more cautious about people."

"*I* need to be more cautious?" I practically spit out. The urge to slap the fuck out of him—even though he's driving and speeding a good twenty miles over the limit right now—is intensifying. He thinks *I* need to be more cautious about people? Is that why he acted so sketchy in front of Selene and Hel? "Is there something you want to say about my friends?" I demand. "You don't trust them?"

He doesn't look at me when he answers. "No."

It's as simple as that. Marcus is quick to judge and even quicker to write people off. It's a surprise he has any friends at all. I sit back against my seat with a grunt.

"This is fucking ridiculous," I growl. "You've been at Hazelwood for three years. You haven't come home to New York in damn near all that time, but the second I show up—the second I try to get even a little bit of my own freedom, here you are, trying to—"

"I'm trying to look after you, Rori," he cuts me off. "I know it's inconvenient. Shit. I fucking know, okay? I don't want to take away your freedom. If anyone's earned it, you have."

I think over his words for a moment before replying. "I'm not going to lie," I tell him honestly. "You transferring isn't such a bad thing—I wasn't looking forward to my big brother hanging over me at Hazelwood, but..." A sorrowful yearning aches in my chest. I've missed him.

Sure, I fucking complain and shit—we fight sometimes—but Marcus has always had my back. Without questions and without fail.

"It feels like you're running from me," I mutter quietly.

The big truck comes to a stop at a red light and he turns to face me. Heat arches up my cheeks and I keep my eyes trained in front of me, afraid to turn and look at the expression he's making.

"Rori." His hand reaches out, touching mine. "Look at me."

"I don't want to."

His chuckle is more breath than anything else. "Yes, you do, brat. Come on, look at me." I suck in a breath and turn to glare at him, blinking in surprise when he lifts a palm to touch my cheek.

"I love you, brat," he says, "and I will always be there when you need me. I promise that everything I do is to take care of you. I will make sure you're safe before I go to Eastpoint. That's why I'm having this meeting with Dean."

"What is it about Damien that makes you so worried?" I ask. "You know they're probably going to get a divorce in the next few months. Her husbands never last long. He's not..." I drift off, not even wanting to say that monster's fucking name, but Marcus already knows. I don't have to say his name to elicit a reaction. His eyes harden and he drops his hand from my face to grip the steering wheel.

"It's just a feeling," he replies vaguely.

I narrow my eyes on him but don't press. It's never *just a feeling* with him, but I let it go. Marcus has his secrets, and ... I have mine.

The truck moves forward again when the light turns green and for the next several minutes, the two of us sit in virtual silence until I notice the direction we're going. The tall skyscrapers and posh restaurants become less frequent and further apart until there are none left at all. The roads become gradually less smooth and I tense when I spot a few haggard-faced people milling about the streets with shopping carts full of stuff.

"Marcus?" I call his name and when he doesn't respond, I look at him. "*Where* are we going?"

Almost as soon as the question is out of my mouth, the truck turns into the parking lot of a one-story brick building with no sign and blacked-out windows and doors. The nicest thing in the parking lot is my brother's truck and what's obviously a rented SUV that he parks right next to. *What the hell is going on?*

"Come on," he says.

Reluctantly, I unbuckle my seatbelt and pop open my door before following him into the building.

The second we step inside, a strong wave of cigarette smoke hits me in the face along with the acrid smell of cleaning supplies. I'm surprised. I would've never expected a seedy place like this to even have cleaning supplies. The cigarette smell is the worst though. I haven't smoked in months and it makes me crave one.

There aren't very many people in the building. A lone, skinny bartender is talking to a guy in a pair of overalls at the bar's countertop and a younger couple in the back, standing around a pool table. As we approach, the girl lifts her head, and immediately, I feel assessed. Almost like she's checking me over as a threat, her cool gray-blue eyes rove over my face and then down the rest of me before they come back up, and she smirks. I don't know what it is about that smirk, but it irritates the fuck out of me.

The guy with her stands and turns when he notices the direction of her gaze. "Marcus," he calls and I watch with a strange fascination as my brother goes towards him without caution and embraces him in a manly hug. *What the actual fuck? Who is this guy?*

"Dean, man, it's good to see you," Marcus says. "How're you doing?"

I blink at the name and then it clicks. Dean—as in Dean Carter of Carter Industries. Shit. My attention returns to the girl as she steps up next to them.

"If he'd just take it easy, he'd be better, but he's a dick that has to keep going," she says.

Marcus releases Dean and steps back before smirking at her. "You're Avalon, I take it," he states, holding out his hand.

"I am." She takes his hand. "I've seen you before, but we haven't had the chance to meet."

"I was a little busy, baby," Dean says, sliding an arm around her waist when she and my brother part. I feel like a voyeur, watching the two of them. Almost like I've suddenly fallen into the background. It's not a place I'm used to—not with someone like my mother dragging me into the limelight constantly in an effort to get people to see her as doting and caring—but I find that I don't mind it.

"Yeah, yeah, yeah," Avalon rolls her eyes before turning to me. "And you are?"

"Rori," I say. She doesn't bother to offer her hand to me and I don't either.

Avalon's smirk widens. "Interesting." That's all she says, and as much as I want to, I don't have an opportunity to ask her what she means before my brother jumps straight into business.

"So, what do you know about Damien Icari?" he demands.

Dean blows out a breath and leans back against the pool table, both his and his girl's sticks and their game forgotten as he pulls her in front of him and wraps his arms around her middle. Something wicked and jealous curls into my throat as he nuzzles against her neck, but I shove that feeling down. Shit like that is for other people.

"I know he's not a good guy," Dean states.

My body stiffens. "How is he not a good guy?" I

demand, blurting out the question with little regard for the fact that I know Marcus only brought me here to listen in.

Marcus cuts me a look, but Dean answers anyway. "Damien Icari might seem like an average businessman and millionaire to the world, but most people who do even the slightest bit of digging can find the truth. He's as dirty as they come."

"Ties to the mafia?" Marcus asks.

Dean nods, and my stomach drops out from beneath me. *What the hell has my mother gotten herself into? No. What the hell could a man who's involved with criminals want with my mother?*

"More than just ties," Dean says with a shake of his head. His hands twine together with Avalon's, and I watch as she adjusts herself against him, trying not to lean too much on one side. A curious part of me wonders why, but I don't ask. Instead, focus on the discussion at hand. "He's practically a member himself."

"Why would he marry my mother?" Marcus demands.

Avalon looks past Marcus and stares at me. Her gaze is impenetrable and kind of unnerving. It makes me want to look away, but my pride won't let me. Instead, I lift my chin and glare back at her which only makes her look harder as her lips curve up even more.

"Think about it, man," Dean continues. "Why else? Your mother has connections to a lot of businesses. Even if she's not directly involved, the Summers name carries weight and it's got money backing it. That, and your Aunt Carmen is a force to be reckoned with. She's the business brains of your family. Either he's married her for a chance to get to Carmen, who otherwise wouldn't have given a man like him the time of day, or..."

Dean drifts off and I jerk my gaze away from his girlfriend's. "Or what?" I ask, calling his attention, and my brother's, back to me.

Dean arches a brow at me once. "Or he's planning on using your mother as a stepping stone to launder his own dirty money."

A sick feeling cuts through my gut. That seedy fucking bastard. He wouldn't dare—but no, he would. Of course he would. My mother can never find a fucking man worth a damn. I might feel sympathy for her if she didn't keep trying and ruining Marcus' and my peace of mind in the process.

Marcus' father split, mine wasn't rich enough for her family or her, and then the other one that had lasted more than a few months ... I don't even want to think about her last utter failure. Why couldn't she just be happy without some sick, twisted, son of a bitch coming in to absolutely wreck our lives?

I bite down into my lower lip so hard, I taste blood.

"That's probably the case," Marcus says as if Dean's last words haven't completely overturned our current situation, but then he's always been good at hiding his negative emotions. Unlike me.

I can't deal with this though, not without losing my fucking shit. I turn away and start walking. I walk past the bartender and her customer and right out the door into the hot California sun onto the broken, shittily lain pavement of the bar parking lot.

"Fuck," I curse as I scrub my hands down my face. Maybe that explains why Isaac Icari was staring at me so hard. Does he know? He has to know. That's his fucking father.

Another thought occurs to me—was that why Damien had pressed so hard to have me move in with his son? A cold feeling rockets through me. My mother is one thing, but me ... what did they expect from me? A hostage? A pawn?

Anger drives up through my body and I feel an itchy sensation in my knuckles; it's overwhelming.

"Want to hit something?"

I jump at the question, startled because I didn't expect anyone to follow me out here—least of all Dean's girlfriend. I turn slowly, incrementally—as if I'm facing off with some dangerous snake. She just stands back, her hands shoved into the pockets of her ripped jeans. She looks like she belongs in a place like this—like she's comfortable with decay and cheap beer. I like ripped jeans as much as the next chick, and as much as I detest the pompous places my mother enjoys, I'm used to it. It's normal to me, whereas *this* is not.

"Hey, I'm talking to you, kid."

I grit my teeth. "I'm not a fucking kid," I snap. Jesus, she can't be more than a year or two older than me, if that. "And I heard you—yes, I want to hit something."

"Okay," she says with a smile. "Then why don't you?"

"What?" I gape at her. "I can't just—" I gesture awkwardly to the space between her and me and then around to the practically empty parking lot.

"Sure, you can," she argues with a shrug, "but I wouldn't recommend hitting rock or brick," she says, nodding back to the bar's building. "It might leave your knuckles bruised, or worse, broken."

I snort. "Speaking from personal experience?" I ask.

She grins. "Yeah."

I shake my head. "You're fucking weird, you know that?"

She shrugs, a lazy movement. "S'not the first time I've heard that. Probably won't be the last."

I look her over, curious. Something tells me a straight-forward approach is what works best on this chick, so I suck in a breath and go for it. "Why did you follow me out here?"

Avalon's smile curves her lips and she tilts her head down toward me. "Thought you might be interested in some free advice."

I sigh, putting one hand behind my neck and leaning it to one side—feeling the need to crack it. "Go ahead," I offer casually. "What would you do in this fucked up situation?"

Her smile cuts through her face and makes a shiver run through my spine. "I'd give my enemies a taste of their own medicine." It's a simple statement, and yet, I know she means something darker.

"What are you saying?" I ask cautiously.

She pulls one hand from her pocket and gestures back. "Your brother and Dean are in there trying to come up with any number of ways to get your mother to divorce this guy," she says.

I'm not surprised. Even knowing that the man my mother has married this time isn't your average perv with too much money and time on his hands, I'm still not convinced they won't divorce on their own soon enough. "So?"

Avalon shakes her head. "From what I know, sounds like Marcus is planning on making a move soon—Dean hasn't told the others yet, but Marcus probably won't be around here much longer. Doesn't make any sense for them to leave this up to him, does it?" No, it doesn't. She keeps talking and finally, I feel like she's captured the breadth of my attention. All of it is focused on her and her words. Her ideas. "Dean's still on the learning curve," she admits.

"To what?" I ask.

"To figuring out that women aren't all pretty objects to be kept and protected. He doesn't think that of me anymore, but most girls..." She drifts off, yet I get her meaning, and she's right.

I love Marcus, but for most of my life, and especially after the catastrophe of my mother's last marriage, he's treated me as little more than a child. Someone to be kept close and protected, just like she said. It probably didn't do anything to change his mind when I called him for help.

"Okay, so what the hell am I supposed to do?" I ask her. "Walk up to Damien and tell him I know the truth?" No, that would not be a good idea. If he really is involved in something like the mafia, that would be a one-way ticket to a Godfather-type ending.

Avalon tilts her head and rolls her eyes. "Come on, girl," she says. "You don't strike me as stupid. What is something you can do that your brother can't?"

And just like that—like a lightning bolt to the head—I know. It hits me like a freight train. It's so simple, it's almost laughable. *Isaac.* A plan forms and my attention drifts to the ground as I see it unfold in my mind. Damien must have seen me as an obstacle—or a key—when my mother didn't immediately return at the start of the summer. That was why he'd tried to force me to move in with his son. As leverage? Maybe. And now that leverage

—me—is free, but he's still having Isaac keep an eye on me.

What for?

I shake my head. Whatever the reason, doesn't matter. What does, however, is that this opens a door. There's a simple solution to this whole issue. All I need to do is make Damien Icari give up on my mother, and what better way to do that than go after his son the way, I have no doubt he's planning on coming after me.

"So?" Avalon's voice makes me jump. Fuck, how the hell does she do that? Make you forget she's there and then surprise you when you least expect it. It's like she somehow manages to mask her own presence, but the second you recall it—it's overwhelming. "Figure it out?" she asks.

I meet her gaze. "Yeah," I say. "I think I've got it."

Her cool, toned eyes slide over mine and she smiles before holding her hand out to me. "Phone," she commands in a tone that brooks no argument. I snort, but reach into my pocket and pull it free, handing it to her anyway. She types something into the screen before handing it back. "You've got my number," she says. "Call if you want more advice or ... whatever."

I almost laugh as I tuck my phone back into my pocket.

"Now," she steps back towards the door, "let's go grab a beer and wait for the guys to make their own plans."

"I'm not twenty-one," I point out.

Avalon throws her head back, her long black hair flying around her face as she roars with hilarity. I blink at the motion and when she's done, she bends over, wiping beneath her dry eyes as if I really almost made her cry tears of laughter. "Shit, neither am I," she says. "Why do you think I brought Dean? He's gonna buy us a beer. Let's go."

I let her reach out this time and take my wrist in her grasp. Although small and feminine as it is, it feels like steel, strength, and something else that I hope like fuck I've got in me, too.

I like this girl, I realize. A hell of a lot.

6

ISAAC

She knows. She has to know. It's the only excuse. It's either that or something I don't even want to think about. Regardless of what she does or doesn't know, Aurora Summers is watching me. The same way I'm watching her—with suspicion and some unnamed emotion that's digging into my head, making me ... curious. Curiosity is dangerous.

I can't even say that I don't like it either. I do. I like her eyes on me. I like her attention, and I find that I want more of it. She is, quite possibly, the least boring chick I've seen or met in a long while, and having her focus on me as much as mine is on her gives me a heady feeling. Like I just smoked a shit ton of weed and every muscle in my body has finally released the tension I've spent years building up. Maybe this will be fun—breaking the girl my father thinks he can use.

"She's in this class too?" Paris leans forward over the back of my seat from the row behind me.

Yeah, she is. Of the seven courses I'm taking this

semester, she's in at least four of them. Statistics 101, Psych 103, Business Admin 100, and now this one—Art Theory and History 200. It's a throwaway class to me—an elective—but to her, I know it's required because she's in the Fine Arts department.

Why?

What could she do with a Fine Arts degree? Most chicks are in this for the potential of meeting their husbands—find that rich upper-class guy that fits what Daddy and Mommy dearest want for their precious *innocent* little girls. It's laughable. Most girls these days are far from innocent. Throw a little money into their background and they're even worse than the guys. Sex. Drugs. Parties. They like it all.

There is no difference between good girls and bad girls. Good girls are just bad girls who haven't been caught.

All except for Aurora Summers, it seems.

From what I can tell, she doesn't party. She doesn't do drugs. She doesn't have sex. But one of her roommates does. Selene Reynolds is exactly the type of girl I expected Aurora Summers to be. Beautiful, though a little empty-headed. Easily influenced by her friends with likes similar to other girls of her class and age. I thought Aurora would be easy to get to, but in the last week she's done little more than watch me in the same way I watch her.

Paris pokes me in the back. "Who's the other one?" he demands.

My eyes go to the girl at her side, and I frown. "Her roommate," I inform him. The one I don't like. Selene will be easy to use, but this one—Helen Argos—is far more difficult. I don't even know how to use her. She's quiet and she's almost always at Aurora's side. The only thing I do know is that, unlike Selene and Aurora, Helen doesn't come from money.

A thought occurs to me. Would money be enough to sway her into spying on my new stepsister?

"She's hot," Paris states, reaching up and rubbing the industrial bar pierced through the top of his ear thoughtfully.

I roll my eyes. "You think any chick with a working pussy is hot," I remind him.

"Not true," he replies. "I wouldn't fuck your new sister if you paid me."

I turn back and glare at him. "She is not my sister," I grit out.

Paris' mouth curves into a knowing smile and his sharp gaze meets mine. "And aren't you fucking happy about that?" he taunts.

Ass. I twist as the door opens and the professor walks in, carrying a small easel under her left arm and a bag overflowing with rolled-up papers on the other. Class begins, and the entire time I'm left sitting there, watching my recent obsession as she ignores me for a change to actually pay attention to the instructor. Is there a reason she chose to sit at the front this time? Every other class she's done her damnedest to get behind me.

I don't like it. She's trying to get herself into a position of power, and that just won't do. It's time to put plans into action. I lean back and tap the front of Paris' table. "How fast can you get to work on the rumor mill?" I ask, lowering my voice as the instructor moves across the front of the classroom with her back to us and her hands on the whiteboard as she writes down a list of names and influential figures in the History of Art.

Paris tilts his head to the side and then glances around

the room. He considers his options and then nods. "I'll have something done by the end of the day." That's it. He already knows what I want from him. I lean forward once more and focus on the back of Aurora's head. Her hair is twisted up into a braided crown today, little flurries of strands hover around her face. The hairstyle leaves the nape of her neck bare. It's a temptation, that naked skin. I lick my lips.

Fuck, Paris is right. It's a good thing she's not my real sister. A damn good thing.

As soon as class ends, Paris is up and out of his seat. "Hey, Jasmine, wait up!" A small smile graces my lips as he slings an arm around the shoulders of a tan blonde near the classroom door and the two disappear out into the hall. Jasmine Thomas is one of the most gossipy girls on campus. She's a good choice to start in on ruining Aurora Summers' reputation.

My phone buzzes in my pocket and I pull it out, scowling at the name on the screen. Briefly, I debate not answering, but I know that'll only make him suspicious. I hit the green button with more aggression than necessary. "Isaac."

My father doesn't even bother with the formalities of a greeting. "What's the girl up to?" he demands.

I blow out a breath, gather my bag, and stride down the classroom steps, heading for the hallway. "She's attending classes like any average college girl," I state.

"And her brother?"

"There's a rumor going around school that he'll be transferring to Eastpoint soon."

There's a beat of silence on the other end and then a low chuckle. "I don't rely on rumors, Son," he says. "Find out if it's true and then get back to me." The call dies.

My grip tightens against the phone hard enough that the plastic creaks. Only then do I loosen my hold ever so slightly. Keeping my father informed on the actions of Marcus and Aurora Summers is not on my list of priorities, but I know if I don't report back—even while he's supposed to be seducing their mother in Italy—the second he's back, my ass will be in the fire.

I can't wait until he fucking croaks, or better yet ... I can't wait until he realizes that all he's done is lead himself into a grave of his own making. Before I can forget, I pull up my phone again and instead of placing a call, I go to the browser and enter an email address into the incognito tab. I type out a quick message, hit send, and then delete the history for the last two weeks, as I've done each time I've contacted this email. It won't keep my father from finding the information he wants if he really digs deep enough, but for now, it'll do. After all, it's not like he really expects betrayal from his own son.

With that done, I shove my phone back into my pocket and heft my bag higher as I stride across campus to the student union. Rumors are one way to irritate Aurora Summers, but it's only one stop in my plan to completely wreck her. This is all about power, and right now, she needs to understand that I am the one with the majority of it.

I enter the library and take the stairs two at a time until I reach the third-floor study rooms. I pass several open doors and even a few closed ones until I come to a room at the very end with the door left cracked. I knock once and push inside. Shep lifts his head and pulls out an earbud.

"Any news?" I ask, shutting the door behind me and flipping the lock.

He shakes his head. "Nothing yet, but I did manage to hack her student account."

"Let me see." I take a seat at his side as Shep flips the computer screen towards me. I take the mouse and scroll down her barren email list. She's a new student, so it's not surprising. I scrub a hand down the side of my jaw.

"What do you want to do?" he asks.

I consider the question for a moment. "How easy is it to get a key to her dorm?" I ask.

Shep arches a brow. "Simple."

I nod. "Do it. I want access to her. I've got Paris working on some rumors."

"You think rumors are going to break her?" he asks with an arched brow. "Knowing who her brother is, I doubt it."

No, but I'm not playing with an unemotional robot here. I'm playing with a human woman. She may not act fragile, but once the real bombardment of my plans starts to hit her—one after another, it'll be only a matter of time. Rumors. Humiliation. Strokes of supposed bad luck. Poor girl. By the time I'm done with her, she'll be begging her mother to leave California.

"Get someone into her space," I order. "I want cameras set up. Hide them well."

Shep gives me a look, but I don't respond to it. I know what he's thinking—he doesn't like it, but he recognizes the necessity of it. In the end, Aurora Summers will either be broken down into nothing and she'll be alive, or she'll be nothing but a pawn in my father's hand, and that—as both he and I know from experience—is a fate far worse than death.

I'm doing this for myself as well as for them. Aurora

Summers is just the tool I'll use to bring my father down from that pedestal of his. Once I light this match, I'm gonna stand back and watch him burn.

7

RORI

Rumors. The bane of a woman's existence. No one can really stop a rumor once it's out there. Plus, I have neither the will nor the desire to change people's minds. That doesn't mean I don't still find it fucking annoying.

I heard she used to sleep around at her high school.

Marcus' sister? Are we even sure they're related? They look nothing alike. What if she's adopted?

They have different fathers. Of course, there's no resemblance. No one as amazing as Marcus could possibly be related to someone as boring as her.

I heard she seduced her mom's last husband.

That last one makes me flinch, though only on the inside. I've perfected the poker face when listening to shit like that. Growing up in elite circles, I had to. What irritates me even more, though, is that some of these rumors aren't even that far from the truth. I can't tell if that's because someone knows something they shouldn't or if they're just throwing darts into the dark, hoping they'll hit

"What the fuck is your problem?" I blink as Selene strides up to where I'm sitting, waiting for class to start. She slams her bag down on top of the desk, turning and glaring at the two girls behind me whispering to each other.

Well … fake-whispering. I know from the tone they're using that they're not actually trying to mask their gossiping. It's almost like they want me to hear what they're saying. Maybe to see if they get a reaction from me. One I initially didn't have any intention of giving them.

"What?" one girl pipes back as Selene continues to glare at them.

"You don't know shit about shit," she snaps. "So keep your big flapping lips shut and mind your own fucking business, bitch."

"Who the hell do you think you—" I turn, locking my hand around the back of my chair, and pivot until I'm facing them. The girl talking is a tall brunette with freckles across her massive nose. She blinks at me as I stare her down.

"Go on," I say, "finish what you were saying. I'm listening."

Red stains her cheeks and she swivels away, gathering up her things as she and her friend hurriedly begin to move seats. "Bitch," I hear the other girl mutter as they hastily move across the room to a new pair of seats before class can start.

I arch a brow. Oh, sure, I'm the bitch because I called them out for gossiping about me right behind my back. I sigh and turn back to Selene, only to realize the target of her irritation has shifted to me.

"If you've been listening to those two talk shit since

you've been here, you should've said something sooner," she snaps.

"I don't care what they have to say," I reply with an offhanded wave, hoping she'll drop it. "I don't know them and they don't know me."

She doesn't drop it. "That doesn't matter, Rori," she huffs as she tosses her bag into the seat next to me. "Rumors aren't good."

"They're just words," I remind her.

"And words can precede you," she says. "They can ruin a reputation."

She takes her seat and I sigh. "I'm not like you, Selene," I say. "I don't need to worry about my image to be able to make it work. You're in the limelight half of the time when you're not at school. I'm just the daughter of a socialite. Nothing special. Not all rich people are famous."

"Yeah, you're right," she says, blowing out a breath. "I just hate hearing people talk shit in general. I think I get enough of that from the magazines and 'razzi. I'm actually surprised they feel confident enough to say anything, though, what with Marcus going to this school too. He's pretty respected here."

I wince and face forward, biting down on my lower lip. The one time I'm hoping she doesn't notice, however, is of course, the one time she does.

"What's with the face?" Selene demands.

"What face? There's no face," I lie.

"There is so totally a face," she snaps. "What aren't you telling me?"

I grimace. "It's nothing major," I start. "It's just that ... *Marcus is transferring to Eastpoint University.*" I lower my voice on that last bit, hoping to just gloss over it.

Not sure what I expected, to be honest. Maybe an 'oh really? That sucks. Sorry, Rori' or maybe a 'that's not a big deal, Rori. Don't worry about it.' What do I get, though? I get the dramatics.

"*What?*" Selene's voice takes on another several octaves. "When were you going to tell me?"

"Well, I was hoping you'd say it wasn't a big deal—"

"Not a big deal?" Selene gapes at me in horror. "Marcus is supposed to be *here*. You moved all the way to California instead of going to Eastpoint yourself because he was here!"

"I came here because of you too," I say in a quiet tone.

She shoots me a bland look. "That's sweet of you to say, Rori, but we both know you really came here because you missed him. He's your brother. You guys have been close since you were kids."

"Not recently," I mutter dourly. Before she can respond to that, though, I shake my head and sigh. "Don't make a big thing about it. I'm trying not to. Besides, this is a good thing now. I mean, I don't have to worry about him going all overprotective big brother on me."

"I just don't understand why he would do something like this to you," she growls. "Doesn't he know how excited you were to finally be able to see him regularly and now he's just, what? Moving? No warning or anything?"

"Marcus does what Marcus wants." I offer a lame half-hearted shrug. "Can we just drop the subject? Please?"

Selene goes quiet for a moment. It's only when I feel the burn of her gaze on the side of my face that I turn to look at her. "And the rumors?" she finally asks. "Any clue where those are coming from?"

I shrug.

"It just seems a bit odd for you to show up at Hazelwood and then a few weeks later to be the talk of the town," she says. "You haven't made any enemies since you've been here, have you?"

I frown. She does have a point. The rumors *don't* make any sense. I haven't been here long enough or done anything extravagant enough to elicit this kind of response in people. That is unless someone is starting them on purpose.

As soon as that thought crosses my mind, the door to the classroom opens, and the face I've been trying to avoid as much as possible for the last week enters. It's like lightning strikes my brain. He tips his head up, an arrogant smirk on his lips as he turns—looking away from the girl he's walking with—and his gaze meets mine. And I know.

That. Motherfucker.

As if he senses my thoughts, his smirk grows. Isaac brushes off the girl talking to him and heads down the first row of desks. He takes a seat directly behind me and I stiffen when I feel his hot breath brush against the back of my neck. I should've worn my hair down.

"Hello, Aurora."

The penalty for punching a classmate probably isn't as severe here as it would be at other universities—but only because most of the students here have been far wealthier as infants than any of the faculty or staff at Hazelwood ever have been or ever will be in their entire lives. That doesn't make my desire to wipe that cunning smirk I know he's still wearing off of his face.

Even if I manage to hold my physical temper back, I can't help the words that come out of my mouth. "Fuck off, Isaac."

His chuckle is dark and something about it makes shivers skirt down my spine. "What's wrong, *Sis*?" he asks. "I'm just checking in and seeing if you've been enjoying your time at Hazelwood. Have you spoken to your mother lately?"

"Rori?" I can feel Selene's confusion as she glances from me to the man behind us. I ignore her in favor of focusing the whole of my attention on *him*.

His words solidify my suspicions. Isaac Icari is the source of these outrageous rumors. My only question is ... *why?*

Slowly, I turn in my seat until I'm facing him. Eyes like icicles meet mine. It's not fucking fair. His beauty is almost blinding and yet underneath it all, I know there lies a man of sinister intention.

"What do you want, Isaac?" I demand.

"What makes you think I want something, Sunshine?"

I blanch at the nickname but force myself to slap on a sickly sweet smile. "The fact that you're here talking to me," I reply with exaggerated amiability. I want to be clear to him that I don't trust him or his father. "But if I'm wrong, then I suppose the only way to ensure that I don't mistake your kindness for something else is to never talk to me again."

He laughs, even slapping a hand to his chest and sitting back as if he's been mortally wounded. "You hurt me, Sunshine," he says. "I was hoping we could become closer."

"I'd rather have sex with a diseased, boil-infected frog," I reply with that same smile. "Make no mistake, Isaac Icari, I want nothing to do with you or your father. *I. Don't. Trust. You.*"

He arches a brow, and I can tell by the way his laughter drifts off and he sits forward, keeping his eyes locked with mine, that my actions have done the exact opposite of what I'd wished for. I've interested him. He's not even sparing Selene a glance—which is a shock enough. I'm not ugly, but Selene is a budding actress who's also landed more than one modeling contract in her search for fame alongside her parents. She's gorgeous. And he's acting like the only two people who exist in this room are him and me. That, too, is a red flag. In fact, everything about him is one giant red flag.

"What makes you think I care if you trust me, Aurora?" Isaac asks. I hate the way he says my name. He doesn't shorten it like I prefer, but says the whole thing as if every syllable is important and nothing can be overlooked. Even if that's what I want—to be overlooked, to be ignored by him, to be invisible to his eyes. Isaac Icari is clearly a man who sets his mind to things quickly and, once they're in his sights, permanently.

"I can't possibly say what," I reply, "but I think we both know that the marriage between our parents won't last. My mother is on her fourth marriage in the last two decades. I can't imagine your father is a man who cares for his wife being so free with her feelings."

He tsks. "So cruel," he comments, "and to your own mother, no less." Something tells me, though, that he cares even less for his father. I may dislike my mother in some— okay, *many*—instances, but I still love her. I'm just honest about who she is as a person, and Emilia Summers is rarely a person who I actually like.

As I stare back into Isaac's cold gaze, though, I know that it's not dislike for his father I'm seeing, but actual hatred. Pure and true.

The only thing that disrupts the moment is the classroom door opening and our psychology professor's booming voice as he enters, already halfway into a sentence and chattering on about today's lesson. Ten minutes late, no less.

I turn away from Isaac and spend the rest of the class with the knowledge that his focus is squarely on me, burning into the back of my head. If there was any doubt before that he was the person behind these crazy rumors, the fact that he approached me today shreds through them.

Fine, I think. If he wants to play games, I can play along. After all, I'm not one to back down from a challenge. Never have been and never will be—as Isaac Icari will soon learn.

8

ISAAC

I'm in trouble. Or rather, I've looked trouble square in the face and I challenged her. A few rumors are nothing but splashing rocks against the surface of her pool.

I take the library stairs two at a time until I meet the third floor study rooms and just like last time, I find Shep at the very end with the door slightly open. I push inside, closing the door behind me and locking it.

"Update," I grit out.

"The cameras are live," he replies without looking up from his computer. I move around the table and slide into the seat next to him. He turns the screen towards me. "We went with just two cameras," he says, pointing at each one as he explains. "One at the front of her door to see who's coming and going. One inside that encompasses the room."

"What about her roommates' rooms?" I demand. "Or the common areas." Unlike other Universities, Hazelwood is geared toward the rich and famous. Instead of white brick walls and two beds squished into a tiny space,

Aurora Summers' dorm room is one in a small apartment. It's about the size of a small mid-level hotel room, with soft beige walls and lush off-white carpet. I point to the screen. "There's a cut off here," I say.

Shep cuts a look my way. "That's the entrance to the bathroom," he says.

"Why don't we have one in there?"

He arches a brow. "Didn't take you for a voyeur," he comments.

Fuck. I'm not—not usually—but something about this girl is throwing me off. Two cameras are not enough. I want more. I want to know where she is and what she's doing at all times. She's like an itch under my skin, one I can't reach or scratch, and it's driving me mad.

"We should have a camera at least in the common area," I say.

Shep is quiet for a moment, but when he speaks, his voice dips low. "What is the goal here, man?" he asks.

I look at him. "What do you mean?"

"You know exactly what I mean," he says. "What are you trying to do? I know you're trying to drive her to the brink, but the cameras aren't gonna do it. I can understand a few just to keep watch but are you hoping to do something else with this footage?" He arches a brow. "I don't give a shit about this chick, you know that, but are we planning on streaming her private life for the world to see, or is this just for your personal pleasure?"

A dark feeling unfurls in my gut. No, I don't like the thought of anyone seeing Aurora's private world. I can feel my shoulders tighten. If I'm being completely honest, I'm not all that comfortable with even him being able to see this either—but he's the tech man. He's learned more about computers than I'll ever be able to understand in my life. I need him. I need this.

"I'm not streaming it anywhere," I tell him. "I'm just being cautious."

He eyes me for a moment before turning his attention back to the screen. "If it's just caution, then let's just leave these two cameras. I don't want to chance them being found by adding more."

I press my lips together, but I don't push the issue. Maybe he's right. Maybe I am being too overbearing. My gaze trails his to the screen as the door to the girl in question's bedroom opens and she appears, tossing her bag ahead of her with more force than necessary. It lands on her bed with a bounce and she turns, shutting the door behind her.

"Is there audio?" I ask.

He nods, leaning over the keyboard for a brief moment. Shep hits a few buttons and then lifts a set of headphones I hadn't noticed before, passing them to me. I slide them into place and already I can hear her curses.

"—fucking asshole. Who the fuck does he think he is?" She growls in frustration and shoves her hands through her long hair, pushing the liquid red gold strands back. On the screen, her face cuts a striking image. Big, wide, light brown eyes. A smattering of freckles across the bridge of her petite nose and long eyelashes throwing shadows down her bone structure.

I lean forward, watching her as she paces back and forth across the room and then finally sinks into the cushy chair in front of her desk and groans. A knock sounds on her door and it pops open. The girl from earlier—Selene— steps inside, holding up two dresses on hangers.

"Hey, I'm picking my outfit for the Gods and

Goddesses party this coming weekend. Which dress do you think I should go with?"

Ugh. Girl shit. I sit back again and let my mind drift as I listen to the two of them talk. At least I know she's irritated by me. She has to know the rumors are my doing —well, Paris' really. I know this won't be enough to drive her to the edge, though. What else can I do? What more is there?

I slip the headphones off and toss them to the desk before scrubbing a hand down my face. "Problem?" Shep asks.

"No," I say. "They're just talking about that stupid God party or whatever." I bend over and set my elbows on my knees, steepling my fingers together and resting my chin there.

"You seem upset," Shep points out.

"I'm not."—*I am.*—"I'm just trying to figure out what to do next."—*I'm just trying to understand this strange girl and what her weak point would be.*

The best friends are a weak point, but going after them too soon could backfire. I don't have to be the one to do it, though. I sit up. "Are we going to that party?" I ask.

Shep shrugs. "Can," he replies. "We're invited." Of course we are. There's a standing invitation on this campus for us. We're legacies, after all.

"Call Paris. Tell him to meet us there."

"You know it's a mask thing, right?" Shep quirks a brow my way. "Required. No one gets in without one."

I groan. "Fuck. Fine. I'll get one. Make sure to be there." If Aurora and Selene are going, then there's no doubt they'll drag their third friend along. And a party is the perfect chance for Paris to make his move on her. He won't mind, after all; I saw how he was eyeing her in front of the coffee shop at the start of school. He may say Selene is hot, but Helen Argos is the one he's truly attracted to.

I pull my phone out and send him a quick text anyway, just to make sure. I rarely ask him for favors, but he knows I'd cut myself open to help him if necessary. Same as I would for Shep. As soon as I get the affirmative text back, I've got the game plan running circles in my head.

It's nothing but a countdown now. Sunshine girl's days are numbered. Friends are weaknesses and strengths. It's just too bad for Aurora Summers that she doesn't know how to make use of hers.

9

RORI

I stare into the mirror of Hel's bathroom and finish brushing on another swipe of gold highlight along my cheekbone. I rarely go for an excessive amount of makeup, but every once in a while, I like it. Because sometimes, makeup isn't just a way to make a girl feel pretty. Sometimes, it makes a girl feel powerful. Tonight, it makes me feel like the goddess I'm pretending to be. Beautiful. Ethereal. *Dangerous.*

I smile at my reflection. I look like a completely different person. Gold glitter covers the upper half of my face, from just above my eyebrows to halfway down my cheeks. My lips are plumped and painted in a shimmery, light pink.

The nearly white-blonde wig that is braided into a crown at the top of my head is frighteningly realistic with a few wispy curls falling against my neck, and with the white floor-length Grecian dress, I look like I really have transformed into a goddess of the night ... or rather Dawn.

A high-pitched whistle reaches my ears and I turn, meeting Selene's gaze as she looks me up and down.

"Damn girl, you look good!" she says. I laugh at the baby pink dress she's wearing. Even though it's Grecian style like mine, someone has obviously adjusted it to look more modern. Instead of being floor length, it's cut to just at her thighs with thick, gold ropes hanging around her waist to emphasize her hourglass shape.

Next to her, Hel looks ready to be going anywhere but to a college party. In lieu of a dress, she's wearing cut black pleather pants that mold to her shape and a matching lace bralette.

"Who's your goddess?" I ask.

Hel holds up her mask, showing a half mask made to look like a skeleton's face. "It comes with a crown," she says, lifting the crown in question in her other hand. My eyes widen. An array of sharp-pointed sticks pokes out of a ring of dead roses.

"Underworld or something?" I ask.

"*Yup.*" She pops the last syllable. "If anyone asks, I'll tell them to guess, but I was thinking Hel—Norse Goddess of death.

"I'm Aphrodite!" Selene pops in.

"Oh, we can tell," I say as I slide past her.

"What?" She puts her hands on her hips and glares playfully at me. "How?"

"You're practically exuding sexuality," I reply. "Are you planning on killing all the guys tonight or fucking them?"

She thinks about it for a moment. "I don't know yet," she finally admits. "I'll decide when I get there."

I shake my head. Lord help whoever tames her.

"Wait, who are you supposed to be?" Hel asks as I pick up my mask from the common room coffee table and slide it into place. I'm glad I went with a soft white mesh instead of something hard and plastic. The fabric molds to my upper face. The glitter looks like it's leaking down—like I'm crying liquid gold.

"Eos," I say.

Selene frowns. "Who's that?"

"Aurora," Hel replies.

I smile. She gets it. "What?" Selene scrunches her face up as she looks between us. "Am I missing something?"

"Yeah," I say, "but you usually are."

Her lips press together and she offers me a bland glare. "Just for that," she says, "you have to dance with me tonight."

I laugh, shaking my head. "Come on," I say. "We're gonna be late."

"Fashionably!" Selene calls after us as Hel and I move towards the door and out into the hallway.

Together, the three of us head out. Half an hour later, the town car Selene called pulls up in front of a luxurious mansion with large Roman pillars spanning the front of the building. Lights twinkle and glitter from all directions. The difference between this place and the bar Marcus had taken me to is like night and day. And yet, I feel as though I'm stuck somewhere in the middle of the two.

Born into wealth and luxury, bored with the fallacy of it all. Craving reality, and yet, also frightened of the darkness it holds. Dusk and Dawn. That is who I am—tonight it's just a little more obvious than usual.

Just before we enter the house, Hel latches onto my arm. "Are you still planning on getting back at that guy tonight?" she asks.

Her words bring me back to reality and remind me of

the real reason why I came tonight. I'd double-checked with Selene and asked her to ask around, and sure enough, Isaac Icari was invited. He should be here. "Yes," I answer her without hesitation. I'm not backing down.

Her hand tightens on my arm. "Just ... be careful," she warns. "I've heard some pretty shady stuff about him on campus this past week."

I tilt my head in her direction. "Shady in what way?" I ask.

Hel looks up at me with wide, dark eyes and slowly loosens her hold until her hand is barely pressed against my arm. "I heard that the Icari head is involved with organized crime," she says on a low breath, barely loud enough for me to hear over the chatter of people and music inside the house.

There's concern in her gaze. I reach over and clasp her fingers with mine. "Even if that's true, nothing will happen to me here," I assure her. "Don't worry."

"Yeah," she says without much confidence in her voice, "the second I stop worrying about you is the second I start acting like Selene."

Almost as if to prove the ridiculousness of that statement, Selene squeals as she pushes through a crowd of people and dives headfirst into the dance floor. Thankfully, she's left me alone, having forgotten her threat before we left. I smile regardless, watching as she makes quick friends and an attractive man with a bare chest and animal mask starts grinding against her back. I wait for a moment to see if she needs help, but she turns and grins at him, putting her own hand against his six-pack as she grinds right back.

"The second you turn into a Selene clone," I reply to Hel, "is when the world ends."

She harrumphs in reply, but I know she agrees. They love each other, mostly because when the rest of Selene's family had scorned Hel's stepfather for marrying her mother, she'd welcomed her with open arms. Still, they've always been and always will be two completely different people.

"I'm gonna go grab a drink," she says. "You want anything?"

I shake my head. "You gonna be okay on your own for a while?" I ask instead. "I'm probably going to head off." *In search of my target,* but I don't voice that last bit aloud. Not that I need to.

She narrows her eyes on me. "I've got my phone on vibrate in my bra," she tells me. "Call or text if you need me. I'll feel it."

I tilt my head down in acknowledgment before watching her disappear into the crowd, her dark slender figure only overshadowed by the black crown of sticks and roses on her head as she takes off.

And just like that, as soon as she's gone, the crowd around me converges. Like sharks smelling blood in the water, the moment I'm caught alone without a buffer, I feel a hand slide around my waist and I'm jerked roughly against a hard chest.

Irritation flares to life as hot, unwelcome breath hits my ear. "Hey there," a deep masculine voice says. "Anyone ever told you that you look like a fallen angel?"

I don't even bother with a response. Instead, I reach around, latching onto two of his fingers and turning the opposite way out of his grasp until he's gasping in pain and half bent over when I tuck his thumb against his back.

"Anyone ever tell you that you need to keep your

hands to yourself?" I ask sweetly before shoving him
forward into a group of guys watching with amusement.

One of them blocks the asshole from falling immediately as he lands against him, but the guy that catches him
surprises me. When I expect him to help his friend up, he,
instead, looks down and steps to the side, quirking his lips
as the guy I just shoved falls the rest of the way, landing
on his ass with a stunned expression.

Then, as if there's not a two-hundred-something-
pound dude cursing up a storm as he crawls up from the
floor, the guy standing across from me puts his hands in
his pockets and looks at me. Like everyone else here, he's
dressed for the theme. His wide shoulders are covered in a
billowy white pirate shirt and his pants are a worn brown
suede. He looks like a farmer or country boy with the halo
of light brown, almost blonde curls on his head, but the
eyes staring back at me through the plain black mask are
anything but innocent. They're downright sinful.

"Did you have to hurt him like that?" he asks and I
stiffen because the second he opens his mouth, I recognize
his voice and I can't believe my fucking luck. "He was just
shooting his shot."

"Yeah? Well, I was shooting him down," I reply casually, crossing my arms. On the outside, I'm cool as a
cucumber, but on the inside, I'm a riot of nerves. There's
no way Isaac recognizes me—not with the wig and
makeup ... right?

Isaac looks back at the guy brushing himself off and
glaring in my direction. "Yes, you were," he says absently,
putting a hand out and stopping the douche when he
moves towards me with a snarl. "Whoa there, my man. I
think she's a bit too feisty for you, don't you agree?"

"You fucking bitch—"

Isaac's hand turns into a fist as he clenches his fingers into the guy's dress shirt, nearly ripping a few buttons off in the process. I press my lips together, but it's only to keep them from dropping open completely when Isaac turns and gets into the guy's face—that smile still in place, though it grows a bit tighter.

"I suggest you *walk away*." Isaac's growl isn't a request; it's a command. One that makes the man pause and take notice. Despite the fact that he's obviously bigger and heavier than Isaac, there's something very acute about Isaac's smile. Something predatory. Sharp. After another moment, the dude nods and Isaac releases him. I watch with curiosity as the guy turns and disappears into the crowd without another glance back.

What is it about Isaac Icari that, even when his identity is supposedly hidden, he commands respect and authority?

I don't know, and to be honest, I'm not sure I want to find out, but it's too little and too fucking late now. The two of us are bound through this thorny maze until we reach the center. I think back, remembering all the little digs and rumors that have been floating around this past week. All because of him.

"Now that he's gone..." Isaac nods and the posse around him disperses without another word. The two of us are left in the front hall of one of Hazelwood University's notorious frat houses, with only the sound of music drifting in and gold glitter fluttering around my eyes every time I blink. I stiffen as he moves towards me, reaching down and grasping my hand. He lifts it and bends. My chest tightens and all of the oxygen in my body freezes as the feel of his lips brushes against my knuckles. They're softer than I thought they'd be. He's such a hard man to read. I thought he'd be hard all over, but his lips are like silk against my skin. And it isn't until his head tips up, those blue eyes looking up at me with curiosity and interest, that I finally force myself to start breathing again. "Can I ask who you're supposed to be, Goddess?"

Do I answer, or will it be too obvious? He didn't react to the sound of my voice. Maybe I really am unrecognizable in this getup. "What kind of goddess would I be if I just gave everything away?"

Those full lips of his quirk up even more and he straightens, getting taller and taller until I'm forced to tip my head back to meet his gaze now that we're little more than a foot away. "A mystery, then," he replies. "I like it."

"And you?" I ask. "You don't look like a god."

Now that comment has him chuckling as he releases my hand from his grasp and takes a step back. "Maybe I am and maybe I'm not," he replies. "Maybe I'm a human in god-like clothes."

"Aren't we all." I don't mean to say the words, but as soon as they're out, I know I can't take them back. It was my own thought and not something said to draw him in. He doesn't seem offended though. In fact, he tilts his head and I feel that gaze of his sharpen.

"If you won't tell me your name, then what am I supposed to call you?"

"I think Goddess is good enough, don't you?"

He laughs. "Fair enough," he replies with a shake of his head. Isaac holds out his hand. "Then, Miss Mystery Goddess, would you care to join me?"

Placing my hand against his feels wrong. It feels like going against nature or stepping straight into the path of a tornado. Yet, I do. I do it because I'm tired of feeling like a child in need of protection. I'm tired of waiting on the sidelines while the actions of everyone but myself—my mother, my brother, a stepfather I never wanted—hold control over my life.

Not anymore.

Hel's warning rings in the back of my head. The Icari family and organized crime. Dean's caution to my brother. All of them are rolling around in my mind, telling me to turn back. Only one voice is screaming above the rest. She's shouting 'Hell yes, bitch,' and unfortunately, that's the one I listen to.

It's dangerous, I know. There's no maybe about it. But I think I'm starting to like the danger.

10

ISAAC

Sneaky. Sneaky. Sneaky. It's impossible to keep my amusement from shining through. Does she really think that she's hidden under half a pound of makeup and a wig? It's a beautiful look for her, I'll grant her that much, but eyes are like windows to the soul and I knew exactly who she was the second she looked up at me.

She can wear all the gold she wants, and exude her confidence behind that pretty little mask, but nothing can hide those eyes of hers. Eyes like dark honey. Rich. Cunning. Tempting.

What is she planning? She has to know who I am. Or maybe she doesn't. I can't quite say what would be more intriguing.

I have to hand it to the girl, though; tonight she has me spellbound. I'm still debating on whether or not I should let her take the lead. I want to see where she'll steer us. I want to see what her angle is. Because there's no doubt in my mind that she has one. I hope like fuck she's planning something naughty—even if that means she doesn't know who she's doing it with.

I'm hungry. Not for food. Not for drink. But for her.

After the fiasco with Javi—one of the fresh blockheads for Hazelwood's defensive line—I lead Aurora out of the main portion of the party and towards the back veranda. "Drink?" I ask as we stop by the bar on the way out where a stone-faced man in a tux and a black mask stands, waiting for orders.

"Tequila Sunrise," she says.

The man doesn't even bother asking for identification —no one cares when money buys silence as easily as liquor. Minutes later, with her glass in hand and a beer in mine, I head towards the staircase leading into the back-yard and she follows.

It's quieter on the back lawn, further from the party than anyone else likely would've been comfortable with. Not her, though. I bet she's thinking that she's gotten a golden opportunity. Me and her. Alone. I find a stone table beneath an open umbrella at the entrance to a large hedge maze and take a seat.

I sit back and tip my beer up, swallowing down a mouthful. *Let the games begin.* It's time to see what she's made of.

"What should I call you?" she finally asks, choosing her words carefully.

I lean my head to one side, watching her through the holes in my mask. "Icarus," I decide. "You can call me Icarus." Seems fitting, considering it's only a few letters away from my real name.

"Icarus isn't a god," she points out.

"True," I agree readily. "But I don't need godly powers to please you, Goddess."

"Oh really?" The slight eye roll she gives me is amusing rather than irritating. "Well, be careful there,

Icarus. Or you might just find yourself burning alive. Maybe you're better off impersonating an actual god."

"The idea of burning doesn't scare me," I say. "Besides, what makes a god *a god*?" I ask. "Power?"

She tips her own glass up against her lips and when she lowers it, that little pink tongue of hers flicks out and licks a drop of orange juice off the rim. The fabric across my lap tightens.

"You could say it's power," she says. "But if that were the case, then you *would* be a god, wouldn't you?"

"The God of Hazelwood University?" I ask. Yeah, she definitely knows it's me. I doubt she'd say that about anyone else. I hum in the back of my throat, my lips twitching in amusement. "I can't say I don't like the sound of that."

She laughs and it's like ringing bells in my ears. "You're a man, of course you like the sound of that."

"What makes a goddess *a goddess*," I challenge instead, switching gears as I lean forward and set my half-finished beer on the table. I steeple my fingers together and regard her with seriousness.

She doesn't react. In fact, she acts as though she can't even sense my hard gaze at all as she lifts her drink and downs another mouthful before pushing it onto the table as well.

"It's not power," she confesses, looking up at me through thick dark lashes. Despite the blonde of her wig and the lightness of what I know to be her natural hair color, her lashes are ink-black like the night sky.

"Then what is it?" I press, curious.

"It's a willingness to do whatever it takes to succeed," she says. I wait, something telling me that those words aren't all she has to say. And after a moment, I'm rewarded for my patience. Aurora blows out a breath, turning her head away. Small droplets of sweat collect on her neck and her collarbone. My gaze zeroes in on one as it slips over the dip of bone structure and down into the cleavage of her dress.

Stepsister, I remind myself. *Tool. Pawn. Baggage. Enemy.* That's all she is. All she's supposed to be.

My cock, on the other hand, doesn't seem to give a fuck. Needy bastard. Maybe I should've let one of the other girls hanging around Paris and me earlier suck me off before this. It's too late now.

"A goddess doesn't need power," she continues. "She already appears weak in the face of a god. No, what she really needs is durability. Perhaps even adaptability—a way to ensure that no matter what happens to her, she can keep going. Keep breathing. Keep living. As if nothing can touch her. Nothing can hurt her."

Silence stretches between us and she doesn't speak again for several moments. Neither does she reach for her drink. "You speak as though you have experience with that," I comment. "On the need for durability."

Her lips pinch together and the skin around the corners of her mouth whitens even beneath the makeup. Then, with careful movements, she looks my way—lifting her gaze to meet mine in challenge.

"Do you always ask your dates such philosophical shit?" she asks, shaking her head with a quiet, almost mocking laugh to herself. "In the end, none of it is real. The only real thing we can count on is what we can see and feel."

The fact that her words are almost an exact replica of something I might have said stuns me into silence. Loathe as I am to admit it, I think Aurora Summers and I have a little more in common than wayward, shittastic parents. Unfortunately, relating to her won't save her. In the end, I'll still use her.

As if she senses the dark direction of my thoughts, she leans forward, pushing her drink away. "What do you really want, Icarus?" She licks her lips. "Tell me, and perhaps I can make it come true."

Several emotions hit me at once—many of them contradicting. Thrill. Disappointment. Arousal. Regret.

Thrill because I know where this is going now. Disappointment because I almost expected more from her. Arousal because my dick doesn't know what to do with itself when an interesting woman sets herself in my path. And regret because I know I'll do it, anyway.

I stand up and hold out a hand. "Why don't you come with me, then?" I offer. "And figure out for yourself exactly what I want."

The feel of her fingers grasping for mine is like a ringing bell of warning in my head. I ignore it, though, because when Aurora Summers—pretend goddess—lifts her honeyed gaze and her eyes meet mine, nothing can stop me from doing what I'm about to do. I want to know what it feels like to walk on the darkest of lines, and I want to see her there with me.

11

RORI

I*carus*. Of course, that would be the name he'd give me.

Sure, Icarus was intelligent—a veritable genius, but he was also arrogant. Ultimately, that was his downfall, as it will be for Isaac.

My heart pounds against my ribcage, fast and fluttering—like a caged bird. Pretty and trapped. Isaac's philosophical words were disturbing. Too much so. His tone was almost poignant behind the veneer of indifference. I relate so fucking hard. I feel like my insides are squeezing me tight, cutting off my blood flow, cutting off my airflow. The world is narrowing down to one pinpoint I can see—Isaac Icari.

Now is the time. The last moment I can turn back and pretend I never intended to get mixed up with him. Despite knowing that, my feet continue forward and my mouth keeps silent. The truth is, even if I were to turn back now, the reality that both he and I are in won't disappear. The rumors will continue. Our parents will remain as they are. They'll always be *who* they are.

So, I let myself be pulled past the point of no return. I go willingly into that dark night and even if a light somehow reaches me once again, I don't think I'll regret these actions. Marcus warned me before he left the first time that people like us will always attract hidden agendas. I didn't know what he meant then. I do now.

The thought that I have nothing to prove is the biggest lie people like me tell ourselves.

I have so much to prove. To myself. To my brother. To my mother. And to Isaac.

I know exactly how they see me—weak, easily manipulated, powerless. It's my job to prove them all wrong and show them exactly how done I am with being treated like a pawn in their games. I am no man's pawn.

Each second that ticks by makes me want to hurry my movements. Like a clock is ticking down the time I have left. If I don't do this—if I don't end this sham of a fucking marriage between Icari and my mother before it's too late —then...

Isaac's hand tightens against mine, pulling me from my internal thoughts. His hand is warm, but not grossly so. There's no sweat—just heat ... and confidence. I look up at him, staring at the back of his head, analyzing his outline.

Has he ever felt out of control before? What will he do when he realizes who I am? What will I do in response?

The two of us slip deeper and deeper into the garden's maze behind the frat house mansion, the lights and the music fading as darkness surrounds us. Silence echoes up into the midnight sky. Stars twinkle down overhead. The soft scents of wet soil and freshly cut grass invade my senses. My skin tingles—invisible needles prickling me—as if waking up from a long sleep.

"So, Goddess..." Isaac stops as he comes out in the center of the garden to a stone gazebo and turns to meet my gaze. "What'll you do now?" he asks.

I tilt my head to the side and pull my hand away, wiping it casually against the side of my dress. *It's a good thing I'm wearing a mask,* I think. He can't see my face and, hopefully, that means he can't discern the riot my emotions are causing.

Right here. Right now. I'm just a girl he's interested in. Not his fake stepsister. Not his enemy. Just an illusion.

I smile. "Why don't we have a seat?" I ask, gesturing to the gazebo.

"Why don't you tell me why you're out here with me?" he counters, stepping closer.

Fine. If he wants to play it that way ... my hands hit his shoulders and I shove, pushing him back until his spine is against one of the hedges. Behind the mask, his eyes widen in surprise and then narrow as I lean up on my toes and bring my face right before his, sliding closer and closer until my lips are a hair's breadth from his.

"Is this what you wanted then?" I ask, smiling when he stiffens—not just his shoulders, but something down below as well. What do you know ... messing with Isaac Icari is enough to make a girl feel powerful. I should be careful not to get addicted to the feeling.

"Done with your games now, huh?" he replies coolly.

"What makes you think I'm playing a game?"

Hands latch onto my arms and he spins both of us in such a quick motion that my lips part on a gasp and before I know it, my back is pressed into the hedge and I'm lifted off my feet. Left with little recourse, I wrap my arms around his shoulders and my legs around his hips, tightening my limbs until I'm not at risk of falling. *Is this what he does to keep girls off balance?* I hate to admit it, but it's working.

His chuckle vibrates against my whole frame. "You and I both know that we've both been playing a game since the moment you looked at me and crooked your little finger." His words are breathy, hot.

Shock hits my system when I feel his lips move against the side of my throat unrestrained. He shows no hesitation, no nervousness as he follows the path of my pulse until he reaches the underside of my jaw and opens his mouth to press a hot kiss to the skin there before pulling away. My thighs tremble and my insides tighten.

I need to get to my phone inside my bra before he realizes it's there. Releasing his shoulders, I push his upper body back and debate for a brief moment on how to pull this off.

"What's wrong?" he asks.

"Nothing," I say quickly. "It's just ... I think my dress is a little too tight." When in doubt, go naked. It's not like I've never been naked in front of a guy before ... just not with the intention to seduce and destroy. Mata Hari, I am not, but I pray it works.

His lips twitch. "Does a goddess reveal her secrets that easily, then?"

I lift my head and regard him curiously. On the outside, it's a simple, teasing question, but I know there's a reason for it. It almost sounds like he's ... disappointed. Almost as if he'd expected something different from me. What else could he have thought, though? I'm not a mind reader and even if I was, something tells me Isaac Icari wouldn't be so easy to understand.

"I didn't say I was taking it off," I say quietly. "It's

tight. I just need to adjust it. Unless ... you were expecting something else?"

His head jerks back. "You..." He stops, lips parted and for a long moment just stares back at me. The two of us are locked in what can only be considered a battle of wills. Who will crack first?

Moments later, I have my answer. Isaac's strong arms release me and he slowly lets me slide down his front, so that I feel every hard inch of him. He takes two careful steps away and then turns his back to me. "Hurry up." The words are said through gritted teeth, a testament to the desires he's shoving down—all because I told him I wanted to fix my dress.

With a sharp inhale, I reach into my inner cup and pull out my cell phone. Turning quickly, I shove it into the hedge, adjusting the height as much as I can so it can span the two of us. A small kernel of regret pierces me, but as quickly as it came, it fades away again. Even if this isn't what I want to do, it's what I *have* to do.

No sooner have I shoved the phone into place, flicked the camera light off, and hit start on the record button than Isaac turns towards me. I jump as he reaches up and rips his mask off, tossing it away before he moves for me. Now, there's no more facade—not from him at least. He's there in all of his Isaac Icari beauty.

I'm back in his arms in a split second, being lifted against a strong chest as my feet leave the ground. With an arm beneath my ass, he keeps me pressed as close to him as physically possible. "You didn't take off your dress," he murmurs as his lips return to their previous position against my neck. The heat he exudes invades once more.

"I told you I was just fixing it." I sigh as his tongue traces a path down to my collarbone.

"No makeup down here," he says.

"What?" I blink, confused by the comment.

He lifts his head once more. "I thought you would've dusted makeup all over," he says. "I half expected my mouth to come away tasting like plastic and glitter, but I guess all this silken skin is purely you, isn't it?"

I don't know what to say to that, but it's okay because it doesn't seem like he's expecting a response. Isaac's head dips down and he reaches around, fingers finding the zipper at the back of my gown. "You should've taken this off instead of fixing it," he says as my dress loosens and the fabric at the front begins to drift down. It was a good call to remove the phone.

"You wouldn't have been disappointed?" What makes me ask the question, I don't know, but curiosity keeps me from taking it back.

Isaac's head moves back once more and cool air filters over my skin. I swallow roughly, nervously. "What makes you think I'd be disappointed?" he asks.

"You seemed like it," I said.

He arches a brow. "This isn't disappointment, Goddess," he says, rubbing his fabric-covered cock against me, between my legs. "It's excitement."

Maybe some of it is, but I'm not that naive. He was on the verge of disappointment. I just don't know why. I bite my bottom lip as his head dips down and his mouth dances between my breasts, igniting a fire inside of me that I haven't felt in a long ass time.

"I think you would've been disappointed," I insist when really I want to slap myself upside the head and tell my inner curiosity to shut the fuck up. Now is not the time to be finding out what he's so fucking disappointed about. It's the time to be catching him on camera, naked and compromised. Something to use as blackmail later.

My breath comes out on a rush and my words are almost swallowed by the wind. But they're there and he hears them. They give him pause and Isaac lifts his head once more, those dangerous blue eyes of his piercing into me in ways that go beyond the surface.

"What is that supposed to mean?" he demands, his voice rough with desire as well as something else I can't name. Frustration maybe? Just how far am I willing to let him go tonight? This is just supposed to be enough to get dirt on him, not for me to lose myself. Yet, with every second spent in his presence, I can feel my resolve fluctuating. Not with my ability to see this through—I know I can and I will—but I almost want to be doing this for another reason and not because we see each other as enemies.

When I answer, the truth pours out. "When you thought I was going to take off my dress before," I tell him. "You were disappointed."

"You think so?" He neither confirms nor denies my statement, and for several long moments, the two of us stare back at one another with a heaviness that wasn't there previously. "Maybe I just didn't know if you were going to be one of those girls who fucks on the first date."

My breath catches in my throat. "Looks like I am," I say pointedly, looking down between us.

He hums in the back of his throat. "It's different when I'm the one taking your dress off," he tells me.

I frown. "If we fuck around, then what makes a difference as to who gets naked first?"

Isaac's breath gets closer as he leans into me, his palm

sliding up my spine as my legs tighten around his waist. "Is that what we're doing, Goddess?" he asks tauntingly. "Are we *fucking around*?"

Silence descends between us after his question. It's a distraction, a clear signal that he's not willing to go into any more detail about why he might have been disappointed in me. I press my lips together and debate letting it go, but in the end, I can't. "What do you want, Icarus?" I ask.

He blinks, pulling his head back again until a ray of moonlight slaps him right in the face he's revealed without his mask. High cheekbones. Thick dark brows. Full masculine lips. He looks like the god he's pretending not to be.

"Why are you calling me that?" he demands. "You know who I am now."

I tilt my head to the side, since I know he can't see the arch of my brow behind my mask. "That's the name you gave me," I say. "I don't want to destroy the fantasy."

His surprised expression morphs into one of amusement. "Are you saying you won't reveal yours to me tonight?" he asks.

"My identity?" No. No way in fucking hell. No one can know what I'm about to do, especially not him, not until I'm ready to use this trump card I'm creating. "No."

"No name and no secrets," he whispers, bowing his head towards me. "You're really making me work for no reward."

My fingers arch up over his shoulders and my dress loosens even more with the movement. Fabric falls away and the tops of my breasts are revealed. Warm air touches my newly unclothed flesh. His eyes go immediately down to my cleavage as the dress droops further.

"That's not true," I say as his gaze eats me up. "I intend to reward the man who's stolen into my garden tonight." It'll be his prize for falling right into my trap.

The quiet laugh that erupts from his throat is enough to shake me to my core. It's dark and sinister, like something forbidden is being whispered into my ear. "If that's how you want to play things tonight, Goddess, then so be it," he replies. "I'll play the part of your mortal lover if you open those divine legs of yours and let me inside."

I don't have a chance to say another word—be it acquiescence or denial—before his head descends and his mouth takes mine. A heat like I've never known consumes me. Fire burns away my thoughts as his tongue intrudes. Dirty. Filthy. Vile. Addictive.

Isaac Icari kisses like a villain. Like he's a mortal trying to seduce the goddess he's found. He plays into my fantasies like no other man could until I'm left breathless and on the verge of a new emotion I never thought I'd feel again. Not after...

I pull away from the kiss, shaking my head and disrupting the direction of my thoughts. No. I don't want to think about that right now. It has no place here. Even if I don't like Isaac, I like this. I like what his body does to mine. Just for right now, I'll let myself forget that I'm supposed to hate him. Just for tonight, I'll play the part he wants from me.

12

ISAAC

A beautiful little liar, that's what she is. An illusion.

I still haven't quite figured out what it is that she wants from me tonight, why she's here, or why she's decided to do this with me. My dick doesn't seem to care. It pulses against the inside of my pants as her dress sags down the front of her body, revealing inch by inch the creamy expanse of skin that she was hiding underneath.

My mouth waters and I dip my head once more, tasting her. When I first put my lips to her flesh, I'd expected the disgusting feel of dusty makeup. Instead, all I got was clean, perfect skin. She smells like the sun. I can't help but take a bite—setting my canines to the column of her throat and sinking deep, digging the blunt edges of my teeth into her until I can feel her whole body stiffen against me and a small moan escapes her throat. She likes a little bit of pain.

My dirty, manipulative goddess.

My cock jumps. It's hard enough to keep my desire at bay, but when her nails sink into my shoulders, scoring me even through my shirt, it becomes impossible. I want to feel her all over me. Her flesh is right there, and she's giving it to me. I'm not selfless enough to turn down the ambrosia before me.

Damn the fucking consequences, but we can pretend later. Pretend that she never opened her legs to me and let me touch her like this. Or maybe this is her plan—it probably is if I give my lust-addled brain long enough to contemplate it.

I don't. There's no point. I want her and I intend to have her. At the very least, I intend to get my release.

I pull back abruptly, not giving her a second to ask what I'm doing before my hands find the hem of my shirt. Her legs tighten around me briefly and then drop completely back to the ground when I force them to part. I take a step back and yank my shirt up and off, dropping it into the dirt before I'm back with her, pulling her against me until I can feel her soft feminine curves under my wanting fingers.

Aurora Summers is hiding something. She's hiding the reason she's sought me out, and I know there's no mistaking it. She *did* seek me out. Why would a girl who never parties, rarely drinks, and doesn't have an ounce of dumb rich girl personality in her be here tonight? There's only one answer: she's here for me.

I half expected her to jump back and reveal her own identity when I pulled off my mask, but she didn't. That tells me she knows exactly who she is seducing. Her lack of surprise and, even more, her unwillingness to walk away should be a huge warning, and it is. The temptation of her, however, is too much for me to listen to logic. Whatever she thinks she can gain from me now, it can't possibly be more than she's willing to give.

I intend to give her exactly what she came for, and if I

get to take advantage of her body in the process then it's her own fault for coming to me. She knows what she's doing. She stepped into this labyrinth. She should know that there's always a monster at the center waiting to eat all who wander inside.

My next kiss is violent, harsh. I grab onto the back of her head and pull her into me with rough, angry movements. Surprisingly, she doesn't get nervous. Instead, she rises to the challenge—meeting me stroke for stroke. She's not shy at all. Her own tongue twines with mine once again. She moans into my mouth and doesn't hesitate to play dirty. Her nails scrape against my skin, driving me higher and higher.

How cute. As if the bite of her nails does anything but make me want to reciprocate the pain.

Unable to take it any longer, I rip away from her devious lips and snatch her up by the wrists. Both of us are panting and breathless.

"You want more, goddess?" I inquire.

"Yes..." The confession is a low whisper that turns into a half-moan, as if she doesn't want to actually show how turned on she is, but at the same time, she knows she needs to if she is to get what she wants.

A grin graces my lips. "How much more?" I press.

"W-what?" Soft eyes stare at me through her mask. Heated and clouded with arousal.

I bend down, brushing my lips along her cheek even as I continue to hold her wrists in my hold, transferring both of them to one of my hands. "Is your pussy wet?"

Her skin warms next to my face. "I..." She stops, tugging lightly at her bound hands.

Can't admit how much she wants me? That's okay. I can just check for myself.

"Why don't I find out for myself?" The question is rhetorical, a fact she's obviously aware of because she doesn't respond as my fingers touch her—moving down her front over the fabric. I skip her breasts and she inhales sharply, her head turning slightly in a panicked motion that I ignore. If she wanted out of this, she would say so.

Instead, I move down, lifting up the folds of her dress higher and higher until they pile up onto my wrist as I slip my hand between her legs. A groan rumbles inside my chest. "Fuck," I mutter, sliding two fingers along the soaked fabric covering her pussy. "You're so hot for me, aren't you? Is this pussy desperate? Do you want something, goddess?"

She swallows, tugging at her hands again. "Let go." The words are a breath. Not a demand, but a gentle request. Arching a brow, I release her and she goes up onto her toes, her mouth moving over my flesh as she suckles and kisses over the side of my throat. Amusement dances within me.

Her soft limbs slide against me, clinging. I like that. I like feeling like she needs me to keep her afloat, and at the same time, there's a little sense in the back of my mind that warns me if I loosen my grip, she'll float away—leaving me forever. I don't want to keep her for that long—I can't—but I do want her for tonight so I tighten my grip and spin the two of us around.

A gasp leaves her lips as I lift her back into my arms, her dainty little feet leaving the ground once more. Her hands flatten on my shoulders and she pushes back when she seems to realize that I'm carrying her away from our original position. "Wait, stop!" Aurora rips herself from my arms, nearly sending both of us flying towards the ground when I adjust my grip to keep her from falling.

I curse internally, irritation sliding through me.

"What's wrong?" I demand, lifting my head and looking around, seeking out a reason for her sudden outcry. I see no one, though, and so my eyes return to her form as she stands before me, adjusting her clothes as a blush stains across her cheeks beneath the gold glitter of her makeup. She looks back the way we came, and her expression tightens. I'm not sure what thoughts are going through her head, but her teeth flash white in the darkness as she sinks them into her plump lower lip. Instead of answering me, she seems to be arguing with herself.

"Do you want to stop?" *Please say no. Fuck, Gods above, please tell me you haven't realized what a colossal mistake this is going to be.*

A moment of silence passes between us and then she straightens her shoulders and turns back to me. I watch as she reaches up and grips one side of her dress and pulls it down. She does the same to the other and suddenly her breasts are bared to my view. My breath stops in my chest. That's her answer, then. A big fat hell fucking no, and I've never been more grateful for a 'no' in my life.

At first glance, Aurora Summers is an average girl that looks no different from the rest. She's neither overly beautiful nor is she ugly. She's normal. Easily overlooked. At least, that was what I'd initially thought.

My original assumption could not be further from the truth. Standing before me like this, she's a true goddess with full round breasts tipped in pink. Freckles stain across her skin going even further down, and I can't help but want to trace each and every one of them with my tongue. They mold over her chest and between her breasts to her stomach and upper thighs.

"I want more," she whispers, her voice carrying across the quiet space between us.

My tongue feels like it has swelled up by at least ten times; it chokes me, clogging my throat so no words escape. It's only when she pulls her arms free of the straps of her dress and then goes to her knees in front of me that my voice seems to come back to me.

"Shit..." I hiss out a breath as her little hands go to the front of my pants and she quickly undoes them.

What the fuck is this girl doing to me? Is it her goal to see me lose my absolute shit?

That thought doesn't seem to be far from the truth because she doesn't hesitate to open my pants and pull my cock free. It rises to her attention, slapping against the underside of my belly button before swaying away from me and right towards her.

Calm the fuck down, I urge myself. *She wants something from you. Don't think this is anything more.* I close my eyes and suck in a breath and then another and another until I feel like I'm further from her and more back in the right headspace. I reopen my eyes and look down at the image she presents.

With curious fingers, she explores my length, her nails scraping slightly against my sensitized skin as she rakes them down the notches on either side of my hips and pulls my pants down a little bit further. Little pops of electricity race through my system. She curves her fingers around me, stroking up and down. Squeezing. Driving me to the brink with little movement or effort.

She's a liar, I remind myself. *She's doing this for a reason, and it's not for her own pleasure.*

That last internal thought hits me squarely in the gut in a way nothing else could. That's right. Aurora

Summers hates me. I'm on the verge of making her life miserable. She knows that. Whatever she's doing here is to get back at me. Or perhaps it's to get back at Mommy Dearest. Whatever the case, though, it's a fact that she doesn't fucking want me. I'm just a means to an end.

A scowl overtakes my face, one I can't hide. Irritation slithers through my skin. I reach forward and palm the back of her head. Big brown eyes look up at me through a white mesh mask. "Don't just stroke it, goddess," I say. "You know what you need to do."

If she wants to play games with the big boys, then she's going to have to learn to follow her little schemes through, because I have no intention of letting her get away tonight without getting a little something of my own.

"Open your mouth," I order, my voice hard.

Her lashes flutter behind the mask, and it takes a second—the longest one in history—for her to do as I command. But when she does, her tongue slides out, an open invitation for what I want to do to her. Fuck me, but she's too much. I fist my cock in my grip and slap it against her tongue.

Precum dribbles out, catching on the flat surface, but she doesn't flinch. *Fucking slut.* How many others has she done this to? I thought she was different—not the party girl others of her status are. This, though, proves that I gave her too much credit. She's not a good girl at all. She's a fucking whore like the rest and there's only one way to treat a whore.

"Are you hungry, goddess?" I ask. The image she presents, on her knees, tits out, tongue against my cock should be criminal. She blinks and, instead of answering, tries to lean forward and capture my cock between her lips.

I pull my hips back, slipping out of her reach and causing her to look back up at me with confusion. I grin, feeling mean. "You'll have to ask for what you want," I inform her. "I don't want to question later if you wanted this or not. I want you to beg for my cock in your mouth."

She swallows again, her throat bobbing with the movement. There's a play of various emotions through her eyes. Confusion. Hesitation. Finally, Resignation.

"Please," she says, somewhat awkwardly. "Please, can I suck your cock?"

I stroke myself, up and down, base to tip and back. "I don't know," I hedge. "Do you think you can swallow me?" I'm taunting her, a fact she realizes as her skin turns pink beneath that stupid mask. Oh, how I wish I could rip it off and be done with this façade. But no, she wanted it this way so we'll play things her way. Until it no longer amuses me.

Aurora leans forward again, and again, I back away. She whimpers. "Wait—" Her hands latch onto my thighs. "Please."

"Please what?" I arch a brow. "You're going to have to be clear with what you want."

"I want to suck you," she says, sharper now, more desperate. "I want your cock in my mouth, on my tongue. I want to taste you. Please fuck my mouth."

This time when she moves forward on her knees, her hands reach for the base of my cock—replacing my own—she licks up the front. "Use me," she pleads.

My smile is full of razor-sharp rage. "I intend to fucking destroy you, goddess," I growl right before I slide my hands to the back of her skull, and the head of my cock disappears between her lips.

My skull snaps back as molten heat wraps around my dick. I force it in faster than I'm sure she intended to take it, but I don't care. When she chokes slightly on the length, I don't stop. Her mouth is like a cavern of wet fire.

"*Fuck.*" I groan. "Just like that. Suck me, baby."

Her tongue lashes against the underside of my shaft. She strokes it, moving down as her lips stretch over the girth. I grit my teeth and hiss out another breath. *Jesus. Fucking. Christ.* Heaven and hell are both a lot closer than I was once led to believe. They're both right here, in her dangerous little mouth.

My fingers move through her wig, an expensive one at that since it feels like real hair. If I close my eyes, I can imagine that it's actually hers. Instead of a flat, ugly white color—I imagine the soft silken tresses of brown and gold and even a little hint of red under my fingers as she takes me deeper into her mouth.

She's not a first-timer, that much is clear. She sucks me all the way until I hit the back of her throat. A grin flutters across my lips when she moves to pull back, but I tighten against the back of her head and hold her in place. I open my eyes and look down with a smile.

"No, no, Goddess," I say, tauntingly. "If you're going to start something, you should finish it. Take me all the way. I want it in your throat."

Her lips tighten around my shaft and her eyes widen with surprise and a little bit of panic. "You begged me to use you, don't get scared now," I say. Before she can try and push back again, I push once more.

A groan hits me when she chokes on my cock again, the muscles of her throat and mouth convulsing as I push past her resistance and right where I want to be. I can hear her breathing heavily through her nose, but she does it. My cock sinks past her mouth that last few inches and fuck it, it's gratifying. Feeling her whole body trembling as she tries to suck me threatens to make me come far too soon.

"That's a good slut," I tell her. "You're right where you want to be, aren't you?"

The eyes that cut up to my face are full of indignation. I grin down at her and use my hold on her head to pull her nearly off my length, with nothing more than my head just past her lips. She turns her face to the side, coughing.

"Don't be a dick," she snaps, drool dribbling from her lips.

I roll my eyes. "You know who you're fucking," I say. "I'm not the one wearing a mask. If you go to Hazelwood —and if you're at this party, then you at least know of it— then you also know who I am."

"Why the fuck does that matter?" Her face blanches, her brow creasing.

I pull her closer, but she doesn't open her mouth again. My cock slides over her cheek, wetting her skin with her own saliva and my precum. I rub it all over her, a burst of amusement hitting me when she grits her teeth. Leaving one hand still at the back of her head, I fist my cock once more, taking it in hand and slapping her with it.

Her lips pop open in shock. Before she can say anything, I turn her face and slap her other cheek and then insert my cock back into her waiting mouth, pushing until she has no choice but to take it.

"Come on, Goddess," I say. "You can do better than that, can't you?" It's a taunt, one that pisses her off. Her nails sink even deeper into the skin on either side of my hips, the sharp pinpricks of pain turning me on like nothing else. That little attitude she shows is nothing compared to what I wish she'd do.

It's no fun hunting prey that doesn't fight back.

Aurora's tongue curls against the underside of my cock as I slowly pull back and drags down the veins there, tracing them and making me see fucking stars. Fuck, but she's good. My other hand moves down until both are against the back of her head. She's going to make me lose control. I've never fucking lost control before, but with her, I can feel my tightly held reins loosen.

The back of her skull presses into my palm when she tries to withdraw. I widen my stance and shove my cock, undeterred, back into her throat. She makes a small choking sound but takes it even better the second time. Soon enough, I'm able to saw back and forth between her full, pink lips without a care. Her throat is tight and every time my head enters, she swallows, squeezing me impossibly tight.

"There you go, Sunshine," I breathe. "Fuck, that feels so good. Yes—ugh, just like that..."

I can't think. My mind fractures, and I tighten all over, holding her down against my groin as I come straight down her throat. "Swallow," I hiss through clenched teeth, hunching over her as I grind her face into my lap. "Swallow my fucking cum, Aurora." I look down at her, locking our gazes together, and grin. "If you're already going this far to blow your stepbrother, you should be good enough to take it all, shouldn't you, sweetheart?"

I can sense her shock, but it's too late. My cum is already filling up her mouth, sliding over her tongue to the back of her throat. It makes me a disgusting bastard to relish in the fact that a little piece of me is in her belly, reminding her of the dirty, filthy things she did here tonight in this garden. As soon as I'm done, I pull out and take a step back, doing up the front of my pants and leaving her sitting there on her knees in the dirt with her pretty breasts hanging free.

Aurora coughs, bending over and spitting out the last of my cum. "What the fuck!" she screams.

I laugh, striding across the space to where I dropped my shirt. Picking it up, I dust off the debris and slide it back into place. When I've turned back, she's already got her dress adjusted.

"What's wrong, Sunshine?" I ask. "Mad because you got caught?"

Her chest rises and falls in rapid movements with her harsh breath. "You fucking asshole," she snarls.

I arch a brow before bending to pick up my mask as well, though it's useless at this point. As is hers, but I notice she doesn't take it off. "I don't know what you were trying to pull here," I admit a tad belatedly, "but I think if you want to piss off your mother, finding out you blew her husband's son will do, right?" I lift my gaze back to hers. "I'll even post a review if you like."

"You knew the whole time," she says, but it's not a question.

Still, I answer like it is. "You're not as good at hiding your identity as you think you are."

Her eyes narrow behind her mask. "Then why did you pretend not to know?"

"Why did *you*?" I shoot back. She has no answer to that. Instead, she just stands there, continuing to glare at me even as her hands clench into fists at her sides. I blow out a breath. "Whatever you did this for," I finally say, "I thought I'd play along to find out, but if you aren't even sure, then ... I guess I'll just say thanks for the nice blow job and be on my way."

Again, she says nothing. So, I turn and walk away, the heat of her gaze following me the entire way.

13

RORI

The squeak of the black marker against the dry-erase board at the front of the classroom is a sharp stab to my ears. I can feel the eyes on me. It's been three days since that stupid party, and the rumors have doubled in size. Now, people aren't even pretending to whisper about me. They're talking openly and rather loudly.

The little ace that I created to take advantage of Isaac sits dormant, partially useless, on my computer in the bag at my feet. The second half of the video, the part when he came down my fucking throat right before calling out my name, needs to be deleted. Or maybe I can corrupt the sound. I haven't really thought that far ahead. Him finding out who I was hadn't been in my plan, and now adjustments need to be made. Whether he realized I was recording or if he truly thinks I seduced him to get back at my mother, he sure knows how to ruin a good fucking plan.

Or maybe it'd been a bad one. Hell, I don't know anymore. All I know is that Isaac Icari needs to back off before I really lose my fucking mind.

Class ends, and I grab the first thing in front of me—my notebook—quickly shoving it into my bag before ripping the strap up and over my shoulder. I'm halfway down the front of the aisle when an unfamiliar girl steps in front of me, blocking my path.

I pause and take in a deep breath, praying that I can maintain my cool. If only Selene hadn't skipped class today, I wouldn't have to worry about beating the ever-living shit out of somebody.

"Is it true?" The girl in front of me is either too stupid to realize that I'm not in the mood to deal with her, or she's got just enough bitchy confidence to believe no one can ever actually touch her. Whatever the case, she cocks out her hip and tilts her head at me expectantly.

"Is *what* true?" I reply through gritted teeth.

"That you fucked Isaac Icari," she snaps.

Shock rockets through me and I whip my head around to stare down the man responsible for this fucking mess. Isaac stares back at me with an arched brow and a smirk. This chick has some serious balls asking me that with him in the room. I pivot to face her once more with a scowl.

"Why the fuck aren't you asking him?" I demand.

She rolls her eyes. "I'm asking *you*," is all she says. Then after a brief moment where I do nothing but grind my teeth together, ruining several thousands of dollars of dental work from years past, she huffs out a breath. "Well?" she says. "Did you or didn't you?"

"Why do you want to know?" I ask. An idea pops into my head and before I know it, a smile stretches across my lips. "Actually, you know what, the reason doesn't matter. You asked me if I fucked Isaac Icari?"

I can feel every eye and ear in the room on me. Even

knowing it'll make them late for their next classes, some of the students have stopped packing their things and are leaning in to listen to what I'll say next.

Oh you stupid, fucking arrogant asshole, I think with pleasure. Rumors are so easy to manipulate, and so easy to lose control of.

"That's what I asked, isn't it?" The girl doesn't seem to realize that she's just given me the opportunity of a lifetime.

"Yeah, I did," I say a little louder than her original voice and her jaw drops in shock, as if she's surprised that I admitted it. I turn to the side, pushing her out of my way before stopping and looking back. "If you're thinking of fucking him, I wouldn't recommend it. He has a tiny dick and I didn't even come. I'll never be able to get those five minutes of my life back again. Huge waste of time if you ask me."

With that final statement, I lift my gaze, meet Isaac's furious glare with a smirk of my own, and head for the exit.

He wants to play with rumors and my reputation? Well, fine. Two can play that game. Rumors, after all, once spoken, can't be stopped. You know what they can be, though? Rumors can be taken and turned on their heads.

He wants to tell people we fucked? Fine. I won't deny it. Instead, I'll fuck him harder than he ever thought he could fuck me.

I stomp down the hallway and head out into the last of the summer air. I make it three steps down the sidewalk before I'm abruptly jerked to a halt by a hand on my arm. Dark, wicked blue eyes glare down at me through the longest lashes I've ever seen on a man, and it takes everything in me not to punch him in his stupid face.

"What the fuck was that?" Isaac demands.

I blink innocently. "What was what?" I ask, lightening my voice to a sickly sweet, almost childish tone.

He growls. "That," he snaps, pointing back the way we both came. I note he's without his bag. He must've rushed after me the second I left the room.

"That," I state, "was me proving to you that I am not to be fucked with, Isaac."

He stares down at me, nostrils flaring. This time, the roles are reversed. Instead of leaving me stuck and unable to say anything, I'm the one with the power. He never even considered that putting him in those rumors about me could bite back. I pull my arm free from his grip.

"When you're ready to call it quits, just let me know," I say. "I'll deliver the divorce papers to my mother personally."

Once again, I make it no more than a few steps away before he stops me—this time, with nothing more than his words. "He won't divorce her," Isaac says.

I consider his expression for a moment. His eyes are unwavering, and though both his jaw and fists are clenched in anger, he doesn't move a single step from where he stands. And he doesn't look away from me.

"They won't last, regardless," I tell him. "They never do."

"I hope you're right," he says.

I should be surprised, but I'm not. All along I got the sense that the two of us have the same goal.

I turn to face him fully. "If that's true," I say, "then why all of the bullshit?" I gesture absently around me, but he has to know what I mean. It's fucking obvious.

"Because hopes don't make reality," he says. "He won't divorce her." There's no hesitation in his words. It's as if they are absolute in his mind. That ticks me off like nothing else.

I cross my arms over my chest as I stare him down. "What makes you think he's any different from her other husbands?" I demand.

"Whatever Damien Icari wants, he gets, Aurora," Isaac says. Something in his tone makes the hairs on the back of my neck stand on end. The bomb he drops a second later explains why. "And right now, his sights are set on Summers' Industries."

My lips part in shock. *Summers' Industries.* Not Emilia Summers, herself. He's practically announcing the truth behind their marriage. "Why are you telling me this?"

Isaac takes in a breath, and it seems to break the spell that has left him motionless in front of me. He straightens and takes a step back.

"Be careful, Sunshine," he says. "Playing with fire will only burn you in the end."

"You started this war, Isaac," I tell him. "I'm only finishing it."

The corner of his mouth tips up. "We'll see."

Isaac doesn't let me respond. He simply turns and strides away, ruining what would've otherwise been a damn good exit on my part. Prick. I grind my teeth the entire way to my next class. By the end of the day, my jaw and my head are both throbbing.

When I walk through the door to my dorm apartment and spot Selene on the couch with her phone in hand, I frown. "I thought you weren't feeling well," I say as I drop my bag next to the dining room table and take a seat.

"Oh, no, I'm fine," she says, her eyes locked on the screen in front of her. "I had a modeling thing in town. I just got back like five minutes ago."

"Okay..." I pull out my laptop and open it up, pulling up the video I'd taken over the weekend. The front door opens, and Hel stomps in, muttering under her breath. "You good?" I ask as she passes me and enters her room.

She doesn't immediately respond and even Selene lifts her head, glancing to the door to Hel's bedroom before meeting my gaze. A moment later, Hel comes back out and slams her laptop on the table across from me.

My eyebrows skyrocket. "Try not to break the table," I say, voice full of sardonic amusement.

She doesn't even look my way as she starts typing furiously and then she flips her computer screen around and presses play. The second the audio hits my ears, I'm up and out of my seat. I grab the top of the screen and stare in horror at the grainy visual of a familiar scene. It's me and an old high school memory I thought I'd buried.

A disgusting sickness curdles deep as, on screen, the younger version of myself stands in the middle of a crowd with an almost absent look of utter humiliation.

"It's all over the internet," Hel says, her voice low and angry. "Some girls in class were talking about it today."

It's hard to tear my gaze away, but when I do, they meet hers with somber seriousness. "When?" I demand.

"Last period," she says. "It hasn't been up for long."

My eyes return to the screen. "Can it be taken down?" Something nasty festers in my throat, threatening to rip open a hole.

Selene drops her phone onto the couch and stands up, hurrying over. She shoves her face in front of the screen and stops. I know when she recognizes the scene being displayed before us because her face goes white and she clasps her hand over her mouth.

"Oh my god..." She looks from the screen to me.

I lick my suddenly dry lips, but no words come out.

Selene turns to Hel. "Where did this come from?" she asks.

Hel sits back with her arms crossed over her chest and a dark look on her face. "Stupid question. You know exactly who it came from."

She's not wrong. I'd heard nothing about this before the last class I'd had with him. That can only mean he already had this information—this ... evidence. This is his payback for what I said. He doesn't waste fucking time, I'll give him that. He must have had someone ready to upload it at a moment's notice. The timestamp of the posted video only marks it as being up a little over an hour ago.

For the first time in a long time, tears prick at the backs of my eyes, threatening to overwhelm me. *Playing with fire will only burn you in the end.* Isaac's earlier warning spills into my mind, almost like an extra dose of punishment to remind me.

I don't want to watch what I already know will happen in the center of that crowd, but for some reason, I can't seem to pull my gaze away. It's like when you're driving down the road and you pass the remains of a gruesome accident. My mind fights it, but my body wants to see. All of it. All over again.

The video, obviously taken on someone's cell phone—an onlooker, someone who can't possibly know what I was thinking at the time—shakes as a bucket of honey and syrup is thrown over the front of my high school prep uniform. It soaks into the front of my white button-down shirt until the bra underneath is visible. The 'video me' crosses her arms over her chest, eyes wide and horrified.

"I didn't know there was a recording," I say absently. My voice sounds like it's coming from somewhere far away.

Selene bites her lip. "I did," she confesses.

Both Hel and I turn to look at her.

"*You* did?" Hel repeats in shock.

She nods with a wince before jumping to explain as she whirls to face me. "I thought your brother had taken care of it, though," she admits with shame. "He was—"

"*Marcus knew?*" That sick feeling blossoms and takes over, invading every fiber of my being.

No, no, no, no, no. I didn't want him to know. I never wanted him to know—or to find out. My horrible high school shame. He knew about everything else, this—the result of pissing off one of the most powerful families in New York—was something I wanted to bury as deep as possible.

Selene looks to the ground. "He still had friends there, Rori." Her voice is quiet but resolute.

She's right. I remember now. There had been a few guys from the football team—players who'd remembered him before he'd moved to California and gone to Hazelwood. They'd been kind enough to cover me with a jacket and break up the crowd. But it'd been too late for their rescue. The damage had already been done.

"The question is, how the fuck did they get something like this?" Hel demands.

"It's a small world," I say. *Especially in the upper echelon.* "I'm sure Isaac has a lot of connections."

"Are you mad at me?" Selene asks.

I blow out a breath and scrub a hand down my face.

"No," I say. "I'm not mad at you." I don't have the energy to be mad at her, and honestly, if I think about it, when had she had an opportunity to tell me? She'd been gone on jobs practically all the time—most of her schooling had been done on the road. She was likely hoping that I would forget that horrible year before I took up kickboxing and learned how to fight back. I, myself, thought I'd left it behind.

"What are you going to do?" she presses.

What am I going to do? I suck in a breath and my eyes turn to my own computer screen. "I'm going to give him a taste of his own medicine," I say.

"Are you sure that's wise?" Selene bites down on her lower lip, glancing back and forth between me and Hel.

The wisest thing I could've done would have been to ignore Isaac Icari the second I landed on Hazelwood's campus. That was then, though, and this is now. There's no use in turning back when the match has already been lit. So, I might as well make use of this fire I've created.

Bile sits in my stomach, acidic and putrid. I look back to Hel's screen as movement pops up in the corner of the video. A familiar face appears.

Megan Wood.

I stare at the girl, watching her laugh as she rips a bag of bird feathers open and starts tossing them in my face. A few of her friends help. Some even go so far as to waltz right up to me and slap them on themselves. Brave little cunts. Old anger flares to life, and my hands clench into fists at my sides.

It'd been Megan's father—another notch in my mother's husband's belt—that had started it all. It made sense that she would take her anger out on me. And because of this, I'd learned my fucking lesson.

Until now. Until Isaac Icari. This video is a warning. Play the game, he's saying, and you'll get burned.

The girl in the video—the three years ago version of me—wouldn't have even thought of fighting back. She would've buried her head in the sand and hoped her tormentor would lose interest. Now, though, I don't feel as ashamed as she did. I have nothing to be ashamed of. Their anger towards me—*Megan's* anger towards me—was unwarranted.

It's not your fault, Rori. None of this is your fault. Marcus' words from back then remind me of that.

I'm not who I was in New York. I'm who I am *now*. Here. And who I am now is not a fucking pawn.

14
RORI

The whisper-like sound of a door opening jerks me out of a deep sleep, but instead of sitting up, something tells me that keeping quiet is better. Keeping quiet is safer. My fingers dig into the sheets beneath me as my ears strain to hear something in the darkness of my bedroom. There's no light save for the soft glow of the moon shining in through the sheer curtains across from my bed.

My lashes flutter against my cheeks. My heart pounds against my chest—faster than it ever has before. My insides tighten.

Please be wrong, I beg my mind as it supplies the reality of what's happening. Please let it be my imagination. But deep down, I know I'm not wrong. If I'm being honest, I could feel his gaze on me at dinner. I just kept hoping I was making it up in my head.

Now, as the bottom of my comforter moves ever so slightly, I know that I wasn't.

Eric Wood—my mother's newest husband—slowly, carefully, takes a seat at the end of my bed. I can barely make out his shape with my narrowed eyes.

Go away, I beg silently. He must not realize I'm awake yet because he just sits there, watching me. His gaze is locked on me and even though I can't make out his shadowed expression, I can see the movement of his arm as his hand goes to the place between his legs.

What do I do? What the fuck am I supposed to do? She's been married so many times, but nothing like this has ever happened. None of them even so much as glanced my way. They just pretended I didn't exist until the divorce papers were thrown in someone's face, usually theirs.

Eric has been different from the start, though. I've always noticed the way his eyes lingered on me. The low touches on my back as I moved past him at some function or another. I'd never felt comfortable being alone with him.

Why is he here? I want to ask the universe. It's a dumb question. I know exactly why a man like him would come to his fifteen-year-old stepdaughter's room in the middle of the night. The real question I want to ask is —why me?

Eric bends low until I can feel his hot breath on my face. I squeeze my eyes shut, feeling ice trail throughout my body. It's childish, but I can't help but hope if I keep my eyes and mouth shut, pretending like I'm sleeping, he'll get up and leave.

A sinking sense of dread tells me that I'm only lying to myself, though. Just like how I lied and told myself that I didn't see his looks or feel those small "innocent" touches. That I was out of my mind to think that he would—

I gasp when his hand slides beneath the sheets and touches my bare thigh.

"I knew it," Eric whispers in a low voice. "You're awake."

No use in hiding it now. I throw back the covers and

scramble across the bed as fast as I can. A hard hand locks on my ankle and stops my escape.

"Stop!" *A hand slaps over my mouth, keeping the shout muffled.*

"Don't scream," *he growls.* "You don't want to disturb your mother, do you?"

I do, though. I so fucking do. If Marcus were here—if he weren't at that stupid college we dropped him off at last month, then I'd go for him, but he's not here now. He can't save me. I have to save myself.

I offer a muffled protest under his hand, but all that makes him do is press down harder. My eyes widen and I realize the actual predicament. I was stupid to think he would just come in and get up and leave if he thought I didn't wake up at his entry.

Why did I do that? *I ask myself.* The answer is simple —because I want to pretend. I wanted him to leave and then I wanted to wake up the next morning and pretend like it was all a bad dream.

Well, it's not, *I chastise myself.* It's happening. So, do something!

I struggle against his grip, yanking my head to the side. "Get off me!" *I yell.*

Eric huffs out an annoyed sound and then the rush of air hits me a split second before the flat of his palm slams into the side of my face. I freeze, shock rocketing through me. Did he just ... hit me?

I don't have a second to react. Eric's slap is still at the forefront of my mind. It strikes me stupid because I don't even feel his hands moving to my sleep shirt, jerking it up and over my head until the wash of cool air hits my chest.

My body begins to tremble. Starting from somewhere deep within me and then moving outward into each of my limbs until my whole body is shaking with the movements. Eric doesn't seem to take any notice. Something escapes my throat—a whimper? A cry? I'm not sure. My ears aren't working right. Instead, there's nothing but a dull ringing. At least, until he speaks again.

"Shut up, you dumb little whore." Each word is vicious, a knife to my throat, stopping me from protesting. "I know you want this. Stop acting like a good, innocent little girl." My lips part, but nothing comes out. He keeps talking. "Walking around in those tight little tank tops and shorts..." His words drift off as he sits back and takes in what he's revealed.

Tears break free and slide down my face. The side of my face that he struck is on fire. Each tear that slips over that cheek feels like it's scraping raw flesh. I sniff hard. "No," I say through gritted teeth. It's a protest to both him and to myself. I can't let this happen. I can't just lay here and take it. I'm not that kind of girl. I'm not the kind of girl who doesn't fight back. I'm—

Eric's hands grip my wrists and slam them down over my head. He's a big man, but I didn't realize how big until now. It's not surprising, though. Like most of my mother's husbands, Eric has a past in something active. He's an ex-pro-athlete turned businessman, and it's clear by the strain in my muscles and the complete and utter lack of anything happening that he's never skipped his workouts.

Fear slams into my body, and I buck under his weight. "No!" I snap. "No! Get off of me!"

Another slap hits my other cheek, but I don't care. I open my mouth, fully intending to scream. Even if Marcus isn't here, my mother is. We don't get along, but she would never let this happen to me. She wouldn't let him—

Eric's hand cups over my mouth, stifling the scream.

He appears over me; the moonlight hitting his face at just the right angle so that I can see the violent expression on his face.

"Keep screaming, Aurora," he growls. "And I'll do so much worse than I'm planning." Worse than what he's planning? I think. What can be worse than rape? As if he senses the directions of my thoughts, he grins, revealing perfectly white teeth.

When I was a kid, I always thought monsters would be ugly, but he's not. There's a reason my mother married him. He's tall. He's fit. He's handsome.

And he's all over me and I think I'm going to fucking puke.

Eric's body lowers on top of mine, squishing the air out of my lungs until there's nothing left inside of me. "Just be a good little girl, Aurora," he whispers against the side of my face as he draws his hand away. There isn't enough room between us or enough air in my lungs for me to even try to scream again. "You've been tempting me for so long. Did you really think I wouldn't notice?"

I shake my head, turning my cheeks back and forth rapidly, denying his claim. I wasn't. But ... if he thinks I have, then do other people think that? If I told anyone about this, if I screamed and called my mom in here, would she believe me?

Eric Wood has a perfect record. No one has ever accused him of this. What if he's right? What if I was unintentionally...

My thoughts derail as one of his hands snakes his way beneath my shorts and two firm fingers touch my pussy. I jerk and whimper. I squeeze my eyes shut. I don't want this. I really don't fucking want this.

"Please stop," I beg, my voice breathless. He's practically sitting on my chest. Spots dance in front of my eyes, my vision narrowing. I can't breathe. I can't fucking breathe! "I'm sorry," I say. "I didn't mean—"

"To tempt me?" he interrupts. "Of course you did. You're just like your mother. You think I can't see that? You're nothing without this—" He punctuates 'this' as he shoves those two fingers right into my bone-dry vagina.

I wince as pain spears through me. Reaching down, I try to shove his arms down to get his fingers to leave my insides. It feels like he's spearing me with hot spikes. "It hurts," I whimper.

Eric doesn't listen, he just pulls his hands back and shoves his fingers right back in. "Be a good girl," he urges. "Just let go. If you remain quiet and let me do this, you'll feel so much better."

More tears track down my face. No, it won't. I know it won't. I can't even lie to myself the way he's trying to lie to me. My legs clamp together, trying to avoid the jerky movements he's making. That frustrates him because he rears back and slaps my face once more.

"Open your fucking legs," he growls, shoving them apart. The sudden shift of movement as he moves between my thighs makes him finally lift up off my chest and for the first time in what feels like forever, I can finally draw a full breath.

My lips part and I suck in as much air as I can, preparing to let out the loudest scream I've ever made in my entire life. I don't care if it disturbs the house. I don't care if people miles away can hear me. I just want someone to come here and stop him.

Eric must sense my intentions, though, because at just the first sounds of my scream erupting from my throat, a pillow is shoved over my face, blocking both the sound and the air from escaping my lungs. I'm flipped over onto my front and my arms are dragged behind me and locked at the center of my back with cotton fabric—something that feels similar to the sleep shirt I'd been wearing. The fabric tightens impossibly, cutting into my wrists, and I struggle to undo the bindings, only it's too late. I'm well and truly trapped.

Shock and horror rip through me as his fingers find the waistband of my shorts and he jerks them down. "Fuck, you're hotter than your mom," he says, as if that should be a compliment.

I struggle again, fighting my way upward as I feel my flesh being revealed. Cool air washes over my skin. Fire licks along my spine. No, no, nonononono. No! This can't be fucking happening. Not to me. Why? No. Please no. But it is, and no amount of begging internally can stop it now.

The more I struggle, the harder Eric presses against the back of my head, shoving my face into the pillow until I can't breathe and start feeling light-headed. A firm hand grips one of my ass cheeks, pulling it open as his fingers slide into the space between.

I open my mouth and immediately it's filled with fabric from the pillow in front of me. I choke and cough, trying to spit it out, but it's shoved so far in, wet and wedged between my cheeks that fighting against it does nothing.

My mind goes hazy and suddenly I'm floating. Perhaps it's a lack of oxygen or panic as my heart gallops inside of my chest, trapped and pounding, but I think I pass out for several long moments.

When I open my eyes again, the world around me has shifted. I look up as my legs are separated. My body feels limp. "Here you go, sweetheart." Eric's voice is soft, almost gentle—completely different from how it was. He pushes a thumb into my mouth, holding it open as he leans forward and kisses me.

My eyes widen, and I flinch back in disgust as his tongue invades. Something hard but quickly dissolving hits my tongue. He shushes me as he pulls back. "Don't worry," he whispers. "It's just gonna make you feel real good."

Drugs. He drugged me.

I start to cry. Fuck. I hate crying, but I can't stop the tears now. My mouth moves, but it feels numb and no words come out. No more protests. The world tips over, and I stare up at the ceiling of my childhood bedroom as he pushes my legs even further apart and moves between them.

I'm completely naked now. Whatever he gave me made it so that I can't move. When I try, it feels like I'm trying to lift a thousand pounds, even though all I'm trying to do is swat away his hand as he cups my face.

"There, now," he says as he moves over me. "That's better, isn't it? You're being so good now. That's all you needed to behave."

The urge to vomit is gone now. I never thought I'd wish for it back, but I do. I'd love nothing more than to puke all over this asshole as he takes himself in hand and pushes the head of his cock towards my core.

Empty. All I feel is empty. Devoid of all emotions. My eyes make their way back to the ceiling. I don't even wince when he breaks through my hymen and groans.

"Fuck, you're so fucking tight." He begins to saw back and forth inside of me, his cock pressing deep and then withdrawing. "That's it. Good girl. What a good fucking girl. Such a tight pussy."

My skin tingles, and it's the only sign that I can even

still feel myself there. His commentary slips through my mind. *Good girl. Good girl. Good girl.*

I don't want to be a good girl; I think. I don't want to be anything anymore. I just want to disappear.

Vanish into the mattress that I can't even feel at my back like I never existed. Maybe if I never existed, this would've never happened. Maybe if I wasn't here, he wouldn't be here—taking everything I never knew he could steal.

I hate staring at my ceiling while this is happening. With its glow-in-the-dark stars that Marcus gave me for my ninth birthday and the soda stain from dumping an entire bag of Mentos into a liter of Coke. It's only a reminder of who I was and who I will never be again.

So, I close my eyes, cutting off the image of the stupid ceiling in front of me, and I just drift away. I do what I do best when something makes me uncomfortable—I pretend.

15
ISAAC

P resent Day...

Even as I stride into the off-campus coffee shop with a baseball cap pulled down low over my forehead, peeking beneath the brim and scanning the wide-open area, my thoughts aren't filled with my reason for being here. Instead, a specific bratty blonde is all I can fucking think about.

Everything about her attracts me. From the way she'd sucked me like she wanted to siphon my soul out through my dick, as well as the way she'd lifted her gaze and glared me down in the middle of campus, showing no fear despite knowing who I am. It's dangerous, this hold she's forming over me.

I stride through the crowd of people waiting in line for their coffee and head to the end of the counter, scanning the mobile orders piled up on the little black stand marked for such customers. I find mine and snatch it up just before a man with his face buried in his phone reaches for it.

"Hey!" He grunts as I half-shove him out of my way and head towards the back of the shop. His irritation disperses just as quickly, though, as the girl at his side gestures to his coffee. By the time he realizes, I've already found my spot, deposited the bag in my hand on top of the table, and taken a seat.

I've got my computer out and my headphones in—sans music—within seconds. I'm not here to play the college student. I'm here for more important matters beyond literary assessment papers and pretending to learn shit I don't give two fucks about. Everything about me today is a facade. From the cap to the nondescript clothing, and even to the cheap, beat-up laptop I grabbed from a low-budget pawn shop on the way over.

I'm doing everything in my power to appear as the middle-class student trying to cram as much information in his head as possible amidst the overcrowded and noisy coffee shop. My eyes are glazing over twenty minutes later as I click away from a search engine for the fifteenth time when a familiar weight takes a seat behind me.

Back-to-back, I can smell the faint scent of menthol cigarettes on him, and it makes me crave one. "Hello, Isaac."

"Malik." I don't look back. Instead, I keep my head trained forward and my eyes level with the computer screen, though I'm not reading anything on the article I've got up in front of me. We hardly speak and even more rarely meet in person, but it's clear that though my father's been away on that bullshit honeymoon of his with Emilia Summers, he's still been hard at work. Otherwise, I wouldn't be here like this at all.

"We received your last message." Agent Malik Brown's voice is sharp and concise. I know without looking back that he, too, is dressed for the part. A business suit pressed to perfection and the cheapest black coffee that I know he's only pretending to drink as he checks his watch as if waiting for someone. That someone is already here. "Has your father made inquiries into your actions?"

I snort. I can't help it. If the FBI thinks I can't fool my own father, they wouldn't have tracked me down and offered me this deal. "Of course not," I reply. "If he was onto me, then I wouldn't be here at all." My mere presence is enough of a statement. I'm in the clear ... for now. "Now, get to the reason why you wanted to meet me."

A beat of silence, and then, "We need you to start gathering more concrete evidence."

I grit my teeth. "What more do you fucking want?" I snap, lowering my tone as a couple breezes past. Thankfully, the girl is laughing loud enough at whatever the douche hanging onto her arm says that my voice is swallowed up by the noise. "I've given you account numbers, locations, and even a list of names. If you can't do anything with the shit I've given you, then what use are you?"

"You've been instrumental, Isaac," Malik states. "But you know as well as we do that Damien Icari is quite good at hiding his tracks. All of those accounts came back completely above board. The locations were empty. They might have been used previously, but they were clean when we arrived. Only the associates you listed were of any real use, but we don't want to risk you if necessary. We can't make a move on them immediately. You're our only contact on the inside and your safety is paramount."

What he's saying makes sense, but it's fucking frustrating. What else can I do? What else will put my father away for good and leave the void of the Icari family open for me to step into?

"We need more," Malik continues. "If you want to help us as you say you do, then we need something that is completely undeniable."

Yeah, I know what they need. Hard evidence. Something that paying off judges or threatening jurors won't be able to get him out of. They need a smoking gun. They need *me* to catch my father red-fucking-handed. I scrub my fingers down my face before reaching back and adjusting my baseball cap.

"He's coming back next week," I say.

"Yes, we heard about his new wife," Malik replies. "Do you think she would be of any use?"

Though he can't see it, my lips twist into an annoyed frown. "Emilia Summers is nothing more than an empty-headed socialite," I reply. "She won't be of any use to you."

"And her daughter?"

I stiffen at the mention of Aurora. "*No.*" The word comes out gruff and violent. Just the mere reminder of how close that girl is to the seedy underbelly of my world makes me want to break something—preferably someone else's bones. "She won't be involved with this."

There's no room for argument. Just the thought of Aurora Summers facing off against a man such as my father after betraying him and informing on him to the FBI sends shivers down my spine. It makes my already cold blood turn to ice in my veins.

I know what I'm risking. My life and future. But for her, it would be so much worse. I may not like the girl, but I won't let the stain of my father's hands touch her. Ever.

"You seem pretty confident that she won't be of help." Malik's tone suggests he seems to think that I'm wrong.

"She doesn't even know what he does," I say.

"Which would possibly make her even more useful than you, Isaac," he states. "He won't ever suspect her. The sexism of the world can sometimes cloud people's minds and make them underestimate the potential of a person based on their gender." I close my eyes. No doubt he's speaking from experience, but no. I don't care if Aurora would be the perfect weapon against my father. My goal is to make her go away, not keep her.

The video I released to the school's social media pages should do the trick. If she's not ready for a transfer after that, I don't know what could break her. Even if she doesn't get Emilia Summers to divorce my father, then at least she'll be out of the way—perhaps to Eastpoint with her brother. She'd at least be safe there.

That thought hits me hard. *She'd be safe?* The whole point of my tormenting her is to get her to convince her mother to leave my father. But as I sit back against the worn cushion of my seat, I realize, I don't necessarily care about that anymore.

To my father, Aurora Summers is a pawn to control his wife, but if she disappears, she won't be on his radar anymore. As far as I can tell, there's no love lost between her mother and her. If Emilia Summers remains behind with my father, she'll end up dead or worse—so much fucking worse—and if Aurora is with her, she'll receive the same. Liabilities. Loose ends. Malik and I both know what happens to those.

When did I start thinking in terms of protecting Aurora Summers instead of wanting her gone?

"Isaac?" Malik's voice is hard, irritated, as if he's been calling me for some time now.

I shake my head, and with it dispel my wayward thoughts. "She's not to be informed," I state. "End of story. You bring her into this, and I'm out."

Malik is quiet for a moment and then he hums low in his throat. "Fine," he says. "I'll keep that in mind. As for your father..."

"I'll figure something out," I tell him. "He has a few meetings when he returns; I'll keep my ear to the ground."

"It'd be best if we can catch him in the act, Isaac," Malik says. The pressure against my back loosens as he stands. "Remember that."

I don't look back as his dress shoes squeak against the tile floor. Once he's gone the noise of the coffee shop intrudes once more and I lean back, shutting my eyes against the pounding in my head. My phone buzzes in my pocket and I groan, reaching inside and pulling it free. Shep's name flashes across the screen and I flick the green button, putting the receiver to my ear.

"What?"

"Have you seen the school socials yet?" is the first thing out of his mouth. The tightness in his tone makes me sit up and open my eyes.

"No. What's wrong? Did she reply to the video?"

He laughs, but it's far from amused. "Fuck yeah, she did," he says, "but not in the way you're thinking."

"What do you mean?" Even though I ask the question, my fingers are already flying over the keyboard and I'm pulling up Hazelwood University's student run social media pages.

"I think it's safe to say that she's not backing down from your threats, man," Shep says, and there's a note of respect in it.

A frown overtakes my face as I search the pages for the video Shep had scoured the internet for, but Aurora Summers' high school humiliation is nowhere to be seen. In its place is a new video.

My eyes bulge as I gape at the screen—at a very familiar setting. I almost laugh out loud. Now, I understand Shep's tone of almost reverent respect. She's a hellion—a fucking genius one. A bolt of adrenaline slides through my veins, lighting me up. How intriguing. How ... addictive this girl is becoming.

Now it all makes sense. The Gods and Goddesses party. Her seduction.

So, that's what she'd been doing. I sit back and stare at my own image reflected back at me—only this time, I look far more douchey. Dressed in that stupid costume, I watch myself strip my shirt over my head and maul the girl on screen. She's smart; I have to give her that. She kept her back to the camera. Her identity is hidden. Some may suspect, but no one can say for sure. The wig looks like real hair and it's not her color. The sound is absent, too, so no one could possibly call her out for that. Even when I say her name, no one can hear it on the video. My face, though, is front and center.

My cock swells in my pants and I shift, adjusting myself as I watch the course of emotions spread over my features. On the screen, I flinch with pleasure, my features growing tight. I know the exact moment that I came; my head rolls back on my shoulders and my lips move on screen.

"This is a problem," Shep says, distracting me.

I roll my eyes. "Why is that?" I ask. "This might be a problem if I was a chick, but you and I both know that sex tapes are different for men."

"Isaac." Shep's tone grows tight, all hints of amusement or respect or anything other than flat-out concern disappearing. "Your father will find out about this."

And just like that, the day is ruined. Because, fuck me, he's right. "Take it down," I snap. "Get it down now."

"Already working on it," he says.

My phone buzzes against my ear, signaling another incoming call. I pull it away and see my father's name flash across my screen. *Fuck.*

"You know, once it's gone viral like this, that's only going to make things worse," Shep continues.

"I have to go," I interrupt.

"What about your father, Isaac? He—"

Already knows, my mind supplies. I don't answer Shep. I don't even let him finish. I just hang up and answer my father's call, sitting back to wait for the verbal beating that's guaranteed to precede a physical one the second I see him again.

Fuck my life, and fuck bratty little fighters like Aurora Summers.

16

RORI

"Well, your little plan worked." Hel's statement makes me smile, but her lack of enthusiasm is a bit of a damper on my improved mood.

"It's what he deserves," Selene says with a sniff as the three of us make our way across campus to the final class of the week. It's been several days since the whole incident went down and I haven't seen Isaac in any of our shared classes since.

"I don't know, something feels off," Hel says.

I glance her way, but she keeps her gaze trained ahead of her. "What feels off to you?" I ask.

"The fact that he hasn't been in class for the entire last week," she says, cutting a look my way.

"He's just embarrassed," Selene says with a shrug.

But no, Hel's right. It *is* weird that he hasn't been in class. Isaac doesn't strike me as the type of man to give a fuck about gossip. If I can take this level of bullshit, then I know he can. I know as well as anyone else that this kind of shit is different for men and women, too. I've been so relieved by his lack of presence in the last week that it hadn't even occurred to me. There's no reason why he shouldn't be in class. He wouldn't have had the same hard time as I would have if people knew the girl in that video was me. I bite down on my lower lip, thinking.

"He hasn't bothered me all week," I admit absently. I'd just assumed that my little ace had done its job. *Had I been too cocky?* I thought I'd shown him that fucking with me wouldn't be as easy as he so obviously assumed, but what if it's something else?

Almost as soon as that idea crosses my mind, my phone rings. I jump and reach into my bag, pulling it free and glancing at the screen. I pause and wave at the two of them. "You guys go on without me," I say. "I gotta take this."

Hel finally looks at me. "You sure?" she asks. Leave it to her to pick up on my practically nonexistent nerves. Or maybe I'm not as good at hiding my anxieties as I think. Maybe just being around Selene and her obliviousness has tricked me into thinking I'm way sneakier than I actually am.

I force a smile nonetheless. "Yeah, it's fine," I say. "Go on. I'll catch up with you guys later."

Selene is the first to respond. She latches onto Hel's arm and waves goodbye before dragging her away, and I've never felt more relieved for her blind, ignorant interference than I am right now. Once they're well out of earshot, I answer the call.

"Hello."

"Darling!" my mother's bright, cheery voice shrieks into my ear like a siren. "I'm just calling to tell you that we're back in town. What are you doing right now? I'm near your campus. We should grab lunch and catch up. I can't wait to tell you all about—"

I'm almost stunned stupid by the volume of her voice and the fast pace of her words. Even if I wanted to, I know I can't get a word in edgewise. But it's always like this. She disappears for days, weeks, sometimes months at a time and when she pops back in, she pretends that we're closer than ever before. Normally, I wouldn't even bother. I'd answer her call—because I know if I don't, she'll show up wherever I am whether I want her to or not—and then I'd politely decline.

The only reason I don't now is because she's got something I want. *Information.* "Actually, I just got out of class," I tell her. "I was going to grab lunch anyway, so if you're close, we can meet up."

There's a brief pause on the other end of the line as if she's surprised by my sudden agreement, but when she speaks, there's nothing but excitement in her tone. "That's wonderful," she gushes. "Where are you? I'll pick you up."

"I'm on campus," I say and then give her a more exact location.

"I'll be there in ten minutes," she says, and before I can tell her to take her time, she ends the call.

It doesn't take her ten minutes to get to me. In fact, it barely takes her five. The reason for that is obvious as a small, red sports car comes careening around the corner at breakneck speed, slamming to a halt a few inches from the curb I'm currently standing on.

"Hey darling!" she cries from the driver's seat. She pulls down the massive shades covering her eyes and smiles up at me. "Hop in."

Even here, on a campus full of rich people, seeing someone dressed to kill and driving like a professional racecar driver is out of the norm. People are staring, but I ignore their curious looks, step off the curb, and get in. Seconds later, I barely have my seatbelt buckled when she slams her foot on the gas and the car rips itself away from the curb, sliding right back onto the road and into traffic. I close my eyes, praying for either safety or a quick death— honestly, whichever hurts less.

Immediately my mother begins chattering away. Her words come at such a breakneck speed, that I can't even hear or decipher them until the wind roaring in my ears dies down and we're pulling into the parking lot of a high-class restaurant off a strip.

"—beautiful sites, and Damien was so attentive the entire time. I really think you'll like him if you spend a little time with him. He's just so—oh, here you go." She pauses just long enough to hand her keys to a valet. With shaky legs, I exit the vehicle and trail behind her into the building.

"Mom," I finally manage to get the word out as we're seated at a bistro table along the patio with breezy bohemian curtains fluttering in the wind around us.

She picks up her menu and directs her gaze to it. "Yes? What is it?"

"I actually wanted to talk to you about something," I start.

"Is this about Marcus?" she asks.

I frown. "Marcus?" Why would she think this is about Marcus? We haven't talked about Marcus in years—at least not past when I'd invited him to meet her new husband without telling her. "What about Marcus?"

"He's transferring to Eastpoint University, isn't he?" she replies, looking up.

"Oh, yes. I ... you heard."

"Yes, he told me," she says.

Shock rockets through me. *He told her?* "When did you start talking again?" I ask.

She blows out a breath. "After you invited him to that luncheon," she says, and as she does, her eyes flick up to me. Her brows draw down low. "I was quite upset about that, but honestly, I think it was for the best. You were right. He would have needed to meet Damien sooner or later, and he seems to like him."

"He—*what?*" I gape at her. "Marcus *likes* Damien?"

"Well, he didn't say he likes Damien per se," she says with a wince. "But he hasn't mentioned anything since the luncheon, so I'm assuming he doesn't disapprove of him." The waiter stops by and drops off a basket of fancy bread and takes our drink order, disrupting the moment. When they're gone, however, I focus my gaze on my mother.

Delusional. That's what she is. Just because Marcus hasn't said he hates Damien doesn't mean he likes him. In fact, I'd say it's pretty obvious that Marcus doesn't like him. At all. But whether or not my brother likes her new husband is not why I'm here today.

The waiter returns and takes the rest of our order and, in true high society fashion, disappears into the background as if they never existed, leaving me alone with my mother. I reach for my drink and take a sip—wincing when the bubbly champagne mixture of the mimosa hits my nose. Fuck. They didn't even bother to check my age. I sigh and finish my sip before setting it to the side.

"So, it sounds like your honeymoon went well," I say.

"Oh, darling," my mother says breathlessly as she puts a hand to her chest in a spot-on romantic manner. "It was wonderful. Quite honestly, it was the best honeymoon I've ever had."

"I assume Damien is back in town as well and back to work?"

She nods absently, taking a sip of her drink. "He's such a workaholic," she confesses. "He spent as much time with me as he could. However, every spare second we got, he was on his phone and last week he got a call about something or other—changed our whole flight plan, and we ended up back here faster than you would've thought."

My gaze sharpens on her. "What did he get a call about?" I ask, letting the words roll off my tongue in a light, almost disinterested tone.

"Oh, I don't ask questions about his work, dear," she says with a scoff. "You should know better than that. It's best just to let men do their men things, and we women do our women things." It takes every fiber of my being to resist the urge to roll my eyes at that. "I do hope you and Isaac have been getting along, though." Her comment has me stiffening, but I feign a smile.

"Oh, I hardly see him on campus," I lie.

"Is that so?" she frowns. "I could've sworn he mentioned that you two had attended a party together while we were gone. Isn't he in a few of your classes?"

I choke on another sip of orange juice and champagne. "He mentioned that?"

She nods. "He said as much when I ran into him at the house earlier this week."

I slam my glass down and look at her. "You've seen him?" I demand.

She blinks at me. "Good lord, Aurora, you act like it's a crime for me to run into my stepson." I wince at the reminder of what he is—not just to her, but to me as well —but keep my gaze on hers.

"It's just..." What do I say? "I haven't seen him in class in a few days, so..."

"Oh, yes, he did mention that he'd been out of class because of what happened."

"What happened?"

She nods and sighs. "He looked quite the worse for wear," she says. "Boys and their arguments, I suppose. He said something about a workout that got out of hand, but there were bruises on his face. I suspect he must've had a falling out with one of his friends." She pauses and puts a finger to her chin thoughtfully. "Or perhaps it really was a workout," she surmises. "I forgot, but he's on the football team, isn't he? That would explain the bruising on his face. He doesn't strike me as much of a boxer, although I'm not sure what teenage boys are all into these days." I don't point out that he's not a teenager for much longer, as she drops her finger and shakes her head. "Marcus was so careful when he played. Perhaps I'm just not used to other young men."

A fight? Bruises? I'm getting more information than I ever expected. It was definitely a good thing to agree to meet with her.

"Anyway," she says suddenly, switching subjects as she leans forward and clasps her hand over mine on top of the table. "I was so excited that you agreed to have lunch. I actually wanted to ask you over to the house."

"The house?" I stare back at her, confused. "What house?"

"Our house, silly," she giggles, slapping the top of my hand before pulling away. "Damien's and mine."

"So, it's really official then." I shouldn't be so surprised. In the past, every husband she'd been with had ended up moving in with her. Not the opposite. It's a little unsettling, but it makes perfect sense for her to live with her husband. They're married, after all. I'd known it was coming since I came home at the end of senior year to find all of our stuff packed and gone. Still, that doesn't make me hate it any less.

I pull my hands off the table and away from her reach as the waiter reappears and begins setting out our food. I stare down at the Eggs Benedict that I'd ordered and suddenly want nothing more than to shove it off the table and watch the expensive porcelain shatter into a million pieces.

My emotions feel like they're pulled on a tight string and I'm balancing, walking the tightrope as my mother digs into her salad and pretends like all is right with the world. I want to press into her, ask more, but I think this is all I'm getting from her. At least I got some information on Isaac. I know the real reason why he's skipping classes —likely to keep the rumor mill from going wild.

The video was one thing. The video he probably doesn't give a single shit about. The bruises on the other hand ... my mother can pretend it's just boys being boys, but I know the truth. Isaac isn't the type to let himself be hurt. Therefore, whoever left those marks on him is someone he can't stop.

Damien Icari.

My hands freeze above my plate at that thought, but it makes sense. His father. It has to be. Who else would Isaac be unable to stop? Who else would have that kind of power over him? Maybe there's more about my dangerous Icarus boy than meets the eye.

I flick my eyes up to my mother as she chatters on, her words drifting in one ear and out the other about her honeymoon. Something I couldn't care less about.

"I'll come," I say, startling her.

Her big eyes rise to meet mine. "What?"

"To the house," I clarify. "I'll come visit the house. I want to meet with Damien again," I tell her. "I think we got off on the wrong foot last time. Maybe I should apologize for asking Marcus to come to the luncheon without warning you."

The sound of metal scraping porcelain as her fork clatters to the plate in front of her shocks my ears as she gapes at me. "W-what?"

It's not that surprising, is it? I wonder. I blink and look down. "It's not a big deal," I say. "I just ... want to be nicer to him," I lie. "He's your husband, after all."

A sniffle makes me jerk my head up as I watch my mother clasp her hand over her mouth, her eyes filling with tears and a familiar haziness that I haven't seen from her in a long time. "Oh my goodness," she croaks. "Rori, darling..." She reaches for me and surprise holds me prisoner as her hands grasp my wrist. "I would love nothing more than for you and Damien to be closer," she confesses. "I know, with our past, we haven't been the best of friends, but this is really important to me. He's not like Eric, sweetheart. I promise."

My whole body goes cold. "It's fine," I lie, staring down at my plate even though my appetite fled the second she mentioned that man's name. "I don't want to make a big deal out of it." Or have her mention that fucker's name again.

As if sensing my internal agony, she releases me without hesitation. "Of course," she says quietly. "Yes, I would love for you to come to the house. Perhaps for dinner next week? I don't want to disrupt your classes."

I suck in a breath and then another and another,

trying to fight off the feeling of my vision tunneling—the world around me growing dimmer and dimmer. *Don't fucking do this, Rori,* I order myself. *Don't fucking lose it now. It's just a name.*

But it's not. It's not just his name. It's the reminder. It's the fact that that stupid dream is still sitting in the back of my mind, like a festering old wound that just won't scab over. I take slow calming breaths until my vision returns to normal and I feel the urge to puke disperse.

Maybe Eric Wood had expected me to keep quiet about what he did to me, but I'm not the silent type. I'd told on him—to both my mother and my brother. Marcus had beaten him to within an inch of his life and when he'd threatened to have him arrested, my mother had stepped in. She'd divorced him without a second thought and quietly informed him that if he so much as tried to come after her son, she'd take him to court for all that he'd done.

She'd been there when we'd needed her, but it hadn't been enough. She'd brought him into our lives and I don't think she even realizes that afterwards, all she'd done was run away. Away from the reminder that I'd destroyed her last marriage. Away from us.

I eat my Eggs Benedict without tasting a damn thing, and I stop when the plate is half empty; I can't stomach another bite. At the end of the day, it doesn't matter what she does now; no one can erase the past. All we can do moving forward is try to keep those mistakes from happening again—starting with Damien and Isaac Icari.

17
RORI

A week passes without a word or a reminder of my promise to have dinner with my mother and her husband. When Isaac shows back up to school, his bruises have faded enough that they're barely there. If I hadn't spoken to my mom, I wouldn't have even known he'd had them. When he reappears, he's all smiles and no one even questions it. The gossip about the videos has all but completely evaporated.

Is that power?

It's almost sickening, or it would be if I didn't know certain truths. Something tells me he's hiding more than he seems to be. Not just his hatred of me, but his hatred of his father. I've rolled the thought over and over in my mind along with something else.

I'm becoming obsessed with him. Watching him in every class. At first, I tell myself it's just because I'm waiting for payback. I'm waiting for his revenge, but nothing ever comes. In fact, if anything, he starts avoiding me like the plague. Every day, without fail—the second the professor ends class, he's gone.

I should be grateful. I got what I wanted. He's left me alone. He's pretending like we have nothing more to do with each other. What more do I want?

The answer is glaring me straight in the face, but I can't accept it.

So, when Selene comes back to the dorm on Friday after classes and asks if I want to head out to a club with her, I throw off my textbooks and study materials and leap at the opportunity. I haven't been out since we got here, but now that Marcus is planning on heading to Eastpoint, it's not like I'll have to worry about people reporting back to him. I miss him, for sure, but perhaps him going to Eastpoint is what's best. We've lived separate lives ever since the incident. Maybe this is just how we're supposed to be from now on.

I finish swiping on one final layer of mascara and tighten the ponytail at the top of my head before turning and adjusting the tie keeping the front of my halter top up. If California is anything like New York, the nightclubs will have a dress code. No shredded anything. No cheap shit. Only the best for the best. My borrowed dress makes me look like someone else, but I don't mind. Tonight, that's exactly what I'm going for—someone else. Someone who doesn't need to think about the possibility of her mother being used by a monster. Someone who doesn't obsess over an enemy who's made her life miserable. Someone who doesn't care.

"I'm so glad you're coming," Selene says as we head to the curb outside of the dorm to the waiting car. The driver steps out and comes around, opening the back door. She slides in first with me following closely, and the door closes behind me. "I mean, if you were worried about me going alone, it would've been fine. I'm actually meeting a few people from the agency, but we haven't been out together in forever."

"Yeah, you're right," I agree absently. I rest my head against the glass as she chatters on about the jobs she's been on this week. It's a good thing Hazelwood is so used to people like her—students who are also minor celebrities. Special circumstances might not otherwise be allowed considering how many classes she's missed thus far. Then again, anyone who would think she's stupid would be wrong because despite all of that, I know she's managed to keep up with the curriculum. "Where are we going tonight?" I ask.

"Oh, it's a new club that just opened up," Selene replies. "It's called *Labyrinth*—very vogue don't you think?"

"I guess." I don't care if it's popular. It doesn't matter. As long as the place has alcohol and music; that's all I need tonight. A way to relax.

Minutes later, the car slows down and I glance out the window, my eyes widening as the vehicle comes to a full stop in front of a massive tower. "Let's go!" Selene squeals in excitement and, this time, the driver opens her door first. As soon as he does, she's out of the car and heading towards the entrance, bypassing the long line of people waiting.

I don't look back as I follow after her. She flashes her ID at the two security guards at the door. "I'm here for the VIP party," she says before turning and locking arms with me. "She's my guest."

"Of course, Miss Reynolds." One of the security guards steps forwards and undoes one side of a velvet rope, gesturing for both of us to step inside. "Enjoy yourself."

She giggles, waving goodbye as we make our way inside. Stepping into *Labyrinth* is like walking into a whole new world. If the outside California air is warm, then the interior of the club is a tropical zone. Already I can feel sweat collecting on the back of my neck as I crane my head back to take everything in.

"Wow," is all I can say. "They really went all out."

Selene laughs. "I know, right?" Her hand tightens on my arm and I nearly stumble over my own feet as she drags me forward, pulling me in the direction of the long bar at the back of the bottom floor.

The club fills the entire building. Each floor circling up from the bottom one has a gaping opening in the middle for those on the upper levels to be able to look down over the edge. The dance floor takes up the majority of the ground floor, with people in expensive designer clothes grinding and moving in time to the beat within a circle of tall Grecian pillars that act as foundational support for the whole building.

Selene leans in close as we hit the end of the bar and stop. "Isn't it cool?" she gushes.

"Yeah," I agree. "Very cool."

She squeals again and then leans over the counter as a bartender steps up to us. "We'll have two screwdrivers," she says.

"And shots," I say. I look at her. "Do you want a shot?"

Selene's face freezes for a moment, and then she smiles. "Uh ... sure."

"We'll have three shots of tequila," I tell the bartender.

"Um ... I know, I should've asked this before," Selene says after the bartender leaves to make our drinks. "But is there another reason why you decided to come out with me tonight? You don't usually do shots."

"I'm fine," I lie. "I just need to de-stress. It's been a long ass week."

"Are you sure that's—" The bartender returns, dropping three shot glasses full of tequila in front of me along with two screwdrivers.

I don't hesitate. I lift the first shot of tequila, down it, and then the second. I know, with Selene, that we'll be sipping on those screwdrivers for the next hour. I can't wait that long to let loose some of this tension already built up inside of me. When I turn back to my friend and push her shot over to her side before reaching into my bra and removing my credit card to hand to the bartender, Selene is staring at me in shock.

"Hey, Rori," she says, putting her manicured hand on my arm, "if something's bothering you, you know you can always talk to me."

I blow out a breath. "Do you want your shot or not?" I ask.

The bartender comes back. "You want to start a tab?" he asks. I give him a nod of confirmation.

"Come on," I say as soon as he's done and we're ready to go. I grab my screwdriver. "You said you were meeting some people here, right?"

"Wait, Rori!" Selene grabs my arm, stopping my escape. "I'm serious. Is something going on? You're being really weird."

I look away and blow out a breath. "I'm just..." I grit my teeth before looking back at her. "I'm irritated by Isaac," I admit. "I'm stressed about Marcus leaving for Eastpoint, and I'm..." I groan. "It's just all complicated. I promise it's nothing more than that. I just want to fucking relax tonight, Sel. Can we do that? Please?"

She sighs and squeezes my arm. "Of course we can. I only wanted to make sure you're not getting ready to go down a dark hole. You know? I mean ... you know the kind of shit I've seen some of the girls in the business get into. I know you're stressed, but I wanted to make sure it wasn't anything that I didn't need to be seriously concerned with."

Oh, she should be concerned. She should be hella concerned, because she's right to worry. I'm not thinking straight tonight. I haven't been thinking straight since my mother walked in and wrecked my life all over again. Not since Isaac showed up and made it his personal mission to disrupt everything that was left over after her announcement. Just for a little while, I want to pretend like none of that exists. And that desire is something that could get me in some serious trouble. But that's something I'll worry about later.

"Tonight's not about worrying," I say, and I know I'm not just talking to her—I'm talking to myself as well. "Tonight's just for fun."

She grins and reaches for her shot of tequila, putting the glass to her lips and throwing her head back in true party-girl fashion. Once that's gone, she grabs her drink and the two of us head up to one of the higher levels with only one thing on my mind—more booze and some relaxation.

18

ISAAC

Labyrinth is Paris' baby. The fruits of several months of labor and money that he's worked on finding investors for. Damn near completely separate from his parents' money and almost completely his own. Full of debauchery and sin, it resembles an actual labyrinth. Everything inside is a mix of modern and ancient architecture and art. Only the ground floor makes any sort of sense. It's almost like a trick to make those who come in thinking that they can handle what comes afterwards.

The upper floors are where the real fun begins, and tonight is its official reveal.

A familiar face joins Paris and me in the owner's personal garden lounge on the topmost floor. "Congrats, man," Shep says as a waitress drops off our drinks and disappears into the background.

"Thanks." Paris is grinning from ear to ear with a doe-eyed girl on either side of him. One already has her mouth latched onto his throat while the other is fiddling with the many piercings that line his ear on the opposite side. Before the end of the night, I suspect he'll have them whisked away to some private room where he'll make all of their 'fuck the owner' dreams come true. Many men would kill to be him.

I turn and look over the rail to the ground floor below. "It's a beautiful club," I comment. "You did good, man."

"I didn't really do much in regards to the layout," Paris admits. "The architect I hired suggested it and I think he fucking killed the design."

He did. This place is like no other. Even I feel like a god among men as I sit up here, looking down upon the mortal realm. One of the lights overhead shines across the raised dance floor below and a familiar head of sunshine-colored hair catches my attention.

"Fuck." I sit up straighter. There's no fucking way—but it *is* her. There's no mistaking that hair. Or those hips as they swivel back and forth in time with the rhythm of the music. Bass jumps through invisible speakers in the walls, her body moving with it.

Everything around me fades as I focus on her. I shouldn't be fucking doing this to myself, but I can't seem to help it. Even the sore spots still lingering beneath my clothes where my bruises haven't completely healed can't keep my mind from straying to her. She's in my head. In my fucking thoughts, every hour of the day, seven days a week. No amount of punches or broken ribs can halt all thoughts about Aurora Summers and how much I should not want her.

"—fucking hell, man? Isaac!" I jerk and turn back to Shep and Paris.

"What?" I scan the area, looking for a reason for their sudden volume.

"What do you mean what?" Paris demands as he gets up from his seat and joins me alongside the back of the lounge couch I'm sitting on where it's shoved up against the railing. "What's going on with you?" His head turns and he follows my earlier attention." "You're—oh, I see." He turns back to me with a knowing look. "Still can't stop, huh? Thinking about getting revenge for that little stunt she pulled?"

Shep frowns but doesn't say anything. If he were to be the one to make a decision, I know what he'd say—*stay away*.

After that last meeting with my father, and the subsequent hospital visit, I was in agreement. Being away from her for over a week has been easier. In class, I've managed to keep from meeting her curious gaze. Outside of class, I've done my damnedest to know where she is and where I will *not* be at all times.

Seeing her like this, though, is temptation itself. Against my better judgment, I let my gaze drift back to the woman who has haunted me for the last several weeks. She's all done up tonight. The short, glittery dress makes her legs appear miles long. She moves well, even in sky-high heels. Her long hair is pulled up and back, showing off her bare shoulders and upper back.

My insides tighten when I watch an unknown guy move in on her where she's dancing with her friend—the model-actress. My thoughts darken as I watch his hand land on her waist, and a split second later, she jerks and turns. Her features grow tight and she turns her cheek, shaking her head. I can't hear her from all the way up here, but I can just imagine the rejection she's giving him. It almost makes me feel better. Almost.

That is—maybe it would've if the guy didn't obviously ignore her and place both of his hands back on her waist. I don't know what the mother fucker is saying either, but from the sour expression that takes over her face, I'm sure it's something disgustingly vile. Likely rejecting her rejection. I stand suddenly, unable to take it a second longer.

"Where are you going?" Shep demands.

I ignore him. "I'll be back," I tell Paris.

Paris arches a brow. "Don't hurry on our account."

"Are you fucking serious right now?" Shep looks between him and me before focusing his attention on our friend. "You're really cool with him going after her?"

Paris shrugs. "Once he fucks her for real, she'll be out of his system," he says.

"Yeah, maybe," I say, nodding, but deep down, I doubt it'll be that easy. I've wanted women before. I've done whatever it took to get them in my bed. I've felt both the relief of my lust and the thrill of winning a game of chase. Aurora isn't exactly running from me. She's not hiding. She's not backing down.

This is different. I know what it feels like to be interested enough in a woman to need to fuck her out of my system, and this isn't it. This is something more. Something dangerous. Despite knowing that, though, I don't let the guys in on my thoughts.

Shep's mouth curves into a scowl, but he sits back. "Fine," he snaps. "Do what you need to do then. Fuck up your own life. See if I give a shit."

I resist the urge to roll my eyes and clap him on the shoulder as I pass by. "I'll make sure to be more understanding when you find yourself obsessed with a woman."

He snorts. "Fat fucking chance of that happening, asshole," he mutters. Still, I'm already on my way to the exit, hitting the button for the private elevator, and imagining what I'm going to say to her when I get Aurora Summers alone.

I didn't come here tonight with the expectation of meeting her, but I guess fate is just funny that way. I can't deny it anymore. Paris is right—I want her. Far more than I fucking should.

The doors slide open revealing the bottom floor amidst its chaos—lights, dancing, free pouring alcohol. It smells like sweat and expensive cologne down here. I step out into the mess of it all and go in search of my prey.

19
RORI

Unwanted hands find their way onto my waist for what has to be the tenth time in the last hour. Fueled by alcohol and irritation, I whirl around on the new offender and glare up into a pair of dull green eyes. The guy is obviously intoxicated. I shove his hands off even as I scowl at him.

"Hands off," I snap. "I'm dancing with my friend. Not you."

I turn to face Selene once more, who hasn't even noticed my absence. Maybe I shouldn't have given her that earlier shot, because she's easily the worst lightweight ever. She's swaying in time with the beat. Her eyes are closed as she leans into one of the other models from her agency, mouthing the words to whatever pop song is playing over the speakers. I barely make it another step towards her when the offending guy grabs my hips once more and directs me back to him.

"Come on, don't be like that," he whispers into my ear. I flinch away as his hot breath hits my neck. "I can show you a good time."

"The only good time I'm looking for," I say through clenched teeth as I grip his hands against my body and quickly push him back, "is one where you're not around. *Back. Off.*"

"I just want to—"

"I believe she told you to get fucking lost."

I stiffen at the familiar voice that interrupts.

Are you fucking kidding me? I wish a hole would open up in the center of the dance floor and swallow me whole. *He* can't be here. There's no fucking way the universe could be that cruel, but as I lift my gaze and meet a pair of stormy, ocean-blue eyes over the guy's shoulder, I know it can. Because it is.

Isaac places a hand on the stranger's shoulder and jerks him away from me. The dude stumbles back and barely manages to catch himself before falling. He does, however, manage to slam into a couple of girls dancing on their own and when they gasp, catching his attention—he grins and redirects the full force of his drunken gaze on them, leaving me alone with my tormentor and unexpected savior.

Isaac looks back at me, and fuck, but he looks good enough to eat. His golden blond hair is pushed back. The lights from the club, as they flow across the room in a circular motion, rise and fall over the plains of his face that only make the sharp angled lines of his features even more prominent; he looks like he could be sculpted from pure stone.

I blow out a breath. "What are you doing here?" I demand, crossing my arms. It's a defensive move. I can't help it. I feel like I have to constantly keep my guard up when it comes to him. Isaac Icari gives me no ounce of peace. He's nothing but danger and darkness. Maybe that's why I can't help but be attracted to him. There's something wrong with me.

"It's opening night," he says, stepping closer. So close, I can smell a hint of mint and whisky on him. It's alluring.

"Don't—" But it's too late, Isaac's hand slides around my middle. He pulls me into him and suddenly, we're dancing. Not the cheap grinding that some of the other couples are doing, but a soft sway back and forth that is far more intense.

Each brush of his body against mine sends my mind careening into full-blown panic. Heat shoots through me, lighting my flesh on fire. The soft stroke of his hands on me reminds me of a time when they were rough. When his cock was in my mouth, down my throat, and he was shuddering above me. I growl out a curse.

"I don't want to dance with you," I say through gritted teeth.

His fingers merely tighten against me as he yanks me harder into his chest at that statement. "Too fucking bad, Sunshine," he says, bending low until his lips are right next to my ear.

I should feel just as repulsed by him as I was by the other guy, but my traitorous body hasn't gotten the fucking memo. She's completely obsessed. Enough that I can feel the dampening of my panties. Jerking my head up, I glare into the twin pools of dark blue that are his eyes. He doesn't need to know what he does to me.

"You're not the type to do something for nothing," I say cautiously. "What do you want for the save?"

Isaac releases a breath and spins me in a circle. It's a precise movement, practiced. He's a good dancer. No uncertain hip thrusts or back and forth shuffle. Isaac spins me away and then back to him until I land against his chest with a breathless gasp. The room is spinning. My head is foggy. I look back across the dance floor. We're getting farther and farther from Selene and her friend, but I don't say anything. If Isaac wanted to hurt me, he would have done so already. And if I can keep her away from him for the time being, I'm willing to do it. I don't trust him and I don't want my friends near him. Not Selene. Not Hel.

"Just dance, Rori," Isaac says. Shock hits me. Rori. Not Aurora. Not Sunshine. Not Goddess. It's the first time he's ever actually said my nickname. That, more than anything else, tells me that this meeting is *different* from our previous ones.

Hesitantly, I let my hands drift up to his shoulders. They're wide—he definitely has the frame of an athlete. I swallow reflexively as on the next spin, one of his legs slides through both of mine and I'm nearly knocked off my feet. He keeps me steady, though, sliding a palm to the small of my back and gently urging me closer. There's no room between us. His chest against mine has my heart beating faster. More sweat collects at the base of my skull and slides down my spine beneath the dress.

"This..." I don't know what to say, but this feels almost wrong. It's strange to be in Isaac's arms and, for the first time since we've met, not be at each other's throats.

"Just let it be," he urges. "It's just a dance."

But it's not. Not really. Maybe he wants to believe it is, but I know the truth and I don't have the luxury of lying to myself. Still, I let my words drift off and close my eyes as the music starts to flow through me once more.

Isaac holds me against him, but his grip doesn't hurt. It's almost like liquid, our movements fluid as we dance together. My mind fogs over as the alcohol I imbibed earlier finally hits me. It's almost like my body waited until it felt comfortable enough to relax. Around Selene, I still felt like I needed to be on alert. But now ... now *he's* here.

I open my eyes and when I look up, I realize Isaac's attention is centered fully on me. The shock of his blue eyes and the sharp intensity in them blurs out everything else around us. *Why do I do this to myself? Why does he do this to me?*

We could be anywhere else in the world—in the middle of a burning building—and I wouldn't even notice. He's that fucking hard to pull away from. He's entrancing. Mesmerizing. *Is he doing this to me on purpose, or is this just how he is?*

"Why are you dancing with me?" Despite the unspoken oath to stop asking him questions, this one comes out all on its own, without my consent.

His lips part and his grip on my side tightens, until I wince at the pain it causes. Immediately, his hold loosens and his fingers brush over the spot he hurt—almost as if the gentle touch is a silent apology.

"I want to call a truce," he says, his words barely audible over the noise of the room—the people talking and laughing, the music playing.

The song ends and the bubble pops. All of the outside world intrudes once more. "Why?"

He shakes his head. "Can't you take the olive branch without asking so many questions?" His lips curl in amusement.

I shake my head. No, I can't. That's not the way I work. It never has been.

Isaac stares back at me and then, slowly, his hand arches up and his fingers brush against my cheek. "Every second you're around me," he says. "You're in danger. I don't want to see you in danger anymore."

My body feels buzzed and numb all at the same time. It feels like he just made an admission that's bound to change everything. A part of me wishes he'd take it back, but now that it's out there in the open, that's not an option. "Is this about your father?"

His eyes flash and he looks up. My attention follows his until I see what he's looking at. His friends stare down at us from a balcony way overhead, their arms folded over the railing at the topmost floor. The auburn-haired pretty boy—Paris, if I remember correctly—smirks at us. The other one, however, looks like someone's shoved a rather hard stick up his ass. He barely pays me a glance and instead chooses to direct the full brunt of his glare at Isaac.

There's some unspoken communication going on between the three of them—a conversation that I'm not privy to. It lasts for several more seconds and then Isaac sighs and looks back at me. "Come on," he says, pulling me off the dance floor. "Let me take you back to your dorm."

"Wait, what?" I struggle against his grip, but Isaac doesn't even blink. He merely drops down, wraps an arm around my legs, and lifts me against his chest like a prince in a fairytale. I scowl. He's no prince and this is no fairy-tale. "Stop!" I command him, smacking his chest. "I can't leave. I came with my friend. I need to make sure—"

"I'll make sure she gets home safely," he says. "One of

the guys will keep an eye on her and she'll be back in her bed before dawn."

"Are you fucking serious?" I frown up at him. "How the hell can you expect me to trust you?" I demand. "We're not friends."

He pauses just off the dance floor and looks down at me. "Do you want us to be?" he asks.

I gape at him. "What? Friends?" I shake my head. "No, I think we're beyond that. I can't be your friend."

My words seem to amuse him because when I expect a scowl in response, he merely chuckles and nods. "You're right about that, at least. What will it take to get you to leave with me right now?" He's tipping my whole fucking night on end. One moment he's reminding me how much of a monster he's been to me for weeks and the next he's being courteous.

I narrow my gaze on him. "I want to talk to her," I say.

He looks at me and then sighs. His arms loosen and slowly—inexplicably slowly—he drops me down and lets my feet touch the floor once more. "Fine," he says, "but I'm going with you. Make it short."

I look up at him and when he stares back, he arches a brow, and I know—beyond a shadow of a doubt—that this is as much as I'll get from him tonight. I sigh and turn towards the dance floor, scanning the room for a familiar head of white-blonde hair. When I catch sight of Selene, I start towards her, shadowed by what feels like my own personal bodyguard.

Isaac's presence at my back is a constant. It sends tendrils of something electric skittering up and down my spine. An awareness inside of me wakes up and takes notice. I don't know how he does it, but there's no denying that he has a way of occupying a space.

When I approach Selene, and she spots me, she blinks and does a double take—pulling away from her friend. "Hey..." Try as I might, it's hard to ignore Isaac. It's no shock that even she can't do so either. Her gaze slides first to him before she looks back at me and raises a single brow. "I'm going to head back to the dorm," I tell her. "Are you going to be okay?"

She frowns. "With him?" Surprisingly, her voice is steady and though she's still swaying back and forth slightly—her body moving almost involuntarily in time with the beat of the next song that comes on—I'm thankful that she's not as drunk as I originally thought.

"Yeah," I say. "We're going to talk."

Selene focuses on Isaac and then, without hesitation, she reaches up and clasps me by my shoulders, moving me to the side. "If anything happens to her," she starts, glaring up at Isaac as she snaps her hands to her hips. "I'll track you down and gut you. You got me?"

Isaac cracks a smile. A genuine one, if I've ever seen one. "Understood," he says.

Selene squints up at him, and I bite my lip to keep from laughing. I don't know what she sees in his face, or if maybe she realizes that there's nothing she can do except let me make my own decisions, but she finally sighs and looks back at me. "Text me when you get home," she demands.

"I will," I promise, taking her hands and squeezing them tight.

Isaac reaches into his pocket and pulls free a card. "Whenever you're ready to go back," he says, holding out the card for her to take, "one of my guys will be more than happy to give you a ride."

"I already have a ride," she says, lifting her chin, but she takes the card anyway.

"Just in case," Isaac says with a grin.

His hand finds my hip and curves around it. "See you later," I call back as he motions me forward and the two of us exit the dance floor for the second time tonight.

"Be safe!" Selene calls after me. "I'll close out your tab for you!"

With Isaac's hand on my side and the hot club air making my hair stick to my nape, I don't know if safe is anything I can be around him. A part of me argues that I shouldn't be doing this. I shouldn't leave with him. I know what it means. Even if we're drawing a line in the sand, giving in to a truce, there's more happening tonight than either one of us wants to say aloud.

Safe? With a man like Isaac Icari? It's almost an oxymoron. But as I step outside of *Labyrinth* and feel the California air on my skin for the first time in hours, I have to think that maybe the two of us have been building to this since the day we sat across the table next to our parents. Maybe there was no other way around this. Maybe we were always going to end up here—no matter what either of us has done to the other.

I swallow reflexively as he hands something to the valet and then pulls me closer to his side. I shiver, catching his attention. Isaac looks down. "Are you cold?"

No. If anything, I'm hot. Hotter than I've ever been in my life. I shake my head, unable to voice the words inside. His gaze remains locked on mine despite the lack of verbal response until the valet returns, pulling up in front of us in a black Escalade.

Isaac reaches for the passenger door and holds it open for me. I take his hand and step inside, letting him help me into the expensive car. Once the door is shut at my back, I watch him slip money into the valet's hands and then circle the front of the vehicle.

This is it, I think. Tonight is both the end of our feud and the beginning of something new. I'm not sure which I'm hoping for. All I know, though, is that tonight is a turning point.

20

RORI

Isaac is quiet. It's the kind of quiet that preludes some serious shit about to go down. My hands clench and unclench in my lap as he drives. The city passes by us in flashes of lights. It's a classic California Friday night. Tourists are out and about, as are the residents. Drunk girls in body-tight dresses stumble across crosswalks with their friends, laughing and cursing as they try to travel to the next bar or club in their sky-high heels.

I half expect Isaac to get irritated at their antics, but he must be a true Californian boy because he barely spares any of them a glance. The whole of his attention is on the road, and when the light before us turns green, he eases his foot off the brake and speeds up. Cars cruise by with their light-up taxi and independent carpool signs glowing in the dark. A glance at the dashboard tells me it's barely past midnight, but the city is still going hard—most are already past the point of no return.

I glance at the man at my side as he silently stares through the windshield, almost as if he wants to ignore my presence. I wish I'd drunk more. I have a sinking feeling that I'm going to need a little more liquid courage before I can deal with him tonight. But it's too late now. I've agreed to this and I need to see it through. Besides, the truth is that we've been circling each other for far too long.

The further we get, the darker the roads get. The fewer people we see. Several minutes pass and the surroundings become unfamiliar after we pass the university and keep going. I sit up straighter and flip around to face Isaac.

"What are you doing?" I demand. "Where are you taking me?"

"I'll take you home," he promises. "But after we have a talk."

I cut a look his way, irritation flourishing in my veins. "I want to know where we're going, *now*, Isaac."

He glances my way once and then returns his attention to the front of the car. He doesn't offer an excuse or even bother trying to assuage my sudden irritation and panic. That's it, just a glance. I'm not getting an answer.

Irritation turns to anger in a heartbeat. "What the fuck is your problem?"

"Have patience," he replies.

Have patience? Oh, I'm freshly out of that, especially when it comes to him. "No." I'm so fucking sick of him dictating my actions. It's been a nonstop fight since the second I stepped foot in Hazelwood. "Pull the car over."

"I'm not pulling the car over, Aurora." His tone is hard. "Just sit there like a good girl until we get there and then you can pitch your fit."

Maybe some girls would have just sat back and done as they were told, but not me. I pride myself on not letting my emotions get the best of me, but when I'm done, I'm *fucking done.* I hit him. Ball my fist up and slam it into his arm hard enough that it jerks his whole body. The Escalade skids sideways—in hindsight, maybe it was a bad idea to hit the driver, but he's so fucking frustrating, I honestly don't see how I had any other choice.

"Fuck!" Isaac corrects the front of the car and then flashes a look at me. "Calm the fuck down, Aurora. What the fuck is wrong with you? Do you want me to kill us both?"

"No," I snap. "I just want to kill you. Pull this fucking car over *now*."

Something dangerous flashes in his eyes and, suddenly, my seatbelt jerks against my front and I'm slammed back into my seat as the SUV comes to an abrupt halt. Isaac directs the vehicle into an empty parking lot and throws the gear shift into park. I don't waste a second reaching for my belt to unlatch it. My hand finds the handle of the door and I throw it open, bolting as soon as we've stopped moving.

"Aurora!" Isaac's irritated roar reaches my ears.

I ignore it.

Fuck him. Fuck his father. Fuck all of this. Maybe I should've gone with Marcus to Eastpoint. Yeah, I would have struggled to find my place there. I would have, yet again, had to live underneath the umbrella that accompanies being Marcus Summers' baby sister. At least I wouldn't be here, dealing with *him*. Maybe then I wouldn't be in this situation. So many maybes. So many what-ifs, yet at the end of the day this is all that I'm left with. A confusing amount of attraction to a man I should fucking hate. A lost sense of what to do. And an undetermined amount of danger circling me at every waking moment.

Hard footsteps sound behind me. I keep walking. A hand grabs my arm a moment later. I close my eyes and let myself be yanked around—I expected it anyway. I use the momentum of the movement to propel my fist. If he's going to jerk me around, then the very least Isaac's going to do is take the damage that comes with it.

My fist flies towards his face and I register the shock on his expression a split second before my knuckles connect with his cheekbone. The skin over the bone breaks. Isaac curses, but instead of thrusting me away as I expect, his hands latch onto my arms and shake me.

"Stop it!" he growls. "Fuck! Just fucking *stop*."

"No!" I scream, dropping my arm as my whole body trembles with the force of his shaking. "*You* stop! Fuck. I'm so goddamn tired of this shit. You think you can just come into my life and boss me around? I'm not your fucking toy, Isaac. I don't know what kind of girls you've fucked with before—which ones had the audacity to get in your way and turn your ire on them, but I am not like anyone you've met before. You mess with me, and you won't just have a fight on your hands, you'll have a war."

Isaac glares down at me. I just don't give a shit anymore. I glare right fucking back at him, daring him. "You drive me fucking insane." He spits out his words like they're poison. Maybe they are and I just don't know it yet because knowing that I drive him crazy in the same way he does me does something to me. It makes me feel good. It makes me feel powerful when all I've ever felt is fucking helpless.

"Welcome to the club." I snort. "You think dealing with you is any different?" My feet move back, but he follows, keeping his hands latched onto my arms. "Let go," I demand.

He doesn't let go, though. Of course not. That would be too easy—giving me what I want. Instead, Isaac moves ever closer until the scent of him—all sharp spices and warmth—fills my nostrils. My thighs tighten.

"Let go, Isaac," I repeat. "Or you'll regret it."

"Don't bother, Sunshine," he says. "I already know what you're planning."

"Oh, really?" Even as the words are coming out of my mouth, I jerk my leg up and aim my knee directly between both of his. In a move faster than lightning, his hands tighten against my arms and he yanks me off balance before my knee can make it to its destination. The two of us go tumbling down in a heap on the pavement and at the last second, he turns, hitting the ground first. My face slams into his chest, my nose crashing between his pecs.

A low, rumbling growl emits from the body beneath me. Self-preservation has me scrambling backwards, but his hold is still there and it's strong. Isaac flips both of us once more until this time, I'm the one with my back to the ground, hard concrete and small loose rocks digging into me past my dress. He hovers, blond curls falling into his shadowed face as he looms over me.

Sweat beads pop up along my spine. My whole body goes cold. My throat closes. "*No...*" What I mean to be a scream comes out as little more than a breathless whisper.

"You are the worst pain in my ass I've ever fucking had to experience," Isaac starts talking. I hear him—the insulting worlds—but they're far away. The rest of me may be here, but my mind has been catapulted backwards.

Phantom hands slide their way up my inner thighs.

I'm going to puke. *No,* I order myself. *Don't puke. Not here. Don't let him see. He can't know.*

"Get off me." Fine trembles start up my limbs, and soon, they've overtaken my entire body. Try as I might, I can't stop them. "Please ... *Isaac.*" I say his name more to myself than to him. It's a reminder of who this is in front of me and who it's not. It's not him. It's not Eric. "Stop. Get ... get off of me."

"—rora." My vision swims in front of me, growing hazy as the panic takes hold—squeezing long tentacle-like tendrils around my neck until my airflow is cut off and I'm gasping for breath.

The shadow above me disappears and a moment later, I can feel my body being positioned, pulled up, and settled back against a hard, warm lap. A firm, wide palm touches the back of my head, cupping it. Isaac says something else, but I don't hear it anymore. The hands touching me no longer feel as restraining and disgusting but rather soft and gentle.

That can't be Isaac, though. He doesn't have a gentle bone in his body. It's that thought, too, that finally pulls me out of the past and out of the bone-numbing panic attack. My vision returns in small increments. I can hear my breaths coming in fast, jerky sounds—but I'm breathing and that's what matters.

I don't know how long we sit like that in the middle of an empty parking lot with rough pavement under us and a warm breeze fluttering against our faces, but when I finally feel like I can move again and the world isn't trying to close in on me, I look up into a pair of eyes so blue they could rival the fucking midnight sky.

"Are you okay?"

Am I okay? I repeat Isaac's question in my mind again

and again until I feel like it's branded on my soul. *No, I'm not okay.* I push back against his chest and this time, he lets me. He releases me as easily as if he was always intending to in the first place, and I climb up from the safety of his arms to stand on my own.

"I'm going home," I tell him.

He gets up, though a bit more slowly than I did. I wait for a response, but all I receive in return is a hard, impenetrable look. "Did you hear me?" I demand. He continues to stare at me, and I feel electrified by his gaze. He looks like a blue-eyed tiger hunting its prey.

I take a step back. He takes one forward. "Isaac."

"You're not going anywhere, Aurora," he says. I blink, but don't respond. He continues. "You can go home *after* we've had our talk," he repeats. "Now, unless you want to tell me what that was all about"—I stiffen as he gestures to the ground we'd just been sitting on before letting his gaze come back to me. There's no doubt what he means and I have no intention of telling him shit.—"then what you're going to do is get your ass back in the fucking car before I strap you down, spank your ass, and throw you in myself."

This is just too much. "Why?" The question slips out before I can think better of it. And instead of sounding angry or frustrated, both of which I'm feeling, it sounds … tired. More tired than I care to admit I actually am—especially to someone like him. Someone that I should have my guard up with.

He arches a brow. "Why would I spank you?" he clarifies. "Or why am I forcing you to talk with me?"

"Why are you even bothering?" I ask with a deprecating laugh. My hands come up and I scrub them down my face, not even caring if it's ruining my makeup. It's waterproof anyway. It should be able to withstand the strength of the rest of my emotions too. "Why even bother to explain anything now? What are you hoping to gain?"

Isaac tilts his head to the side and considers me. "What makes you think I'm trying to gain anything from you, Aurora?"

"Don't bullshit me, Isaac," I say. "You've been trying to torment me into doing what you want since the day we met." I blow out a breath. "I'm tired," I admit. "I'm fucking sick and tired of it. What do you really want?"

"I want you to get in the car," he states. "I want to take you somewhere safe, and I want to sit down and have a civil conversation for once."

When a laugh comes out of my throat, it echoes up into the sky and it doesn't sound anything like amusement. "Civil?" I'm shocked he even knows what that means. "We passed civil a long time ago, Isaac. What we are is nothing but two warring sides. You made us this way."

"You didn't seem too keen to stop the fight," he points out.

"You're right," I admit. Why? Probably because he gave me a reason to prove to myself that I wasn't the scared little girl in need of protection anymore. But I don't want to fight if there's no real reason to. "We both want the same thing," I tell him. "We want our parents' marriage to end. So, why are we even bothering to do this?" It's fucking stupid.

"I have my reasons." His words are vague and they make me want to punch him again. My hands clench into fists at my sides.

"You want to talk?" I ask. "Then tell me. Give me your fucking reasons because I don't get it."

"Not here," he says. Isaac steps forward and, this time,

I stand my ground. He comes at me, step by step, inch by inch until he's standing in front of me and only then does he stop. "Get in the car, Aurora." When I open my mouth to deny him once more, his head dips, and my eyes widen as his forehead touches mine in the lightest brush. "*Please.*"

There's a whole host of emotions in that final word. A plea. A wish. My lips part and hang open, but when he says it in that tone ... I find it hard to deny him.

My eyes slide shut. My insides riot, but even so, I turn and walk away from him. He doesn't come after me because he knows where I'm going. I head to the car, where the passenger side door is still hanging open, waiting for me. I grip the handle and climb back inside, shutting it firmly behind me, and it's only when Isaac rounds the front of the Escalade and gets into the driver's side that I speak.

"Tell me where we're going, Isaac." It's not a request.

Isaac's hands grip the steering wheel and he turns the key in the ignition. "Away, Aurora," he answers. "Far, far away."

21

RORI

I saac's 'far, far away' isn't actually that far. At least, physically, it isn't. But as we pull up in front of a hotel several minutes later, it feels like both of us are lost in a haze of our own thoughts. Maybe he meant that the two of us would eventually escape this cycle we were born into—fighting for dominance when all we are meant to be are pawns in someone else's game.

"Come on." I don't fight him this time as he parks at the entrance and gets out, tossing the keys to a valet. We enter the building and I trail behind him, passing the front desk without stopping. We enter a private elevator and remain silent all the way up to the top floor. The penthouse suite, of course. I would expect nothing less from the Icari heir.

"What is this place?" I ask as we step out onto marble, tiled floor and the elevator doors close behind us. My voice echoes around the vast space. It's all whites and blacks. Monochrome and lifeless.

"It's the place you were meant to move into," Isaac

says. "With me." Right. I'd almost forgotten Damien's "offer."

So this place was meant to be my cage, then. I take a look around, moving farther into the living room. The only sign of life aside from the two of us are the various plants around the room. The contrast of so much empty space next to vibrancy almost makes my eyes hurt.

"Okay," I say, my voice echoing in the quiet open space. "Well, you've got me here, now, Isaac." I turn towards him, my back to the wall of windows and the glass doors that lead out onto the rooftop patio. "Say what you want to say."

He looks at me for a brief moment and when he doesn't immediately respond, I scoff. "What? Is the place bugged?"

It wouldn't surprise me. Damien Icari strikes me as the kind of control freak who wants to know everything about everyone at every second of every day—including his own son.

He shakes his head. "No, I wouldn't move into a place if I thought it was bugged. I have a team sweep it regularly." His words confirm my suspicions. My eyes narrow on him. I'm starting to develop a larger picture of what's going on.

Damien and Isaac, despite being father and son, are at war. A far more brutal and bloody war than the one between him and me.

I exhale and look back to the room, scanning it until I find what I need. The second I spot the alcohol cart, I make a beeline for it. I pop the cap on the decanter sitting there and pour myself a hefty dose of whatever's inside. It doesn't matter what it is—all alcohol numbs the senses eventually and I hadn't had nearly enough back at the club.

"What the hell do you think you're doing?" Isaac doesn't move fast enough to stop me. Before he can make it across the room, I've got the glass half full and placed at my lips. I swallow back a mouthful, wincing at the burn in my throat, and then down the rest. When his hand lands on my shoulder and his fingers pluck the glass from mine —it's too late.

"What the fuck am *I* doing?" I repeat with a laugh. "What the fuck are *you* doing? Dancing around the subject?" I let him take the glass and place it back on the cart before I jab him in the chest. "You brought me here, Isaac. Time to spill the fucking beans. If there's a point to the cloak and dagger shit, I'm ready to listen."

His eyes turn cold as he looks down at me. "No, I don't think you are. You're just angry. You want to get drunk—"

"You're damn right I want to get drunk," I snap. "And you want to know the reason?" I grab him by the front of his shirt, sinking my nails into the fabric as I drag him with me. I stomp towards the space we just left—right in front of the elevators where there's a massive mirror hanging there for all who come through those doors to see. "Take a good long fucking look," I say, shoving him towards it.

Isaac's head lifts and his dark eyes glare at me through the reflection. Slowly—so fucking slowly—he turns back to me. The intensity of his gaze sends shivers down my spine, but I don't back down. There's no point. I've already shown vulnerability to him and I hate that. I don't want to do it again.

So, what do I do? I do what I've always done. I push.

"The subterfuge doesn't suit you," I tell him. "The lying, the sneaking around, the social torment." I lower my eyelids and stare back at him through slitted eyes. "What's wrong? Are you that scared of a little girl?"

That does it. His hands clench into fists at his sides. "You think I'm scared of you?" he asks through gritted teeth.

"It would explain a few things," I reply. "Like how you treated me in the garden that night."

He stiffens, shooting me a dark and thunderous glare. "You knew who I was," he snaps. "Don't act like I'm the one who took advantage of you first. *You* sought *me* out."

"Maybe I did," I concede, "but you can't deny that you were rougher with me than you would've been with anyone else." Because he'd been trying to punish me.

"And you know that, how?" He growls. "How would you know how I fuck someone, Aurora?"

"You've been fucking me since day one," I snap back, "fucking me over."

The low chuckle that comes out of him sends warning alarms blaring through my head. "You think I've been fucking you all this time? Oh no, Sunshine. I haven't even begun to fuck you. Yeah, maybe I was a little rough with you, but you can't deny you deserved it. You're the one who got on your knees and put yourself in that position. I didn't force you. You wanted my cock."

"I didn't want to be treated like a whore!"

"If I treated you like a true whore, you wouldn't be here right now."

My lips part, words hanging right on the tip of my tongue, but no response makes its way out of my mouth. What can I say to that? I shake my head. "We're getting off topic," I say. "You're trying to distract me."

Isaac's face screws into a dark mask of anger. "I'm not the one standing here bringing up the past."

"Past. Present. Future—all of it has to do with you," I reply. "So long as this bullshit keeps going on and your father stays married to my mother, then it matters."

"Don't act like you didn't fucking like it, Aurora," Isaac says. "You might not have gotten to come, but you drooled all over my cock like any other slut begging for attention."

My hand connects with his face before I even realize I've moved. For several long seconds, the two of us are catapulted into shocked silence. His head stays turned to the side from the force of my slap, and my body remains frozen in front of him.

Shaking, I lower my palm back to my sides. "Don't assume I'll let you fuck with me like anyone else might," I warn him. "The only reason I let you get away with it is because—"

"You wanted revenge," he finishes for me.

I don't answer.

"That might be true," he continues, "but that doesn't mean I'm not right."

I cross my arms over my chest. "Tell me the truth." I grit the words out through clenched teeth. "Why the fuck are you even bothering with me? Why are we even playing this game to begin with?"

"I'm not playing—"

"The fuck you're not." I cut him off, casting him an exasperated look. Does he truly expect me to believe that he hasn't been moving his pieces around on the chessboard between us the whole time?

The words seem to strike something within him. His dark gaze finds mine and without realizing it until it's already happened, I take a step back. "You want to know what I'm doing? Fine, I'll tell you, you fucking bitch. I'm trying to fucking protect you!" His responding yell chills me down to my bones. It vibrates the mirror hanging on the wall.

There it is, I realize. The crack in his once impenetrable armor. I keep my eyes on his as he advances on me in quick stomping steps. "You fight me and you fucking fight me," he seethes, striding forward as my arms drop and I keep backing away. "But Aurora you are in far more danger than you realize."

He's not done. Something seems to have snapped within him, and I feel like I'm finally seeing *him* for the first time. His insides are just as shredded as mine. His eyes are wild, his nostrils flare, and his chest pumps up and down with effort.

"You want to know why I brought you here?" He doesn't stop until he's a shadow looming over me, his hand slapping the wall next to my head. "I brought you here to warn you. You should be fucking terrified. Of me and of my father. You're right to be wary of both of us, but between him and me—*I* am your only salvation. So do both of us a favor and keep your fucking mouth shut and your head down. Stop fighting me. If you want to do something to help, convince your mother to divorce him. As soon as possible. The sooner the two of you are far away from Hazelwood and Damien Icari, the better."

"Why?" The tops of his cheeks are stained red, not with embarrassment but fury and something else, but it can't be fear ... can it?

Lightning strikes in his blue eyes, clear as day and dark as night. "Why?" he repeats quietly, sounding stunned. "Fucking, why? Because he will fucking *kill you*,

Aurora. That's why." There's a flash of that enigmatic emotion within him at the roar that erupts from his throat.

Small trembles start up and move throughout my whole body, taking over. "Why the fuck do you care whether or not he kills me?" That's the question that I can't help but ask.

Why is he dancing around it? Why won't he admit it? Is it really that fucking hard to just come right out and tell me everything? Does he not think I can handle it? Does he think I'm some pathetic little girl in need of his protection? There are all these questions and no answers. I'm alone here in the dark, confused—not just by his words but the *reason* for them. *Why does he even care if I live or die by his father's hands?*

I need it in plain words. I need to know if it's the truth or if I'm just fucking crazy because being around him makes me feel like I am; like every second spent in his grasp is another second I'm slipping free of my carefully maintained facade that everything is alright.

"Why do you care, Isaac?" I repeat the question, looking up into his gaze. Daring him to continue. Daring him to open his perfectly sculpted lips and tell me another lie. Is this really about his father, or is he afraid of me? "I'm not important," I continue, stabbing at his ego. Pricking his pride. He's close enough to the edge that I know if I keep it up, something will break, and maybe, I'll finally see a little bit of the real emotions of Isaac Icari spill out. "I'm nothing but a pawn, right? I'm just your stepsister." The last word is a fucking taunt, a barb I know he won't be able to resist biting back against. "Not your friend and certainly not your lover."

He pulls back and this time instead of the flat of his palm, his fist hits the wall, making the paintings and mirror nailed into it shake and tremble with the force of his anger.

"Shut. Up." His words are dark and violent. Shaking with an inner fury that I knew he had to possess yet haven't seen him release in front of me.

I tilt my head back, chin up, with my eyes on his, and I do something I never thought possible. "Make. Me."

Silence and seconds stretch between us. I don't know who moves first, but I'm afraid it's me. It *is* me. I can't help it. All I know is that we have been building towards this moment. I've been climbing the mountain that is Isaac Icari for what feels like all of eternity and I'm tired. Tired of fighting against our natures.

I push up and slam my mouth against his. There's a stunned moment where he doesn't move and I open my eyes to find him staring back at me. I don't move away. I don't apologize. If he denies me now, if he rejects this, then I'll know the truth. I *was* crazy.

But he doesn't do any of that. In fact, the slow curve of his mouth reveals that I haven't, in fact, lost all sense of reason. Not at all. His anger turns into pleasantly surprised amusement. He smirks against my lips and then he reaches down, cupping the back of my neck, and his eyes slide shut.

Tongue against tongue, he delves inside of me and sucks out the very last breath of resistance lingering between us. And fuck him. He's a good fucking kisser. I may have started this. I may have been the first to give in, but if Isaac is anything, he's a control freak. To him, he has to be the one to finish it.

He pushes me back into the wall until my skull is flush with the plaster and then, he consumes me. A leg slides between both of mine, his knee pressing up against my pussy, and a whimper escapes me as the rough feel of fabric presses right against my clit. Now I know what that smirk was about. It was almost like he was saying, *Oh, Sunshine, you're going to regret choosing this path.*

But I don't.

"You should've run when I told you to," he tells me. "You should have run so far and so fucking fast..."

"Why?" I taunt. "So you could watch my ass?"

He barks out a laugh and shakes his head before bowing towards me. His hands are hard on my body, their hold unbreakable. I squirm under his strength, my insides clenching and unclenching as need pulses through me and goes nowhere.

"I'll make sure you're safe," he promises. "It'll be painful. It won't end here. Just remember—as you suffer in the fire you lit—you wanted this."

"I know." It's the only thing I can say. I can't deny his words because he's right. I *do* want this. Even if he burns me alive, I won't regret this. Because this is the most alive I've felt since that night three years ago when a man who should've never touched me thought he could take without consequences.

No. I shut that thought down without remorse. I don't want the past to intrude on this. This isn't for *him*. This is for me. This is *all* for me.

I shove my hands up into his sandy blond hair, the mixture of brown and gold tangling in my fingers as his curls twine around the digits and I kiss him back. He wants to eat me alive? Swallow me whole? Own me? Fine. He can, but he'll have to fight for it first.

22

ISAAC

Aurora Summers kisses like the world is ending. She opens her mouth and lets me sink deep like this will be the last time anyone shows her any sort of affection. She's all hard lines and jagged edges—a princess trapped in an incredibly high tower, surrounded by walls of thorns and even a fiery dragon or two. When she finally decides to break free and step outside, she bursts to life.

Feminine hands shove up into my hair as she yanks me closer, demanding more. I reach down, cupping under her thighs and lifting her against me. And just as I expect, she doesn't hesitate. Her legs open willingly and she wraps them around me. Once she's decided she's going to do something, she doesn't second guess it—she just goes for it.

"You're so greedy," I murmur against her mouth. "Don't worry, I'll make sure you get off this time."

"I don't know if I can trust that," she replies, panting. "I'll just have to take it for myself."

Her chest pushes against mine. I can feel the rapid

beat of her heart. Her scent is in my nose. Her hair in my face. Her hands on my skin. I want more. I want it all.

"Oh, you'll take it," I warn her, rotating my hips as I press my cock up between her legs, letting her feel my desire. "You'll take every last inch of my cock and your pussy will never be the same."

Cheeks flushed, eyes glazed over with lust, she stares back at me with her back to the wall. "Prove it." The words are a challenge and I've never been one to back down from a challenge.

Her dress has hitched up her hips. I grab the hem of it and pull it even higher—up and up until it catches at her waist. Only then do I stop and reach around, finding the zipper and yanking it down. The damn thing snaps under my fast movements. I don't fucking care as I rip the straps around her neck keeping the top up. I'll buy her a new one ... and then probably shred that off her as well.

"You said you weren't a whore," I comment lightly as my hands move over her. She stiffens at the term, but I don't let her get too far into her thoughts. I push her legs down and the shimmery fabric of her dress falls to the floor at my feet—along with her phone. "But I should warn you now," I tell her, kicking away the dress and toeing the phone along with it. "I intend to make you question that tonight."

"Isaac." My name is a warning on her lips.

I shake my head. "I won't do anything you don't want me to," I assure her. Tonight, anyway.

"I don't want to be treated like a whore," she snaps as my eyes take her in.

My cock pounds behind the prison of my zipper. "Yes, you do," I say, breathless. "Otherwise you never would've let me treat you like I did in the garden. Maybe you want to deny it to yourself, but some part of you loved the harshness. You liked the control you gave me. You liked the power you held."

She snorts, rolling her eyes. "I think you held all the power."

"If you think that, then you weren't paying attention." I move against her, grabbing her hand when she means to pull away and sliding it over the front of my pants. "This is all your doing," I tell her. "You're the reason."

Standing before me, wearing nothing more than a pair of peach-colored underwear and so much perfect skin, Aurora Summers looks like a goddess ready to sacrifice herself to the fires of mortal lust and desire. I decide, in this moment, that she shouldn't ever wear clothes again. I want her naked always—cooking, studying, exercising. It doesn't matter what she does, I just want unimpeded access to this body at all times. It's unreasonable, I know. Impossible because the second another person sees what's mine, I'll go on a murdering spree, but the thought is still there.

I release her wrist and her hand remains, cupping my cock through my pants as her lashes flutter. Her breasts call to me. I touch them, sliding both hands around each one, lifting them in my grasp.

"Beautiful." I don't realize I've uttered the thought aloud until she chuckles. Her fingers retract and trail upward along my arms as I squeeze each breast in turn, flicking against her hardened nipples. *They would be so pretty with a little jewelry*, I think. *Something to remind her of me.*

"You only say that because you want to fuck them," she says and suddenly my thoughts switch. The image of her laid flat out on her back, holding her tits together as I slide my cock between them and straight up towards her open, waiting mouth crosses my mind.

Fuck. I groan and lower my head, pressing my forehead against her shoulder. She's gonna make me come in my pants like a fucking virgin. The first time had been nothing like this. At the party, we'd both been trying to act as someone else, hiding our true intentions. There's none of that now. This time, she's not doing this for some fucking revenge video.

I stand back. When Aurora lifts her gaze and meets mine, she doesn't flinch away. She doesn't try to cover herself or act shy or reserved. She stares back at me with expectation, and fuck if that's not the hottest thing in the whole goddamn world. Confidence. The knowledge of her own worth and beauty. It's a heady mixture that turns me on and makes my cock throb inside my pants.

"Turn around," I say. "All the way. I want to see you."

She arches a brow, but we've come too far now. There's no backing out. Slowly, in small incremental movements, she pivots until she's facing the wall. I close my eyes briefly. I didn't get to see her like this the last time, so I couldn't have known it then, but seeing what I see now ... *how the fuck have I managed to stay away from her as long as I have?*

Her ass is a work of art. It's practically begging me to get on my knees and worship it. My hands fly down to the hem of my shirt and rip it up and off, discarding it along with her dress. The belt comes flying off next, landing on the floor with a hard thump. My shoes follow. When she's finally completed the turn, I've got everything but my pants off. I advance on her, and as I do, she opens her arms to reach for me.

Her legs are back around my waist, ankles locked at

the small of my back as her breasts press against my pecs. "There's no going back," I whisper against her lips as I carry her through the penthouse.

She arches up against me, pressing herself as far into me as she can. "Good," she replies. "Because I never look back."

I don't think that's completely true. Not from what I saw earlier—in the parking lot—but perhaps she means that if she can help it, she doesn't look back. Maybe she doesn't want to look back but some things force her to. Whatever the case, it doesn't matter right now. All that matters is that she and I, in this moment, are as connected as we've ever been and there's no prying us apart once I get inside of her the way I plan to.

Our lips meet once more, mouths clashing in a dance as old as humanity itself. She tastes amazing, like liquor and sunshine. It's heady and addictive, just like the woman in my arms. She's closer than she's ever been, even at that stupid party. She might have had my dick down her throat, but she was never quite this near. I can see each and every individual freckle across her high cheekbones and the bridge of her nose. They litter her skin. Down her face. Over her shoulders. There are even a few on her upper chest, though fewer there than other areas. The result is the same—she's been marked by the sun.

And I want to leave my own mark.

I pull away from her mouth as we enter the bedroom and then press her back into the massive king mattress across from the wall of windows that overlooks the California coast and city beneath it. My body finds its place on top of her and I come down hard, letting her feel every inch of my arousal through my pants against the small of her belly. She stiffens, at first, her breath coming out in harsh pants. I go back to that moment in the parking lot.

I raise up. "Aurora?" Her name is a question but also a comfort.

She shakes her head, unresponsive. Her body trembles against mine, but she doesn't go back into that full-blown panic she'd been in earlier. "Open," I command. "Look at me. Look at who's on top of you."

For a brief moment, her eyes remain squeezed shut and then after several tense heartbeats, her lashes flutter and she lifts them, meeting my gaze. Once again, I press down on top of her, harder. I settle myself against her in increments, waiting for any sign that she's not okay. Her hips shift under me. Her legs part, allowing me room, giving me her unspoken permission. My lips touch her throat and I grin when she arches up, unaware of my intention.

A cry of surprise echoes from her throat as I sink my teeth into the soft, delicate flesh between her neck and shoulder, biting down hard until I'm sure there's a perfect indentation marking her skin—one that won't be going away anytime soon.

"Fuck!" she cries out, slamming the flat of her palm against my chest as she pushes me back slightly and reaches up to feel the wound. "That hurt."

"Good," I say, still grinning. Her hands turn to claws as her nails sink into my chest and she glares up at me. I arch a brow. "What's wrong?" I ask. "Want a little payback?"

Before I realize what's happening, she hooks her leg over my hip and shoves up on one side, pushing me over. We flip and she ends up straddling me from above, her nails still digging their way into my flesh.

"Yes," she answers with an easy, almost evil smile. She leans down and my eyes find the place that I marked. It's blossoming into a pretty red color and I know before the end of the night, it won't be the only wound either of us will be sporting.

I spread my hands out even as my dick jumps between us, ready and willing to do whatever she wants so long as it means it can sink itself inside the place between her legs. "Then do your worst, Sunshine," I say, offering myself up to her.

"Oh, I will, *my dear Icarus*," she replies, reminding me of the name I gave her at the party. Her smile grows wider as she leans over me, putting her lips to my right pec, right over my heart. "It seems all you do is bring out the worst in me."

And as her own blunt, little teeth sink into my skin, all I can think is, *thank fuck for that.*

23
RORI

Isaac is like liquid heat beneath my fingertips. Everywhere I touch is warm. He's all wiry muscle bunched beneath tight, hard skin. He acts so differently than he did before. It's almost like I'm doing this with a completely new person. It isn't until we're already on the bed and practically naked in each other's arms that I realize that it's not so much that he's a different person but that he's finally let down those guarded walls of his.

It shouldn't touch me the way it does—knowing he's opened himself to me—but it does. I kiss him again, letting our tongues battle with one another. It's a fight, and it's not. We both want this. Yet, we also like the little wounds we inflict on each other. It's fun to leave little possessive marks.

I find the front of his pants. It's already half open, unbuttoned, and unzipped. I push my fingers inside, setting them flat against the ridges of his cut abdomen and sliding them beneath the fabric of his underwear and pants until my fingers meet the iron-hard cock beneath. It was dark the last time I touched it, that last time I'd taken it in my mouth. I'd almost forgotten how big he is. Even as I circle my fingers around the hard length of him, I can't believe I somehow fit him all the way in my mouth, my throat.

How the fuck didn't I choke?

As if he can hear my thoughts, Isaac chuckles and a moment later speaks. "Is that all you're going to do, Sunshine?" he challenges as I lift up and look down at him. "Give me a handjob? I thought we were past cheap teenage party favors. Or are you getting cold feet?"

With him? Always. He frightens me far more than I'm willing to admit—especially out loud. But with this? Ha. We're already too far gone.

"You're the one who left your pants on," I tell him. "Maybe you're scared I might defile you."

He laughs and I blink at the sound. It's shockingly beautiful, loud, and full of such real, genuine amusement it makes me realize he's never actually laughed like that in front of me before. He reaches up and locks on my arms and once more, we're spinning until my spine hits the mattress. Then he disappears long enough to shuck his pants onto the floor and toss a condom onto the bed at my side.

The next thing I know, thick fingers find the outside of my panties and he pulls those off as well. Instead of just chucking them to the floor with the rest, he lifts them like the filthy degenerate he is and presses the crotch to his face, inhaling as he fists his cock over me. Isaac takes up the space between my legs, and I spread them wider to give him room, not even aware of what I'm doing until a wash of air strokes over my soaked pussy. By then, it's too late. I'm too far absorbed in what he's doing.

He wraps his hand around his dick and pumps it from

base to tip and back as he presses the soaked fabric of my panties to his nose and mouth with a groan. The muscles of his abdomen ripple as his hips roll into his hand and he puts the drenched spot of my panties right over his mouth and nose.

When he catches me staring at him, he smiles and then tosses them over his shoulder before releasing his cock and using his hands to spread my thighs even wider —until my muscles strain and ache. "The smell of your pussy is an aphrodisiac, Sunshine," he informs me. "You smell like pure heaven."

"Pervert," I mutter as my face heats up.

"Your pervert," he replies. "Just as you're my greedy little slut, aren't you?"

It should not turn me on the way he keeps calling me that. Slut. Whore. Those are bad words—degrading terms. Yet, from his mouth, they sound almost like endearments. *That's fucked up, isn't it?*

His low chuckle rockets through me as he bends and shoves his shoulders beneath my knees, hooking them over his back. "Say it," he orders.

"W-what?" My brain short circuits as the heat of his breath touches me. My insides contract and I'm terrified that he can see it with how spread out I am, that he can see the way my pussy is pulsing with need for him.

"I want you to say the words," he says. "Tell me what you are."

I'm shaking my head before he's even finished. "I don't like those words."

"Yes, you do," he insists. "You've just been conditioned not to like them."

"They're degrading."

"You like to be degraded," he says.

"No, I—ah!" I scream in surprise as he cuts me off by lifting a hand and shoving two fingers into my pussy. No warning. They slide right to the hilt—a testament to how wet I already am.

"I promised you that you'd get to come tonight," he says, "but you've got to be willing to put in the work too, Sunshine."

My hips roll automatically as he thrusts his fingers in and out, curling them up at just the right angle so that stars begin to dance in front of my vision almost immediately. "Oh, fuck!" I groan, my chest arching and my back bowing as he fucks me with his hand.

Almost as soon as it started, though, it's gone. Isaac's fingers pull free of my pussy and I jerk up in shock, staring down between my legs where he grins up at me, a string of fluid still connecting his hand to the opening of my body. "Isaac..." I whine.

"Tell me what I want to hear, Aurora."

I groan, angry, and so fucking turned on. They're just words, I tell myself. They mean nothing. "I-I'm your greedy little slut."

His fingers return to my core, but hover just along the outer lips, stroking up and down, completely ignoring my entrance and my clit. "Louder."

"I'm your greedy little slut!" I say a bit louder.

"Are you?"

"Yes!" I scream. "I'm your greedy little fucking slut! Please, Isaac. Please." I'm half fuckin delirious as his fingers stroke closer and closer to my pussy. His thumb moves up over my clit. I'm sweating, panting, shaking. My whole body flares to life, tightening all over as it anticipates his next move.

Warm breath filters over the outside of my pussy and

a second later, Isaac's fingers are at my core once more, spreading me open. "So fucking wet," he whispers against my flesh, and just the brush of his words across my clit makes my back bow. "So fucking ready for me."

I've had guys do this for me before and all of them had made me feel like it was just a part of the foreplay they had to get through in order to fuck me. This, however, is different. Isaac's words are spoken with a low reverence that sounds almost holy even though they're anything but. Shivers skate down my nerve endings. Little pops of electricity spark up beneath my flesh.

"So juicy, baby," he continues as he thrusts back and forth into my cunt. Disgusting, wet vulgar sounds reach my ears and hot, molten embarrassment floods my face. Still, I can't stop the way I squirm towards him, pushing my bottom half into his hand as he slides his fingers into my pussy.

"You're soaking my fingers," Isaac says. "You're dripping onto the bed." My cheeks are on fire. His words are dirty, but I can't stop replaying them in my head. Each one only makes the problem worse. I can practically feel myself leaking around his digits. I know he's not exaggerating.

I tremble as his head descends. My body locks up at the first touch of his tongue against my pussy. He proves just how dangerous he actually is as he spears into me, sucking me dry, lapping me up like I'm the last drop of water in the world and he's dying of thirst.

My teeth sink into my lower lip, biting down hard enough that blood floods my mouth. I can't help it. It's so fucking good. Better than I've ever had in my goddamn life. Unwillingly, my hips start to rock against his face, seeking out the pleasure he gives me. With shaking hands,

I reach down and thread my fingers into the blond locks at the top of his head. He doesn't seem to notice. He's far too focused on sucking down every fresh gush of wetness that spills out of me. His mouth opens and his tongue slides through my folds and above it all, his fingers press down on either side of my clit, both holding me open and reminding me that he can end it all in a heartbeat.

"Fuck!" I gasp for breath that never seems to come. All of the oxygen in my lungs has evaporated, leaving nothing behind, and I'm left to shake and tremble beneath his ministrations and hope like hell that he ends my life with pleasure before the suffocation does it for him.

A moan erupts from me as he hits a spot inside that sends my mind reeling. My thighs lock around his head and a fresh wave of heady pleasure hits me. I can't take it for much longer.

"Isaac," I rasp. "Isaac, oh god, please…"

He devours me. His fingers pinch down harder on my clit and send me into an explosive white light that tears through my mind. A scream is ripped from my throat as my hand clenches against his head and an orgasm over-takes me. There's no controlling it.

I lose track of everything from his mouth on my pussy to the air against my flesh. My eyes slide shut, and it isn't until I feel him pull away that I notice the waning of my orgasm. It's hard to notice anything past the quivering of my own limbs. Isaac slips up my body, gripping my hips and yanking me down until my lower half is in his lap.

My eyes open to mere slits. Fine trembles still shiver along my skin and spine as he looks down at me, mouth coated in wetness. He takes his cock in hand, slips the condom on, and directs it towards my still throbbing, contracting pussy, pushing just the head inside.

"There you go, Sunshine," he says, his voice hoarse as he licks his lips and moans. "Open for me."

There has never been a command that I've wanted to follow as much as that one. My legs spread and I even reach down with shaking fingers, cupping them beneath my thighs as I hold myself open for him, giving him everything. His lips pull into an off-kilter smirk that does wicked things to my insides.

"Good girl," he praises me as he sinks inside. "I knew you would be. My good fucking girl." I gasp, arching into the movement as he stretches my hole. "Fuck, you're tight." *Of course I am,* I think with a wince. I haven't done this in a long time. I'd been willing to do so much to get back at him, but it isn't like I've slept with that many guys. This is different. *He* is different.

Isaac's face scrunches up and he releases the base of his cock to punch the mattress next to my head as he bends over my body, slowly but surely sawing his way into my cunt. One hand comes up to cup my face. My thighs are trembling with effort.

"There we go," he whispers, holding himself above me. "Just like that. Oh, fuck ... Rori. You take my cock so fucking good, Sunshine. You're squeezing the shit out of me."

The stretching burn of his dick makes me bow up towards him once more. "It hurts," I whimper.

His gaze clashes with mine and he bares his teeth at me. "How does it hurt?" The question sounds more like a command. My throat goes dry.

"It burns," I say, panting. "It's too big."

"You like the burn," he says, pushing harder, grinding his hips into me.

I snap my head back. "Ugh, fuck! N-no, I don't."

"Then why are you so fucking wet?" he growls. "Why are you soaking my cock in your pussy juices, Aurora?"

I shake my head back and forth, a physical denial to his words. One of his hands shoots down to my pussy and I clench up, forcing a groan out of his chest. His fingers slap the top of my mound, right over my clit.

"Ah!" I scream.

"Don't fucking test me," he growls, shoving his fingers into my pussy, stretching it even further as his dick invades. The burn increases, growing hotter. His fingers don't stay, though. As quickly as he thrust them in, he pulls them back out and then holds them in front of my face.

"You see this," he says, separating his fingers enough for me to see the wetness sticking them together. "You fucking love it. Your mind might believe one thing, but your body knows the truth."

I can't hold myself up any longer. I release my thighs and instead reach for him, wrapping my arms around his strong shoulders.

"Please," I beg as my chest aches with need. I burrow my face against him, trying to hide from both his words and the intensity of his gaze. "Isaac, please, fuck me."

A growl erupts from him—something animalistic and dark. His hands return to my hips. "I shouldn't let you get away hiding, Aurora. Don't think you'll get away with it every time."

"I just want you," I whine. "Please, I just want ... ugh, yes. Right there. Please, oh please. Fuck me. Fuck me. Fuck me." I can't stop chanting the words over and over again, until my throat feels raw.

I didn't realize what those words would do to him or me. I didn't realize how much he was actually holding back. But as the last sound of my voice fades into the room, Isaac cups my hips and pulls back, nearly ripping his cock from within me before slamming completely forward—filling me up.

Light flashes behind my eyes at the sheer force of it. It stings. It fucking *burns*. He doesn't stop there, though. Isaac rails me, fucking into me with harsh movements. His cock cuts me deep, slicing through my pussy and into places I've never felt before. He keeps me exactly where I am with intention. Locking his hands on my waist, keeping me from slipping away as he thrusts back and forth. The muscles in his back bunch beneath the hard grip of my palms as I hold on for dear life and he drives me back up the same mountain I'd just come down from.

My nails sink into his skin, scoring across his shoulder blades as he fucks into me, jerking my whole body with the forcefulness of his thrusts. Every time he slides into my pussy, I feel him hit something deep inside. A whimper escapes my throat.

"You're creaming on my cock, Sunshine," Isaac grits out. "So fucking tight and wet. It's like you were made for me to fuck you."

I've never had a guy talk to me like this. It's almost as if Isaac's words are magic—a spell he's weaving over me and the damn wand is his dick. I cry out as he fucks me harder, slamming into me as if he loves hearing the sound. A split second later, he proves me right.

"Scream," he growls. "Come on, Rori. I want to hear what I do to you. I want to know you feel every bit as fucking insane as I do."

I shake my head back and forth. "You're ripping me apart," I snap, panting. "I can't—it's too much."

"You can," he urges, never stopping. "You're a big girl,

aren't you? You wanted this. You wanted me to lose my control. You wanted my cock in your cunt. Well, you got it. I told you that you were going to take every last inch."

I clench my teeth and squeeze my eyes shut as the next thrust sends me even higher up the bed. I swear to God he's bruising my insides, but sex has never felt so good before. He's deeper inside of my body than I ever even knew was possible, and his words, whether he realizes it or not, only serve to drive me higher.

"Isaac..." His name pours from my lips. A plea. A curse.

"That's right, goddess," he says, his words sliding over my ears with heat. "Call my name. Scream it. You're taking me so good. Taking me to the fucking edge. You're going to burn me."

He's not the only one on fire. If I'm burning him, then he's burning me right back. We're flying directly into the sun. No stopping. No fear. The two of us are setting each other on fire and soaring through the flames like we're fleeing something dark and dangerous. The whole while I'm chasing this new release, one much bigger than before.

It isn't long before I'm gasping through the fluttering of my second orgasm. "Isaac," I cry out. "I'm gonna ... oh fuck ... I'm gonna fucking come. Please don't stop. Don't stop. Don't stop. Don't stop."

I can't seem to help it. I mutter the words on repeat like a broken record, terrified that he'll start to slow any second and I'll lose this momentum. Whatever is on the crest of this orgasm I know is going to destroy me, and I'm ready and willing to go. I want it. Whatever it is, as long as it lets me feel this way for just a little bit longer, I'll take it.

"Shhhhh." Isaac cups the back of my head, never slowing his movements, keeping pace with each passing stroke. "I've got you," he promises. "Almost..." He cuts himself off and pulls his head back, forcing our faces right up against each other.

His mouth opens and slams down on mine, his tongue pushing past my lips without reserve. He doesn't ask. He takes. He violates. I swear to God I'm going to bite down on his tongue when I come, though. It's right there—I can feel it cresting, just out of reach.

Struggling away from him, I plant my hands on his shoulders and arch up. "Look at me." His command is more of a plea than an actual order, and it makes me follow it.

My eyes clash with his, tears leaking out of the corners of mine as he drives me higher and higher. "I want to see you come on my cock, Aurora," he says, breathless, as his hips continue to piston into me. "Don't you fucking close your eyes, or I swear you'll regret it."

I want to ask him how. I want to know what his threat could mean, but I don't have a choice anymore. My eyes widen as the tidal wave of release crashes over me and I tighten, my pussy clamping down on him as my orgasm reaches its height. He reaches up, holding my head and forcing me to stare back at him as it slams into me.

It's a different level of intimacy, letting someone else watch you come apart. I struggle to keep my gaze locked on his even as my insides clamp down around his cock. His upper lip pulls back and I can practically hear him grinding his teeth.

My nails sink harder into the flesh covering the muscles of his back. I can feel wetness—blood—but I can't release him. My body won't let me. I've never had an orgasm feel so painful and yet so fucking good. I'm left gasping for breath once more and it isn't until I finally regain control of my limbs and manage to loosen my hold that Isaac finally eases back, giving me enough room to breathe.

The gentleness only lasts for a split second. I stare up at him as hands land against me and push. Isaac practically shoves me back into the mattress and my eyes widen as he pulls out of me completely, ripping the condom off as he palms his cock and strokes it above my mound. I bite down on my lower lip as I watch his hand fly over his shaft in hard, violent movements. A part of me wonders if it hurts, but then again—with the pain that he gave me, maybe that's what we're both into.

"Spread your legs open," he growls. "Hold them."

Blinking, confused, I do as he commands. My thighs tremble as I pull them apart and hold myself open as he squeezes his cock, the veins on both it and his throat standing out with each passing second. It doesn't take long for him to erupt.

Cum shoots out and hits my lower belly, startling me with how hot it is. Isaac doesn't stop there, though. He directs his cock down further as another stream of it lashes out and hits my pussy, soaking through the wetness so that I can feel it before he then aims it upward. The next volley arches up and lands on my breasts. All over, he coats me in his release. Groaning as he paints me in his cum, Isaac marks me, emptying himself all over my pussy, stomach, and tits until his arms are trembling and I feel the sticky evidence seeping into my flesh.

Only then does he seem to regain his senses. Panting and flushed, Isaac looks down at me and smiles—a true, pure smile. Even coated in sweat with loose, exhausted limbs, I feel the fluttering of more arousal slip through me.

Fuck no. How? After two back-to-back orgasms? How can he do that?

Isaac leans down, brushing my damp hair back as he presses a close-mouthed kiss to my stunned lips. "You look so fucking pretty covered in my cum, Sunshine." The words he whispers against my mouth shouldn't make me hot, but they do.

When he pulls back, his eyes open and lock with mine. "There's no going back now," he tells me.

My lips part, but no words come out.

"Say it," he orders. "Tell me that there's no going back."

"Th-there's no going back," I answer, numbly. I know he's right, but, this ... this sex can't really fix everything. He has to know that.

He nods. "Who do you belong to?" he demands. I press my lips together and when I don't immediately answer, his hands tighten on my body. "Aurora." My name is hard on his tongue. "Who do you belong to?"

I shake my head. "*Isaac, I—*"

"That's right," he cuts me off without letting me finish. His blue eyes burst to life. "Me," he whispers. "You're mine, Sunshine."

My stomach hollows out and the reality of what I've just done hits me sharply. Just like that, I know there really is no going back. He and I are past the point of no return. This one decision has locked us together. Suddenly, a true fear springs to life in my mind.

What does this mean?

Isaac and I are like day and night. One night of hard-core fucking doesn't make a relationship. His possessiveness isn't reality. His demanding behavior, and his desire to protect—none of it cures the fact that there are still too many secrets between us. How do I make him understand that, though? How do I proceed?

We may have given in to the attraction we both couldn't stop, but there's so much more at stake. So much more we have to worry about. I reach up and my fingers brush his. I make a split-second decision. One I doubt he'll like, but it's one I have to make. Whatever we are— whatever this is between us—we'll have to discuss it later. What's important is everything else. His father. My mother. The danger he spoke of. The war that's brewing.

"What now?" I ask.

There's no running from my meaning. No hiding it. His jaw clenches and unclenches. His lashes flutter and I can practically see the thoughts spinning through his mind. "We'll figure it out," he promises me. "Whatever happens, though, I swear you'll be safe."

"It's not just me I'm worried about," I tell him. "What about my friends? Will he use them? Or what about my mother? What happens to her after he's done?

His grimaces and I have my answer. "If he thinks they'll work in his favor, then yes," Isaac answers regardless.

"I won't have my friends involved," I tell him. "I can't let that happen." It's too late for my mother, but for them, I can still do something.

"Do you trust me?" Isaac asks.

I blink. "What?"

"Do you trust me?" he repeats.

I stare up at him, my eyes glancing across his face, trying to seek out a motive for this question, but all I see is a cool determination. I want to say yes, but even the purest of relationships have fallen before, and our relationship is anything but pure. I bite down hard on my lower lip, forgetting that I've already cut it. More blood fills my mouth.

Isaac reaches up and presses down on it. "Don't," he whispers. "Don't think about it. Just let me handle it. I won't hurt you anymore, I promise."

I shake my head. "I'm sorry," I reply. "I can't."

He frowns down at me before releasing me and sinking back on his heels. "You can't what?"

I swallow and lean up, keeping our gazes connected. "It's not that I can't trust you," I tell him. "But it's too soon. It's too early. Whatever you have going on, whatever you think you can do against your father ... the only way we can move forward now is if you involve me." Even if we're not forever, the least we can be is allies.

"No." His tone is hard, his face angry, but I push forward.

"It's the only way," I argue.

"No, it's not," he argues. "You don't want to get involved with him. It's too dangerous."

I sigh. "I'm already involved," I remind him.

He stiffens, but he knows it's true. Blue eyes look down and then back to me. He considers me for a moment. "You don't have to be," he says, shocking me.

"What?" I gape at him. "What the hell is that supposed to mean?"

"You can escape his path," Isaac tells me. I can see the thoughts working through his mind in the expressions that play out over his features—worry, consideration, realization, acceptance. I don't know what he's thinking, but I have the sneaking suspicion that I won't like it. "Follow your brother," he tells me. "Go to Eastpoint."

My hand snaps out before I even realize what I'm doing and I cup it around his throat, holding him as I shove my face close. My words, when they come, are low and angry. "Fuck. That," I spit back at him. "You are not sending me away like someone in need of protection."

"You *are* in need of protection," he replies coolly. He doesn't even flinch or make any sort of reaction to my hand as it clamps down harder.

"I'm. Not. Leaving." I say the words with precision.

He shakes his head. "You're not putting yourself in danger either."

We're at a stalemate, him and I. Neither one of us is willing to budge. A rock and a hard place. I'm not even sure which of us is which. "Be careful, Isaac," I warn him. "Be very fucking careful. Just because we fucked doesn't mean you get to tell me what to do."

He chuckles, his full, masculine lips spreading into a wicked grin. "You admitted you're mine, Sunshine," he says, leaning into my grasp as if it doesn't bother him at all. I didn't, not really. He just heard what he wanted to hear, and I ... let him. It doesn't mean I'm truly his. Even as I think that, though, guilt pricks at me.

"That more than anything fucking means you should do exactly what I tell you to do, but I get it," Isaac continues. I blink. "You're not used to being out of control. It'll take time for you to realize that you can hand it all over to me." His hands clamp down on my hips and he lifts me, depositing me back on his lap—despite all the sticky, sweaty aftermath still all over the both of us. His lips descend and take mine.

It's powerful, this kiss. It's commanding. It's mind-numbing. "But fine," he whispers when he pulls back. "You win ... for now."

My hand falls away from his throat and he takes my mouth again, but in the back of my mind—despite the slack he's given me now—I know it can't last.

How long will I keep winning? Or is this even a true win?

Whatever the case, something tells me that the next part of our journey is going to be more perilous. If I want to be ready, I need to do more than demand inclusion. I need to be able to protect myself and my friends without Isaac's help. I won't stand next to him as a damsel in distress. I will stand as a fucking goddess, and should I fall, Isaac Icari will fall with me.

24

RORI

Isaac looks like a fallen angel when he's sleeping. The bronze gold of his hair shines in the dim lighting as dawn crests through the windows and I pause in my efforts, my clothes clutched in my hands, as I take a moment to just look at him. My chest tightens.

This was a fucking mistake. An error in my judgment. I wish I could blame it on the alcohol, but I know deep down in my soul that wasn't it at all. It was all my choice. *He* was my choice. A dangerous one.

The air conditioning kicks on above my head, blowing a blast of cold air over my shoulders and shocking me out of the moment of reverie I'm locked in. I shake my head and turn away from the image the man on the bed presents. I take what little clothes managed to end up in the bedroom with us and head out into the hallway, collecting my things as I go. I pull it all back on, frowning as my dress catches at the back.

Did he break it? The zipper gapes open and I growl in irritation, snagging what looks like a slim gray hoodie off the back of the couch in the living room and tugging it on to hide the fact.

I slap the button for the elevator, praying that I can make it out of here before he wakes up. Thankfully, it arrives without any sound from the bedroom. I pull out my cell phone and curse when I see the barrage of text messages from Selene, asking where I am and why I didn't come home.

Quickly ordering a car as I head down to the lobby, I switch back to my messages and send a text, letting her know that I'm okay and on my way home now. Thankfully, Selene is less prone to freakouts than Hel. Once she sees my text, she'll be okay. It's early enough that there aren't many people in the lobby as I hurry from the elevators to the outside. When I reach the rounded driveway, a slender black town car is pulling up.

I don't wait for the driver to get out before I'm yanking the back door open and sliding inside. "Hazelwood Campus," I bark. "Dorm side."

The man in the front is quiet as he nods his acquiescence, and the car pulls out of the hotel parking lot. My anxiety is making me act up. I'm far more irritable than I should be—odd considering that I just had possibly some of the best sex of my life last night. Unlike my mother and peers, I never speak to people like that.

The guilt eats away at me with every mile that passes under the wheels of the vehicle. By the time the driver pulls up in front of my dorm, I'm already pulling up my phone and adding a generous tip on my card by way of apology.

Neither one of us says a word as I climb out of the back and head for the front doors. My heart hammers as the quiet of the hallways echoes in my ears. I press my key into the lock of the front door, turn it until I hear the lock click, and then withdraw it before easing the door inward. I step into the open kitchen of my dorm's apartment, pausing in the doorway as a familiar figure stands up from the couch.

Hel crosses her arms over her chest and tilts her head to the side as she takes in my haphazard appearance, from the club heels I wore last night to the new—and definitely borrowed—hoodie I've got on over my dress. I'd almost rather it were Selene. Selene would be easier to fool. I glance at the floor as the door closes quietly behind me and snicks shut.

"What happened?" she finally asks.

I blow out a breath and scrub a hand down my face as I move further into the kitchen, tossing my keys onto the counter. She moves to the side as I kick off my heels and then sink onto the couch of our combined living space.

"I made a mistake," I say honestly.

"You fucked him." It's not a question, but a damn good guess. One I can't hide from.

"Yeah..."

Hel is quiet for a moment and I sink my face into my hands, bowing forward over my knees as the gravity of my actions finally slams into me. It isn't until I feel the couch cushions sink beside me that I realize she's taken a seat next to me. Warmth hovers over my spine for a split second before I feel her press a palm to my back.

"What are you going to do now?" she asks.

After everything Isaac told me? I'm not sure. There's so much I don't know still. What I do know, however, is that I have to warn Marcus. I'd like to tell my mother, but she wouldn't believe me. Once she's in a man's clutches, she likes to remain there until she comes to her senses on her own. Nothing I can say will make her see the truth until she's ready. Isaac thought that I could get her to leave his father, but that's not true. My mother never listens to me. The only one who might be able to break through to her is Marcus.

"I don't know, Hel..." I blow out a long breath. "But things can't go on the way they have been."

"Are you two..." I lift up when her voice wavers, hesitating. I meet her curious gaze. "Together?" she finishes.

Are we? I open my mouth except no words come. There's no answer. Instead, I'm left with only more questions. "How would that even work?" I ask.

She shrugs. "I don't know, Rori," she says. "What does he think?"

"I..." I lean back and she withdraws her hand as my spine hits the back cushion with a thump. "I didn't stick around to ask."

"You snuck out?"

I gesture down at my appearance and give her a half-hearted smile. "Does this not look like the outfit of the walk of shame?" I answer before groaning. "I fucked this all up so bad. I should've never gone with him last night."

"Selene came home and said that you disappeared with him," Hel states. "I was worried."

"I'm glad she made it home okay," I say.

Hel sighs. "Does this at least mean that he's going to stop torturing you?" she asks.

"Maybe?" Hell, I don't fucking know what's going on in Isaac Icari's head. Having his dick inside me doesn't necessarily mean that suddenly he's become an open book. What terrifies me, though, are his words from last night. The claiming.

You're mine, Sunshine. His words echo through my skull like the ringing of a bell announcing the plague has arrived. The plague of the Icari family. His father. Him.

"He wants me to leave," I admit. "He wants me to go to Eastpoint with Marcus."

Hel frowns and leans forward to take a good long look at my face. My expression, whatever it is, must only confuse her even more as her brows draw down lower and lower over her big eyes. "What does that mean?" she demands.

I lift my shoulders and let them drop back down. "I have no clue," I lie. "But I'm not doing it. There's no way I'm going to tuck my tail and run away now."

She eyes me for a beat. "There's more you're not telling me, isn't there?"

Damn it. I press my lips together, but she's not an idiot. My lack of answer tells her everything she needs to know.

"You need to be careful, Rori," she warns me, pushing up from the couch. "You need to be incredibly careful with him. Whatever is going on between the two of you, I doubt it's over."

She's right. It's not over. Not by a long shot. I didn't realize it until after the fact, but Isaac is obsessive. The way he looked at me when he laid down his claim. Even now, I can recall the heat and intensity of his gaze. He meant it. Every. Fucking. Word.

As Hel shakes her head at me and moves back towards the hallway, I let my head drop down to rest against the back of the couch and curse to myself. I have a feeling that once Isaac latches onto something, it'll take an act of God to make him let go.

Right now, I'm his newest focus and the only god around is the God of Hazelwood, himself.

Isaac Icari.

My Icarus.

25

ISAAC

She's running. I smirk as I watch her in her bedroom at the Rozenfeld Dorms, poring over textbooks and scribbling something into a notebook. While, initially, I'd been more than a little irritated and disappointed waking up without her in my arms—I can't help but feel like that's exactly how it was meant to be. Maybe if I'd woken up with her curled against my chest, I might have felt some form of regret. Instead, I'd been left without even the opportunity. She'd stolen it from me and left me wanting more. Craving more. Needing it like I need my next breath.

Aurora is running from me, but it only makes me want to chase her that much more. I caught her once. Does she really think I won't catch her again? Does she think that next time I won't chain her up to keep her by my side?

The desire to go to her eats away at me as I watch her in what she thinks is her private space. Golden strands fall over the corner of her shoulder as she leans forward and writes something on the top page of her notebook before turning her gaze back to another textbook. The cameras, though originally placed in her space for more cruel purposes, have become my salvation. They're the only reason why I haven't tracked her little ass down and dragged her back.

Instead, I'm letting her think she can run. I'm giving her space—or at least the illusion of space. All the while, I'm observing her, soaking in her sunlight as she walks around her room in tiny shorts and tank tops, thinking she's safe—thinking that she got away from me, even if only temporarily.

A sharp knocking rap hits the door of the small library study room. I look up from my phone as Shep's familiar face appears in the doorway. He pushes his way inside, dropping his bag next to the chair at my side before slapping the door closed once more. Dark hair is pulled away from his face and tied up with a small leather band, revealing an unusually unshaven jaw.

"Bad day?" I inquire absently as he grunts his way through, tearing open his backpack and withdrawing his laptop.

He shoots me a dark look. "It'd be a little better if someone warned me that he was going to get his dick wet with his stepsister."

I shrug and lean back against my seat. "Why's that gotta put your panties in a wad?"

Shep's laptop lands on the table and he snaps it open, glaring my way. "Because I had to be the one to go back through and edit the video feed your father has on you," he growls. "The least you could do was give me some advance warning—I could've just run a fake feed instead of having to go back through it. Spending the weekend reworking that shit wasn't exactly on the list of dreams come true."

"You don't seem to mind sharing your partners," I say absently. "What's the problem with playing voyeur every once in a while?"

Shep scrubs a hand down his face and for a brief moment, guilt nips at me. He does look tired—dark circles under his eyes, unshaven face, and all. I sigh. "I'll be more mindful in the future," I tell him. "I'm sorry."

He crosses his arms over his chest and leans back. "Does she know she was on camera?" he inquires.

I shake my head. "She didn't ask," I reply. Well, that's not entirely true. I told her the place wasn't bugged. That was true. The video doesn't have audio.

"Is this another way to get to her?" Shep asks. "Are you planning on spreading a sex tape of her after what she did to you?"

A month ago, the thought would've been at the forefront of my mind. In fact, even now, I have to admit that it's not a bad idea. Sex tapes are different for men and women. It'd definitely have her contemplating a move. Now, though ... the thought of someone seeing Aurora Summers the way I'd seen her—wild, untamed, open and so fucking sexy it drove me half out of my mind—makes me want to put my fist through a wall.

My eyes go to my friend. The only reason I'm not contemplating that with him is because this is my own fault. I hadn't stopped to consider every ramification.

"No." There will be no sex tape. "Delete it. Get rid of the evidence."

Shep arches a brow, but releases his arms and bends over his laptop as he strokes the keyboard. Seconds later, he sits back and nods my way. "Done."

My muscles finally release and I relax back into the chair once more. "Thanks, man."

He shakes his head. "What are you thinking?" he asks. "Seriously. What is it about her? She's just a girl. Fuck, she's not even a girl—she's a liability. Have you forgotten what you're trying to do here?"

"I haven't forgotten anything," I say, dropping my tone. "I met with Agent Brown a few weeks ago and he says they need more. They want hard evidence of Damian Icari's less than legal dealings."

"Fuck." Shep's curse mimics my own internal thoughts. The harder the evidence, the riskier the feat. And now ... my eyes go back to my phone screen and the girl there. Now, there's more at stake. "What fucking use are the Feds if they can't use what you've already given them?" Though it comes out as a question, I know it's not.

I close out the camera app and shove my phone into my pocket. "They want to catch him red-handed to make sure there's no way their worm can wiggle off its hook." It's smart on their part but makes my job a hell of a lot more dangerous.

"So, what's the plan then?" Shep asks, leaning forward, his hands on his knees.

I contemplate the question, but I already know there are few choices I'm left with if the FBI isn't able to do anything more. Unfortunately, I don't like any of my options. I hold up a finger.

"Option A," I start, "is to get close to Emilia Summers. She wants a family and now that she's married Damien Icari, she considers herself my mother."

"Damien will be suspicious," Shep points out.

"I'm aware." It's exactly why I don't like option A.

"He'd rather you get close to the girl," Shep says. "It's why he wanted you to watch over her to begin with."

I nod my agreement. "He wants to use Aurora to control her mother, but from what I've seen they don't necessarily have that close of a relationship."

Shep shakes his head. "That doesn't really mean shit," he argues. "Mothers are different and considering how much Emilia seems to want a perfect family—I have no doubt that, regardless of the state of their relationship, Aurora would still make a good pawn."

I clench my teeth at that comment but don't say anything. I don't have the right to disagree. Up until a few nights ago, I would've said the same damn thing. Hell, if I remove myself from my own obsession for two seconds, I know that's exactly what Aurora is in all of this—a pretty little pawn. The fact that I know it's true doesn't stop the vein in my forehead from pulsing.

Shep arches a brow my way. "You good, bro?"

I slowly release a breath, whistling sharply as I press my spine against the back of the pathetically padded library chair I'm in. "No," I say honestly. "Things have gotten more complicated."

"What other options are there?" he prompts.

I shoot him a dark look. "Send myself into the mouth of the beast," I say with a sigh, "and let him swallow me whole."

He flinches back and scrubs a hand down his jaw, scratching at the stubble there. "That's not a good idea."

"No fucking shit, Sherlock." A groan locks in my throat and I shove the soles of my shoes against the floor, tipping the chair onto its back two legs. "I need to be closer to his business to find the evidence they're fucking asking for."

"You know that the second you step into Damien's world ... there is no coming back."

I close my eyes. Of course, I fucking know that. If anyone is aware of the world Damien Icari presides over, it's his heir. My father is swallowed by the darkness he reigns over. He's soaked in the blood of his enemies. When I was younger, he wasn't the one to hide it. My mother was. And then, when she was gone, the nannies were. At the end of the day, they all knew what he was capable of. Yet, they remained.

As his son, I can't live my life with one foot in the darkness and one in the light. I have to make a choice. It was bound to happen someday. I just never expected it to come this soon. Silence stretches out between Shep and me for long moments. He doesn't say anything, content to let me roll through my own thoughts until I figure something out. I appreciate that about him. His ability to just let me be when I need him to.

"He's planning a party," I finally say. "To celebrate his new bride."

"Do you think you can find something there?" Shep asks.

I let the chair drop down on all fours and uncross my arms. "There's no telling," I say with a sigh. "But it'll be as good a time as any. If I can find some documents or contracts—"

"Those won't be enough," Shep says, cutting me off. "But you can probably look for information during the party while he's distracted. If you can tip off the Feds to a place where they can catch him red-handed, then you're in the clear. You don't necessarily need to be the one to catch him."

He's right, but he's also wrong. "The only way to

catch him and ensure my own safety is to get involved," I say. "I need to be caught *with* him."

Realization hits Shep and he leans back. "To make sure he can't suspect you," he guesses.

I nod. *Fucking bingo.* Never did like that damn game. I'd prefer a good hand of poker any day.

"Then what about the girl? Are you just going to leave her alone then? What was last weekend about then? You fucked her ... now what?"

"I want more." The confession spills out of me before I can stop it, and I can tell by Shep's silence that it shocks him. I shake my head and bend down, ripping my bag up from the floor as I stand and throw it over my shoulder. "She's different," I say.

"She's in danger," Shep points out.

Another true statement and the nagging crux of my issue with her. I want her. I have to have her. But will having her kill her? That's the question. I warned her, but she refuses to leave. She refuses to abide by my commands and as much as it irritates me, it also enlivens me. It sparks something deep inside of me that I didn't know I had. Possessiveness.

As if he sees that very fact in my expression, Shep shakes his head and turns away from me as he refocuses on his laptop. "You're insane," he says. "But do whatever the hell you want—I know nothing I say can convince you anyways."

I snort. "Thanks, man. I appreciate the support."

I head for the door and pop it open, stopping as he calls out once more. "Just one thing"—Shep turns in his seat—"make sure she's trustworthy. Test her if you have to, but we can't have her fucking shit up when you're this close to nailing the bastard to the FBI's wall of most wanted."

A smirk tips my lips up. "Test her?" A brilliant idea. I mean, in a lot of ways, Aurora has already cleared test after test. I know she's got the steely courage needed to stick around. She hasn't been run off by me yet. I know she's got loyalty in her blood. That much is clear by her friendships and her relationship with her brother.

"Make sure she can handle the pain of being with you before you throw her in the fire," Shep continues. "Because I can't help but feel like I'll be picking up your pieces if she cracks under the pressure. You can't be with a weak-hearted girl."

Aurora is anything but weak-hearted, but I also can't say that the idea of pressing her more—of seeing what shape she molds into—doesn't appeal to me. I lick my lips as an idea pops into my head.

"Are you and Paris still going to the shop this weekend?" I ask.

Shep arches a brow. "You want to bring her?"

I nod. "Yeah."

"Shit, man. She's not the kind of girl you bring there. Plus, Paris is in a fucking mood—you know how he gets. Any time he throws those little parties, it's because he had a fight with his family. Besides, you never come."

"I've come before," I argue.

"Yeah, but you don't get pierced," he reminds me. "You just come by for some of the weed and drinks."

I shrug. "She should be introduced to our world sooner or later."

Shep groans. "Nah, she might be a socialite princess, but she ain't like us."

"She will be." Because I have no intention of letting her go.

He blinks. "Are you..." His brows draw down low over his eyes as he drifts off, staring at me with an expression full of disbelief. "You're not actually thinking about keeping her, are you?"

I roll my shoulders back. "Maybe I am." Maybe that's the only choice I've got left. "I can't see this obsession going away any time soon."

"Then make it," he snaps. "She's a liability. Fuck, man, she's your *stepsister*."

"I don't need to be reminded," I grit out. "But that's not forever. Her mother and my father won't last. They will divorce—the second he has what he wants from Emilia Summers, she'll be gone." Hopefully, it'll be by way of papers and prenup rather than death.

Shep continues to stare at me, his lips parted in shock. "No." He shakes his head. "No. *Fuck no.* You can't be serious."

I am serious, though. As serious as a heart attack. There's no explanation for why I feel the way that I do. Only that the thought of letting Aurora get away makes my chest ache something fierce. There are so many reasons not to get involved with her. My father and the precarious position I'm in between him and the Feds is only the tip of the iceberg, but *fuck*. Can't I just have something for me? One piece of sunlight in this otherwise shitty fucking world?

"You're right," I say. Shep glares at me, knowing I'm not about to switch shit up and tell him I'll stay away from her. That's not gonna happen. Not now. Not after everything. "I need to know if she can handle our world." If she can handle me.

"First of all"—he holds up a finger—"that is *not* what I said. Secondly"—his fingers separate as a second one joins the first. "That's different and you know it."

"I'll be the one to decide that."

Shep throws his hands up and swivels back to his laptop. "Fine, do whatever you want. Yeah, we're going to the shop on Friday. Paris will have his usual posse of girls."

I lean against the doorframe, liking this idea more and more. "And you?"

He shoots me a dark glare over his shoulder. "Don't fucking ask if you already know the answer," he growls my way.

I back up out of the doorway, lifting my palms in surrender. "Cool your jets, Shep," I tease. "Just making sure you're both there when I bring my girl."

"You're fucking crazy, asshole," he replies without heat.

He's probably right. I *am* crazy. But that was Aurora's mistake. She fucked me even knowing that I could break her apart. She kissed me first. She leashed me to her side and now, I want to leave my own mark on her. Now, there's no getting away.

26
RORI

The weekend passes and Monday comes and goes, lulling me into a false sense of security when I don't hear anything from Isaac Icari. Maybe he hadn't really meant his words. Maybe they'd just been spoken in the heat of the moment, on the cusp of orgasm. Guys say stupid shit when they're horny like that. It wasn't like he'd professed his love for me—I honestly don't know what I would have done if he had—but it had felt a little deeper than two people smashing uglies. Especially when he'd demanded me to tell him who I belonged to.

I belong to myself. Not him.

Because of his recent absences, it's almost a shock to see Isaac sitting pretty at the top of the classroom when I walk into my first class of the day. I stop in the doorway, eyes wide, and Selene slams into my back with an *oomph* and muttered curse.

"Sorry," I say as I step out of the way.

She eyes me as she steps into the classroom, rubbing her nose. Once inside, though, her eyes turn to the general direction of my gaze and then flick back to me. "You never told me what happened between the two of you over the weekend," she says as I shake myself and head towards the front row, as far from him as I can get.

I slide all the way down the row until there's no seat to my left and only one open on my right—the one Selene takes for herself. "It's nothing," I answer her quietly.

She arches a brow but surprisingly doesn't press the issue. I set my bag down and pull out a notebook, slapping it on the table in front of me. A moment later, I realize my mistake. It doesn't matter to Isaac if there's not a seat on my left; as long as there's an opening, he'll take it.

"Morning, Sunshine." The vibrato of Isaac's voice slides across my nerves with the same smoothness as molasses, making every muscle beneath my flesh jump and shiver. A chair scrapes across the floor and all talking in the room ceases as Isaac pulls it right up to the end of the table I'm sitting at in the *front fucking row* and takes a seat. "I know we didn't spend much time together this weekend, but what's with the no call?"

He wouldn't. I reject it. The very idea that Isaac Icari would play this card is preposterous. Then I realize something—I have exactly no fucking idea how he plays his cards. I hardly know him.

Selene's soft perfume wafts my way as she leans over the table, openly watching the two of us. Once again, I see I've been played for a fool. It was odd that she hadn't pressed me for more information about what had gone down between Isaac and me over the weekend. It was because she'd been expecting something like this. Now, she's got the first seat at my side to watch this little circus act go down.

"Go sit somewhere else, Isaac," I hiss between clenched teeth.

When he reaches for my hand, the grip on the pen I just pulled from my bag tightens. Carefully—as if he's half expecting me to stab him with the pointed end—he pulls it from my grasp. Smart of him, really, because stabbing him is exactly what I'm contemplating at this moment.

Of all the pig-headed, dumbass things for him to pull, this has got to be the worst.

He lifts my now pen-free hand to his lips and presses a kiss to my knuckles, grinning as he does so. "Now, why would I want to be away from you, Sunshine?"

Because if he doesn't get away from me, right now, I'm going to kill him. I don't say that though. I don't have an opportunity because the classroom door opens and the professor walks in as two more students scramble in after him, their notebooks falling out of their bags as they hurry to the only available open seats so as not to be counted late.

Even the professor, too, pauses at Isaac's placement—seated at the edge of the front row with his hand holding onto mine. He leans back and props his ankle up on his knee as he smirks at the professor—as if daring him to say something. Of course, the studious man doesn't. He knows as well as anybody that Isaac Icari is the law on campus. It's easier to let the man get his way rather than tell him he's being inappropriate. No one will reproach him. No one is going to tell him he's being absolutely ridiculous.

No one except me of course.

As the professor launches into his lecture, I pry my fingers out of Isaac's and shove his arm off the side of the table. "What the hell do you think you're doing?" My words, although angry, are low and cutting.

"You left me," he replies easily, keeping his gaze trained forward like he's some model student. He's well aware that everyone in the vicinity can hear his words. *Prick.* "I'm simply reminding you that after that night together, there's no getting away." He leans back even more, popping the two front legs of his chair off the floor as he arches back. "It's you and me now, Sunshine. I'm just making sure the rest of the school knows it."

Conniving, manipulative son of a—"This is not the place," I grit out as calmly as I can muster.

Despite my words, I know that he's managed to accomplish his goal. I have no doubt that the soft click-tapping of nails on phone screens whispering through the room are signs that by the end of this period, the whole of Hazelwood University will know that Isaac Icari and Aurora Summers were seen all over each other—or rather *he* was seen all over *me*. His words have already made their mark and there is no getting away.

Isaac doesn't reply to my comment, so I'm forced to lean closer and drop my tone. "Don't you think you're leaving your friends behind?" It's practically a plea for him to go back to his original row, but Isaac doesn't take it.

He catches my hand once more on the tabletop and even when I try to rip it away, he pulls it against him. Pressing another soft, close-mouthed kiss to my knuckles. My heart pounds against my ribcage, electricity racing through my bloodstream. I swallow roughly.

"There's only one way to get me to leave you alone right now, Sunshine."

"What is it?" I know I shouldn't ask. Whatever he wants, it's likely too late, anyway.

He smiles against the back of my hand. The scrape and feel of his lips against my skin make me shiver. It was one fucking night—one time. Yet, somehow, the last two days have done nothing to quell the memories of Isaac all over me. Of the way his hands had driven me to the brink or of his cock sliding between my legs as he'd stolen the oxygen from my lungs. He's doing it right now and all he's touching is my hand.

Fuck, I'm lost. So fucking lost.

"Meet me somewhere this weekend," he says, "and I'll go back to my seat."

I blanch. "Where?" I demand.

He arches a brow. "You'll find out if you say yes."

I shouldn't. It's such a bad idea. Saying yes to Isaac Icari is like making a deal with the devil. An increasingly hot and dangerous devil. I suck back a breath and shake my head. "Isaac—"

My words evaporate as he parts his lips and sinks his teeth into my knuckle. Sharp sparks shoot up my arm, slipping beneath my skin and stabbing at my nerve endings. With my free hand, I grip the edge of the table. Isaac's teeth scrape lightly over my flesh before a glitter of something wicked enters his eyes, and he bites down. Hard.

I gasp out my answer. "*Fine.*" His teeth release me and he offers a brilliant smile. I blink at the way it makes him look so much younger than he is. It's almost ... innocent. And I know better than most that he's anything but.

"Good girl," he whispers, pressing a kiss to the bite mark he left before he sets my hand carefully back on the table.

I'm feeling floaty—like I was a puppet all along and someone has just cut my strings. I'm so lost in the vibe of it that I barely recognize Isaac reaching down and pulling out my cell from my pocket. Instead of stopping him, I just stare as he grins my way before unlocking the screen. Of course, he knows the code. Asshole probably looked over my shoulder at some point. He fiddles with it for a few seconds before setting it back on the table next to my bite-marked hand.

Finally, his chair slides back—making the professor pause once at the sound before he shakes his head and continues with his lecture. Isaac leans over and presses a kiss to the top of my head with a grin before he sidles away. I can't help it. I turn and watch him go as he strides up to the back row where he'd originally been seated.

It could be seconds, it could be minutes, hell, it could be fucking hours later—I don't know—when Selene leans over my side and prods my arm. "What the hell was that about?" she demands.

My voice, when I answer, is as breathless as I feel. "I wish I knew."

27
RORI

He has my number. I should've known that's what he was doing when he grabbed my phone in class. As I stare down at the phone screen later that night, I rub my thumb over the bite mark left on my knuckles. It still stings, but at the same time, it does funny things to my insides.

Isaac: 221 Brendon St. Friday night. 8 pm

It's a bad idea. I shouldn't go. My fingers hover over the screen of my cell. Instead of replying, however, I switch over to my maps app and type in the address, curious. After a moment, my screen reflects a boring-looking shop front. Blacked-out windows with a logo that has two needles crossing over one another within a bejeweled circle and the name of the store. *Needle Point Piercings.* A piercing shop? What the hell does he want me to do at a piercing shop?

The door to the apartment opens and Hel strides inside, looking like a woman on a mission. I drop the phone onto the coffee table and reach for my drink. The second she sees me, though, her long afro of dark corkscrew curls bounces as she slams to a stop. We look at each other for a long moment.

"What happened today?" she finally demands.

I blow out a breath and set my drink back down. "Isaac cornered me in class," I say.

She continues into the room until she's standing in front of me and drops her bag next to the couch. She carefully pushes the coffee table back, moves my drink to the side, and plops down right in front of me. "Tell me."

I grimace. "I don't know what to tell you," I admit. "He was upset that I left and he wanted me to promise to meet him somewhere this weekend."

"Where?"

I sigh and point to my phone on the table. "A piercing shop." She frowns and picks up my phone. She doesn't have to ask for my password. She already knows it. She swipes the screen open and stares at the location I just pulled up.

"That's suspicious," she concludes as she clicks across the screen—likely pulling up the website or the reviews or something else to gain more information. I don't know how much it'll help. Isaac is probably planning something, but what I don't know.

"So far, nothing else has happened," I say.

"They're rumors," Hel replies.

"Yeah," I agree, "but I doubt he started them himself. They're all probably circulating around the fact that he wouldn't leave me alone in class this morning. There are no more videos or taunting."

"That's not to say it'll last, though," she points out, flicking her dark brown eyes up at me briefly before she goes back to the cell phone screen. Her lashes lower as she scans the screen, swiping up with her finger. "Have you talked to Marcus?"

A beat of silence passes and when I don't answer, her eyes find my face again. "Rori ... tell me you told your brother about this."

"He didn't answer his phone," I hedge.

"Oh my god." My phone slams down on the table, the sharp clack making me jump in my seat. "I thought you were going to warn him—tell him about whatever went down between you and Isaac. What the hell happened to you?"

I stand abruptly and reach for my phone, grabbing it and shoving it into my back pocket as I move away from her. "*Nothing* happened," I reply. "I'm still going to tell him, but he hasn't answered any of my phone calls." Not that I'd tried calling all that much.

"Then *text* him!" Hel's voice grows closer as she follows me into my room. "Rori, you can't go meet him without telling your brother."

I stop and whirl around to face her as I reach the doorway of my bedroom. Hel jerks back as she nearly collides with my front. "Why?" I demand. "He's not even here. He left. Or did you forget?"

She scowls at me. "I didn't forget," she snaps. "But you don't seem to recognize that Isaac Icari is not someone you should be getting involved with. What about the video he shared of you? The rumors? He's been fucking tormenting you since you showed up on Hazelwood's campus. The effects of that shit don't just go away overnight. He can't be trusted."

"I can take care of myself, Hel," I say.

"Can you?" Her words are a slap in the face. I blink down at her as my jaw drops open. Almost immediately, guilt and regret cross her expression. "Fuck ... Rori, I didn't mean—"

I don't say anything and I don't let her get her apology out. I step back into my room, grab the edge of my door and slam it shut. Her hand slaps the wood from the other side.

"Rori, come on, I'm sorry! I didn't mean it like that."

"How could you have meant it?" I shoot back, turning as I lean against the frame. I'm being unfair. I know that the words probably just slipped out without her ever meaning anything cruel by them. Yet, I can't seem to calm the rising old pain that blossoms inside my chest. She knows better than most how fucking hellish life was after Marcus left. "I survived that fucking high school," I remind her, shoving the words out more for myself than for her. "I survived Eric, and I'll fucking survive this."

Another thump lands against the wood and I hear her sigh. "Rori, I just want to help you. You don't even know if you can trust him. You said it yourself—he was out to get you and you were looking for a little payback. What if this is just another tactic? I want to make sure you're not making a mistake."

I already made one. I close my eyes and sink my face into my hands. Stress makes the muscles in my shoulders bunch as my nerves jump beneath my flesh. My phone buzzes in my pocket. I ignore it.

She's entirely right—this could be a new strategy on Isaac's part. He could be softening me up only to make the knife he drives into my back hurt that much more. It's not like I haven't been betrayed by supposed friends or boyfriends before. I've been cheated on. I've been fucked over. The second Marcus had gone off to college, high school had turned into a war zone. His absence had left a void where a leader was supposed to be, and as his little sister, I was the target many chose to prove that they were bigger and badder than Marcus ever was.

This is different. I'm not that scared little girl anymore.

"Can you just go?" I say through the door. "I'm sorry. I just ... want to be alone right now."

Silence, and then, "I really am sorry, Rori," she repeats. "I know you can handle yourself—I'm just worried. I love you. You know that, right?"

I blow out a breath and drop my hands away from my face. "I know," I answer her. "I love you too, Hel."

"I'll be here if you need me," she offers, and after another beat of silence, I hear her retreat—the soft pad of her footfalls echoing through the hallway on the other side of the door.

With a groan, I turn and flop down onto my bed. My phone buzzes again and with irritation, I reach down and yank it out. I slap it onto the mattress next to my head and turn my cheek to check the caller.

Isaac. *Motherfucker.* I answer the call.

"What do you want?" I snap.

"Come outside."

I bury my face in my pillow and repress a scream before lifting away once more. "I'm not doing this with you, Isaac," I say. "I'm tired. Go away."

"Baby, either you come out or I'm coming in," he replies, "and as much as I love the chase, I doubt you'll like what I do when I catch you."

I contemplate that. "You don't have access to Rozen-feld," I reply. "Only students that live on campus can enter the dorms."

He chuckles and I hate the way it makes my stomach

twist up in knots. "Fine then, Sunshine. If you really believe that, then wait your pretty little ass right there, and I'll be up soon. A quick warning though, if we're anywhere near a bed—I intend to get you naked again very quickly."

I shoot up into a sitting position. "Stop it," I growl.

His breath comes in soft bursts over the line, like he's walking or something. "I warned you," he replies. "If you think I can't get to you, then you're in for a rude awakening."

Shit. Shit. Double shit. I don't want to do this. Not right now—not after my conversation with Hel. "Hold on —*please*—Isaac. Just stop." I lift the phone to my ear and hold it to the side of my face.

"You're upset," he says.

I grit my teeth. "Gee, I wonder who could be upsetting me."

"It wasn't me," he replies. "You were angry when you answered the phone. Did you fight with one of your roommates?"

I glance around the room. *How the hell could he know that?*

"Are you looking around your room?" The soft chuckle that reaches my ears following his question makes my cheeks burn with heat. "I'm not there yet, baby."

"*Isaac.*"

"Come out, Aurora," he says. "What are you scared of?"

I glance at the window. "I shouldn't even be talking to you right now," I say, more to myself than to him.

Still, he answers. "There's nothing stopping you from hanging up right now," he points out. "Give in, Aurora, you know you like this. You like me."

"You drive me insane," I reply.

"You didn't deny me, though, did you?" His voice deepens. "In fact, I recall your nails in my back as I fucked your tight little pussy last weekend. You really telling me you don't want a repeat of that?"

"Maybe I am." I turn my head and press the phone between my ear and shoulder as I stand up and reach down to my jeans. They're too fucking tight. I unbutton them and shuck them off, kicking them into the corner of my room as I reach for my dresser and yank it open to pull out a pair of thin leggings instead.

"You're so sexy when you lie, Sunshine," Isaac says. "You barely even miss a beat. Makes me wonder what else you're lying about—maybe you're lying to yourself."

I lean back against my bed as I yank the leggings up first, one leg and then the other before standing again and pulling them up to my waist. "What do you want, Isaac?" I finally demand. "What's this really about?"

"I want what I said," he says. "I want you to come outside. As much as I love the sound of your voice in my ear, I want to see you in person."

"That's not a good idea." I move to the closet and pull the phone from my ear, quickly switching it to low volume and putting it on speaker before setting it on the shelf above my hangers.

"I'm just making sure you're not trying to back out of your promise to see me this weekend." Isaac's words make me flinch.

"That's not a good idea either," I say. "Besides, what the hell would you be doing at a piercing shop?"

"You looked up the address." He chuckles. "Smart girl, and if you're really that curious then you'll find out when I pick you up on Friday."

"I thought you gave me the time so I could meet you there." My fingers find a long-sleeved mint green fleece sweater and I pull it off the hanger.

Isaac hums in the back of his throat before responding. "No, that time was for you to be ready by. I'm a gentleman, baby. I'll be picking you up for our date—just like I am right now."

"We're not dating." I yank the sweater over my head until it drops down past my ass.

"So, what then?" he prompts. "You're just using me for sex? I didn't expect you to be that kind of girl."

A growl of frustration erupts from me and I snatch the phone from the shelf before dropping onto my ass and reaching for a pair of sneakers at the bottom of the closet. "You're just trying to get under my skin," I say accusingly. "I don't know what you're planning, but I'm not falling for it, Isaac."

The ties of my sneakers get tangled as I yank them out and grunt in irritation. "Don't make me wait too long, Aurora," Isaac replies. "I'll give you ten minutes to get your pretty ass out the front door of your dorm and if not, I'll be coming after you."

"I'm not going on a date with you, Isaac," I repeat.

"It's too late to back out of this now, goddess." Isaac's words dip again, and his low baritone sounds like both a dangerous warning and a promise of something sinful. Shivers skate down my spine and I suck in a quick breath through my nose. My muscles bunch. My fingers go still against the ties of my shoes.

"And what if I don't come," I say. "What then? You're going to break into my dorm? What would your father have to say about that?"

Silence, and then... "Just for that little comment, I'm

cutting down your time. Five minutes, Aurora. I'll see you soon."

He doesn't give me a chance to respond. A second later, the line clicks and goes quiet. The reflection of my phone screen shows that he's ended the call. I groan and rework my sneaker ties again, hurriedly untangling them and putting them on.

Isaac Icari is going to be the death of me, I just know it.

28

ISAAC

When Aurora emerges from Rozenfeld, she's got her long blonde hair thrown up into a messy bun. She's wearing an oversized sweater that hides the curvaceous form I know lies beneath her clothes and she's scrubbed her face clean of makeup. Fuck, she's still gorgeous—even if she is a little liar.

She spots me across the parking lot and scowls. I wait, leaning back against my Escalade as she makes her way over to me. I can't help but watch her, eating up the long length of her legs encased in black leggings as she approaches. She stops a few feet in front of me and crosses her arms.

"Alright, I'm fucking here," she snaps. "Now, what do you want?"

I smirk and step to the side, pulling open the passenger side door of my car. "Get in."

She eyes me before flicking her gaze to the interior of my Escalade. I can see the war going on behind her eyes, the battle of if she should trust me and if she should walk away. I let her think about it for several moments. It doesn't really matter what she decides in the end. Even if she refuses, I'll just pick her ass up, toss her in and lock the doors. But I hope she makes this easy on me. I hope she makes the right choice.

With a fresh sigh, she deflates, dropping her arms to her side as she steps forward and catches the door frame. "I can't be out too late," she mutters. "I have homework."

"I'll have you back soon," I promise her. I'm not sure yet if it's a lie.

Aurora reaches up, latching onto the 'oh shit' handle, and pulls herself into the much higher seat. I quietly shut the door behind her before rounding the front of the vehicle and climbing into the driver's seat. I can feel the heat of her gaze on the side of my face as I start the car and put it into reverse.

"What's this about, Isaac?" she asks again. "I promised I'd see you on Friday; do we really have to do this?"

I grip the steering wheel tightly in an effort not to reach for her. She really has no fucking clue what she's done to me. It's almost laughable. My obsession with her has put me squarely under her spell and yet, she doesn't know yet how to use that power. I should be grateful, really. If Aurora ever finds out just how fucking captivated I am by her—if she ever figures out how to use that weakness against me—my advantage against her will come to a fiery, crashing end.

When I don't answer her, though, Aurora's claws come out. "*Isaac*," she snaps my name and even that makes me want her.

"You wanna know where we're going?" I prompt her, shooting a grin her way. "Then sit there and wait like a good girl. We're not going far."

Ocean blue eyes narrow on me. "I don't trust you."

Few people do, so her little hissed comment doesn't hurt me. I return my gaze to the road ahead without responding. Aurora thumps back against her seat, arms crossing again as she stews in her thoughts. Whatever she's thinking, though, she keeps to herself as I drive and the rest of the trip is spent in relative silence.

Less than a half hour later, I'm pulling up in front of a dingy-looking brick building. The parking spots in front are so faded that the white lines are barely perceptible and the only way I know which place to park is because I've been here so many times before—that and the fact that there is a line of second-hand vehicles already lining the small lot.

"Where are we?" Aurora asks as I shut off the engine and get out.

I don't answer. Instead, I circle the hood of the vehicle and frown as she pops open her own door and hops out without waiting for me. God save me from independent women. I grip the door and shut it behind her before reaching for her hand.

The second my fingers close around hers, she jerks back. "What do you think you're doing?"

I lift her hand up to my mouth and press a kiss to the bite mark I left there earlier in the day. I love that it's still there. Maybe if I bite her somewhere else—somewhere more noticeable, it'll show others she's out of their reach. I can't help but like that thought.

"Come on, Sunshine," I say, tugging her towards the front entrance.

She hesitates, but eventually gives in to my careful prodding and follows me towards the blacked out front glass door. Just as we approach, it swings open and a tall man with a shaggy beard slips out, his plaid shirt swaying open to reveal the stained wife beater beneath. Aurora's eyes widen as he passes us by.

"Isaac?" I close my eyes and relish in the timid little tone of her voice.

"It's alright, Sunshine," I say, pulling her closer to my side as we enter the building. "I've got you. There's nothing to be scared of."

I half expect her to bite back a retort about her not being scared of shit, but the second we step inside, her mind is occupied. She turns her head and scans the dark, smoke-filled room with curiosity and confusion. I would do the same if I were her.

She's not a scholarship student or some bar bunny. I doubt she's ever been to a place like *Goon's*. I turn my eye back to the building, taking it in. It's not my first time, but it's hers and I have to wonder what she must be thinking.

Along the back wall, there's an opening for a separate room and a step down into it. It's filled with a line of pool tables, a dart board on the side wall, and a jukebox that likely hasn't been dusted since it was put in thirty years prior.

"Want a drink?" I ask as I push her further inside.

She shoots me a look. "I'm not—"

I cover her mouth before she can say it. "Yes or no, Aurora," I say. "I'm buying."

She sighs and I feel her muscles relax. "Fine," she replies. "Long Island, but if we get in trouble—I'm blaming you."

Another grin graces my lips. "I would expect no less from my good girl."

The way her face scrunches up is so adorable, but I don't tell her that. Instead, I lead her over to the grease-

and-condensation-stained countertop bar across from the similarly dirtied tables in the main room. I order a beer for myself along with her Long Island and pay before gesturing her towards the back room where two out of the five pool tables are already taken up by other customers.

Whether it's curiosity or anticipation—whatever the case, Aurora remains quiet until the two of us are sequestered at our own corner table in the room furthest from the entrance. She takes one deep draw of her Long Island as I move over to the empty pool table closest to us and slide in a few quarters to release the balls.

"Are you ever going to tell me what we're doing here?" she finally asks. "Or why you brought *me* of all people here?"

The balls release and I pick them up, setting them in the middle of the table as I start to rack. "You ever played pool?" I ask instead of answering her question.

She replies after a beat. "I don't like pool."

"Good, I can teach you."

I slip the triangle over the balls and roll them back and forth until they're all stable. Aurora huffs. "Isaac."

"Yes, baby?"

Her lips press together at the nickname. She's gotten used to both sunshine and goddess, but any time I call her 'baby' her hackles raise. "Answer me," she demands.

"Hmm." I hum, contemplating her request. I move over to the wall of pool sticks and grab two off the stand along with a small square of chalk. "How about a bet instead?" I offer.

Her eyebrows raise. "A bet?"

"If you beat me at a short game of pool, then I'll tell you everything you want to know."

"Everything?" she repeats. "Even if I ask about your

father?"

It takes effort to keep my face from reacting to that, but I manage. If she's never played pool before, then the chances of her beating me are slim to none. I've been playing with Paris and Shep since I was practically in diapers after all.

"Anything you want to know," I assure her.

"One game?"

I chalk a cue stick and then the other before holding the second out to her. "One game," I assure her. "You win, and I'll tell you anything you want to know."

Her lips press down hard against each other and she eyes the stick I'm holding out her way. *Come on, goddess. Take it,* I urge her silently. I want to see her here—in this dark, grungy world. A normal girl with a not-so-normal background. For a night, I just want it to be her and me. Isaac and Aurora.

Not Icari. Not Summers. Not the complexity of our relationship. Just a man and a woman.

Her fingers grasp the pool cue and she pulls it from my grasp. For the first time all night, a full-fledged smile breaks free. My lips stretch and I take a step back as she glares at me as she moves towards the table.

"One game then," she replies. "You better keep up your end of the bargain."

"I will," I say, but a split second later, my smile falls away.

Aurora steps up to the opposite end of the table, with the triangle of balls pointing right at her. She grabs the cue ball and adjusts it to her liking. Horror descends as she smirks at me and lines up her stick. Just before she cracks the shot, she looks up at me. "I call stripes."

Mother fucker.

29

ISAAC

Aurora can play pool. Not just that. She can play it *well*.

Fuck. Me. That's hot.

I watch as for the dozenth time, she bends over the pool table and lines up her next shot. Her ass pokes out, grabbing my attention as well as the attention of several onlookers that have scooted closer to watch our game.

One man whistles low under his breath as he stares. If she hears it, she doesn't react. The whole of her focus is on the game. But I do. I hear it, and it makes my blood boil. I scowl at the man, glaring at him until his gaze lifts and he spots me across the table.

His expression turns smug. My stomach bottoms out as my fingers squeeze tight to my own pool stick and I step away from the wall too late. He steps forward just as Aurora adjusts herself, the soft sweater she's wearing lifting up to reveal the lush curve of her ass. She jerks when his hand lands on the small of her back and he bends over to whisper in her ear.

"No thanks," she snaps.

The desire to break his hand pulses like a living thing inside of me. It takes all of my control to maintain my calm facade as the man says something else and she scowls, standing up to push him back. Only then do I step in.

"I said no," Aurora growls. "Now back off, asshole."

Before the idiot can say anything, I step between them and give him a smile. "You heard her, dipshit," I say. "I recommend you leave."

He scowls at me and then takes the beer in his hand, and tips it back until it's drained before slamming it on the surface of a nearby table. "Fine," he slurs. "Keep your cunt. Bet she's dried up, anyway."

With that, he turns and stumbles back to the bar. A few of the onlookers sigh and shake their heads, but none seem particularly surprised. This man must be a regular—worse than that, he must have a reputation for being a sleaze.

Carefully, I urge Aurora back to the pool table. "Shoot," I order. "I'll be right back."

"Isaac." Her hand latches onto my arm as I move away from her. "Don't."

I pause and look down at where her fingers grip my flesh, her warmth against my own. "Hey." I slide back towards her, resting my pool stick against the table as I grip her waist and bring her closer. "It's okay. Everything's fine. I'm just gonna step out for a sec—he pissed me off and I want to cool my head." Aurora eyes me, her cute brow puckered with mistrust. I smirk and rub a thumb over that little v. "Don't worry so much, Sunshine."

"You're lying." Her accusation is on point, but she has no way of proving it if she stays here. Knowing what I do about Aurora Summers, though, I doubt she will now that she's suspicious.

"Fine." I sigh. "You want me to stay?"

She nods, her gaze flickering from me to the asshole that had his hand all over her as he stands against the bar across the room. Why she thinks a bastard like him deserves her protection, I don't understand, but if it'll make her feel better, I can pretend.

"Alright." I press a kiss to her brow and then move back, releasing her as I pick my stick back up. "Play. I'll watch."

Her frown remains in place. I'm sure she's wondering why the hell I've decided to listen to her now. That's alright. All I need to do is distract her for now. I'll take care of things soon enough.

Aurora moves back into place and bends over the table. This time, as I scan the onlookers, all eyes remain decidedly away from her ass.

The crack of balls reaches my ears and I look back at the table to see that Aurora has sunk yet another striped ball—the last one. Fuck. She's gonna beat me. It'd be hot if there wasn't so much at stake. I've got to stop this. Thankfully, at the next round, she scratches and misses a pocket.

My turn.

Aurora steps to the side and holds her cue stick in front of her as I sink several balls one after the other. The more points I hit, the more antsy she gets. Her fingers moving along the stick as she taps her foot and even goes back to the table to suck back more of her drink. I focus hard, pushing myself for a win harder than I ever have with one of the guys. It all comes to an end as I sink all of my own balls and then the 8-ball last.

"That's a tie," Aurora says as I stand up after my last shot.

I glance her way. "I think I won, Sunshine."

Her scowl is too cute. She bites her lower lip and glares at the table as if it's offended her. Sure, it was close. *Too close*, but I'd won. And even if I give in and let her have her tie—a tie doesn't mean she gets her answers. Not concerning my father anyway.

I rest my pool stick against the wall again and lift a hand to one of the waitresses walking through the room as the rest of the onlookers go back to their own tables and games now that ours has ended. "Are you hungry?" I ask her as the waitress catches sight of my hand and starts towards us.

"No." Aurora's 'no' is biting and irritated. I chuckle, not surprised that she's a sore loser.

"Two burgers and a basket of fries," I say as the waitress approaches, ignoring Aurora's answer.

"Any substitutions?" she asks, glancing behind me to Aurora.

"No, but you can grab her another Long Island and another beer for me." I hand her a hundred. "Keep the change."

The waitress tucks the bill into her apron and nods, quickly walking away as if she's afraid I'll take back the money. Only then do I turn back to my date. Aurora is sucking down the last of her first drink and chewing idly on the straw as she bores a hole into the wall. I take a seat across from her, stepping right into her line of vision. Her scowl deepens.

"You told me you didn't know how to play pool," I say.

She rolls her eyes. "No, I didn't," she replies. "I said I didn't like it, not that I didn't know how to play."

My mouth opens, but she's right. She never said she didn't know how to play. That was my own assumption. Damn. "You knew what I'd think."

She shrugs. "Your arrogance is not my fault," she replies. "Besides, I still didn't win."

Maybe not, but she'd certainly used my own arrogance against me and given me a run for my money. *Sneaky bad girl.* I tip my beer back and drain what remains in the bottle in one go.

"Ask your questions," I say. "But I can't promise I'll answer."

She lifts up and eyes me. "Seriously?"

I arch a brow. "If you want me to take it back..."

"No," she says quickly. "No, I want to know—"

I lean closer, across the table. "You want to know what?"

"About your father."

I sit back. "No." I shove my beer to the side, sliding it to the edge of the table for the waitress to pick up when she returns. "Ask something else."

"Fine." She sits back. "Then let's start with why you brought me here?" Aurora turns and gestures to the bar.

"We're on a date," I tell her honestly.

She blinks back at me. "That's it?"

I shrug. "That's it."

"You brought me ... to a bar ... for a date?"

"*Yup.*" I pop the word and lean back against the wall, crossing my arms over my chest. The way her eyes go to the stretch of my t-shirt over my biceps doesn't escape my notice, but it does ease the hardness in my chest caused by her initial question about my father.

"Why?" she demands. "Why here? I mean you're..." Her head shakes and a strand of hair slips free from her bun, falling to the side of her face, and sliding along her cheek. She doesn't seem to notice it. "You're you—you're Isaac Icari. I'm sure you go to places that are so much more..." I wait, listening to her words as she fumbles over how to explain her thoughts.

"You expected something expensive?" I ask. "Something that stinks of wealth and privilege?"

"Well..." She blows out a breath. "Yeah."

I shake my head. "What about you?" I reply. "You're not poor. Why'd you follow me into this building even after finding out what it was?"

"Because I don't care," she says easily, "and I wanted to know what you were planning."

"And now that you know, why haven't you left?"

"Uh, because you drove me?"

I chuckle under my breath. "You have money, Aurora," I remind her. "You could've called a car to come pick you up. Hell, you could've refused to meet me at all, but you didn't. You entrusted yourself to me."

"No," she snaps. "You threatened me."

"Did I?"

Before she can respond, the waitress appears and drops off our food. The smell of greasy meat and ketchup reaches my nostrils, making my mouth water. The basket of fries, piled high and laden down with salt, is slipped onto the table between our burgers and the waitress high-tails it away.

"You did," Aurora presses as I pick up my burger, squeezing the sides, and bite into it.

I chew thoughtfully and swallow. "Maybe," I give her, "but did you really believe me?"

Her mouth parts and I reach forward, plucking a fry from the basket and sliding it between her lips. Her lips close around it and she pauses, eyes widening as she realizes how fucking good it tastes. There's really nothing like some backwoods, hole-in-the-wall bar food. It's ten times better than that garbage my father shells out hundreds of thousands of dollars a year on a personal chef for.

"Oh my God," she moans, reaching for another as if she can't help herself. I doubt she can. *Goon's* fries are some of the best I've ever had. Even as picky as Shep is, he loves it here.

"Why don't you just relax," I suggest. "Eat and enjoy the date. Don't think about it too hard."

Aurora's gaze lifts and meets mine as she swallows her next fry. "Don't patronize me, Isaac," she replies tartly. "You're planning something. I know it."

I grin and lean forward. "Maybe I'm planning on getting you back in my bed."

"Maybe you are," she agrees. "Maybe you're just after me to piss off your father."

I sit back again. "Eat your food, Aurora," I command. "Let's drop the Daddy and Mommy issues for the night, shall we?"

Her eyes bore into me as she lifts her burger to her mouth. A moment later though, as she bites down on the bun and meat, another moan lifts from her lips. Whatever thoughts she had of pressing me for more information disperses as she begins to consume her meal.

I watch her as she eats, and when our next drinks arrive and Aurora dives for her Long Island to help with the salty taste of the fries, I think that this is exactly what I wanted. Ease. Normalcy. Casual touch.

It's only a temporary reprieve. Come tomorrow, she'll

remain suspicious of me. Come next week, I'll still have to find an answer for Agent Brown. This won't make our problems go away, but we can put it off for now. For this brief moment in time, I can have my date with Aurora Summers and pretend like we're just two normal people.

30
RORI

Isaac's plan is working. The day after our date, I can feel eyes on me. Even if I don't have any classes with him on Tuesdays, I still feel like he's right next to me. Even Hel and Selene notice the newfound interest everyone on campus is starting to show me.

"Just smile and pretend like you don't see them," Selene advises. Unlike Selene, the feeling of being stared at was one I never quite got used to, and it doesn't make me comfortable. I can't just "smile" and "pretend." It bothers me, and I have no way of masking that.

As if the attention I'm garnering isn't the worst, I get a text from my mom halfway through the day, telling me more about her plans now that she's back in town. The last two months have seen more contact with her than I have in the last two years. She used to go months with no contact, but now it's pictures every day. Her with Damien. Her on his yacht. Her at a fancy dinner hosted by one of Damien's business partners. I don't care. I don't trust the guy. After what Marcus' friends said about the man as well as from what I've learned from Isaac, I have no doubt that Damien Icari is using my mother for something nefarious—that much was clear when Marcus took me to meet his friends, but I've yet to figure out how to convince her of that fact. "What's with the face?" Hel asks, sliding her tray next to mine as we suffer through the strange looks and curious whispers spreading throughout the school cafeteria.

"My mom," I answer with a sigh, clicking the screen of my phone off without replying to her latest message.

"What's her damage this time?" Selene asks as she takes a seat across from us.

I glance over the basket of fries sitting next to her salad. "Are you even going to eat that?" I ask, pointing at them with my fork. "I thought you said you had to diet for your next shoot."

Selene blows out a breath. "A girl can't live on lettuce forever," she mutters. "I'm just going to have a few."

Hel shakes her head. "Eat the whole thing, babe," she advises. "I'm starting to worry."

Selene stares longingly at the fries. "My mom said that I'm looking a bit pudgy," she admits quietly.

I blink. "Your mom's back in town?" Why hadn't she said something before now?

Selene nods, continuing to eye the basket of fries. "Yeah, she was at my last shoot and she's coming to my next one too. She said I need to be more mindful about my size since the industry is really leaning into the athletic look these days—the freshman fifteen happens to everyone and it'll happen to me, too, if I'm not careful."

"Selene." Hel leans forward. "You *are* careful. Fuck— you're the healthiest of all of us. Don't fucking starve yourself to make your mom happy."

"She's just trying to look out for my career," Selene

replies quickly, pushing the fries away as she dumps a packet of light dressing over her salad. "Models are only good for a short time before companies move on to something newer and younger."

I roll my eyes. "That's bullshit," I snap. "You're eighteen. You've still got several years in the industry before that becomes a worry."

Selene stabs into her salad with the edge of her fork a bit too hard and sighs. "I know, I know," she says, shaking her head. "But I can't help but think about her words. She's one of the longest-lasting models in the industry. There's a lot of pressure to keep up appearances. Everyone looks at me as Melinda Reynolds' daughter. They have expectations."

"Fuck their expectations! Have you actually gained any weight?" Hel demands.

Silence, and then, "No..." Selene focuses on her food. "I've actually lost a few pounds since we moved into the dorm."

"Then eat a damn fry," she snaps. "It's not going to kill you, and I swear to god, if you try to work out as punishment, I'll shove you in a closet and lock the door."

Selene snickers. "You wouldn't."

"Oh, yes, I fucking would," Hel argues. "In fact, I'll keep you in there for a week, and the only thing I'll slide under the door to feed you will be chocolate bars." She points her fork at Selene meaningfully. "So, it's your choice. A few fries now or a week of chocolate bars."

With a mock look of exasperation, Selene drops her fork and pointedly reaches for a fry. I laugh and Hel gives a nod of approval as Selene pops the greasy goodness into her mouth and grins at us as she chews.

I shake my head, so focused on the two of them that when a shadow falls over the table, I only catch it for a brief second before a strong, masculine arm slides around my shoulders. "What are we laughing at?" Isaac's deep baritone rumbles against my back as he pulls me back against him and leans down.

My mouth opens to ask him what the hell he thinks he's doing when he drops down and captures my lips with his. I mean to pull away—really, I do. The thought is in my mind. My body, however, has other ideas. It's addicted to him already and it relishes in the feel of him, in the taste. My lips part under his and his free hand comes around, clasping my throat to hold me in place—and I know it's just in case my mind catches up with what I'm doing. He's keeping me where he wants me. His tongue invades, marking me as his as he sweeps away all rational thought with this kiss.

This is exactly what I need to be avoiding—very public displays of affection.

Finally, he frees me, pulling back and staring down at me with a wicked, knowing grin. I try to grasp at the tendrils of logical thought as he strokes my jaw with his thumb. "Having a girl's day?" he asks.

I blink and pull away. "No." I turn in my chair, but he's already scraping a chair from a nearby unused table and pulling it up close to me. "What are you doing here?"

"It's the school cafeteria," he replies as he glances over the table and reaches for a carrot stick on my plate. He pops it into his mouth, crunching down as he leans ever closer. "I'm here to eat," he finishes, swallowing.

My thighs tighten at his statement. To anyone else, it would seem such an innocent comment—perfectly appropriate in a place where people congregate to get food. But to me, it's anything but appropriate. There's nothing about this man that screams 'innocence'. If anything, he's the epitome of immoral.

Hel scowls as she scoots to the side, further away from Isaac as he practically shoulders her out of the way and reaches for my plate once more. "*Isaac*," I snap, innately aware that all eyes in the cafeteria are on us. What little ambiguity I might have had is being wrecked and erased.

"*Aurora.*" Isaac doesn't seem bothered by my discomfort at all. In fact, his hand lands on my side, hard fingers wrapping around my waist, and just ... rest there as he eats another carrot. The heat from his palm is driving me mad. Whatever spell he cast on me, it needs to stop here.

I stand abruptly, and his hand falls away. "I'm leaving," I say, shooting a look at a wide-eyed Selene and an obviously irritated Hel. "I'll see you guys later."

Slinging my backpack over my shoulder, I pick up my tray, practically ripping it out of Isaac's reach as I turn and stride across the dining hall. I drop it off in the window along the farthest wall away from the exit, hating that I have to return the same way I came to leave and suffer the looks and whispers all over again.

Almost as soon as that thought crosses my mind, Isaac appears at my side and I press my lips together, grinding my teeth as he ignores my obvious irritation and swings his arm around my shoulders once more.

"Why do I get the sense that you're trying to avoid me, Sunshine?" he asks pleasantly, a smile on his face.

"I don't know, maybe because *I am*," I snap.

He clasps his free hand over his chest. "Oh, you wound me, baby," he says. "How cruel."

"Stop it," I practically hiss at him, dipping my head

low as I pass a particularly full table of girls from one of my classes, all of them openly gawking. *Fuck, what am I? A zoo animal?* It fucking feels like it.

When we make it outside, I feel marginally better. There are fewer people and, therefore, fewer eyes on us. Isaac still follows me, though, all the way to the front of Rozenfeld Dorm. I stop in front of the steps and turn to him.

"Why are you doing this?" I demand, pushing him back. "What are you plotting?"

"Plotting?" He arches a brow and ignores my outstretched palm. I could be warding off a ghost for all the good it does; he seems to walk right into me, gripping my wrist and holding it up and out of his path as he sidles up, close as ever. His chest to mine.

"I'm not an idiot, Isaac," I say, glaring up at him. "No one just flips a switch that quickly. You can't torture me for weeks, threaten me, and then the second you get some ass—pretend like all is forgotten and forgiven."

"Do you think I see you as a piece of ass, Aurora?" The question is insulting, but that's exactly how I've phrased my own responses. A large part of me says 'yes.' That's exactly how he sees me. Another part of me wonders...

And as if he can read my thoughts, Isaac's fingers squeeze my wrist. "If I wanted ass, I can get it wherever," he states. "I don't need to chase after someone as stubborn as you."

"Then why are you?" I demand.

Isaac pulls me closer. "Why don't you answer that question yourself?" he prompts. "If anything, I should be avoiding you. Isn't that right? Considering our own *familial relation,* you are not someone I should even be pursuing like this."

I flinch at the reminder and turn my cheek, not wanting to stare into his impossibly dark and violent gaze. "If you know we shouldn't be doing this, then why are you pushing?" I ask. "It's not like we can be anything, so why try?"

Isaac's sigh blows over my face. Shockingly, he leans into me and drops his head against my shoulder. With the height difference, his back has to bow and his knees have to bend for him to do so, but it warms my shoulder. When his breath fans over my throat as he turns his head, my pussy fucking throbs like the annoying, lusty bitch that she is. *What the hell is wrong with me?*

"Forget them, Aurora," Isaac finally says. "Forget my father. Your mother. Everyone on campus. What do you want? Do you want me the same way I want you?"

Each word is another breath of hot air on my skin, scrambling my thoughts. He's a drug, I realize. Dangerous and addictive. I shake my head. "I can't forget," I say. "It's not that easy."

His grip on my wrist moves, his thumb rubbing over the pulse there before moving down as he twines our fingers together. "It can be," he says. "It can be as easy as we make it."

My head drops back and I resist the urge to groan. "You're asking for the impossible, Isaac," I tell him. "Our parents are fucking married. Legally bound together."

If my mother were to find out that I fucked her step-son, she'd be wrecked. She'd do what she's always done, only this time, it wouldn't be through silent looks and long extended periods of absence. She's always blamed me for the loss of her last marriage, but this time it really will be my fault.

Maybe that's for the best, though, a snide little voice in my head says. It's clear, after all, that Damien Icari is only using her. Isaac had all but said so the night we crossed the line. Damien is involved in something insidious and corrupt. Maybe this is exactly what I need to use to ruin their relationship—if only to protect her.

"Stop." I jump as Isaac's voice hits my ears and his hands reach up, clasping my face. He leans in and presses another kiss to my lips. "Stop thinking." He breathes the words against my mouth, practically pleading as he takes my bottom lip between his teeth and suckles on it, swiping his tongue across the sensitive flesh there.

I whimper, my legs weakening as I lean into him. I should say no. I should push him away. Deny him. But I can't. It doesn't matter if I know right from wrong. What I want overpowers everything else. My greed is a monstrous little thing, consuming me. Making me lift my arms and wrap them around his neck as his mouth takes mine.

His hands grip my waist, pulling me against his front until I can feel the evidence of his arousal against the small of my stomach. I want him again. His cock. His mouth. His hands all over me. I want him to eradicate all of the reasons we shouldn't do this and remind me of how good it feels to have a man worship my body.

This time, when he pulls away from me, I'm panting and gasping for breath. My panties are soaked and my hands grasp at him, needy and clingy. Isaac gently pushes me away.

"Friday night," he grits out between clenched teeth. "Don't fucking run from me, Aurora. I'll come after you. Be ready."

With that, he turns, leaving me shivering and trembling on the front step of my own dorm. It hurts knowing what Isaac wants *is* me, but I can't see how it's possible. I might be an obsession to him right now, but it'll pass. It's bound to. It *has* to.

31

ISAAC

Bart Pollack. That's the fucker's name. I watch the bitch ass motherfucker as he stumbles out of another bar late Wednesday night. A folder with his life history sits in the passenger seat of the cheap thirty-year-old sedan I paid cash for earlier in the day. I won't need the car after tonight, but I will need a damn good drink after I deal with this fucker.

An alcoholic with a history of harassment both in his professional and private life, Pollack is the quintessential gutter rat with a rap sheet several pages long and a string of broken relationships and battered women that had the unfortunate luck to end up with him. Perhaps if I were a more level-headed guy, I'd be able to go on my way knowing his life is as pathetic as the man that lives it.

Unfortunately for good ol' Bart, I've got the blood of the Devil in me, more money than God, and an obsession with the pretty blonde he thought he could fuck with Monday night. He's going to learn today that keeping his hands off things that don't belong to him is more than important—it'll probably save his fucking life.

My target weaves back and forth across the parking lot as he makes it to his beat-up old Ford truck that has the back bumper practically rusting off. He manages to pull himself into the driver's seat and start it up. White headlights flash over the front of the bar as he backs out in sharp jerking movements—slamming on the brakes before he can hit one of the other vehicles parked in the lot.

I watch all of this with an eagle eye and when he's far enough ahead, I turn on my own lights and crank the engine, following after him. The digital clock on the dashboard blinks back, showing that the time is edging past one in the morning. I'm honestly shocked he didn't stay until the bar's closing time, but maybe it's my luck. Luck that doesn't seem to be stopping anytime tonight.

Bart's truck gets farther and farther from the city, until the lights grow few and far between. The shop buildings disappear, giving way to trailer parks and dilapidated apartment complexes. I wait until there's a long stretch of road with no lights, no buildings at all. Nothing but him and me.

I speed up, pressing down on the gas, and swerve into the opposite lane to pass him. When I assume he catches my headlights and sees the darkened car moving up on his side—curving up the wrong side of the highway, he lays on his horn. A man with an ego like him can't stand feeling any sort of inadequacy even if it's the thought that someone thinks he's driving too slow.

The second the back of my vehicle makes it past the front of his, I swerve back into the lane and slam on the brakes. Tires shriek against pavement and I relax my muscles, preparing for the crash. Just as I planned, Pollack's truck slams into my car and his horn blares again. Metal groans. The twin beams of light that pierce through the back windshield of my car waver and then go out as the glass and bulbs shatter against my bumper. Both cars come to a halt and I yank the emergency break up before slapping the vehicle into park.

Reaching into the console, I withdraw the pair of black gloves I put there earlier and tug them on along with the black ski mask I stashed with them. Cursing reaches my ears as I pop the driver's side door. It's dark behind me, the only light on this long road comes from my own headlights. Pollack's truck shudders as he clambers out of the vehicle and slams his door shut, rattling the tin can on wheels.

"What the fuck is wrong with ya, numbnuts?" Pollack slurs as he stumbles towards me. I appear out of the car and crack my knuckles. He doesn't even seem to notice the mask or gloves as he veers towards the front of his truck and curses again. "Do ya even know how much this'll cost?"

With calm, unhurried footsteps, I move slowly, precisely as I approach. When I get close, his head lifts and his bloodshot eyes widen when he realizes that I'm not just a dumbass driver. I'm his worst fucking nightmare.

"Hey!—" He doesn't get anything else out as I grab the side of his head and slam it down into his truck hood. Pollack's skull cracks against the metal, denting the old material and he sags onto the ground like a sack of potatoes, groaning.

I crack my knuckles again and move over him. I straddle the man and slam my glove-covered fist into his face, smashing my knuckles into his jaw again and again until he starts to fight back.

"Fucking—*bitch*—" A fist comes my way too late. I

dodge it and grab his wrist, twisting him until I can slap his face into the pavement. Then I press down, grinding his already bloodied nose and cheek into the hard ground. He curses some more, squirming beneath me as he tries to get free, but that's not fucking happening.

Beneath the mask, I grin with malicious excitement as I grip the back of his head, clenching my fingers in the greasy mop of hair on the back of his head, and using that hold, I lift him up and smash him back down. Blood pours out beneath his face, but I do it again just because I liked it so much the first time.

His hands scramble against the pavement as he pushes up and back. "Motherfucker!" Pollack spits out a wad of blood and then bucks against me. I lift him and step back, giving him the opportunity to get on his feet. He comes up swinging wildly and I get a chance to see the damage I've done to his face.

With the alcohol still in his system, he's running on pure adrenaline and while I can't say I'm not affected, I know I'm a damn sight more composed. I'm calculated and as such, I'm a far more challenging target. He throws a fast right hook and I step aside, watching him go flying after his own arm and stumble right into the back of my car.

I don't think, I attack him while his back is turned. Grasping at the back of his head again, I slam his face against the back window and when I pull him back, my free hand goes for the door's handle. I rip it open as he's cursing and bowing against me again—sputtering out blood-filled words. As if he thinks I'm about to kidnap him, he grabs onto the door frame, fighting back against me—that's fine in any case. It works out perfectly.

With Pollack's fat, sausage fingers wrapped around

the door frame, I slam it shut and he howls in pain as his fingers crunch into the door. I open it again and this time, he pulls his arm back. That won't do. I grab his hand—the same one I just crushed and shove it back into the door frame, slamming the door hard enough for it to bounce off of his now-broken fingers.

More howls, cursing, and this time, sobbing echo across the dark empty expanse of road. I'm not done though. Even as Pollack's legs collapse out from under him and he cradles his broken hand against his chest, I grab his other hand and perform the same vicious action, shoving it into the door and slamming it until more bones crack and more howling ensues.

"Why!" he screams once I'm finally done. "Why are you doing this!"

He recoils as I close the back door of my car and step over him, staring down at the sniveling mess I've made. Only then do I crouch down and answer his question.

"Keep your fucking eyes and hands off my girl," I grit the words out, growling as my voice deepens.

"I-I don't even know who your bitch is," he blubbers.

It doesn't matter. I straighten and put my booted foot right between his legs, stepping down hard and twisting my ankle until he whimpers and shakes. "Then I guess you better not touch anyone's girl in the future, eh? Keep your fucking hands to yourself, or next time you'll have more than broken fingers to worry about." I lift my foot up, and before he can move back or realize what I'm about to do, I kick him squarely in the crotch, hard enough that his head turns and he fucking pukes like the prick he is.

I spit on his face and kick him out of the way as he huddles and balls himself up, his broken hands going to his crotch. The sight is enough to give me a high, that adrenaline from earlier roaring to the forefront as I move back towards the driver's side door. I pop it and get in, twisting the wheel as I throw down the emergency brake and put the car in drive.

The revving engine hits my ears as I make a U-turn and speed back the same way I came, passing the man on the ground. As I pull off the ski mask and toss it onto the folder in the passenger seat, my phone rings.

I give the cell a half glance before hitting answer. "Speak."

"Where are you?" Shep's voice echoes into the interior of the car.

"Taking care of some business," I hedge. "'Bout to drop off a car and head your way."

"You might want to hurry," he says.

"What's up?"

"Paris."

Fuck. That's all that needs to be said. If Shep's calling on Paris' behalf, that means something's gone down with the Troy Family. They couldn't have chosen a worse night. I scrub a hand down my face and then pause as something wet lands on my cheek. Sliding to the side, I check my face in the rearview mirror.

Blood smudges against the upper side of my face. Damn it. I grimace. "I'll be there soon," I snap. "Let me get rid of this car and I'll be right there."

There's a pause on the other side of the line and then, "What do you mean get rid of the car?" Shep demands. "Isaac? What the fuck did you do?"

"Tell you later," I reply, "but it's fine. I've taken care of everything. There won't be repercussions."

"This is about the girl, isn't it?" Shep snaps, but instead of giving me a chance to answer, he continues. "I don't like this. You need to screw your head on right. Whatever's going on with her, let it go."

Never. I scowl. "I'll be at yours soon," I snap. "Talk then." I shove my thumb against the screen, ending the call before he says anything else that's sure to piss me off.

Whether or not he approves of it, my relationship with Aurora has already gone past the point of no return. He'll have to learn to accept it sooner or later because if tonight has proved anything ... it's that I'm too far gone.

32
RORI

I contemplate making myself unavailable when Isaac shows up to pick me up on Friday. In fact, I plan it out. I pack a bag. I pull up the website and phone number to a local hotel with a reputation for being tight on its security, since it often houses celebrities and other people in important positions.

In the end, however, I find myself standing outside of Rozenfeld wearing a loose gray sweater tucked into a tight black pleather skirt and knee-high matching black boots. The changing of the seasons might have some people regretting the skirt, but this is California—not New York. Even in the fall, it's hot here.

Isaac's black escalade rolls up less than five minutes after I step outside and instead of letting him get out and open the door, I step up to the passenger side and nearly rip the handle off in an effort to get in. The sooner I get this over, the better. Or so I tell myself.

Isaac arches a brow as he grips the steering wheel, watching me struggle up into the seat. "Having problems there, goddess?"

"Shut. Up." I lock my fingers around the 'oh, shit' handle and yank my body into his Escalade. "Why do you have to drive such a massive fucking car? I'd ask if you were compensating for something, but..."

I let the words trail off as my ass finally hits the seat and I turn, releasing the handle to shut the door behind me.

"Oh, I'm compensating alright," he says, putting the vehicle into park as he leans across the console.

I straighten, pressing my spine into the back of the seat as he reaches across my front and grabs the seatbelt. He tugs it lightly and then moves it over my body, the backs of his hands brushing my breasts as he clicks it into place. My nipples tighten beneath my bra and sweater and I pray that he can't see them in the darkened interior of the car.

"Compensating for your shitty personality?" I bite out, forcing the words out as a distraction.

Isaac smirks at me. "Sure, Sunshine," he replies easily.

It's gotta be his personality because I know damn well he's not compensating for a small dick. I've had that monster inside of me. And fuck me ... now I'm thinking about it. Sex with Isaac.

I suck in a breath and shake away those thoughts. "Why are we going to a piercing shop?" I ask.

Isaac puts the car into drive and pulls away from the curb. "Paris likes to have little get togethers there every once in a while," he says. "He's been in a foul mood this week so he's throwing a party."

I frown. "In a piercing shop?" I eye him. "Is that even legal?"

Isaac chuckles, the sound going straight down to my crotch. "You should know what money buys, Aurora," he replies. "The people who run the shop are professionals. Close friends of Paris by now, but with enough cash on the line, they'll close up early and give him access to whatever the fuck he wants so long as he signs an NDA with a clause stating neither himself nor anyone he brings will threaten to sue them."

I roll my eyes. "As if that would stop you if you really wanted to fuck them over."

He shrugs, unrepentant. "Whatever makes them feel safe," he says off-handedly as if the very thought of an average person trying to protect themselves from the upper echelon is a futile effort. I almost feel sorry for the shop owners.

There's so much more I could ask—why does his friend choose to go to a piercing shop of all places to relieve stress? What is he doing joining him? How long has he been doing this? What else does he do that I don't know about?

I don't ask any of them. I simply keep my mouth shut and rest my head along the cold window as Isaac drives us through the California streets, heading further and further from campus until he steers the front of his Escalade into a parking lot in front of a semi-familiar building.

Needle Point Piercings.

My hands twist in my lap as he parks the car and I reach for the belt buckle. Just as I press down on the button, Isaac's hand comes out and lands on mine and I jerk, my eyes moving to his face. "Wait there," he orders.

I blink, but before I can ask why, he's already turned off the vehicle and is out of the car. I track him as he moves around the hood until he stops in front of my door. The belt I've already unbuckled slides back over my shoulder as Isaac opens the door and holds out his hand. He catches my confused expression and grins, the expression transforming his face from one of brooding darkness to boyish amusement.

"You ruined my chance at helping you into the car," he answers my unspoken question as he takes my hand and leads me out, helping me use the running board beneath the door to get down to the pavement unscathed. "I couldn't let you do it again."

Self-consciousness eats away at my insides. He doesn't release my hand even when I no longer need his assistance. Instead, he pulls me from the doorway and shuts the door at my back before lifting our combined hands and kissing the back of my knuckles. "Shall we?"

My heart is pounding in my throat as he leads me, unspeaking, to the front of the shop. The sign hanging in the glass is turned to 'closed', but Isaac doesn't even hesitate. He pulls the glass door open and holds it for me to duck beneath his arm and enter the building. My inner warning bells are going haywire, but it's too late to back out now. I'm too curious to know more about this man, too deep into him to keep my head above the water. I might as well see if I can take advantage of what he's showing me. See if there's anything to use against him when the time comes.

The inside of the shop is well lit. A tall, bulky guy with stretched lobes and tattoos up both arms stands behind the counter. He looks up when we enter, and I can see the words on his lips before he says it. He's about to tell us that the shop is closed, but then his eyes move past me to Isaac and his whole demeanor changes. He straightens away from the counter and sets his phone down.

"Hey, Cooper," Isaac says, stepping up to my side. "Paris already here?"

Cooper nods and gestures to the open doorway, leading further back into the shop. "Yes, sir," Cooper says. "Already in the back with some friends."

Isaac pushes me forward and I start walking. "Thanks, man." He nods to the man, who steps to the side of the counter as we pass.

"Your private room has been reserved," he says, his gaze flicking from Isaac to me—a curiosity in the depths. *Me too, buddy,* I want to say. *I'm curious to know what he's planning too.* "Everything's been set up there too, but Paris asked that you stop in and say hi before you, as he put it, lock yourselves up in the room of shame."

Isaac laughs. "Room of shame?" I repeat.

Cooper looks at me. "I assume he meant—" he starts, only to be interrupted by a new masculine voice.

"Paris is a dick," the new man says. "And worse, he's a fucking exhibitionist—he thinks anyone who likes to do private shit behind closed doors is ashamed of themselves."

I look up and blink as I'm forced to look even further up at the man that steps into the open doorway leading to the back of the shop. "Shep." Isaac releases me to hold out a hand to the new man.

The vague familiarness of the man's features has me thinking back to where I could have possibly seen him before. Then it hits me—Hazelwood. This is one of Isaac's friends. I'd seen him that day at *BeanBerry* and again multiple times across campus and in various classes.

Shep clasps hands with Isaac, his gaze flicking to me. "You can go back to whatever you were doing, Coop," Shep says. "I'll take 'em back."

"Alright," Cooper agrees easily, nodding as he slips back behind the counter and picks up his phone once more. "Let me know if you guys need anything."

"Will do," Shep replies.

"Aurora, this is my friend." Isaac releases the man's hand and turns to me, holding out his arm, and I feel compelled to take it.

"Shepherd Hunt," the man introduces himself, holding out a hand that looks at least twice as big as Isaac's. *Jesus. What the hell do they feed him for him to be that big?* "You can call me Shep."

I take the proffered hand gingerly, but to my surprise, he's gentle as he closes his fingers around mine and squeezes once lightly before immediately releasing me. "Aurora Summers—Rori," I say, correcting myself a second late. I've gotten too used to Isaac's use of my full name.

"I'm aware of who you are." Shep steps to the side as Isaac urges me past him and down the hallway.

"The blue room," Shep calls after us as he trails behind.

I don't know what he means until Isaac takes a left turn and stops in front of a door, twisting the handle and pushing it open. "Wait here," he says. "I'm gonna go say hi to Paris. I'll be right back."

I turn and look at him. "Why can't I come?" I don't know what makes me ask the question, but it feels strange that he would bring me here and then keep me away from the very people he came to see.

Isaac winces and glances over his shoulder before returning to me. "You sure?" he asks.

I shrug. "I assume you brought me here to meet your friends, right?"

Behind him, Shep leans against the opposite wall, his massive tree-trunk-sized arms crossed over his barrel chest, watching the two of us. "Let her," he says.

Isaac's expression darkens, and he whirls to face his friend. Something passes between them. I couldn't say what it is, though, since neither of them says anything and Shep's face doesn't change. He merely stares back at Isaac until whatever it is that they're silently communicating is concluded. My lips part, ready to offer an out—a take back—but Shep pushes away from the wall and turns down the main hallway, striding out of sight.

"—if it's that big of a deal..." I start, unsure.

Isaac turns back to me and shakes his head. "No, it's fine," he says. "Shep is just being an ass."

I arch a brow. "Seems like you two have that in common."

He rolls his tongue into his cheek to stop the smile that comes to his lips, but I see it, and it does funny things to my insides. "Come on." Isaac practically pushes me towards the main hallway and then back towards the way Shep had gone.

The sound of low throbbing rock music emanates from a smoke-filled room and the closer we get, the stronger the scent of weed gets. I wrinkle my nose but keep walking. There's no stopping now. Isaac's hand is warm on my back, a direct contrast with the chilly air conditioning that floats across my skin.

Unlike the front of the shop, the back room is cast in near darkness. The only lights are the glowing neon signs on the wall and the wraparound blinking LEDs on the ceiling. There are several couches around what looks like a private waiting room. Each one is occupied by people—women. Tattooed. Untattooed. In nearly every variation of undress. The only men, it seems, are Shep, Isaac, and ... the one lying back in a wide, cushy chair with a woman straddling his lap.

"Paris." Isaac stops me as he steps closer to the man I recognize.

A dark crop of auburn hair pops up, pulling away from the woman's chest as he looks around her and grins. The stench of weed burns in my nostrils, but he doesn't seem to notice. "Isaac!" Paris slaps the girl's ass and mutters something to her that has her edging back and getting up to allow him to stand. He wavers on his feet before heading towards us. "You made it!"

Isaac doesn't speak again until Paris is standing right in front of us. "Yeah, thought I'd stop in to check on you."

Paris snorts at that. "Are you getting pierced tonight instead of just watching this time?" Isaac doesn't get an opportunity to answer before Paris' attention switches to me. "What about you, sweetheart?" He leans forward, looking me up and down. "You ever been pierced?"

"I ... uh..."

"Paris." Isaac's voice is hard. Rather than being offended or even defensive, Paris laughs, raising both hands in mock surrender as he backs away.

"Come on, I'm just asking, man," Paris says. "Besides, you ain't been 'round much lately. The least you can do is let me have a bit of fun."

I frown and cast a look at Isaac. *He hasn't been around? Funny, I feel like he's always looming right behind me.* I turn away and scan the others in the room, my gaze taking it all in.

The girls in the room are all heavily pierced. Belly buttons. Ears. Noses. Brows. Lips. Some of them even have piercings anchored in places I didn't know could be pierced—like hips and above the collarbone. Are they all here to get high and pierced again? It's a little weird to me, but who am I to kink shame?

"Thirsty?" A girl in a skin tight tank top and low hugging shorts steps up to my side and offers me a bottle of vodka. I blink at it. No cup. Just the whole damn bottle. A glance behind her, though, tells me why. There's plenty of alcohol spread around the room. More than alcohol, in fact, since there are two girls straddling each other on a couch in the corner, leaning down to snort lines of white powder from each other's tits.

"Uh..." I take it, not wanting to feel awkward. "Thanks."

She smiles and then turns away. My eyes widen as they fall to her chest where the distinct outline of pierced nipples are clearly visible. I hold onto the bottle of vodka, but let my arm drop to my side. *Wow. Just ... wow.* There's really no other thought in my head than, *holy shit. What the hell have I gotten myself into?*

"Aurora?" I jerk in surprise as Isaac's hand lands on my back and I realize that he and Paris have finished talking and his friend has returned to his chair and allowed yet another heavily pierced woman to climb onto his lap. "Let's go."

I don't ask why we're not staying behind. This might be a party by their standards, but it's obvious that this is something more private—more exclusive—to their little group and whoever the hell they decide to allow into their world for a night.

The vodka clinks against my side as I carry it back the same way we'd come until Isaac pushes me back into the room we'd been at earlier and quietly shuts the door before releasing a breath. Feeling increasingly awkward and standoffish, I carefully step further into the private room. I set the bottle on the table next to the medical chair at the center of the room, and when I turn back around, Isaac is facing me. His eyes are on me, watching me, and I feel like he's analyzing each movement. I shift on my feet.

"So..." I start, glancing away from him to scan the room. "What's this supposed to be then? Another date?"

"Sure," he answers. "You can think of it like that."

My attention returns to him as he passes me and heads for the counter at the back of the room. "How else am I supposed to think of it?" I ask him. Goosebumps rise up along the stretch of flesh revealed between the hem of my skirt and the tops of my boots.

Isaac doesn't answer. Instead, he starts opening cabinets and pulling things out to set them next to a towel laden down with what looks to be piercing equipment. "Should you be messing with that stuff?" I ask as he pulls out a brown bottle and cotton pads, setting them next to the ... clamp? I edge closer, looking over his shoulder to get a better look.

His head turns and the corner of his mouth tips up. "Are you scared?" he asks.

I blink and shake my head. "No," I say quickly. "Why would I be?"

Again there's no answer. Instead, Isaac turns to me and then wraps both hands around my waist, making me gasp as he lifts me up and sits me down in the chair. "*Isaac.*" I can't stop the trepidation in my tone. "What are you doing?"

He grins as he turns back to the equipment and picks up what looks like a wicked looking needle. He pops the brown bottle open and then holds the needle over the sink to the side and pours the liquid over it.

"I'm getting ready," he says.

"You are not using that on me," I say quickly, a warning in my tone.

Isaac looks back at me and grins. "We'll see about that," he replies, "but for now, you're right. I won't be using this on you."

"Why are you—" I don't get to finish my question as he holds up the needle and then picks up what looks like a bar with a small metal ball on either side.

He arches his brow and then drops the bomb he's been holding in. "You're going to use it on me, Sunshine."

33
RORI

"The fuck I am!"

Isaac doesn't even blink at my outburst. When I push up, ready to jump off the chair—a firm hand lands on my shoulder, keeping me down as he hooks a nearby rolling stool with his foot and drags it closer. He plops down in front of me and captures my chin in his grasp.

"Hey," he says, holding me steady. "It's okay. Don't worry."

"Worry? Why the fuck would I be worried?" My words come spitting out at a hundred miles a minute. "It's only like you're wanting me to take a dangerous weapon and stab you with it, and then what? Slide a piece of jewelry through your—where do you even want me to pierce you?" Maybe if it's just the ear, I could do it. But that bar—I shoot a look at the counter—it looks too big for something like his ear. He wouldn't want me to pierce him anywhere dangerous ... would he? My eyes shoot down to his crotch and then back to his face. I shake my head. "No." I reiterate the word to myself as much as to him. "No fucking way. I'm not doing this." I twist my shoulder, trying to rend myself from his grasp. "Let go, Isaac. You're crazy!"

Isaac grins and captures my hand, holding me in place. "Come on," he says. "You can't say you never wanted to get back at me after all I've put you through. It's only a little pinch."

"A pinch?" I gape at him. "You still haven't answered my question. What am I piercing?" He opens his mouth and sticks out his tongue, his teeth flashing white as he smiles as he does it. "Your tongue?" I look at the needle on the counter. "You want me to pierce your fucking tongue with *that*?" It seems far too big, but that could just be my anxiety making it worse than it actually is. The tongue, though, that's better than ... other places.

"We have the clamp too," he says. "It's supposed to keep me from pulling my tongue back when you 'stab me', as you put it."

"Why?" I just don't understand. Why could he possibly want me to do this? I try to think back to that night—the night I got him completely naked and all over me. But even before that, in the garden at the party—I try to think of all the times I've seen him naked or even semi-naked. I've never seen any other piercing. I look at his ears. Even those are clean of any holes.

Isaac shrugs and releases my chin as he reaches for the towel and tugs it closer across the counter until it's within reach. He's serious. Holy fucking shit. He's actually going to make me do this. He's going to put a needle in my hand and make me pierce his fucking tongue. My hands start to shake.

"Hey, hey," Isaac cups my cheek and directs my attention away from the piercing equipment and back to him. "What's wrong, Sunshine? Are you really that concerned?" His head tilts as he looks up at me. This position is so different from the norm—with *me* looking up at *him*. It feels ... like something is being traded. Something more than physical intimacy. "I didn't know if you truly cared for me that much, but if you're scared..."

I suck in a breath. *Scared?* "I'm not scared." Lie. Big fat, fucking liar. That's what I am.

He arches a brow. "Then let's do it." He grins. "Besides, I like the thought of you leaving your mark on me."

Leaving my mark on him? My thoughts center on those words as he releases me and turns back to the equipment. With careful, precise movements, he picks up each and every one of them, ripping open the plastic packaging and dumping them onto the towel. I swallow roughly. A buzzing forms beneath my skin as I watch. Like something inside of me is heating up, vibrating beneath my flesh.

Do I like the thought of leaving my mark on Isaac Icari? I'm afraid I do. All the shit he's put me through until now? It fades into the background in the face of my curiosity. Why is he even offering to let me do something like this? What is his goal? What's his aim? Is this some sort of psychological torture?

"Even if you manage to fuck it up," Isaac says as he rips open the last package, a long pair of what looks like thin scissors, except instead of sharp blades, the ends are flat and circular, leaving an opening for the piercing, I assume. "It'll heal."

"Okay." I don't know what else to say to that, so I just sit there quietly as the buzzing under my skin takes over.

It rolls through my body. I glance to the side, the bottle of vodka grabbing my attention.

Before I can think better of it, I snatch it up. Isaac pauses, maybe in surprise, maybe in confusion. Whatever the case, he doesn't stop me as I unscrew the top and tip it back, dumping a mouthful of the liquid fire down my throat. It fucking burns. I cough and gasp for breath as I lower the bottle and wipe my lips with the back of my hand.

"Feel better?" Isaac asks.

The buzzing quiets marginally. "A little," I admit.

He smirks and finishes setting things up. "Good, then I'll explain how you're going to do this."

"Do you have any other piercings?" I ask.

He blinks. "No, I don't."

"Then how do you know how to do it?"

"I've seen Paris get his done, and I've seen many of his ... well to call them girlfriends might be a bit of an over-statement, but suffice it to say—I've seen it done many times."

"But you're not a professional," I point out, "and neither am I. Are you really sure you want me to do this?"

"Aurora." The buzzing is back. Violently slamming through my system. How the hell does he *do* that? I've always hated my full name—it sounds like I'm in trouble. Coming from Isaac, though, it sounds special. Different. He's the only one who doesn't call me Rori. Damn him, but I know he's fully aware of how it makes me feel. It's there in the glittering cerulean blue of his eyes. "I'm sure." He hands me a pair of black gloves. "Now, put these on."

Nerves jump and dance along my spine, but I do as I'm commanded. I pull the gloves on, making sure my fingers are all the way through their little holes and pulling the latex tight. "Take the clamp." I'm moving on autopilot as I unclench my fingers and take the clamp.

"Good girl." He strokes my hair back away from my face. I shiver under the intensity of his gaze and those words. "Now, here's what you're going to do." I stare right into his face as he explains the process and when he's done, he makes me repeat it to him twice. The longer he talks, the less my nerves jump. It's like there's some sort of audible drug in his voice that calms me. He's got the kind of deep, soothing tone that could either put someone to sleep or make them think of dark rooms, cool sheets, and sweat soaked bodies.

Isaac tips his head back and pulls on gloves himself. "Put the tube on the needle," he orders. As I follow his orders, I realize ... I'm not shaking anymore. My hands are steady. Maybe inside, I'm rioting, but outside, I'm calm. It's a strange paradox.

"Why are you wearing gloves if I'm the one doing this?" I ask as I finish putting the tube on the needle.

He arches his brow as he takes the piercing bar and unscrews it, setting the two parts on the towel next to us before turning back to me and tipping his head back and opening his mouth. "Don't worry about it, Sunshine," he says. "Let's do this."

My gaze flickers from his eyes back down to his tongue as he lets it hang open. I slide the ends of the clamp handles through my fingers and hold on tight as I lift it and then tighten its hold on his tongue. Isaac watches me, his tongue completely still. Is that normal? I wonder absently. I thought tongues were always jumping and moving. I thought the muscles just had to.

Not Isaac's though. He's completely still. The only thing moving are his eyes and the fingers on my thighs.

He strokes me gently, his thumb rubbing back and forth as I clamp him and then lift the needle, pointing it to the underside of his tongue.

One. I take a breath.

Two. I meet his gaze.

Three. I pierce his tongue.

The needle slides through his flesh easily—too easily. It kind of surprises me. The tube goes up with it, and I quickly take the needle out, dropping it onto the towel. I reach for the long part of the bar piercing and slide it into the tube through Isaac's tongue.

I concentrate on the task at hand, repeating the process Isaac explained to me over and over again in my head. Pull the tube back through with the piercing. The tube lands on the towel. Isaac doesn't even flinch as I remove the clamp. His eyes are centered squarely on me. I drop the clamp and pick up the ball, screwing it onto the bottom of the piercing bar. Blood smears my latex covered fingers, lingering on the top and bottom of his tongue.

Now, I have to clean it. But...

I look at the bottle of piercing cleaner sitting next to the used tools and then over to the side.

"What are you thinking, Sunshine?" Isaac's voice is slurred with his tongue hanging slightly out.

"Marking you..." I murmur as I pick up the bottle of vodka. His eyes widen ever so slightly as I keep my gaze on him and tip the bottle back. This time, though, I don't swallow.

I grab ahold of his chin and lean over him. My lips part and he keeps his mouth open for me. Blood smears on his chin from my fingers as I hold him steady and release the stream of vodka directly onto his tongue, from my mouth to his. The alcohol flows over the top of the piercing and then down further into his mouth.

Isaac's eyes grow darker, the cerulean blue turning to midnight as his pupils dilate, overtaking the color. His hands clench and unclench as I finish and his mouth closes and he swallows what I've given him.

When he opens his mouth once more, the flash of his new piercing under the fluorescent lighting draws my attention. "More," he rasps.

I tip my head back again, dumping more alcohol into my mouth and he edges closer. His body takes up residence between my legs. He tips his head back and opens his mouth, waiting. I hover over him, letting the vodka dribble onto his tongue. This time, when he swallows and opens his mouth again, he doesn't say anything. Instead, his hand comes up and grasps at the back of my head and he draws me down until our lips crash together.

Isaac's kiss is hypnotic. It tastes like rust and vodka. Raw and unfiltered. I close my eyes and set the alcohol to the side before wrapping my arms around his shoulders. Pressing closer, I let myself be taken by his kiss. His confidence in everything drives me crazy everywhere else but here. Here, in his arms, it's hard to get myself to remain steady.

It must hurt him, I think, as he slides his tongue into my mouth. But he doesn't act like it. It's a fresh piercing. Still, some blood leaks as he kisses me, invading my senses with his taste. I should be worried. *His* blood on *my* tongue? It's ... definitely not something I should let happen. Yet, I can't stop it. I don't *want* to stop it. It makes my insides throb.

"Isaac." I gasp his name when he pulls back and whatever expression he sees on my face has him gritting his teeth and then reaching back. He yanks his shirt over his head and drops it to the side.

I am entranced by him. My hands drop down to his chest along with my eyes. He's ripped. His body honed and muscled likely from football. He's not a man with massive shoulders, but they're enough to encompass me. Then there are the two lines leading like arrows down into the top of his jeans, pointing towards his still hidden cock. I swallow. I've already had it—in my mouth, in my pussy—so I know how big it is and exactly how it makes me feel.

His hands move to my thighs, the feel of black latex startling as he pushes the skirt I'm wearing up higher and higher. He tilts his head down. "Aurora." The tone of his voice combined with the electric feel of his hands on my skin has me jumping slightly as I look up at his face. "Do you like marking me?"

I press my lips together, but there's no denying my answer. I nod. Yeah, I did like it. Whatever is going on between us, I liked leaving a hole inside of him. A wound that I created. A reminder of me for him.

He groans and dips his head down again until the silky locks of his hair are brushing against my breasts. I've never wanted to strip my clothes away so much in my life. Behind the fabric of my shirt and bra, my nipples pucker and harden into tight points. They reach for him, craving his lips and tongue.

"I want to mark you too," he confesses. His head moves again and he looks up at me, eyes full of light and a strange sort of innocence. Isaac Icari? Innocent? No. That adjective doesn't fit him. Yet, he looks boyish and youthful like this. His curls flop to one side of his forehead as he clings to me, almost begging. "Let me..." He pauses as his fingers stop moving on my inner thighs and I realize what's made him stop.

They're wet. My thighs. They're absolutely soaked with the evidence of what he does to me—of what piercing him and marking him did to me.

"You're going to let me," he says, changing his words as his fingers slip through the wetness, making my breath catch in my throat. It feels strange with the gloves. It should make his touch less potent considering his flesh isn't on mine, but that's not the case. In fact, it makes the intensity skyrocket.

With my hands on his shoulders, he feels the trembles that encase me as he moves up further, towards the throbbing place between my thighs. "Yes, you are..." he whispers.

Isaac pushes me back until my spine is flat on the table and my head hangs over the opposite side. He shoves my skirt hem over my stomach, flipping it out of his way before he hooks one thigh over his shoulder and then the other.

I'm gasping for breath. Shivering with each passing second. My skin feels both frozen and on fire. *How does he do this to me?* I close my eyes, counting down from ten as I try to suck in as much oxygen as I can. His hot breath brushes over my panties and my insides clench in anticipation.

"That's right, goddess," Isaac breathes against me. "Just let me take care of you. Don't move. Let me feel you. Let me mark you just as you marked me. Good girl."

I put my wrist up to my mouth and rip my gloves off with my teeth, tossing the first one over the side of the table and then the second. I know what's about to happen and he might be alright to fuck my pussy with his gloves on, but I want to feel his hair in my grip when he makes me come.

Isaac pulls my underwear to the side and my hands shoot into his hair as his head dips and just before the fireworks explode in my head, I hear his last words. *"Good fucking girl."*

34
ISAAC

Aurora is burning under my fingertips. She's alive. Fiery. Red hot. Every brush of her flesh against mine lights me up inside. She is a craving. A desire I've never known. To need someone is to risk yourself. Needing someone isn't healthy. It's wrong. Yet, here and now, I *need* her like I need my next breath. Like denying myself her taste, her body, would be to drive the final nail into my coffin.

She drives me to the brink of insanity and instead of taking a step back, instead of saving myself and doing the *right* thing, I let her push me over. I pull Aurora's panties to the side and get my first hit of her gorgeous pussy. Just as I expected, she's ready and ripe for the taking. I don't want to rush this, though, I want to savor my victory.

I know well enough that this is breaking all sorts of rules. It's a damn good thing Paris pays the owner of this shop enough that he doesn't ask questions. Truly, if I actually gave a fuck about the damn piercings, I'd be careful with them. I'm not supposed to do this, but the need for

Aurora's cunt—her come all over my tongue and down my throat is too much. It's greater.

Despite the soreness in my tongue, I lean down and grin as her thighs clench around my ears. I lick a path straight up her soaked opening. Her back bows off the table and a choked sound escapes her throat as she squirms on my face. Warm, ungloved fingers slide through my hair. Ahhh, that's what's wrong. My hands remain gloved—that's alright, I need to keep them on for what comes after.

I flick the tip of my tongue over her pearl-like clit and relish the feel of her fingers tightening in my hair a split second before I finally give up teasing her and take her pussy the way I want to. I drive my tongue into her opening, lapping her juices up and swallowing them as they drain into my throat. It's only a touch, only a taste, and already she's sensitive.

Her moans echo in my ears as she rubs herself against my mouth. A needy little goddess, indeed. She's practically begging me with her movements, and her body, to take her. My tongue lashes back out, first up one side of her labia and down the other as she trembles all around me. I return to her clit and as if it's the easiest most natural thing in the world, I clamp the bar now piercing my tongue between my teeth, pushing the little ball at the end out of my mouth as I rub it along her clit.

I'll have to get a vibrating one soon just to do this all over again and see how long she lasts on my mouth. A fresh wave of wetness gushes out and I reach up to her hole, swirling my fingers into her juices and pushing them back up inside of her. Even through the latex, I can feel her inner muscles contract.

"Isaac!" A choked scream escapes her mouth above

and her fingers tighten in my hair. I'm not done. I won't be, not until that scream of hers is free and loud. I want to hear what I do to her and I want to hear it fucking ringing in my ears.

I thrust my fingers in and out of her pussy as I torture her little clit with my lips and piercing. When it's not enough, I dive down and suction my mouth around the hard little nub, gently scraping it with my teeth ever so lightly—giving her the tiniest brush of sharpness combined with the softness of my tongue.

That does it for her. Her gasps turn up and a groan of release pours out of my girl as my fingers thrust faster. Her orgasm floods over my digits, soaking my hand and her thighs all over again. She shakes. She clamps her legs around my head as if she means to trap me here forever. Perhaps another time, I'd let her, but with how rock hard my cock is in my pants, there's no way I'm letting her get away from me tonight without a little more.

As much as I don't want to, I unlock her legs from around me and drop them back to the edge of the table. Eyelashes fluttering and cheeks flushed, Aurora props herself up on the table on her elbows. Her face is so dewy and fresh that it makes me want to ruin her.

My hands dive beneath her skirt and I strip her panties down her legs, lifting them as they slide up her thighs and calves and off her feet. Instead of tossing them to the side, I carefully lift them up to my face and inhale her scent. I've done this before, and fuck, it's just as good the second time around. Aurora's eyes meet mine and widen, and I grin as I tuck them back into my pocket and then reach for her again.

She comes willingly, letting me divest her of her shirt and bra, dropping them over the side of the table. Her breasts are round and full. I heft them in my hands, cupping the flesh in my palms as I bend my head and take first one nipple in my mouth, sucking and flicking it with my tongue until it's shiny and wet from my saliva before delivering the same treatment to the other. A thought strikes my mind. Perhaps a clit piercing is pushing things too far, but her nipples are hard and perfect. Just right for what I want to do.

I release the latest one from my mouth as I hover over her, holding them as her gaze touches mine. "You're a fucking naughty girl, goddess," I tell her. "Coming all over my mouth like that. Did that make you feel good? Did you feel like you shared your divinity with me? Do you want to do it again?"

Pink heat steals across her face, but instead of getting shy, Aurora's head tips back and her lips part. "You always say such filthy things," she muses.

"You like it."

The smile she gives me is all I fucking need in this world. "Yeah," she admits. "Maybe I do. I'm sure that makes me a..." She drifts off, that blush burning brighter. How adorable, she still struggles to say it. Slut. Whore. Filthy little goddess. *Mine.* She swallows roughly and her smile falls away. "What does it make you though?" she switches topics. "A pervert?"

I chuckle. "Yeah, I'm the worst pervert imaginable." Bad enough that I know what to say to get her where I want her. "Now that you've marked me, what do you say I mark you back?"

She pulls back slightly, frowning as her brows lower over her eyes. "How?"

Her tits fall away from my palms as I reach for the equipment to the side of us. I know exactly where everything is in this room. I've been in it enough times and have watched enough people get pierced in damn near every fashion imaginable. Though it never truly appealed to me before now, I can't stop picturing Aurora Summers with her tits glittering at the tips with little silver piercings. I flick one nipple as I pick up the clamp and set it next to her.

"Isaac?" Her voice trembles as she watches me reach into a drawer and withdraw a few more needles and piercings wrapped in plastic packaging. She seems nervous, but after that orgasm—one I can still taste on my lips—she's not quite as jumpy as she was before. Maybe the alcohol helped some.

"You would look so sexy," I say, "with your pretty nipples pierced."

"I don't know, Isaac." She shakes her head.

"Did it look like you hurt me?" I press. "Are you still scared of me?"

Aurora's soft amber gaze hardens and her lips twist. "Don't do that," she snaps.

"Do what?" I feign innocence as I begin ripping open packages.

"Manipulate me," she says. "I know exactly why you're doing it. I don't want a piercing."

"Oh really?" My hand lands between her tits and I shove her back down on the table, climbing on top of her.

She struggles as I take her arms and pin them beneath my legs. "Isaac! Stop it!" Aurora's face grows redder with anger as her yells turn to frustration.

"I'd prefer to pierce your pretty clit," I tell her honestly, watching her face go slack with shock and apprehension as I prep the materials.

She gasps. "*No.*"

I take a clamp and pinch it around one nipple. She flinches. "Yes," I tell her, "but if I did, I'd have to leave you alone for a few weeks. I'd have to let you heal before I could torture you further."

"Isaac—I don't—stop, *ahhh!*—" She tries to twist her upper body, but as she does, I tighten the clamp and she gasps and stills.

"Careful, Sunshine," I say with a grin. "This bites."

I settle the needle against the side of the clamp as tears prick at her eyes. She watches my hands with wide, concerned eyes. It makes me such a fucking bastard to see her fear and get off on it, but I can't help it. I allowed her to mark me and this is the price of that.

"Isaac, *please.*" Aurora's eyes bore up into me, hopeful and almost begging. It gives me pause.

I flick my tongue against the roof of my mouth, feeling the metal bar there scrape my hard palate. "Everything I give you comes at a price, Aurora," I tell her gently. "I let you mark me, now it's my turn."

"Ahhh!" Aurora screams as I shove the needle through, her head tipping back over the table again. I go through the rest of the process, putting in the piercing bar and screwing it on before removing the clamp. A bit of blood drips over her breast and as her head lifts again, I keep my eyes anchored to hers as I lean down and lick it away.

"One more, Sunshine."

She shakes her head as tears slide down her temples. "You fucking asshole," she snaps. Her chest is splotchy, her pretty nipple red with abuse. It looks like a delicious ruby with twin silver balls on either side of it. I clamp her other breast as she curses me.

"Ow, you bastard! That hurts," she hisses. Eyes made

of burned soil glare at me. "I will fucking hurt you for this, Isaac. I don't want it!"

"Really?" I taunt, reaching down between her legs. She bucks beneath me, but I hardly move as my fingers slide over her pussy and when I lift them again, I hold them in front of her reddening face. "Does this look like a 'no' to you?" I ask, pressing my fingers together and pulling them apart slowly so she can see the string of her own juices sticking to the latex.

"That means nothing," she argues.

"And this?" I stick out my tongue, rolling my own new piercing—sore and still tasting of a mixture of her come and my blood—around in my mouth. "You marked me, baby. It's my turn. This is justified."

"You made me!" she screams, bucking against me once more. I pinch the second clamp tighter and a tear leaks from the corner of her eye as she flashes me a look that could flay a man alive.

"Keep looking at me like that, goddess, and I'm liable to come," I say.

She growls as I wipe my gloves clean and then pick up the needle again. Only then do her eyes widen once more and she starts to shake her head. "No, no, no!"

I smirk and ignore her words as I slide the next needle through her other nipple. She screams again and shakes under me. More tears descend from her eyes as I slide the jewelry into her nipple and tighten the ball until she's matching. I clean the area around her new piercings and finally just sit back to take her in.

"Gorgeous..." I don't necessarily mean to compliment her, but the truth spills out as I cup her round, full breasts and squeeze them in my hands.

"Fuck. You," she grits out.

My gloves come off and I slide my hand back down to her pussy, just to make sure, and *ah ... fuck,* she's still so fucking drenched. "I bet you want to," I reply snidely, pulling my hands free from her cunt.

A smile twitches my lips and I meet her gaze as I lean over her. She turns her face from me the second she realizes what I'm after, but that won't do. I grab her jaw and twist her to look at me once more. Aurora kicks at the table underneath me, throwing her legs up and down in a fit. The bottle of vodka next to us tips over.

My hand snaps out and grabs it as some of it splashes across the table and over the edge onto the floor. She clamps her lips shut as I lift it to my lips. The first mouthful goes down like liquid fire, burning into my esophagus. The second, though, is held complacent on my tongue as I bend back over her, pinching her cheeks and jaw.

Our eyes clash, wicked and devious. Still, she refuses to open to me. I can't help it—I like the fight in her. But I'm determined and I always get what I want. I let the bottle go and pinch her nose shut. Ten seconds. Twenty. Thirty. I don't fucking care how long I have to wait. We're repeating this process. What she did to me is what I'll do for her. Tit for tat. A tradition I didn't know we needed. If she passes out and I have to pry her lips apart to spit this vodka in her mouth then so be it. She makes it almost a full minute until it becomes too much for her.

Aurora's lips part as she gasps for breath. I give her a second, letting her suck in one breath, two, and then I open my mouth and let the vodka fall against her tongue. Eyes promising retribution, Aurora has no other option but to swallow what I give her. She takes it and just when she thinks it's about to end, I shove two fingers between her lips. The same fingers that had been inside of her.

She chokes in shock, eyes going wild and round. "That's right, goddess," I say. "Suck your cum from my fingers. Taste how fucking wet I make you. How all that struggling still didn't turn you off."

Her gaze narrows. Oh, yeah, she wants revenge. She feels humiliated. Degraded. My proud goddess. It's not quite over just yet though. I pull my fingers free and then lower them to my jeans. I unzip and free myself from the confines of my pants.

"What do you think you're doing?" she demands, gasping for breath.

With one hand, I reach down and squeeze one of her breasts as I use her juices as slick for my cock. I stroke myself over her, from base to tip and back again. With her lying under me, my cock practically throbs with need. I don't answer her, but I don't need to. She can see exactly what I'm doing.

I thrust myself into my fist over and over again and with her skin right there. Her beautiful face and pierced tits, red and swollen because I made them that way. The tears still lingering in her angry gaze as she promises to fuck me just as hard as I fuck her makes me strain into my hand. It doesn't take long for me to lose my tightly leashed control. When I come, it jets out of my cock in long ropes. It splashes across her tits and up her throat. Aurora shuts her eyes as I groan and more cum shoots out onto her face. Streaking her cheeks and over her lips until she's marked by more than piercings.

My hand flies over my shaft, pumping it, and I direct the last of my orgasm down. From one nipple to the other, I cover her in white ropes. When I'm finally spent and shaking from the aftermath of my own orgasm, she peeks her eyes open at me.

"You look so fucking good covered in my cum, Sunshine," I tell her with a grin.

"You better relish it while you've got it, Isaac," she replies. "Because the second you let me up, I'm going to make you regret your selfish fucking actions."

"Are you?" I ask. With gentle fingers, I tweak her nipple, scooping a fingertip of my cum off her breast and painting her lips with it.

She parts her lips and I sink my finger back into her mouth only to flinch as she locks her teeth around it and bites down hard. She releases me quickly enough and smiles up at me when I turn my hand over, seeing the blood she's drawn on my knuckle. I didn't think it was possible for a woman to look so threatening from such a submissive position, yet she manages it. She's a spiteful goddess.

I don't crawl off of her just yet, not when I know I need to clean her up. After all the blood and piercings and cum, it's only right that I take care of what's mine after I've so thoroughly corrupted it. With movements as gentle as I can manage, I grab a towel and wipe most of my cum from her skin, a little disappointed in myself for not thinking better of it and just shoving my cock into her mouth and coming down her throat.

Her fresh nipple piercings need better care than I've given them. Still, even as I clean her with the appropriate supplies and gentle swabbing, I can't say I regret it. If given the choice, I'd probably do it all over again.

After all, there's just something animalistic about her and I. Something that makes me lose my fucking mind.

"Just remember, Icarus," she says, using my pseudonym from the garden as she distracts me from my chore. "You put your hand in the fire and you'll get burned."

I pull away from her, getting off the table and then reaching back to help her into a sitting position. Though she tries to yank her arms from me, I grasp her wrists and yank her against my chest—savoring the feel of her hard, pointed nipples scraping across my pecs.

"Then burn me," I tell her. "Or better yet, Aurora ... burn *with* me."

35
RORI

Just when I think Isaac isn't as fucked up as he portrays, he goes and does something that completely fucks me in the head. My boobs hurt. They're sore and they ache. So much so that I hesitate to even wear the thinnest of bras in the days following the night in the piercing shop. I could've taken them out. After that night, I looked up to see if it would cause any problems and I know that if I just remove the piercings, the holes will close and heal. Only ... I'm struggling to do it. Instead, I found myself switching my research to care. How to clean them. How to care for them.

Maybe Isaac was fucked up for doing what he did, but I'm just as fucked up for not erasing the evidence and letting it remain behind—like both a badge of honor and sexual humiliation.

After the research, I spent the weekend sequestered in my room—away from Hel and Selene both. Sure, after the little sex session, Isaac had cleaned me up thoroughly. He'd taken extra care disinfecting the piercings—both mine and his. His attention to detail is so like him. One thing I've learned is that he's a control freak. Just remembering the way he'd pinned me down on the table beneath him and how he'd stroked his cock to completion over my face and tits makes me shiver.

Am I a pervert? It's a legit question. Before Isaac, my response would have been an absolute and confident 'no,' but since hanging around him, my confidence is waning. I'm starting to think I'm more like him than I ever believed possible.

I toss my pen down on my bed and groan. There's only so much homework I can do when my head is full of nothing but an asshole that won't leave me alone. As I slide off my bed, a knock sounds on my door. I glance down at my t-shirt, noting the little pricks of my new piercings sticking out beneath the fabric. Quickly snatching up a loose-fitting sweatshirt, I throw it on and open the door.

Hel stands there with a frown and a deep v in her forehead. "Hey, what's up?" I lean against the door jam.

"Have you heard from Selene?" she asks.

I tilt my head to the side and turn back to my room, leaving the door hanging open as I go to grab my phone from the bed. I open the last messages I received and scan down until I find Selene's name. "No," I answer, turning back to Hel. "Not since Friday."

Hel crosses her arms over her chest and bites her lower lip. "I've been texting her all weekend and she hasn't replied," she says.

"She said her mom was coming into town," I remind her gently. "She's probably just locked up with work and catering to her." Hel blows out a breath but doesn't seem put at ease by my comment. I slip my phone into my back pocket. "Is there a reason you're worried?"

She shrugs. "I don't know. I just have a weird feeling."

"I'm sure she's just busy," I say. "You're probably just worried because you know how her mom can be."

The eye roll that follows that statement is exactly what I'm talking about. I chuckle as Hel nods. "Yeah, you're probably right. She's such a fucking bitch. I can't believe Sel was worried about her weight. She only ever gets like this when her mom is around."

I agree, but I don't say as much. Instead, I gently push past her to head through the living room and into our small kitchen. My stomach grumbles as I pop open the fridge and listen to the soft pad of Hel's footsteps following after me. "Are you hungry?" I ask, pulling out a few containers of leftover pasta from earlier in the week.

Hel doesn't respond immediately. I pop open the top and sniff the contents before slipping them into the microwave and hitting an estimated time to heat them up. When I turn and arch my brow at her, it's to find her watching me with careful consideration.

"You good?" I ask.

She tilts her head down. "Depends," she replies.

"Okay..." I frown. "On what?"

"You," she answers.

"What about me?"

"Well..." She leans against the counter, her gaze never dropping from mine. "Sel isn't the only one who's been acting a little off lately. You've been locked in your room all weekend. That's not like you."

I press my lips together and glance away from her penetrating gaze. "It's nothing," I lie. "I just have a lot of homework to get done. I want to catch up as much as I can because I know that once my mom gets back to me about her stupid reception, I'll have no time to focus on school."

While normal mothers concern themselves about their children's grades and school lives, mine would rather the attention go to her—when she's available anyway.

"Uh huh." Hel's tone suggests her disbelief. I ignore it and instead turn my attention to the microwave as it beeps. I pull out the pasta and stir it with a fork, watching steam rise as I try a bite. Cheesy Alfredo touches my lips and I flinch at the temperature, but cover my mouth with my free hand and blow out the excess heat before swallowing.

"Alright, cut the bullshit." I nearly choke as Hel steps up to my side and turns, propping herself up right next to me as she levels me with a clearly frustrated look. "What's going on between you and that guy?"

Swallowing the mouthful of food, I inhale sharply and push the container across the counter. "It's ... complicated," I admit.

She rolls her eyes again. "When isn't it complicated regarding men?"

That's a rhetorical question if I've ever heard one, but I choose to answer it, anyway. "When they're too dumb to play mind games."

She laughs and shakes her head. "Don't think you're getting out of this conversation with jokes, Rori."

I groan. "It was worth a try—you're like a pitbull when you latch onto a topic."

"More like a chihuahua," she replies. "Pitbulls are big babies. It's the ankle biters you gotta look out for."

"Is that what you are?" I smile. "An ankle biter?"

"I don't know," she says, eyeing me. "Depends on if you piss me off. Now, enough fucking around—*spill.*"

Shit. I go to cross my arms over my chest in a protective measure, only to pause and wince when I accidentally rub my sore nipples. She picks up on the small flinch immediately and her eyes slide down to my chest. "Rori?"

Oh fuck it, she's going to find out anyway. I groan and then slip my arms out of my sweatshirt. The second I pull it over my head and drop it onto the kitchen counter, her eyes go round. I don't need to completely strip for her to see exactly what I'm about to tell her.

"Holy fucking shit!" she snaps. "Did you pierce your nipples?"

"Not exactly," I reply. "He did."

She blinks at me. Honestly, the slack expression on her face would make me laugh if it weren't for such a serious reason. Her gaze goes from my breasts back to my face. "He did?" she repeats as if she can't believe what she just heard. "Isaac *pierced* your nipples?"

"If it's any consolation, I pierced his tongue." Except he'd wanted me to pierce his tongue and him piercing my nipples hadn't exactly been my choice.

"What the fuck?" Hel gapes at me as if I've suddenly sprouted a second head with a dozen eyeballs. "You—he— you let him—" She stops and shakes her head, and I have to admit that if I were in her position, I would be just as flabbergasted.

I turn back to my food and pick it back up. I watch her push away from the counter as I shovel more pasta into my mouth. Hel paces back and forth, muttering to herself as she goes. She doesn't turn back to me, though, until I'm more than halfway through my meal. By then, I'm feeling stuffed. I dump the last of the pasta into the trash and toss the now-empty container into the sink.

"What does this mean?" Hel demands. "Are you two together?"

"It's..." I roll my tongue against the inside of my cheek, trying to come up with an answer that doesn't make me sound crazy. There isn't one, though. "I don't know," I finally say with a sigh.

She stares at me. "You let a man pierce your nipples and you don't know if you're even together?" she repeats. "Who are you and where's the Aurora Summers I know?"

I give a halfhearted shrug. "Listen, she's—*I'm*—just as confused as you are."

"Oh, are you?" She flips away from me and more muttering ensues. She's talking so fast and quietly, but every once in a while, I catch a curse or two. Yeah, I get it. She's always been the mom of our friend group and now she's watched me dive off the deep end. Hell, *I'm* the one in the water and even I'm concerned.

Hel finally stops her pacing. "This is ridiculous. You need to stop seeing him."

I blink at her—not unlike the way she'd done to me earlier. "Are you suggesting or telling me?"

She crosses her arms back over her chest and glares back at me. "Telling."

"And you think that's going to work?" I scowl. "That you just tell me what to do with my life and I'll just agree and do what you say?"

"He's dangerous, Rori!" Hel snaps. "You have to see that—plus he's your *stepbrother*—"

"I know what he is!" I yell back. Fuck that word. I hate it. Fucking stepbrother. His father's marriage to my mother won't even last, but Isaac ... Isaac will ... I stop myself. Isaac will what? He'll last? He'll stick around after they divorce? Will he? Can I count on that?

"See!" Hel points at my face. "You're not even sure about him yourself. Otherwise, you'd know what the two of you are. There's not even a label there. Are you going to date him? After everything he's done to you? What about that video? Does he even know about why they treated you like that? Has he asked you anything about yourself that didn't somehow lead to him getting in your pants?"

I scrub a hand down my face. "Stop," I say. "Please, I just—I need to think." I turn away from her.

"Thinking is what got you into this mess," she continues. "You need to end things. Whatever is going on between the two of you, you need to walk away. It's only going to get more complicated from here."

"I asked you to fucking stop!" I snap, whirling back on her. "Can't you just listen for fucking once instead of judging me!"

Hel's brows lower over her eyes and her lips twist. "I'm not trying to judge you."

"Oh no?" I scoff. "That's all you fucking do. You stay quiet and you judge everyone around you. All the rich bitches who don't know what it's like to live in the real world. Well, guess what, Hel, you're a rich bitch now too. You're just like the rest of us."

Hel inhales sharply and straightens her back. "I've never fucking judged you for your family's money," she says quietly. "Everything I've ever done or said to you has been for my friend. You're my friend. I'm worried about you and I think you don't realize how easily you're being manipulated. Isaac Icari is not your boyfriend. He's a guy who's fucking you to get back at his dad."

"Didn't you hear a word I said? I told you that it's complicated," I snap. "There's more to it than his fucking dad and my mom. His dad is—" I cut myself off. I can't tell her. It's not right. Everything Marcus knows. What Isaac said. It's too dangerous. She's right about one thing —this whole situation is dangerous, but I don't have a choice anymore. As much as I wish I could walk away, the time for that has passed.

"If you want me to stop caring, fine." Hel steps back and throws up her hands. "I hope you know what you're doing, Rori. For your sake, I hope he doesn't break your heart."

It's not heartbreak that I'm worried about, but I can't tell her that. The situation with Isaac is more than the two of us. His dad is dangerous. I know that much, but there's still more that I don't know too. More that I need to find out.

My phone buzzes in my back pocket and I rip it free as I hear the door to Hel's bedroom slam shut. At first, I think it's him. It seems like whenever I think of Isaac, he appears in some form. I stare down at the screen, but the number that's become so familiar to me accompanied by Isaac's name, isn't the one I see.

It's Marcus.

36

ISAAC

Twenty or thirty years ago, a bar like the one I'm currently sitting in would have been overwhelmingly filled with a cloud of cigarette smoke. Now it's filled with the scent of too much cologne and desperation. I lift the last of the whiskey in my glass to my lips and down it, waiting.

With the baseball cap drawn down low over the upper half of my face and my usual brand-name clothes traded in for a cheaper t-shirt and pair of jeans, I know I don't look like myself. Even the bartender, despite how long I've sat here, hasn't come back. It's amazing to me how much a change of clothes can alter people's perceptions.

When I'm dressed like I have money, the amount of attention I receive is so natural. Now, it feels as though I've become invisible, and even though that's exactly what I'm going for, it's enough to make me pause and think a little deeper on how external the rest of the world is. How many assumptions affect the way we think and act.

A stool two spaces down scrapes out as a familiar man

takes his seat. Like me, Agent Brown has altered his look as well—in the opposite direction of my own facade. I don't know where he got the Armani suit he's wearing, but he draws the bartender's eye almost immediately. I'm the only one who looks out of place in a ritzy hotel bar like this—a traveler likely here on someone else's dime. Whereas Agent Brown appears every inch the well-off businessman.

"Manhattan," he says before the bartender has a chance to open his mouth. Unsurprisingly, too, the bartender nods and heads off, not even bothering to slide a glance at my now-empty glass.

"You're late." My words are low, barely audible, but Agent Brown hears me.

"You're not the only one being careful," he replies. A moment later, the bartender returns and sets his Manhattan down before him.

I lift my glass and shake it at the man. "Hey, I think this was too rich for my blood, man," I say. "You mind if I get a Bud Light?"

The bartender's shoulders drop and I see the slight twist of his lips as he reaches under the counter and produces a brown and blue bottle. He pops the cap off and sets it in front of me before striding off. I smirk and lift the bottle to my lips. Whether it's liquor or beer, all alcohol eventually does the same thing.

"I heard your father's back," Agent Brown states.

"He's hosting a party to celebrate his nuptials. I'll be in attendance," I reply. "I'm sure I'll be able to find something there that you can use."

Agent Brown lifts his glass and stares into the amber liquid. His lips twist. "I hate Vermouth," he mutters absently, almost to himself.

"Next time, go for something easier and not so pompous, then," I reply.

"Yeah, probably a good idea." He sets the drink down without taking a sip. "Unfortunately, I've got some bad news for you."

My spine stiffens, and it takes every molecule of effort I possess to force myself to relax back into my original leisurely pose. It's hard enough to pretend to be someone else. I feel like I'm playing some sort of spy game in which I've been given very little information and not a single weapon with which to protect myself. Focusing on my role is the only thing keeping me from cracking.

"Tell me." Despite the forced laxness in my body, my tone is stern.

"The brass isn't happy with how long it's taken to get shit done," Brown states. "They've added on a new agent."

"A partner?"

He shakes his head. "No. They want him to work a new angle and I'm supposed to keep working mine."

"Who?"

"Who doesn't matter, all you need to know is that he's already contacted Marcus Summers."

Aurora's brother? I frown. "Why? He's not even at Hazelwood anymore. He transferred to Eastpoint."

"Yes, we're aware." Brown finally lifts the glass as the bartender comes back over and asks him if he's enjoying himself. Brown nods and takes a sip and the bartender smiles and disappears once more down the line. He waits until the man is out of earshot before he speaks. "The new agent is working from the outside in, and I remember how..." He pauses, his gaze sliding my way before it skitters away and he continues, "*disinterested* you were in bringing Mrs. Icari's daughter into it, so I thought you should be warned. This new agent won't be as accommodating as I've been. He'll want to bring her in under any means necessary."

Well, now I suppose I understand the pause. He was trying to figure out the best way to word himself in such a way so as not to offend me. I'm familiar enough with the process of tiptoeing around a more powerful opponent that I can see it in others as if I'm looking in a mirror. My fingers squeeze around the beer bottle in my hand until I don't feel the cold anymore.

"Aurora Summers is off limits," I say, forcing casualness into my tone.

"To me," Agent Brown agrees.

"*To everyone*," I clarify.

"I tried to shut down the notion, but this new guy isn't exactly on the up and up. He's doing what he wants and he's willing to do whatever it takes if it means taking down Damien."

"Even if it means innocent people are killed in the process?" My words are cold, but my insides are on fire. Rage descends like a haze over my vision. "If she dies, you get nothing. If Damien kills her, we're done. *Do you understand?*" I hiss the last words through my teeth.

Brown is quiet and then he sighs. "I have no intention of putting innocent women in the line of fire, Isaac, but I have no control over this new agent. We might be working the same case, but we're *not* together. My bosses are fed up with waiting. Even if Marcus is absent from the city and outside of Damien's current purview, he's still connected. He'll come back for this sister, and he's got connections there too. Marcus might not be an extreme threat to Damien, but he's got friends in high places. There are plenty of connections from Eastpoint to Hazelwood and the Icari empire. Plenty of angles to work and the bosses want every single one seen through."

"I don't give a rat's ass if Marcus Summers is used in your bid to get to my father—it won't work, certainly not with the distance—but I'm warning you now, Brown, if anything happens to Aurora because the Feds don't know their heads from their own asses, I will ensure that neither you nor this new agent of yours has a job left."

Brown's head turns slightly towards me. "I'm surprised by you, Isaac," he says. "I didn't think you'd pull the rich kid 'I'll have your job' threat."

I meet the man's gaze. "I'm not threatening your job, Brown," I tell him quietly. "If something happens to that girl, you'll be too fucking dead to worry about your employment."

"Are you threatening a federal agent, Icari?" Agent Brown's voice deepens.

My smile is full of teeth and promise. "Yes," I say. "I am."

With that, I reach into my back pocket and pull out my wallet. I slam a hundred on the counter and leave my unfinished beer, turning and striding through the hotel and out the lobby doors until I reach the parking lot across the street. I'm practically vibrating with repressed violence and I don't notice my phone ringing until I'm already in my car.

When I take a glance at the screen, a brief bolt of panic hits me. There's no time to quiet it, though, or pretend. I take a look around the lot as I answer, wondering if the fucker is having me followed or if his sudden call is nothing more than a coincidence.

"Isaac." I crank the engine and reverse the vehicle from my parking spot.

"Emilia is hosting our reception this weekend," are the first words out of my father's mouth. "I wanted to make sure that you would have Aurora attend."

I grind my teeth together, briefly wondering why he hasn't contacted her himself when it hits me. A smirk rises to my lips. "She won't answer your calls, will she?" I guess.

His brief moment of silence is my answer and I have to repress a laugh. That's my girl. So feisty. "Regardless of whether she approves of this marriage or not, she will attend," my father states. "You will make sure of it. Emilia wants to see her daughter."

And I just bet he's already becoming quite tired of playing the doting, romantic husband. "What if she refuses?"

"Isaac." The tone of his voice drops. "I'm sure you understand just how important this relationship is to me— to my business."

"You've never quite explained that," I remind him. "All I know is that you need Emilia's connections. Perhaps I'd be more affable to your demands if I understood *why* it is that you need them?"

Come on, old man, I silently urge. *Give me something. A reason. A path to follow to catch your ass.*

My father chuckles darkly. "It's been quite a while since you've been so rebellious, Son." God, how I fucking hate it when he calls me that. "Perhaps you're done with your childish bullying of your new stepsister and have now moved onto a different form of torture?"

"What?" He can't know. There's no fucking way...

"You forget, Isaac," Damien says quietly. "I have eyes

and ears everywhere. Even if they're not in your penthouse, I know what goes on at Hazelwood University—especially when it concerns my son and his stepsister."

"I don't know what you're talking about."

Damien chuckles, and the very sound sends chills up my spine. Yeah, he fucking knows. What else does he know? He can't know about Agent Brown. There'd be more than a small chat over the phone if he knew I was working with the Feds. There'd be no fucking mercy. Still, my muscles contract as if the man, himself, is standing right before me.

"I don't care if you're fucking the girl, Isaac," my father tells me. "In fact, considering the entertainment her mother has provided—if the two are anything alike—I completely understand the appeal." *Fucking bastard.* My hands tighten further on the steering wheel until it creaks beneath the pressure. "Just make sure not to get too attached. Women have their uses, Isaac, but that's all they have. None are worth keeping for the long term. You use them and you move on. If I've taught you anything in life, it's that you need to understand when to let go of your pawns and pick up new ones."

Pawns. I grit my teeth. That's all they are to him. That's all my mother had been and all Aurora and her mother are. When I don't say anything, Damien continues.

"Have Aurora dressed appropriately at the Icari estate Saturday at eight. I expect to see her there or else."

I don't have to ask what he means and he doesn't offer any more of his threat before the phone call ends. With a curse, I toss my cell into the passenger seat and press down harder on the gas. The engine of my car revs as the tires squeal on the pavement.

Adrenaline pumps through my system and alongside it, fear. There's no telling how much he knows about Aurora and me. From his words, he knows enough to make certain assumptions. Correct assumptions. When I pull into the parking lot of the hotel and get out, tossing my keys to the valet, I snatch my phone back up and click across the screen until I get to the secret camera app Shep installed for me.

I pull up the black and white image of Aurora's bedroom. In the dark, she's curled up on her side, clutching a pillow to her chest as she breathes evenly beneath her covers. As the elevator ascends to the topmost floor, I watch her. Counting her breaths, I stroke my finger along the screen.

She's alive. She's breathing. She's okay. That's all that matters for now. That's everything that matters.

37

RORI

My phone buzzes for what feels like the thousandth time in the last hour, vibrating against the scratched surface of the coffee shop table. I take a quick glance at it and blanch, reading Isaac's name at the top before I swipe away from the dozen or so texts he's sent me. He keeps calling, but I don't answer those either. I'd like to block him, but something always holds me back from going that far.

It's been several days since the piercing shop incident, but my tits are still a bit sore. My only saving grace is at least I'm able to wear bras now without wanting to either cry or rub myself into an orgasm. I've never felt so sensitive from just my nipples before, and it's disturbing.

Instead of responding to him, I type out a quick text to Selene, asking her where she is and to give either Hel or me a call because we're worried about her. She hadn't responded to either of us over the weekend, and come Monday she'd missed out on her classes, but after a quick talk to the professor—we found that she'd at least emailed her instructors letting them know she'd be out of class for work for the next week.

Even with the tension at the apartment between Hel and me, we're both worried about her. At least we know she's alive, but it still worries me that she hasn't seemed to come home.

The coffee shop door jingles as it opens and I lift my gaze away from my phone screen to see Marcus step into the shop, a brown leather jacket draped over his shoulders. I stand quickly and lift a hand, stopping his quick scanning of the room as he spots me and heads my way. When he arrives, he closes an awkward arm around my shoulders and gives me a quick hug.

"I got you a coffee," I say, gesturing down to the table. He releases me and we both take our seats. I let him take a sip of his coffee before I jump into the reason for his visit.

"Okay," I say, leaning forward and crossing my arms over the lip of the table. "Now, are you going to explain what the hell that weird phone call was all about?"

Marcus' gaze moves away from me and towards the rest of the room. We're a considerable distance from Hazelwood—a good half hour's drive—but that doesn't protect us from anyone we might know. I can understand his hesitation and caution, especially considering the information he relayed to me over the phone, but that doesn't make me any less anxious to hear it.

"This might not be the best place," he says.

I blow out a breath. "You wanted to meet somewhere off campus," I remind him. "What are you even doing back in California? What about Eastpoint? I'm sure you've got shit to do back there. Football practice and school. You're in your senior year, you don't have the time

to be flying back here all the time." Which he under-
stands—so that must mean it's important.

"I told you that an FBI agent approached me at Eastpoint," he says, reminding me of our phone conversation
from a few days ago.

I nod quickly, my fingers tapping the scarred wood.
"Yeah, you warned me that someone might try to talk to
me, but I haven't seen or heard from anyone like that."

"What about Damien?" he demands. "Has he tried to
contact you?"

I grimace. "Yeah, but it's about the party that he and
Mom are throwing—their belated reception or whatever
it is."

Marcus leans back in his seat and lifts his coffee back
to his lips to take a long gulp. Now that I look at him, he
seems tired. Dark circles rim the skin beneath his eyes and
his hair is casually shoved back but clearly unbrushed.
There's a shadow of beard growth on his jaw that is
normally well-shaven. When he sets his cup back on the
table, I reach for his hand.

"Are you okay, Marcus?" I ask. "What's this really
about? What's going on?"

"Damien Icari has been sticking his nose into Mom's
businesses," Marcus says with a tired sigh. He scrubs his
free hand down his face even as he turns over my palm
and lets me lace our fingers together. I tighten my hold
on him.

"Aunt Carmen is smart," I remind him. "She's the one
in charge of Summers' industries—Damien can't do
anything."

"Yeah, I talked to her," Marcus admits, "but she didn't
even know Mom got married."

I blink and lean back, our fingers separating. I bite

down on my lower lip as confusion fills me. "That doesn't make any sense," I say. "Even when she flew off, she always told Aunt Carmen about the men she was with."

"Yeah, and usually Aunt Carmen gives us a heads up, but she didn't this time."

I shake my head. He's right. I haven't heard from Aunt Carmen in months. "So Mom got married without telling her..."

"And I looked into what Dean told me about Damien Icari," Marcus continues, nodding. "He was right. The man is involved in some shady dealings—the FBI agent only confirmed our suspicions. He's involved in organized crime and now, Mom is too."

My phone buzzes on the table again, drawing our attention. I know, without looking, that it's *him*. Isaac. I blow out a breath. He's warned me how dangerous his father is. So did Marcus' friends. I'd been holding out hope that my mother would come to her senses and divorce him before it became too big of a problem. Now, it seems, though, we've already crossed that line.

"Mom needs to leave," Marcus says.

"She won't," I say. "She's convinced he's the perfect man and you know you can't tell her anything she's not ready to hear."

My heart beats loudly in my ears as I speak. *Don't.* My internal alarm goes off, warning me away from the inner resentment that festers inside of me. Something must show on my face because Marcus' brow puckers and he leans forward, reaching for me.

"Rori?"

I pull my hands out of reach and shake my head, looking away. "I'm fine." It's a lie, but one I have to say—

because if I tell the truth, then we'll have to go down the path that I really don't want to see again.

Marcus is quiet for a moment, but when I look back at him, he's retracted his hand and is watching me with a careful expression. Careful. Ha. He's always careful with me. Considerate. As if I'm some piece of fragile glass. He and his friends have always been like that towards me.

Marcus' little sister. Innocent. Breakable.

The only fucking man who hasn't treated me like that is ... my phone buzzes again and Marcus curses, ripping it up from the table before I can snatch it from his reach. He takes one look at the screen and his expression twists. When his gaze raises to mine, I scowl and make a grab for the phone.

He lets me. It's the reason that I actually manage to snatch it from him. Because if he really wanted to, it'd be all too easy for him to keep it away from me. "Want to explain to me why Isaac Icari has sent you twenty-two text messages and called you thirteen times?" He crosses his arms and eyes me.

I roll my eyes and tuck my phone into my back pocket before picking up my latte. "Not particularly," I say. "I'd rather talk about what we're going to do about Mom."

"Rori—"

"Don't, Marcus." I hold up my hand and glare at him. "You don't have any right to judge me. You haven't been here."

"I'm not judging you, Rori."

I snort and shake my head before taking a long draw from my latte. First Hel and now Marcus. "I'm sure you've already made your assumptions, Marcus."

A beat of silence passes between us and then Marcus speaks. "Are you sleeping with him?"

My spine stiffens. "I don't think that's any of your business," I say carefully.

"You are."

My eyes shoot to his face. "I didn't say that."

"You didn't have to," he replies.

"Then why did you even bother asking?"

"I wanted to know if you'd tell me the truth."

"I didn't lie to you," I point out.

"No," he agrees. "But you don't want to tell me regardless."

I huff out a breath. "Can you fucking blame me?" I demand. "You're my big brother. I don't exactly want to get into my relationship status with you—especially not when it concerns him."

Marcus arches a brow. "So, it's a relationship, then?"

I level him with a dark look. "Whatever it is, it is none of your business," I say.

"Everything about you is my business, Rori," Marcus replies. "You're my responsibility."

My hand clamps around my cup as my jaw tightens. "Well, I absolve you of your *responsibility*, Marcus." I spit the words out. "Don't bring it up again."

"I'm just worried about you," he says. "Damien is a problem, but his son is just as bad."

"Damien and Isaac are two different people," I point out, but even as I say the words—I know that Marcus isn't wrong. Isaac and his father are connected and even if we manage to get Mom away from her new husband, if I'm still around Isaac, then we're right back where we started.

I never wanted to become like my mother, but is that what's happening? Am I falling for the wrong man and becoming just as obsessed as her?

"Rori, have you thought about moving away from Hazelwood?"

Marcus' sudden question startles me into looking up at him. "What?" I gape at him.

"If we manage to convince Mom to leave, what about you and this guy?" he says. "If Damien is involved in shady dealings, then his son is, too."

Shockingly, Marcus doesn't even seem that particularly upset by the reveal of my relationship with Isaac. He doesn't seem angry or even particularly surprised, only put off. Frustrated. My mind rolls over with that information and as I stare back at my brother, the thought hits me.

He already knew.

"Have you been watching me, Marcus?"

His brows raise sharply, as if he's shocked by my sudden question. He doesn't deny it, however. Instead, Marcus sighs and scrubs a hand over his face. "Rori..." Who could have told him? Selene? No, she hasn't even been responding to me, and we haven't talked about Isaac since—another thought occurs in the middle of my last one.

Who had told my brother about the bullying in high school? About the videos.

Hel.

I stand abruptly, shoving back from my seat. I don't even let Marcus finish his thought before I'm grabbing my keys and striding toward the exit.

"Rori!" he calls behind me, but I ignore it as I storm towards the doors.

How fucking *dare* she? How dare *he*?

I make it out the door and halfway across the parking lot before Marcus catches up with me. His hand closes around my upper arm, bringing me to a halt. Before he can say anything, though, I round on him, shoving at his chest until he releases me.

"Using my best fucking friend, Marcus?" I bare my teeth at him in a snarl. "I thought that was beneath you, but I guess not. You're trying to do what you've always done—you're trying to control me without even being in *my* life."

I shove a hand up through my hair, pushing the strands back even as I want to take a handful and yank it out.

"Rori, I'm just trying to protect you—"

"Protect me?" I laugh. How hilarious. "If you wanted to protect me, then do it your fucking self, Marcus. Don't use my friends to keep tabs on me."

"Hel was just looking out for you; she was worried!" Marcus snaps, growling. "You've been fucking around with someone dangerous. Someone who humiliated you to the whole campus."

"So you know about that, too." I nod absently. "Of course you do. What else has she told you?"

Marcus presses his lips together and I snort. "Oh, don't get shy now," I say. "It's too late for that."

"All I know is that you're fucking him," Marcus says. "That's bad enough."

"Bad enough?" I repeat the words. Is it bad? Isaac? Is he really that bad? He's the one who's been here. He's been trying to protect me. He warned me away from his father. Maybe he hasn't told me the whole truth, but even my brother hasn't. Won't. Who can I even trust anymore?

"You think a man changes that fast?" Marcus demands, sounding frustrated. "How can he go from spreading rumors and posting videos to being in love with you? Men don't do that unless they want something and you're giving it to him."

"Giving it to him? Yeah, maybe I am," I say. "I'm fucking him, but that doesn't mean anything."

"Oh, Rori..." Marcus looks at me and shakes his head. "You're not that kind of girl. Sex means something to you. It has to."

"Why?" I scream. "Because I'm fucked up? Because I was raped? Because Mom invited some asshole into our lives and then didn't even think about what he'd do when he was put into a house with a teenage girl who wasn't related to him?"

Marcus' face goes pale and his jaw drops. We've danced around this for years. Too many years. And I'm fucking tired of it.

"Maybe I like sex, Marcus," I continue. "Did you ever think of that? Maybe fucking Isaac does something for me. Maybe it gives me a little bit of freedom. At least he doesn't fucking lie to me."

"He's definitely lying to you, Rori. Don't be fucking—"

"What?" I demand when he stops. "Don't be fucking stupid?" I guess.

He presses his lips together and refuses to say anything. That's all the answer I need.

"It's good to know what you think of me."

"Fuck—Rori, don't take it the wrong way."

"How am I supposed to take it?" I ask. When he doesn't answer, I nod. "Right, then. I'll see you later, Marcus." I turn to go, only pausing when I reach the car and my fingers close around the driver's side handle.

"What about Damien?" Marcus' question is pressing.

I shake my head. "Figure it out yourself, Marcus.

Hell, let her burn in the mess of her own making. I don't know if I even care anymore."

Everyone always chooses to lie, cheat, and steal to get what they want. At the end of the day, everyone considers everyone else possessions. Friends. Lovers. Family. It doesn't matter. I slam the door behind me and start up the car, speeding out of the lot, and ignoring Marcus standing there as I pass him.

It itches at me to call Hel. To tell her off and to tell her to mind her own business, but instead, I direct my attention elsewhere. I direct it to Isaac, steering my vehicle in the direction of Hotel Theós.

38

RORI

I saac Icari is an enigma. One second he's burning hot —a threat, a weapon pointed straight at my heart. The next, he's cool. He's soft and comforting and everything I'd ever wished a man would be towards me. I don't know which is the real Isaac, but I'm going to find out.

If anything, the conversation with my brother made it clear that someone needs to make a decision, and that someone is me. No one likes the thought of Isaac and me together and that should be a warning to me.

I press down harder on the gas, powering through a light that flashes gold and then red just as the top of my car speeds beneath the heavy swing of the yellow form. I'm angry. I'm confused. I'm seeking a release for all of this pent up energy inside of me.

What's the real reason I'm going to Isaac right now? I shake my head as that question forms in the back of my mind. I've been avoiding him for a reason. The reminder of why sits heavy on my breasts, warmed by my own skin.

He's crazy. He's obsessive. He's hot and cold. Isaac is a confusing powerhouse that drives me insane and makes me question everything I've ever believed about men and relationships. When I pictured my life four years ago, I would have thought I'd find a nice guy—maybe a jock, maybe a business nerd—but whoever it was, it would've been someone who didn't torture me upon our first meeting. Someone who was fully honest with me and even comforting when I told him about my past. Someone Marcus would have comfortably threatened without actually believing he'd ever follow through with his words because I'd found someone real—someone genuine. Someone ... normal.

Isaac is anything but normal.

Hotel Théos appears, the fancy swirling sign of its name backlit and glowing in gold at the front of the parking lot despite the fact that the sun hasn't set. I pull through the drive and stop in front of the dozen or so glass doors. A tired looking valet hurries around the front of his stand and opens my door for me. I leave the keys in the ignition, taking the tag he hands me as I stride towards the front doors. I bypass the desk and head straight for the penthouse elevator.

It's a good thing my memory isn't trash because I don't need to call Isaac or give him any sort of warning as I type in the code I'd watched him use the night I'd first come here. The doors slide open and I step inside, turning and slamming my thumb into the button that will send me directly up to the floor I need.

My foot taps against the floor in a repetitive motion—it's calming. I count each tap. One. Two. Three. Four ... by the time I reach the twenties, the elevator is slowing. It dings and the doors slide open.

"Shep!" Isaac calls, "I'm in here."

I roll my tongue into my cheek. I guess he was

expecting one of his friends. I don't say a word as I follow the direction of his shout until I find him in the living room with his head bent over the coffee table in the center of the room, a sheaf of papers spread out in front of him.

They're everywhere. Papers. Pictures. Documents. On the table, couch, and even some on the floor in various patterns and stacks.

"Expecting someone?" I ask, keeping my tone light and casual.

Isaac's head jerks up, and for the first time, I see him truly surprised. His eyes widen, and he straightens before standing up from his position perched on the edge of the couch. "Aurora..." He frowns but approaches, stepping around each stack with care. "What are you doing here? How did you—"

"Get in?" I finish his question for him as he comes to a stop in front of me. "With the code, how else?"

I glance behind him and he tilts his head to the side, watching me carefully. "You're upset." Good for him, at least he can read the room.

"Around you?" I ask with a tight smile. "When am I not?"

I take a step around him and lean down, pausing only slightly when he doesn't move to stop me as I grab a stack of papers and lift it to my face. "Aurora, what's wrong?"

What isn't wrong? My mother is married to a mafia boss. The FBI is after my brother. And I fucked my stepbrother. This whole fucking thing is wrong. Everything about it. So ... why can't I seem to stay the hell away from him?

My eyes scan the papers in front of me. They're lists—names, numbers, dates, locations. I can't seem to make heads or tails of what any of it means without some sort of clarification or direction. There's no context to them. I drop them right where I picked them up and turn back to Isaac.

"Marcus came to see me today," I say.

Isaac's frown deepens. "Marcus is back in town?" He glances away, back towards the elevator, before returning to me and scrubbing a hand through his hair. "Is this about the party this weekend?"

"You knew about that?" What am I asking? Of course he knew. Before Isaac can answer, I shake my head. "I suppose that's probably part of it, but it's definitely not the entirety."

Isaac watches me, his eyes following as I stride across the room, stepping around the handfuls of documents spread out. I want to ask him what they're for, but I can't get distracted from my reason for being here. I stop when I hit the edge of the room, right in front of the long windows that face out over the city and the sun in the distance, turning the sky a mirage of colors as it starts to sink over the edge of the land.

I turn back towards him. "He was contacted by the FBI." Isaac's whole body—his demeanor—changes. The concern in his expression smooths out and hardens. His lips turn down further and his muscles contract, his shoulders swelling larger. I cross my arms and scowl. "Is there something I should know?"

Surprise of all fucking surprises, Isaac shakes his head. "It's not a good idea, Aurora."

"Consider me bad then," I say. "Because—despite how politely I asked—what I meant to say is that it's time to tell me the fucking truth, Isaac." I scowl at him. "What the hell is going on?"

Isaac curses beneath his breath and turns away from

me as he bares his teeth and blows out a frustrated breath. It irritates me enough that I can't fucking watch it anymore. I turn away and make my way across the room to the bar. Just like last time, I pull out a glass and uncork the crystal decanter—pouring a hefty amount of alcohol into my cup.

"What are you doing?" Isaac's footsteps echo loudly as he stomps towards me.

I stop when the alcohol is almost at the rim. "Measuring with my fucking heart," I say, setting the top on the decanter back in place.

"If you really want to have this conversation, I'd rather you didn't drink through it," Isaac says.

"Yeah? Well, I'd rather everyone in my life stop lying to me, or at the very least stop hiding shit, but that hasn't happened." I lift the glass to my lips and take a long sip—letting the burn hurt my insides until the alcohol is far enough down that it doesn't threaten to spill over the top with every movement.

"Aurora."

I turn and face him. Isaac stops in front of me, the heat of his body so near and so fucking distracting.

"Isaac." I mimic his tone as I lift the glass again and take a big gulp. He curses again, his gaze lingering on the glass in my hand. I can see it—the contemplation. The thought in his mind. He wants to take it from me—just like last time. I'm waiting to see if he'll follow through. Surprisingly, he doesn't.

Instead, his hands reach out and land on my hips. "Aurora, what's this all about? Why are you so upset? Is it the FBI? What did they say to Marcus? What did they ask?"

"I don't really know," I admit. "We didn't get past the

fact that they were solely focused on Damien Icari." I meet his gaze and set the glass back down on the bar counter behind me.

His expression darkens at my words, but his hands don't leave my sides. "I'm sorry, Aurora," he says. "I really didn't want you to be involved in this mess."

Well, at least now I know that he knew about the FBI. That's a consolation at least. He's not hiding that from me. Other things, probably, but it's a start. Against my own better judgment, I let my hands touch his chest, feel his warmth, his strength. His heart beats against my palm, sharp and fast.

"I'm tired of being lied to, Isaac," I say quietly, looking up at him through my lashes. "You told me once that your father was dangerous. I know he's a criminal, but that's all you give me. Vagueness and nothing more." I know why Damien Icari married my mother. To use her. But why does that concern him so much? "I don't know why *you're* so cautious about him. Why you suddenly changed."

Isaac captures my hands and holds them when I move them up. He presses my palms harder against his pecs and I feel the shift of his muscles beneath his shirt. "I never wanted to hurt you." Isaac's confession doesn't ease the tightness in my chest. "I wanted you to leave. To convince your mother that marrying my father was a bad fucking idea."

"So you tortured me to ... what? Save me?"

He nods. "It doesn't make anything I did right, but—"

"But you thought that would be better than telling me the truth?" I arch a brow up at him.

"I didn't know you, Aurora." Isaac pulls me forward. With his fingers clamped on my hands, he forces me to wrap my arms around his middle. "You were just baggage attached to Emilia Summers—baggage I didn't even know about until just before I met you. You think I'm privy to my father's schemes?" He pauses and shakes his head. "I'm not. He doesn't trust me like that. Not like you seem to think."

"And the FBI?"

A vein in Isaac's forehead pulses at the reminder. "I'm sorry they approached your brother," he says through a clenched jaw. "But I didn't have any power over that."

"But you know they're after your father?" I gaze up at him, thinking that through. "Are you working with them?"

Isaac doesn't answer. In fact, he doesn't even react. His face goes a careful calm—a distant and almost indifferent look enters his eyes. The only way I'm even assured that he's still very much aware of my presence is the solid heartbeat next to my face and the way his hands hold onto me.

"I'm tired of the manipulations, Isaac." I try to pull away, but his hands become like iron shackles. "Let go." I yank at my wrists as his fingers circle them.

"No." The denial is a growl, low and deep and dangerous. My eyes widen as he presses me back against the bar. "Never."

I grit my teeth and glare up at him. "You lie to me. You manipulate me. You don't want me around and then you do. What the fuck am I supposed to do here, Isaac?"

"Trust me." His answer is sharp and ready as if there's no doubt in his mind that I should just accept the bread-crumbs of information he feeds me.

"Not until you trust me," I snap. "Tell me everything."

"I..." He closes his eyes, his upper lip pulling back

away from his teeth like an animal ready to bite. "Fuck, I can't. Sunshine, I..." His words trail off.

"If you can't tell me the truth, then I can't trust you." The words are true, but they still don't stop me from asking my next question. "Are you using me to some end?"

Isaac's eyes open and he looks down at me. As the sun sets behind me, his face is thrown into shadows. It's there —visible—but not completely illuminated. "I wouldn't do anything that would hurt you, Sunshine."

That's not an answer. I shove hard at him, squirming enough that he finally drops my hands and latches onto the counter on either side of me. He presses me back harder as I push against his chest, growing more and more frustrated and angry the longer I'm locked against him without any give on his part.

"Fucking ... let ... me ... go!" I scream. He turns his head when I ball up my fist and punch his chest. His head snaps to the side on my next strike and still, he doesn't fucking move.

I'm panting, my chest rising and falling in rapid movements. Oxygen squeezes into my lungs but never quite makes it all the way in, leaving me breathless. Isaac's head drops until his forehead touches my shoulder and I stiffen all over as his hips move forward, trapping me harder against the counter.

"Sunshine..." His voice is gruff, tortured.

The elevator dings behind him and for a brief second, neither of us moves or makes a sound as footsteps enter the penthouse. "Yo! 'Zac!"

Isaac's friend, Paris, comes around the corner from the direction of the elevators, followed a split second later by Shep. The two stop when they spot me and Isaac. This time, when I press against Isaac's chest, he takes a step back and frees me.

"Oh, sorry 'bout that, man," Paris says, looking from me to Isaac. "Didn't realize you had your girl over."

"I'm *not* his girl," I say sharply, stepping away from Isaac. His hand shoots out and latches onto my wrist. I pause and look back, but Isaac doesn't say anything. Quietly, I reach down and pry his fingers off of me. "Besides, I was just leaving."

I make it halfway across the room before Isaac finally speaks. "You need to be careful, Aurora," he says. "You have no idea the kind of man my father is. Whatever you're thinking, don't—don't try anything. Or at the very least, tell me before you act rashly. Don't get yourself fucking killed."

"Unless you can tell me the truth, then you don't deserve any insight into my plans, Isaac," I say. "I'm not stupid. I won't do anything without thinking it through, but until you stop making me feel like a toy you're using just to piss off your father, I don't want to fucking hear a damn thing about what I do."

I stomp past his friends, the burn of their attention and curiosity flaming the side of my face as I make my way to the elevator. The sting of unshed tears fills my eyes, but I hold it in. I wait and it isn't until the doors close behind me that I cover my face and finally lose it.

I didn't think it would hurt this much—being denied even the common decency of answers. I thought I didn't care—not about Isaac. Not about people's bullshit anymore. But I guess that, too, was a lie. A lie I fed myself day after day.

Because if the shredding pain in my head and gut is anything to go by—I care. I care a hell of a lot.

39
ISAAC

"You good, man?" Paris' voice cracks me out of my head and slams me back into the present after Aurora's sudden entrance and subsequent exit.

Does he want the true answer? No. I'm not good. I'm as far from fucking good as a man can possibly be. I scrub a rough hand over my face and turn away from both him and Shep. Their attention bores into the back of my head. They've got questions. Of course they do. I've been so absent from a lot of things—if not in body, then in mind. Aurora has me fucked up, and she doesn't even seem to realize that the reason I'm not telling her shit is because I fucking care about her. Too much.

Should I go after her? Should I just let her calm down on her own and then approach later? I've never felt so confused in my life.

"Isaac?" I blink and turn back, realizing both of my friends have come further into the room, carefully avoiding the papers that linger across the floor. They are watching me with varying expressions.

Paris' brows are drawn down low and there's a slight v

forming between his eyes, the look of concern. Whereas Shep has his arms crossed as he glares at me. One is worried, and the other is pissed. Makes sense—that's how it's always been. Paris rarely gets angry. He just pushes everything down and moves on to the next addiction of self-harm—tattoos, piercings, drugs, alcohol. Shep is always pissed. Only now, he's lost the will to control it on the outside.

"Enough is enough." Shep is the first one to speak. He drops his arms and steps closer to me, walking across the room until he's standing only a few feet in front of me. "I think it's time you come clean and tell us what's going on?"

"Are you in love with that girl?" Paris asks.

I raise my head and meet his gaze. Am I in love with Aurora Summers? "I ... don't know." It might not be the answer they're looking for, but it's an honest one. I don't know what love even means.

Paris tilts his head to the side. "Then is it obsession?"

"I ... maybe?" I curse silently and grit my teeth. "I don't like her being away from me," I admit, "but with my father—it's complicated." More than complicated, it's downright wrong. Even if our parents' marriage is only temporary, we're still technically step-siblings. That knowledge, however, doesn't seem to have any bearing on my own volatile emotions. Regardless of knowing how we're connected, I want her. More than anything some-times. More than my next breath, more than I want my father to die.

That last thought hits me like a freight train. My jaw drops and my hands clench into fists at my sides. Do I want to protect Aurora more than I want to see my father pay for his sins? The answer should be simple. It should be a flat-out no. I've spent years hating him, months working against him with the FBI to try and get them solid evidence. I've put my life on the line without a second thought, but putting hers on the line? It's out of the question.

"This is fucking ridiculous," Shep snarls. "I told you she was going to distract you and get you hurt, and here you are—following her around like some sick, sad puppy." He shakes his head. "Does Damien know already? She's not going to stick around, Isaac. You know this. Even if, by some miracle, all he does is divorce her mother rather than kill her, she'll be gone. Shit like this—relationships built on lies and backstabbing ... they don't last."

"I don't want to lie to her."

Silence meets that statement. When I look up, it's to find Shep slack-jawed as he gapes at me. "You can't tell her the truth," he says.

I bite my tongue. *Can't I?* It's a risk, for sure, but if she knows then maybe she'll finally start to listen to me. Maybe she'll stay away.

"Isaac!" Shep steps forward and grabs ahold of my shoulders, shaking me slightly. "You cannot tell her who your father is or what he does. If Damien ever finds out, then you've essentially signed her death warrant. He doesn't leave loose ends. You know this."

"She already knows some of it," I tell him. "She knows he's dangerous."

"But does she know what he's involved in? Does she know *why* he married her mother?"

I shake my head and he blows out a breath—a relieved breath. "Listen," he says. "We're here for you." He gestures back with one hand at Paris. "Both of us. We'll do whatever you need us to do. We'll follow you and swallow the backlash without question, but her ... she's just a girl, Isaac. She doesn't belong to this world. You know it. I know it. I know you like her. I know you want her but ignore your obsession. If you want her to survive Damien Icari—Let. Her. Go."

Let her go? My stomach riots. My chest caves inward. My mind fogs over. *Let her go?* A million thoughts race through my head. My skin prickles as if a million tiny insects are crawling all over me. *No. Never.* My whole body rebels at the idea.

Paris strides across the room, the soft, quiet whisper of his footsteps drawing both Shep's and my attention. Paris doesn't usually insert himself between us, but when he does, it's because he's got something to say. Shep's other hand falls away from my shoulder and he takes a step back as Paris stops at our sides.

"You want to keep her?" he guesses.

I nod.

"Is she trustworthy?"

I shoot a look to Shep, who presses his lips together. Damn it. I don't know. An angry Aurora is unpredictable. The way she'd seduced me at the Gods and Goddesses party is proof. Her meager, albeit amusing, attempts to fight back when I'd been trying my damnedest to get her to leave the school were biting and ingenious. Where others might have backed off and shrunken into themselves, she stepped up and fought back. I lit a fire under her and all she'd done was make it burn hotter.

The lack of an answer has Paris sighing as he anchors his hands on his hips and looks down, a barrage of emotions flittering across his face. "If you can't trust her, then you just need to take care of the issue at hand. Up your timeline so to speak."

"The Feds—"

Paris holds up a hand, effectively stopping me as he levels me with a look. "The Feds are part of the problem. They are as much of a danger to you and her as Damien is."

"I agree," Shep says with a nod.

"It's too late to back out of the deal I've made with them now," I tell them.

Paris sighs. "Yes, so there's really only one option you have."

"The party," I agree as he meets my gaze. Paris stares back at me, unblinking. "I need clear red-handed evidence, and I have no doubt that my father is using this reception as a way to conduct business he otherwise wouldn't be able to."

"Using Emilia Summers' business connections?" Shep clarifies.

"Yes."

Paris frowns. "I was under the assumption that Emilia wasn't very involved in her businesses and that it was her sister that ran things."

I turn away from them and move back to the papers scattered across the room. "I've done my own investigating," I tell them, "and you're correct, Emilia isn't directly involved in the businesses—but she has a position on the board of directors and as Emilia's husband, my father now has the contacts that she had with overseas materials providers."

"Couldn't he have gotten those contacts without her?" Paris asks as I lean over and pick up a specific batch of documentation.

I turn and nod. "Yes, but the Feds would have been all over him if he'd reached out himself. Now, he can make it look like his innocent wife is the one setting up these meetings. He's using her as a cover, not necessarily for the connections. He's trying to smuggle goods into the country using these material providers. Barrels of gasoline can be emptied and changed out. Oil companies from the Middle East—I have a list of the ones he's been keeping an eye on for the last few years."

Shep takes a step forward and holds out his hand. I give him the papers and watch as his eyes scan the information printed there. It's not enough to prove my theories, but it's enough to warrant following up. "Damien is patient," I continue. "He knows that the Feds are watching him, and he most likely knows that they've contacted Emilia's son, Marcus."

"So your plan to is to find this evidence at the party?" Paris confirms.

"Some of the executives will be there," I say. "If my suspicions are correct, he's going to try and set up a private meeting with them during the party. If I can get into that meeting or get near it and set up some recording devices, then the Feds will have at least enough evidence to investigate him openly instead of this cloak-and-dagger bullshit they've been pulling ... or I can use what I find to lead them to the actual materials."

"What this paperwork doesn't tell you, though, is what he's trying to import," Shep states. "What exactly is it that he's trying to do? What kind of goods is he involved in?"

I suck in a breath and blow it out. "Tax evasion. Corporate fraud. Money Laundering. These are the things he's been involved with thus far. But this is bigger, this is more dangerous."

Paris frowns. "Isaac?" Drugs. Guns. Those would be

bad but better than what I know he's planning. "What is he importing?"

It's been so fucking long—looking into his background. The companies he's had his eyes on. The countries he's been obsessively trying to involve. I don't want to admit it. That my own father has stepped so far into the dark that there's no coming back. Murder and killing would have been kinder. It would have been more humane.

"People," I finally say.

"People?" Paris and Shep repeat the word, their confusion a testament to their goodness. Their humanity, but it gets worse. So much fucking worse.

"Yes," I say, "but not just people—girls. Young girls. Women." I have no doubt that his plans for these women are anything but innocent. There's only one reason a man like my father would bring undocumented young immigrant women over from impoverished, third-world, or even misogynistic countries. Human trafficking.

"Shit." Shep's sentiment is my own. So I choose not to say a damn word.

"This is big, Isaac," Paris says. "This is bigger than anything he's done so far. This will catapult him to a new level."

"It'll make him wealthy beyond belief, and that's all he cares about," I say.

"It doesn't make any sense," Shep argues. "Why now? He's been fine with everything else. He's been clean, and the Feds are struggling to catch him. Why would he risk his safety for more money?"

"There's a void in the underground market," I say. It started a few months ago. Barely perceptible—certainly invisible to the common man or woman—but it's quickly growing, and the upper echelon is taking notice. They're realizing it because they are the customers and their product is gone. "An organization has undergone a change. I don't know who's behind it, but the products and services they provided have been put on an extended hold and there's a shift happening."

"What organization? One that specialized in trafficking?" Shep asks.

I nod. "It's all there." I gesture to the other papers. "I couldn't find a whole lot of physical or paper evidence, but from what I understand there's a load of people that are supposedly dead popping up here and there."

"Dead?" Paris moves across the room and starts looking at the other papers, stopping to pick up a stack. "Dead people coming back to life?"

"More like they've faked their death," I tell them, "in order to perform some of these services. Their connections are what tell me it has to be an actual organization. They sell everything from people to hitman services. Over the course of the last few months, though, the people have disappeared and they haven't popped back up."

"They could be laying low," Paris says as he absently flips through documents.

"I'm sure that's true for some of them, but not for so many," I reply. "No, my guess is that someone else has taken over, and with an organization like that—it can only mean it was done in a bloody fashion."

"And because of that, there's a gap in the underworld's illegal goods exchange," Paris guesses, looking up. "Your father is trying to fill that role before whatever organization was originally running it returns."

It's a guess, but an educated one. Knowing what I

know about my father and his greed, his damn near obsessive need to be bigger, more threatening, more powerful, to have more—this is his golden goose. His next step and nothing will stop him from taking what he wants. Certainly not his wife's daughter.

"What do you need?" Shep's words have me looking up. Clear golden-brown eyes meet mine.

"I need Aurora to be safe," I confess. "I can't do shit until I know that she's going to be okay. She's in my fucking head all the time, and she's so damn stubborn. She scares the life out of me. She's going to draw his attention and if she's too much of a threat, you know what he'll do to her."

Shep nods. "He'll kill her."

Without hesitation. And that's something I can't let happen. "I know I'm fucking stupid," I admit. "I know she's become a weakness, but I can't..." There are no words, no excuses for how absolutely dangerous my feelings for her are. My hands clench into fists at my sides, my nails stabbing into my palms as if to wake me up from the hypnotic trance she's got me under. "She knows he's dangerous, but she doesn't know *how* dangerous. She thinks I'm using her—and maybe that's how it started— but I can't continue knowing what it'll do to her." Knowing I could get her killed. "Damien knows, he knows about us."

"He'll use her against you," Shep states. It's not a question but a statement of fact. At least, it is to him.

"You have us," Paris says, dropping the papers from his grip to the coffee table. "Whatever you need, we're here."

"I can't say that I'm happy she's involved," Shep says as he, too, lowers the documents in his hand. He sets them next to Paris'. "And I can't say you shouldn't walk away from her. Abandoning her would be the easiest and safest course of action."

"I can't." Not won't, but physically—I don't think I could leave Aurora behind even if I wanted to.

Shep sighs and groans as he rocks back on his heels and crosses his arms. "Then, fuck it." He grits the words through his teeth, closing and then reopening his eyes before leveling me with a dark look. "Yeah, we're in. *I'm* in. We'll help you get the evidence you need. Whatever you fucking need."

"It'll be dangerous." I offer the warning, despite already knowing their response. It's only fair that they understand the risks. "The reception might seem safe because it's semi-public, but the second Damien finds out about any of this—that I know, that I'm working with the Feds, that Aurora is close to this—it could mean him choosing to take us all out."

Shep arches a brow at me. "Doesn't fucking matter," he says. "I said we're in—Paris said we're in. That's the end of it." He lowers his arms. "Isaac—we're brothers. Maybe not by blood but by fucking fate." He claps me on the back. "Now tell us how the hell we're gonna pull this shit off."

If I thought I was insane before, Shep and Paris only confirm it. I'm absolutely out of my head, and maybe ... maybe it'll be easier to answer Paris' earlier question. What else would make a man risk his damn life and that of his brothers if not love? Love for a woman that threatens to kill me herself.

40

RORI

In all the myths of the world, the worst of the worst, the fallen, the damned, the betrayed—there is one common enemy. *Hubris*. Pride. In each story, the consequence of too much hubris is downfall. Isaac's one true enemy is himself. The same can be said for everyone else —Hel and my brother included.

As I swipe a fresh coat of lipstick across my lower lip, I lean back and stare at myself in the mirror. Baggage. Pawn. Tool. Unassuming. I know exactly what Isaac's father thinks of me. It's there in his actions, in his barely restrained distaste for me. I'm nothing but a connection to my mother, a way for him to control her.

What is it with men and their control? Isaac. Damien Icari. Even my own brother. Each of them *wants* to control me. Yet, with each invisible chain they drape across my shoulders, all I want to do is fight back, rip them off, be free.

Maybe Isaac was right in the beginning. Maybe I should've walked away and never looked back. I can't say it wouldn't have made things easier, less complicated. It's too late for that now. As much as I've hated the decisions my mother made in her past, as much as I've resented her absence and neglect, I can't let this go on.

Tonight, it ends. Tonight, she knows the truth. Damien Icari is using her and she needs to get out before it gets her hurt. Or worse. Killed.

A knock on the dorm door has me hurriedly finishing my makeup and putting it all away. I stride out into the living room to find Hel and Marcus already there, awkwardly shifting on their feet. I pause and frown.

"No need to be uncomfortable on my behalf," I say snidely. "Now that I know the two of you are in league with each other, you might as well talk about me in front of me instead of behind my back."

Hel's face blanches. "Rori, you know that's not what—"

"Don't get mad when you know we're just worried about you," Marcus says, cutting her off.

I hum in the back of my throat but don't offer a response. Nothing I could say would change them, anyway, or make them feel remorse for their actions. Sure, maybe Hel feels bad, but she still thinks she's right. Marcus, on the other hand, doesn't even seem to feel guilty. I've never been so irritated with him in my life.

"Come on," I snap, reaching for the jacket I've got draped over the back of the couch and pulling it on over my glittering cocktail dress. "Let's get this over with."

Marcus shoots me a look, but turns and gives Hel a nod of acknowledgment before striding back out into the hall. I check that my phone is in my jacket pocket and then stride through the room towards the front door, pausing only when Hel reaches out and gently touches my arm as I try to pass her.

"I'm sorry that I upset you, Rori," she says quietly. "I know you're mad that I called Marcus and told him stuff without telling you, but—"

I hold up a hand and move away from her touch. "No buts, Hel," I say. "You know what you did and even if you apologize, it still doesn't make me trust you. I'm not mad you told him, irritated maybe, but not mad. I'm pissed that you didn't tell me. I'm your best friend. Not Marcus. I'm the one you should've brought your concerns to."

"I did," she replies. "I told you—repeatedly—that Isaac Icari was dangerous. You wouldn't listen."

"Because it's *my* choice to make," I remind her. "Everything I do is my choice to make. What happens the next time I do something that you don't agree with?" I ask her. "Are you going to run to my brother for every little thing?" When she goes quiet, I shake my head. "I love you, Hel. I do. But I just can't trust that you won't do something behind my back again. Informing on me to my brother? At the very least, you should've told me."

Hel bows her head forward, her dark curly hair falling over her face. "Yeah, I know," she admits, "I should've told you that I was going to tell him." She lifts her head and dark, almost red-brown eyes meet mine. "I can't promise I won't call him if I think you're in danger, but I can swear to you that I'll tell you if I do."

I press my lips together as a slight burn in my nose warns me that tears are coming. I suck them back. Not right now. There's no time. "We'll talk later," I say, turning away from her.

"Rori!" As I step out of the apartment door, Hel calls my name and I pause when I feel her small hand close around mine, pulling me to a dead halt. I turn back as Hel grips the door, keeping it open, and stares back at me. "I am sorry," she says again, "for betraying your trust."

I could throw her off. I could turn away and give her nothing, and for a moment, I contemplate it. Then I inhale a breath and slowly release it. My own anger isn't worth it and the hurt it stems from will heal. Gently, I turn my hand over and squeeze hers back.

"I know." It's all I can offer her for now. An acknowledgment, if not an acceptance. If not forgiveness. Hel looks hurt, like she's about to cry, but when I pull away this time, she lets me go. The door to the dorm closes and I turn, my heels clicking across the floor as I make my way down the hallway to join my brother at the elevators. Tonight is about more than my friends. It's about my family and Isaac. It's about finding out if his hubris will be both of our downfalls.

Damien Icari's California Estate is massive. If west coast lavishness could be put into a building, it's the sprawling Grecian mansion that is his home. As Marcus pulls through the long winding drive, following the already extensive line of black town cars and expensive foreign sports vehicles, I take a second to scan my surroundings.

Neither of us has said a word the whole drive. I've been so focused on the tense silence, but the moment we pass through the gates, all of that evaporates. The front is nothing but white stone and pillars. Twin square fountains mirror one another on the front lawn, sparkling blue and lit up from within. Despite the dusky sky and the sun sinking behind the building, the water practically glows.

The statues in both are different depictions. One is a strange beastly man with a bull's head and a woman captured in his arms. The other is a man with melting wings; his arm outstretched towards the sky as if he's falling.

There are lights encircling each pillar on the front porch, glittering as they're intertwined with vines and greenery that have obviously been placed there rather than allowed to grow naturally. Our car moves forward, and the closer we get, the more my stomach sinks. I pull out my phone and check for messages, but once again, there's nothing. Not from Isaac, and strangely enough, not from my mother either. The only other person I half expected to message me would be Selene, but unfortunately, we're still in the dark. She seems to be getting her assignments from professors, but there's no word to her actual friends. It's concerning.

After tonight, I'll have to finally track her down and demand answers, I tell myself. If it's about her mother, then something needs to be done. Whatever the case is, though, I hope I can resolve my own problems sooner than later and refocus on my friends—maybe rebuild my friendship with Hel.

Marcus grits his teeth as his fingers squeeze the steering wheel of the dark SUV he's driving. Finally, we reach the front of the line. A valet in slacks and a white button-down hurries to my door, popping it open and offering me a hand. I take it gratefully, as the heels I'm wearing tonight are exceptionally high and sharp as hell. All the better to stab someone with if I feel the urge. At least, that's what I told myself when I forked over my credit card to purchase them.

I step out onto the cold stone walkway as my brother

rounds the front of the SUV to take my arm from the valet. As much as I want to rip myself away from him, I let it slide and link my arm through his as we make our way through the front pillars, following the crowd of equally dressed guests.

We make it through the front doors and I hand over my jacket to a woman dressed much the same as the valet. Eyes turn as the golden hue of my dress is illuminated by the bright lights. I've always avoided making a scene around my mother, but this is a statement.

To Isaac. To her. To Damien.

I'm no one's pawn, and I won't stay quiet. Not this time.

"You're not usually one for ostentatiousness," Marcus comments lightly.

"Yes, well, playing the wallflower hasn't exactly gotten me anywhere," I remind him. "So, I thought I'd change things up."

"I don't think that's a good idea, Rori."

"You're welcome to think whatever you want, Marcus," I reply. "But just like everyone else, you don't control me. I control myself. Besides..." I gently ease my arm away from his the second we're in the grand space meant to be the reception's main room and turn to face him with a half-smile. "It's just a dress."

"It's not the dress, and you know it," he replies. "You're drawing attention to yourself on purpose."

I am. I'm doing it because I know it'll shock my mother. It'll lead her to ask questions and be the perfect excuse to get her alone. The perfect excuse to give her my warning. I only hope she takes it. My brother opens his mouth to say something else but is curtly interrupted by a familiar voice.

"Aurora? Marcus?" I can see my brother's brows rise in slight surprise and I can't fault him for it. The two of us turn as a tall woman approaches with a glass of champagne in hand.

"Aunt Carmen?"

Her heels click across the marble flooring as she approaches, a loose, reserved, black floor-length gown swishing around her ankles. Despite the high neckline, the sleeves stop at her shoulders and the spot of color flashing at her feet draws my attention down to the bright red Jimmy Choos. They look like the shoes from *The Wizard of Oz,* and that brings a smile to my face.

"It's so good to see you." Aunt Carmen moves forward and envelops me with a strong half-hug as she holds her champagne out of the way. Once she's done, she moves to Marcus, who greets her with the first genuine smile I've seen from him in a while. He gently kisses her cheek as she pulls away.

"It's good to see you too, Aunty," he says. "I didn't know if you were coming."

Aunt Carmen huffs but nods. "That's fair. I've been to so many of Emmy's damn weddings, I've grown tired of them, but considering I didn't actually go to this one, I thought I could at least come to the reception."

"Have you seen her or talked to her?" Marcus asks.

Aunt Carmen sighs and then slams back the entire glass of her champagne before answering. "Of course not." She sets the now-empty flute on the tray of a passing waiter before turning back to us. "But that's nothing new. I want to hear about you two. It's been so long. Rori, honey, how's college treating you?"

It's a startling change to have an adult treat me like a child again, and while it might upset or irritate others, it only evokes a smile from me in the way Aunt Carmen always manages to. "It's fine," I answer. "The classes aren't as hard as my high school teachers led me to believe."

Aunt Carmen laughs at that. "They never are," she agrees, shaking her head. "But you're a smart girl; I'm sure you're just flying through them." She turns to Marcus. "And you, boy." She pops both of her hands on her hips, the short length of her shoulder-length hair swishing with the movement of her head. "You transferred to Eastpoint! Shame on you for not telling me."

Marcus blinks and has the audacity to look sheepish as he offers her another smile and chuckles. "Sorry, Aunty."

She huffs out a breath. "Well, I hope you're at least managing to keep up with classes."

"I am," he assures her before frowning. "How did you find out anyway?"

Aunt Carmen grins. "You think your mother is the only one with male connections?" she asks with a shake of her head. "I know the head coach at Eastpoint, honey. He told me all about his new player. What a shock for me that was."

"Coach?" Marcus blinks at her. "You and Coach are—"

"Oh, don't look at me like that, Marcus Summers," she stops him. "I'm a grown woman and fully capable of having a little fun on my own."

I snicker and turn my head as Marcus grimaces.

"Of course," I hear him say as my eyes catch on a figure at the other side of the room.

The man's head turns, and cool, blue eyes scan the room. He doesn't see me. Not right away. My throat tightens, though, the closer and closer his eyes move as he searches the room. What is he searching for? I wonder. Is it me?

Isaac looks like a modern god with his blond curls brushed out and slicked back. He looks darker, older. His black-on-black suit makes his frame appear particularly intimidating in a room full of otherwise bright and lavishly dressed men and women. When his gaze finally touches mine, I'm relieved to see the quick response.

His lips tighten, his eyes widen, and his nostrils flare. It says something that I notice all of that from across such a large room, but maybe it's because I know him so well now. Each breath. Each change. It's like a neon sign glaring at me. The two men he's standing with turn their heads slightly and I recognize them—Shep and Paris. His friends. Paris offers me a smile and a surprising little wave. I blink but nod his way. Thankfully, Shep doesn't follow his friend and merely watches me with infinitely enigmatic eyes.

"Rori?" Aunt Carmen's voice pulls me away and I turn to find her frowning behind me. I peek over my shoulder and feel my body go stone cold.

"I'm going to kill him." Marcus' words are low and full of wrath.

There's no fucking way. No way in hell my mother would let him come to something like this. They haven't spoken in years. Not since … but there he is. The man of my worst nightmares strides into the room with his head held high like he has every right to be here, a young woman on his arm that looks to be his daughter's age. She's reed thin and is dressed in a skin tight gown, the front cut so low that the swells of her small breasts peek out on either side of the fabric that clings to her form.

Despite the gorgeous outfit, she appears bored—almost detached in her role of what's about to be a shitshow. I feel nothing but pity for her.

"She can't know," Aunt Carmen says quietly. "She doesn't know." Oh, how I wish I could have the same confidence in my mother that she seems to.

"How the hell can she not?" Marcus snaps.

"Icari must have invited him," she replies. "Emilia would never welcome him here. Not after…" Her words drift off, but I can feel the heated vibe of her stare on me. No one questions what she means.

My question, though, is … why? Why the fuck would Damien Icari invite my mother's ex-husband to his wedding reception? Why would she let him? And why the fuck did Eric Wood show up?

41

ISAAC

Aurora is so close and yet so fucking far. It's maddening to see her and know that I can't touch her. Not here. She's dressed to kill in a glittering gown with straps dangling over her shoulders that would be so easy to snap. I can picture it now. One quick tug and they'd rip clean free and I'd be able to pull that already dipping neckline down further to reveal her pretty breasts and the jewelry I put there.

Every step she takes into the room has her entire body shining as whatever fabric her dress is made of shimmers under the light of the chandeliers. I want her. I crave her. It's a sickness in my gut that is slowly driving me to insanity. I'm so focused on her that when her demeanor changes, I know it. I watch the way her head turns, and the following tension as it fills her entire body.

"Something's wrong." Paris and Shep both glance at me as the words leave my lips. For once, Aurora is not focused on me, but on something—some*one*—else. I follow her gaze to find an older, middle-aged man with a young woman strapped to his side.

"Who is that?" I demand.

Paris answers immediately. "Eric Wood," he says. "That's Emilia Summers' ex-husband."

My eyes flash back to Aurora and her family. Marcus steps closer to her at the same time the woman with them does—as if they're protecting her. *From him?* I wonder. It certainly appears that way. My gaze returns to the man in question and narrows. He doesn't seem to realize the attention he's drawn as several heads turn and watch him walk in.

A tinkling laugh draws my focus away from the newcomer as horns blare and Emilia Summers and my father appear at the top of the staircase that leads into the ballroom they've set up for their reception. Aurora's mother is dressed in a floor length white gown—a modest wedding dress that's less ostentatious, but no doubt just as expensive as everyone else's attire.

My father—for his part—is dressed much like me. Black suit. Black button down beneath the jacket. Black tie. He keeps a pleasant and fake smile as he descends the staircase with Emilia in tow. The two of them enter the room and all heads turn to them. A champagne flute is shoved, unceremoniously, into my hand as the waiters around the room begin handing them out. They don't even check IDs as several of the younger attendees are given the alcohol without care. It's not their business to know who should be allowed to have what.

I turn back to Shep and Paris. "Why would Emilia's ex-husband be here?" I ask.

Paris shakes his head, his lips turning down into a deep frown. "I don't know," he answers, lowering his voice as the rest of the noise in the room drops. He moves closer. "But from what I do know about the couple—her son assaulted him and she filed for divorce within days. There were rumors that he attempted something with..." Paris' eyes scan away to something over my shoulder, but his meaning is clear.

Cold rage swallows me up. My eyes snap back to Aurora, but she's sequestered behind her brother and the woman now. I can only catch glimpses of her pale face as she stands between them. Shep steps in front of me, a casual movement to the average onlooker, but to me, it's calculated. It disrupts my line of sight.

"Don't do anything here," he warns me. "If you want to go after him, do it later. We have more important things to focus on tonight."

He's right. Goddamn it, I know he's right. Whatever happened between him and Aurora, I'll have to find out on my own. I knew she'd been bullied in high school long before she came to California, to Hazelwood. I knew Emilia had been married many times before and divorced, but I'd never looked deeper.

I already know without having to ask what the story is. That night in the parking lot when I'd chased her down, tackled her to the ground, and the panic on her face. The way she'd screamed and cried—and none of it was because of me. I know because it's such a common fucking story; but I want her to tell me. I want her to open up and reveal all of her secrets. Not because she has to, but because she trusts me.

"Focus on the job at hand," Shep whispers, keeping his face tilted up as my father takes center stage in front of his audience.

I suck in a breath and turn, returning my focus to him as well. My father lifts his flute and takes the small utensil from a nearby waiter to clink it against his glass as a sign that he's ready to speak before he hands it back and addresses everyone.

"Thank you all for coming tonight to celebrate the joining together of our two families," he says. "When I met Emilia Summers, I knew, in an instant, that my life had been forever changed." Emilia leans into him and smiles. He glances down and I have to admit, he plays the part well. The doting, love struck husband. "Emilia, you're the key to my future success, I just know it. You are the one thing I was missing, and with you, I'll reach new heights—heights no one even knew existed."

Applause rings loud throughout the ballroom as everyone raises their glasses in response. I put the rim of mine to my lips and take the lightest sip. What a fucking con artist. His words were calculated, precise. No doubt Emilia didn't hear it, and no doubt no one who doesn't know the man, himself, could understand. But I know—I know him so well.

Those were not words of love but of greed. To Damien Icari, Emilia Summers is nothing more than a tool—his 'key,' as he proclaimed her. To me, Aurora is so much more.

I bide my time, though, as people swarm the 'happy couple' to offer their congratulations. I'm increasingly aware of eyes on me—attention I've never sought but has followed me from birth. For Emilia's guests, this is nothing new—another wedding, another marriage that they all assume will end in failure. For my father's guests, however, marriage comes as a complete surprise. They're all asking the same thing: *What does this mean for his heir?*

"Isaac, it's so wonderful to see you." A tall, potbellied man calls out as he approaches. I dimly recognize him as an associate I've seen at the house a time or two, though his name, I can't recall.

"You too, sir." I nod with a smile.

Paris and Shep both take a step back and I wave them away. Now that the party is in full swing, they know what to do. My presence will be missed, but theirs won't.

"Your new stepmother is quite the pretty thing, isn't she?" the man says with a laugh.

My lips tighten, but I don't respond to the comment. Instead, I quickly down my champagne and hand it to a passing waiter. "If you'll excuse me, speaking of the couple—I have to go pay my respects."

I head one way and out of the corner of my eye, I watch as Shep and Paris head the opposite. The distinct lack of security for an event this big at the main Icari estate concerns me, yet we don't know when we'll get another chance like this.

Straightening my back, I march forward, cutting around several people obviously waiting in line to address my father and his new bride. He sees me coming. "Isaac."

"Father." I nod to him before turning to Emilia. "Emilia, you look lovely. Congratulations and welcome to the family."

While Emilia is vastly different from her daughter, the two do share the same soft brown eyes and when I lift the back of her hand for a chaste kiss to her knuckles, a light blush stains her cheeks. Very similar to Aurora, though without the caustic retort no doubt my Sunshine would respond with.

"Thank you, Isaac," Emilia says. "Your father's been so wonderful. I hope we'll get a chance to bond too."

"Of course," I reply easily. "Just let me know whenever you have free time. I'd be happy to take you to lunch."

Emilia chuckles as she takes back her hand. "I also need to thank you for taking such good care of Rori. I know she can be a little distrusting and hard to get along with, but your father tells me that you've befriended her. I can't tell you how much that means to me."

My smile falters and I slide a quick glance at my father. His face, however, reveals nothing. "Aurora is quite easy to like," I say. "There's no need for thanks."

Emilia's smile is blindingly bright, but before she can respond, my father cups his arm around her side and leans down. "I think that's enough, darling," he whispers. "We have plenty of other guests to attend to. Let the boy go—" His eyes lift to mine even as his head stays tilted towards hers. "I'm sure he'd like to spend some time with his friends and new siblings."

We lock eyes for a continued beat before I straighten away from the two of them and flash Emilia another smile. "Enjoy the rest of your party," I say.

"Thank you, Isaac." Emilia's voice follows me as I turn and head away.

In my pocket, my cell phone buzzes. I know I need to check it, but as I'm striding through the center of the ballroom, the glittering flash of Aurora's dress catches my eye again. Without a second thought, I change direction and make a beeline for her.

Her voice, lowered into a whisper, reaches me as I move closer. "I don't want to make a scene," she says.

"I don't give a fuck if you want to make a scene or not," Marcus replies. "The second I find him, I'm going to drag him outside. Obviously my last warning didn't take."

"Now, now, calm down," the older woman standing

between the two of them lifts her head and raises her brows at me. "We have company."

Marcus turns as I stop in front of Aurora. "Get the fuck away from her," he snaps as I reach out.

Aurora looks up at me, her eyes clouded with emotion. I watch them as they flit across her face. Surprise. Confusion. Fear. Resignation. My hands itch to touch her, but when I try, she takes a step back, leaning away from me as her arms come up and close around herself.

"Aurora—"

"Did you not fucking hear me?" Marcus steps between us and I clench my fingers into a fist, dropping it to my side.

"I heard you, but I was under the impression that your sister was an adult in her own right who could speak for herself." I cock my head to the side, keeping my voice cold and steady.

Still, Aurora doesn't look at me.

"Marcus." The older woman steps forward, her short choppy hair swaying above her shoulders as she takes me in. "Would you introduce us?"

Marcus keeps his mouth shut, so I sigh, reaching forward to offer a hand. "Isaac Icari."

The woman takes my hand. "Carmen Summers." The aunt, I realize. Emilia's sister.

"Nice to meet you." The words are automatic, but her smile isn't.

She tips her head to the side as I take back my hand. "Is it?"

"Excuse me?"

Carmen's eyes go from me back to Aurora and Marcus. "It seems to me that there's more to your relationship with your new step siblings than my lovely niece and nephew have told me."

Aurora finally speaks. "Aunt Carmen."

"It's alright, dear," Carmen says, keeping her tone light. "Unlike your mother, I have no intention of pressing for things you don't wish to tell me, but for you—young man—let me make something very clear." I meet her cool gaze and wait. Her smile drops away. "I advise you to respect my family to the utmost of your ability."

"I do—"

"And walking up in the middle of a private conversation and inserting yourself is not respectful," she continues, cutting me off. "It seems clear to me that my nephew" —she cuts a look at Marcus before looking back at me— "doesn't like you. You'll have to forgive him, he's quite protective of his sister."

I sigh and bow my head slightly. "I meant no disrespect, ma'am," I say. "I only wanted to check on Aurora. She..." I look past the woman to meet Aurora's flat gaze. Her chest pumps up and down in short, rapid movements. Though she tries to conceal it, her eyes keep bouncing around. She looks past me and then back again. The muscles in her arms tense and relax as she continuously tightens her hold on herself and then realizes what she's doing only to do it all over again. "She hasn't answered my calls lately."

"*Good*, take that as a sign," Marcus snaps.

Carmen arches a brow at me. The intensity of her gaze is brutal. Unlike her sister, I feel as though she's seeing through me, picking me apart with nothing more than a look. After another beat of silence, she looks to Aurora and does the same. Finally, she seems to come to a decision.

"Marcus, I think it's time I go say my congratulations to my sister," she says, taking a step out from between Aurora and me. "Walk with me?"

Marcus gapes at her and then, glancing around to make sure no one is listening, he leans closer. "You're not seriously going to leave her alone with him, are you?"

"He has a point," Carmen replies with a shrug. "Aurora is a grown woman, and I highly doubt that he'll try anything untoward here in a room full of people."

Marcus curses under his breath before turning back to the woman in question. As if sensing her aunt's resolve, Aurora sighs and shakes her head. "Just go," she says. "It's fine."

Her brother clenches his hands into fists before turning away. His shoulder smacks into mine as he passes, pausing for only a moment to whisper his last warning. "Make no mistake," he hisses into the side of my face. "I don't care who your father is. If you hurt her, I'll make you wish for death."

42

RORI

I'll make you wish for death... Well, at least I know my brother isn't a complete asshole. Not if he's willing to threaten Isaac Icari like that on my behalf. I'm still mad at him, but it makes the anger in me ease somewhat. He doesn't look at me as he stomps off with Aunt Carmen, and I'm left to my own devices with none other than the product of my darkest wet dreams and nightmares.

I sigh and slowly lower my arms. "What do you want, Isaac?" I came in here tonight expecting to throw my head back and brazen my way through yet another bullshit wedding reception. Faced with Eric Wood's arrival, however, I probably sound far more tired than I was hoping to be the next time I saw Isaac.

"I want to know what Eric Wood did to you."

My insides contract with shock. My lips part and my eyes snap to his. Intense. That's the only word I can use to describe his expression. Now that there's no one around us to pay attention, he's relaxed into the perfect facade. Now, he looks ready to kill someone.

"That's none of your damn business," I say.

"Anything about you is my business," he retorts.

I snort. "I'm honestly shocked you don't already know. I would've assumed you and your father had done your research."

"My research wasn't as in depth as you'd have thought," he replies. "I could find out, but I don't want to. I want *you* to tell me yourself."

He wants me to tell him, myself? Why? Because it's by far another piece of proof that he owns me? What the hell is with his obsession? I shake my head. I genuinely don't understand it.

"How did we get here, Isaac?" I ask, truly curious. "At the start of all of this, you were tormenting me. The rumors. The video." I stop and swallow around a tight throat. My hands clench into fists. "You found that video but you don't know why it happened?"

"The why wasn't important then."

I laugh, but it's anything but amused. "But it is now?" My voice raises an octave. "No." I shake my head again. "You're giving me whiplash, Isaac. I don't know what changed things. I wouldn't think sex would do that to a guy—certainly not a guy like you."

"A guy like me is full of insecurities, Aurora," he says. My skin comes alive as he steps closer. The low timbre of his voice rolls over my flesh. "I might not seem like it, but I'm actually quite simple. I have my own fears just like everyone else. The difference is that I've been taught to hide those fears. To bury them until no one could possibly unearth their remains."

I lift my face and feel my lashes brush my skin as I tip my head back to keep my gaze on his. "So?" I prompt him. "What's changed?"

"You," he says. "You changed me." He hovers,

blocking out the rest of the room and the light. Despite the fact that I know where we are, he always seems to make me feel like we're alone. Like I'm the only one in the room with him.

"How did I change anything?" I wish I could swallow the words right back up. Take them away and pretend like they never escaped. To ask him for answers feels like I'm asking for more.

Isaac's breath brushes over my face. Hot. "I wish I could pinpoint one exact thing, Aurora," he says. "I wish I could give you the answer you seek, but I can't. All I know is that you're like fire to a man dying in the arctic. I've been cold for so long. I want your warmth."

I shiver at his words. A pang in my chest makes my whole body lean into him. This is not the place to have this conversation, but then again, Isaac has never been the type to conform to anyone's expectations—save for maybe his father.

The reminder of Damien has me glancing to the side, past Isaac as I scan the room. My eyes widen when I spot Eric Wood standing before my mother and Damien. My lips part in surprise. For once, my mother's smile falters. She recoils from Eric as he extends a hand to Damien, who takes it with what appears to be the most genuine of expressions I've ever seen on the man. Smugness. Victory.

His head lifts even as Eric seems to be chattering on. Damien assesses the room and I know exactly who he's looking for when his eyes meet mine and lock. The corner of his mouth tilts up. *He* invited Eric Wood. I feel fucking sick.

Is it a warning? Is it something else? Any of the onlookers who don't know my history would assume that Damien is simply playing the jealous, prideful new husband—rubbing his marriage in the face of my mother's ex.

"Aurora?" Isaac looks back and follows the direction of my gaze. Damien tips his head down in response and I feel Isaac's body stiffen at the silent, barely there acknowledgment.

Fucking bastard. My limbs begin to shake. They tremble with barely repressed rage. *How fucking dare he?*

Isaac turns back to me and pushes me further towards the back of the room until my view of Damien and my mother and Eric fucking Wood is disrupted. "Don't," he hisses. "Don't look at him."

How can I not? He ruined my fucking life. My childhood. My mother never forgave me—she might act like she gives a shit, she might have divorced him after everything went down, but after Eric, she stayed away longer and longer. At first, it was just weekends alone, then extended weeks, months, holidays ... Marcus was away at college, and I ... I was left to bear the brunt of the local scorn. Eric never even got jail time. She thought it was good enough to divorce him.

No. Even prison wouldn't have been enough for me.

Isaac lifts his hand and touches my side. I jerk in response, but he doesn't release me as a normal person would. Of course not. Isaac is anything but normal. "What do you want, Aurora?" he asks, lowering his voice. "Do you want him gone?"

I swallow, my throat suddenly dry. "Why?" I demand, my voice coming out harsher than I intend. "Are you offering to get rid of him for me?"

"Yes." One word. That's all it takes for the whole of my attention to return to him. I stare up into his eyes, dark and wicked. Midnight deviousness reflects back at me.

My lips part but I don't speak. Instead, I inhale a breath and another and another until I feel like I'm so full of air that I could fly away.

"He bothers you." It's not a question, so I don't answer it. I exhale as Isaac's hand moves down my arm to my elbow and then even further to my hand. "Come with me."

I shouldn't. I know I shouldn't, but when he takes my hand and pulls me with him, I go. Isaac leads me around the edges of the ballroom, behind potted plants and tables stacked high with catered food and large luxurious ice sculptures. At first, I think he doesn't actually mean for us to leave the room and he's just planning to get me somewhere within the confines of this horrible place—still close and yet unseen by others.

Surprisingly, though, that's not his plan. Isaac takes me to a side door I hadn't noticed before and as a waiter comes out with a tray laden with drinks, he catches the edge with his hand and holds it open before pulling me inside. We don't stop there. Together, we make our way through the back hallway and then into an open kitchen.

The sharp jarring sound of dishes clinking together and pans being yanked off of burners, dumped, and then tossed into a sink full of water—the heat sizzling and steaming up the space as it hits—is so different that it makes me jump. Isaac doesn't give me room to pause. He keeps going, gently tugging me along until we're out of the kitchen and into another small hallway.

We move so fast, taking so many turns, that I know without him, I'll be lost in this house. I'm dizzy. My stomach is churning and my head hurts. I was so confident when I first came here but seeing Eric again—I shut my eyes as they begin to burn.

Pretty girl ... so soft ... shhh, don't make a sound. No one has to know what you like. I can make you feel so good. Just lay there and let me—

"Aurora." Isaac's voice jerks me out of the old nightmare that passes through my head and I realize we've stopped moving and are now in a quiet, study of some kind.

The lights are off, but the vast floor-to-ceiling windows behind a massive desk on the other side of the room face out towards the front of the house, where I can see the distant fountains and their odd statues. From here, they look like monsters, even the man with wings. The light from the outside glows, spilling into the otherwise darkened room.

"Why did you bring me here, Isaac?" I ask. "I hope it's not to apologize. What's the point anymore? You're never going to tell me the truth."

"If I did, would you stop fighting me?" I blink at his question, shocked by the insinuation that he'd even give me the slightest bit of hope for the truth.

"I..." Would I? If Isaac tells me the truth does that mean I'm finally giving in to whatever is going on between us? That I'm going to follow him and trust him?

"You can't even give me an answer," he says, sounding more tired than anything else. "That's why I can't give you what you want, Aurora. Sunshine..." His hands land on my shoulders and I finally look up at him. His expression is twisted. His brows practically meet the crease forming between them. His fingers are cold on my skin. There's a visible war going on inside of him. It's strange. A heavy weight settles in my chest.

"I'm mad at you." It's a confession.

In the dark, his lips twist into a weary grin. "I know."

My heart picks up pace. Speeding through my chest until I swear it's going to rip itself free and escape through my ribcage.

"Isaac..." His head dips. I shouldn't. Fuck me, but I know I shouldn't. I just can't help it. I tilt my face towards his and when his lips touch mine, pure, liquid lightning fills me. It spills through my system. Alive. Spreading. Latching onto every blood cell to be carried through the rest of my body until I'm entirely consumed by the feeling.

His lips move over mine, light at first and then firmer as he grows impassioned. His hands move over me, cupping my back, sliding down. My mouth opens and his tongue invades. Warm metal clicks against my own tongue and I jerk. I'd forgotten entirely about the piercing.

Isaac pulls away but keeps me near, his hands refusing to give me any room. "Do you like that, goddess?" he asks. "The sign of your marking?"

I'm panting. Hot. Dizzy. I swear Isaac Icari makes me feel like I'm in an eternal descent. I'm falling. Dying. Grasping at the air with nothing to hold onto. He's like a sickness I can't escape. A drug.

Several heartbeats pass without an answer. I extract myself from him, removing his hands from my skin when they become too much to bear and it's clear he won't do it himself. Being so close makes it hard to think. *He* makes it hard to think.

"You need to tell your mother to leave him."

My heart drops at those words and I look up at him quickly. His face has fallen back into that mask, though. Unreadable. "Did you..." A wash of cold air falls over my spine. The hairs on the back of my neck rise. "Did you bring me here—did you kiss me just to ask me that?"

He doesn't say anything immediately, but that's all the answer I need. I laugh. It's just too fucking funny. It really is.

"Oh, you almost fucking had me, you asshole."

"Aurora—"

"No!" I snap, jerking away from him when he reaches for me again. "Don't fucking touch me." I'm a damn idiot. I should've known better. This was all just another manipulation. "You don't fucking care about me," I accuse. "You just wanted me to think you did, so I'd do whatever you want."

"*No.*" He growls out the word and advances on me. I stumble back, my heels catching on the area rug beneath our feet. A gasp escapes my lips, but hard, broad hands grab onto my hips, stopping my fall before it even completes. "I've never faked what I feel about you," he murmurs, lowering his head. "I do fucking care, Aurora— Rori ... please."

"Fuck you!" I snap. "Where the fuck do you think you get the right to tell me what to do?"

"You want her to anyway," Isaac continues, ignoring my question. "Now is the time. Before it's too late."

"Are you going to tell me why?" I press.

He looks away. *No, of course not.*

I shove against his chest, wanting his hands off of me. "I am not one of your goddamn lackeys, Isaac!" The anger takes over and I shove him again. All of it fills me, pouring into my veins. "You don't get to order me around without giving me answers. You don't get loyalty without loyalty. You probably couldn't even manage to be loyal to one woman if you tried."

I push and push until his back hits one of the book-shelves along the side of the room. The second his spine hits it, he suddenly grabs me and spins the two of us. The room tilts and my own back hits the shelves as we switch positions and he presses into me, his face shadowed by the lack of light as he leans down against me.

"*I am loyal,*" he hisses in my ear. "The second I knew you were mine, my loyalty became unquestionable—don't you ever fucking question that. Ever since I fucked this sweet pussy"—My breath catches and I arch up onto my toes as his hand moves down the front of my dress to cup me right through the fabric—"it became the only thing I wanted."

Damn him. "Well, you can't fucking have it."

"Oh, I can, baby." Isaac covers me entirely, my chest to his. My hands snap down to his wrist as I try to shove his fingers away from that place. He doesn't let me. Instead, he captures both of my hands, crossing them over at the wrist, and pins me back against the shelves. Once he's sure I'm immobile, his fingers return to my body.

He moves down as I squirm against him, cursing and fighting even as the heat of his palms gets hotter. He moves down to the hem of my dress and pushes it up, his fingers stroking the soft skin of my thighs. I gasp and wiggle.

"No—stop!"

"You know what's funny?" he asks, the question confusing in the already overwhelming mix of emotions pouring through me. "That first night—when I pinned you to the ground in the parking lot, when you tried to run. You freaked out on me. Lost your shit, but now... you're not."

I freeze as his words penetrate my brain. His fingers

continue their path despite my lack of response. His thumb strokes right between my legs, over my cloth covered pussy. I hate to admit that I'm already wet. Angry and horny. Confused and ... distraught.

He's right, I realize. I'm not panicking. I blink up at him. In fact, I haven't panicked like that with him since. *Why is that?*

As if he hears my internal thoughts, Isaac leans down, brushing his lips along the top of my ear just lightly enough to make me shiver. "Whether you can admit it to yourself or not, Sunshine, you want me," he whispers as he continues to stroke me. Up and down, back and forth until I know my panties are soaked through. "You're not scared of me. Your body trusts me, even if your mind doesn't."

"Y-you seem real sure of yourself, don't you?" I gasp as he pulls my panties to the side and his fingers make their way against my flesh without that thin barrier. I rock up onto my toes again as he inserts the first finger, all the way to the knuckle. "Fuck!"

"There you are, Sunshine." Isaac's voice dips lower. Deeper. Darker. I whimper as he withdraws his finger and another joins it. Two fingers thrust into my pussy, curling against my insides as my juices weep down the inside of my thighs.

It's filthy and vile and it feels so fucking good.

"I fucking hate you, Isaac Icari." The words are cruel, meant to hurt. I hope they stab into him like daggers. I hope he bleeds.

They don't—however—stop his movements. Instead, they seem to rile him up even further. He adds a third finger, stretching my opening as he fucks me with his hand. His thumb strokes over my clit and I gasp, gritting my teeth as the sound erupts from me.

"No, *nonono*." I shake my head back and forth as he breathes into my ear, his hand moving faster and faster. He presses down on my clit as he fucks me with his fingers—slamming up into me until I swear my feet leave the floor every time he thrusts in. I bite down on my lower lip, forcing back the moans that threaten my sanity. They pile up inside my mind.

Sparks dance under my skin. Violence sings in my blood. I hate him. I want him. Fucking Isaac Icari is the goddamn devil.

"Come on, Sunshine." At his urging, my hips start to rock against him. I can't stop it. My body has left all sense of dignity behind. All of my self respect has fled in favor of the sensations coursing through me as Isaac's fingers fill me to the brim. I close my eyes on the next upward thrust as the world explodes around me.

My lips part and a groan fills the space between us. Low and long, I shudder as my orgasm overcomes me. I never thought it was possible to come just from a man's fingers, but I'm starting to realize that a lot of things are possible with Isaac where they wouldn't be with others. The power with which he controls me is god-like. Dangerous.

I scream as his thumb slides over my clit again and instead of coming down from the first part of my release, I'm sent screaming into another one. Isaac slams his lips against mine to muffle the sound, swallowing my screams as I come apart under his ministrations.

My eyes roll back in my head and I shiver and shake against him. His tongue fills my mouth as his fingers fuck me into oblivion. I'm burning alive. He set me on fire and poured on the gasoline. It's so good, it hurts. Tears leak out the sides of my eyes. I'm sure it's ruining my makeup, but I don't care. I'm drooling, sopping. A wet mess. Certainly not something any man would find attractive, but Isaac laps it up. He drains me of everything and eats it. Devouring me like a starving man.

When I've come down from the high of my second orgasm, I'm panting, my chest heaving up and down as I try to suck in all the oxygen that seemed to escape me in the last several minutes. I'm dimly aware of the fact that his fingers are still inside of me, that his hand is still between my thighs. Isaac carefully pulls free, and I wince as he leaves my body. My thighs are soaked and uncomfortably trembling as he lifts his hand.

The glint of the window's light as his fingers hover between us makes my whole body flush with heat when I realize they're absolutely covered in my wetness. He doesn't hesitate. Isaac locks his eyes with mine and then slowly brings them to his lips. He sucks each one, individually, into his mouth, licking them clean.

"You taste like fucking nirvana, Aurora."

I'm going to do it, I realize. More tears prick at my eyes as I shut them. Slowly—gently—he releases me. My hands drop back to my sides and his fingers find my hips to keep me upright. I'm trembling like a newborn calf.

"Shhhh." Isaac pulls me into his body, offering his warmth. His hand touches the back of my head, stroking through my hair. I sniff hard. He's probably getting my cum in my hair. I snort. What a stupid thing to think of. "Are you okay?" he asks, leaning back.

I turn away from him and wipe a finger under each of my eyes, brushing away the lightly smeared makeup. "I still don't trust you, Isaac," I say, "and whatever I tell my mom has nothing to do with you."

"But you agree that she needs to get away from him?"

I don't answer him. I don't even look at him. I half expect him to stop me. To force a response when I turn away. He doesn't stop me. He doesn't say a word as I head towards the door, open it and step out into the hallway.

Don't look back, Aurora, I tell myself. *Just keep walking.*

Even as I do, though, my chest feels like it's caving in on itself. That fire from earlier is all but burned out, and I was right.

I fell. He pushed me over the edge and I fell fucking hard.

43
ISAAC

Aurora's tears make me feel like the worst kind of shit in the world. Like scum that isn't even fit to touch the bottom of her shoes. I anchor my hands on my hips as I rock back and stare up at the ceiling, not really seeing it.

I hurt her. Let her believe that everything that happened here tonight was another manipulation. I could have told her the truth, a part of me wants to. It would be easier, but then she'd be in far more danger. If she knows what Damien is planning, then she's as good as dead and I'll be the one who signed her death warrant.

My phone buzzes again in my pocket. I can't say how many times I felt the damn thing move in my pants as I'd fucked her with my fingers against the bookcase, but I'd ignored it all in favor of watching her body come apart under me. This time there's nothing to distract me. I yank it out, swipe the green button and put it to my ear.

"Isaac."

"We have a problem." Shep's hard tone is enough to get my ass moving.

"Where are you?" I leave the study and step out into the hall.

"Left wing," he states. "Third floor. You were right." I turn at the end of the hall, towards the emergency staircase I know is beyond the door at the end.

"He held a meeting?"

"Not exactly," Shep hedges. "Paris went back to the party to make sure he was staying put—you weren't answering your phone."

"Sorry," I mutter, picking up the pace. "Something came up with Aurora."

"Yeah, well, I figured that to be the case."

"What did you find?"

Shep blows out a breath. "I can't explain over the phone. You'll have to see when you get here."

"Alright, I'll be there soon."

"I'll be out in the hall waiting," he says. "Unless someone comes. Keep a low profile, but make it quick."

"On my way." I hang up the call and slam into the emergency staircase exit. My feet pound stairs as I take them two at a time. I reach the third floor in no time, but I'm all the way on the opposite side of the house. Once I'm in the hallway, I slow my pace, scanning and pausing at each intersection.

No one appears to be up here and even the sound from the party doesn't reach these quarters. Still, it's better to be safe than sorry. Once I finally reach the third floor, left wing, I spot a figure hovering outside of a door towards the opposite end.

Shepherd.

His face is etched into a dark mask. "I'm here," I say as I approach.

He nods and turns towards the door he's standing in

front of. He pauses for a moment, drawing in a breath before turning the handle and leading me inside. I stop in the doorway as he takes a step to the side to reveal the contents.

"Fucking ... Christ."

"Yeah," Shep says. "My exact sentiments."

"Did you open them?" I take a step closer to the containers. There are at least a dozen of them. Large holes drilled into the tops of wooden crates lined up on the other side of the room.

When Shep doesn't answer, I look back at him. His gaze trails across the room to the furthest container. The answer is sitting right there—the top pried off and set to the side, on top of the box next to it. He grits his teeth.

"I don't know what we're going to do with this, man."

As I move towards it, I curse internally. I have a distinctly awful gut feeling as I approach, as if I know exactly what I'm going to find. The revelation inside turns my stomach. My fingers curl over the opening, tightening as the wood digs into my palms.

A small girl—a fucking child—lays in the crate, curled into a ball, her lashes fluttering as her eyes move back and forth behind closed lids. I look from the girl to the wires attached to her arm, a large bag dripping clear liquid into the tube attached to her hangs from the side of the crate. Drugs. No doubt to keep her asleep until she can make it to her owners. In her other arm, a similar tube is attached and a second bag hangs next to the first. Water? Nutrients? How fucking long can a human survive in a crate like this?

A thousand thoughts race through my mind. No doubt the rest of these crates are filled with others. We can't leave them ... but we can't extract them. To do so would put all of us at risk. There are likely others.

"That arrogant ass..." I grit out. How fucking cocky is he to think he can bring this into his own estate? The answer: extremely.

"I've already taken pictures," Shep says. "You can send them to your Fed friend."

I shake my head. I'm not stupid. "Pictures can't do shit for these girls," I say. "By the time he gets them, they'll be long gone."

"So what do you want to do?"

I don't know. *Fuck!* I have to think. *What do I do?* My hands squeeze the rim of the crate harder. A splinter stabs into my palm. I hardly even feel it beyond the rage consuming me. I take a step back, turning away from the box.

"Close it up," I snap through gritted teeth.

Shep stares at me. "Dude, are you serious?"

"Do you have a better plan?" I demand. "We can't get caught or no one can help them. Releasing them puts everyone at risk."

"So you're just going to let them go?"

I shake my head. "No." I breathe through my nose. "We'll go back to the party—show our faces. I've got some bugs and trackers in my car. Text Paris. Have him grab them. We'll mark each of these boxes. I'll give Agent Brown the tracking information and we'll let him handle the rest."

Shep continues to look at me, but I can't even meet his gaze. He moves past me and my body tenses. He lifts the crate's lid back into place, the wood creaking. Unsurprising, the girl inside doesn't make a sound. Vomit threatens to come up my throat. Behind me, Shep slams something into the crate's lid, likely making sure it's solid and that it won't be revealed that someone's already opened it.

I move towards the door, but Shep's words give me pause. "You knew he was planning something," he reminds me. "You told us it was trafficking."

My head lowers as my hand lands on the doorknob. "Yeah," I say. I look back at him. "It's one thing to *know*, but it's an entirely different thing to see it for myself." There's no more denial. I thought I'd long left hope that Damien was better than I expected in the past but apparently not.

Disgust rolls through me. Knowing his blood runs through my veins makes me feel sick down to my bone marrow.

"We'll help them, man. We'll set them free." Shep's words are meant to be an assurance. Instead, I take them as a vow.

Whatever Damien Icari does, I swear to myself—and to whatever Gods are left in this forsaken world—I will fucking stop him. Even if it kills me.

44
RORI

The first person I see upon my return to the ballroom is none other than my mother. Thankfully, her new husband is not at her side when she spots me and hurries my way. I glance over her shoulder, searching the room to see if Isaac has returned, but I don't see him. Another figure I don't see is Eric. Good. Maybe he left. I can only hope so.

"Rori!"

I swallow and straighten my shoulders, pasting on a bright smile as my mother approaches. "Mom."

Her brows pinch together and when she reaches for me, I subtly move back to keep her from automatically trying to enfold me in a hug. "I've been searching everywhere for you, darling," she says. "Where have you been?"

"Fixing my makeup," I half-lie. I'd ended up stopping by the bathroom on the way back—after finding one of the employees to lead me since I did, in fact, get lost. At least it gave me the opportunity to pull myself together and fix the mess that my face was after what happened with

Isaac. "Was there something you needed? I'm sure Aunt Carmen could've helped you."

"I thought you might've left," she says, biting her lower lip. "I wanted you to know that I didn't invite Eric. I had no idea he'd be here."

Her words seem sincere, and for a change, they actually make the pain in my chest ease. At least she's not that far gone as a mother. My shoulders slowly lower and I nod. "I know, Mom," I say quietly.

Her lips press together and she folds her hands in front of her, the knuckles whitening as she tightens her grip. "I can't believe Damien would invite him," she confesses. "I'm *so* sorry. I don't even know why he came in the first place."

She shakes her head as if she can't believe it, but I can. Damien is a controlling bastard and he's vindictive. At least, that's what this little action of his has proven to me. He's angry that I didn't conform to his desires and he wanted to see a reaction, no doubt. Damien can't outwardly punish me or he risks upsetting my mother, but he still wanted to do something. It wouldn't have taken a genius to delve into my background and that of my mom's ex-husbands to find out that there are issues between Eric and me.

Eric Wood, for his part, is a pompous asshole. Marcus might have beat the shit out of him, and my mother might've divorced him, but he still eventually got away with it. There was no trial. Only rumors. Only speculations. A man can survive under that. A fifteen-year-old girl, though? Yeah, no one fucking believed me. No one but my family.

When silence stretches between us, my mother unclasps her hands and touches my shoulder. "I'm sure

Damien was just jealous or something—you know how men can get. I hope you can forgive him."

Jealous? Yeah. Maybe. Doubtful, though. Damien Icari knows exactly what he was doing when he invited Eric Wood to his reception. The Icari men have a way of twisting their actions to make everyone around them play right into the palms of their hands. Unfortunately, I'm no exception.

"Actually, Mom, I wanted to talk to you about him."

"About Eric?"

I shake my head. "No, about Damien."

"Damien?" she repeats, her brows lowering as her lips pucker.

"Yes." I look around. "Is there somewhere we can talk privately?"

My mother frowns down at me. "What's this about?"

"I'd really rather discuss it somewhere else. Not here," I hedge, wincing when a couple passes by with glasses in hand. They smile and pause to congratulate my mom on her recent marriage. I'm forced to stand back and watch the shift come over her. Her confused expression disappears quickly and she smiles brightly, laughing as she thanks them and tells them to enjoy themselves.

It's only once they're gone that she turns back to me and the facade drops away. "I'll make sure Damien knows that Eric isn't to be invited to anything ever again," she states. "So, please don't worry, darling. We don't need to make it a big thing."

"It's not about Eric," I repeat through gritted teeth. "It's about *Damien*. Forget Eric."

My mother blows out a breath. "Do we really have to do this here?" Her tone turns pleading. She reaches out and touches my hand, holding it in hers. "If you have any issues with him, I'm sure I can talk to him, but can we discuss it later? Maybe you, me, and Carmen can go for a girl's day?"

"No—Mom—" I flip my hand over and grasp hers tighter when she tries to pull away. "It needs to be now. You need to know—"

"Know what?" I freeze as the semi-familiar deep voice intrudes, interrupting my next words.

Damien Icari appears out of nowhere, like a monstrous creature sliding out of the shadows. He steps up right behind my mom and slides a hand around her waist, pulling her back into his chest with such a quick movement that her hand is ripped from mine before I realize what's happening.

"Damien!" My mother giggles gleefully. The sound makes my insides churn, and I have to resist the urge to reach for her and yank her away again.

"I missed you, dear," Damien says, dipping his head towards her throat. Despite the fact that his body covers her, that his arms encircle her, his eyes remain on mine.

My mother laughs again. "We were just together," she says.

"Seconds are far too long to be apart from you," he says.

Liar. I narrow my gaze at him. The dark look each of us gives the other is interrupted by none other than my mother as she smiles and turns, her white dress swirling around her legs as she lifts her hand to his face and strokes his cheek. Damien's eyes immediately go to her.

How can she not see it? The lies. The deception. Why? I don't understand. Does she want love so badly that she allows herself to be controlled by such a man?

Two figures step into my line of sight, right over

Damien and my mother's shoulders. Isaac. He's back, but this time, he's different. His face is pale as he readjusts his suit coat. His friend, the taller one—Shep—is at his side, a similar expression of abject discomfort on his face as well.

I can't stand it anymore. All this fakeness. My mother's own naiveté. It's pathetic. It's depressing. It can't go on. Fine. If she only believes lies ... then lies she'll get. I know it'll hurt, but maybe ... it's better than the alternative.

I blurt out the worst thing I can think of, the one thing that I know she couldn't bear from a partner and the reason many of her marriages in the past had fallen apart. "He's cheating on you."

Four words. I'm not even sure if they're true or not. I don't expect that Damien would be a loyal man. He'll do anything to get what he wants. Just like his son. Neither of them can be believed, but one thing is for sure, this marriage can't continue. And there's one surefire way to get my mother to question everything she knows about a man.

"What?" My mother's hand falls away from Damien's face and his jaw goes slack with shock. She turns to me as I clench my hands into fists at my side.

Like a record scratching, the nearby surroundings come to a halt. My words hadn't been a shout, but they certainly hadn't been quiet either. The room is too big for everyone to have heard my claim. But every head in the vicinity has turned our way as if they're sharks sensing freshly spilled blood.

"He's not loyal," I say, more confidently. "You think he loves you, but he doesn't. He's just using you."

My mother blinks at me, her eyes watering slightly. The hurt on her face makes me ache, but it's for the best.

"Emilia." Damien tries to reach for her.

She blinks rapidly, reaching up quickly to wipe away the evidence of her sudden tears. When Damien's hand touches her arm, she jerks away. She stumbles and I jump forward, catching her before she can fall.

"No." Despite my words, she shakes her head and turns to look at me. "No. Aurora, darling. You must be mistaken. Do you have..." Proof? No. I don't. But I've sown the seed of doubt and that's all that matters.

"I'm sorry, Mom," I say instead of answering her unspoken question.

A glittering of tears lingers on her lashes. Damien's expression darkens when he looks back at me. "She's lying," he growls. "Emilia, you can't truly believe that I would ever—"

"I-I need a moment..." My mother bites down on her lower lip as she cuts him off and once again avoids his touch when he moves toward her.

"I wanted to tell you in private," I say, making it up as I go along. "I didn't want to say it like this, but—"

"Please, Aurora." She lifts her hand, stopping me. "Not now." Her head pops up and she glances around. "Carmen? Where's Carmen?"

"Emmy?" As if she was waiting for precisely this moment, Aunt Carmen appears with Marcus at her back.

My mother leaves me and lurches towards her. I watch her go, feeling bereft and helpless. It was cruel but necessary, I tell myself. Whatever it was, though, I don't have long to contemplate it because as Carmen's arms go around her, my mother stumbles from the room. Carmen looks back with a frown creasing her brow. The moment she's out of earshot, a hard hand grabs my arm, roughly jerking me to the side.

"You little fucking cunt," Damien snaps, his voice lowering.

A sharp pain squeezes my bicep as he squeezes to the point of twisting my skin in his grip. I resist wincing in pain as I glare up at him. "Is that mask of yours finally dropping?" I taunt him.

"You have no idea what you've just done," he says.

"I saved my mother from a man like you," I reply. "I know exactly what I've done."

His grip tightens further until I can't hide my grimace. Damien leans in, dropping his voice until only I can hear. Even as Marcus approaches, his expression raging—Damien speaks, "You just earned yourself my wrath, little girl," he says, "and I assure you, the wrath of a man such as me is not to be taken lightly."

I recoil from him, and when I pull my arm from his grasp, he lets go. "I'm not afraid of you," I snap.

"Rori." Marcus steps between us as Damien arches a brow at him once before returning his attention to me.

Damien looks like he wants to say something, but instead of doing so, he merely straightens his suit coat and then turns away, striding off with his head held high like the blue blood that he is.

Marcus and I both watch him. My arm aches and when I glance down, I note the red marks that will, no doubt, grow darker over time.

"Are you okay?" Marcus asks. Before I can answer he glances around and gently takes me by the shoulders to turn me towards the exit. "Come on, let's talk outside."

I look back, scanning the room for Isaac, but he's gone. I don't see him at all. Or his friends—either of them. Marcus pushes me towards the exit and out into the hallway.

"What the hell did you say to him?" Marcus barks, distracting me. "What did you say to Mom?"

My heels click along the hard floor of the corridor as we head back the same way we came at the beginning of the night. I sigh. "I told her that Damien was cheating on her," I admit.

Marcus jerks to a stop, but when I keep walking, he hurries to catch up. "He is?"

I shrug. "I don't know," I say. "Maybe. Probably."

Marcus is quiet for a moment as I head towards the coat check. He doesn't say anything as I retrieve my coat from the lady behind the counter and then he does as well. In fact, he stays silent until we reach the abandoned front porch of the mansion.

"So, you lied to her?" Marcus clarifies. "You told her that Damien was cheating on her to get her to divorce him?"

I pull my coat closer and wrap my arms around myself. "I don't know that she'll divorce him over what I said," I reply. "I don't have any proof, and while I can't believe that Damien really loves her, without proof, she won't have a real reason to leave him."

Marcus stares at me. I can feel the heat of his gaze against the side of my face, but I don't turn to meet his gaze. "Then what was the point?" he asks.

"To sow doubt," I tell him. "Maybe he isn't cheating. Maybe he is." I tilt my head up to the night sky, gazing out past the two statues on either side of the round drive-way. "Either way, she won't be able to stop thinking about it now. It will always be in the back of her mind for however long they're together. Every time he goes away—every time he has to work—she'll wonder to herself."

"Rori ... that's—" Marcus is interrupted by a valet's approach.

"Do you need your vehicle, sir?" the man asks.

Marcus starts to shake his head, but pauses to look back at me. For a long moment, neither of us says a word, and then Marcus looks back to the man and nods. "Yeah, here." He withdraws a ticket from his pocket and hands it off.

Once again, we drift into silence. Finally, he speaks. "Rori. Mom is going to find out that you weren't honest."

"Is she?" I ask. "When are we ever honest with each other—her and I?"

"I know you and her don't get along, but—"

"What?" I pivot to face him. "What do you know about whether or not we get along?" I demand, following it up with my own answer. The real answer. "Nothing," I say. "You don't know shit about our relationship because you haven't been around. Then, when I finally move closer to you—you leave. Are you running away from me? From her? Us?"

He shakes his head. "That's not fair."

"No," I agree. "Life isn't fair. Doesn't matter."

"My point is," he says, "we could've talked to her together—told her the truth and told her that he was using her. We could've—"

"She won't listen," I say, stopping whatever other excuse he's got. He still doesn't get it. Even if he's been away for four years, he should know our mother just as well as I do. "She only hears what she wants to hear," I tell him, "and I don't think we have the time to wait around for the honeymoon phase to fade out."

"Why? What do you know?"

"It doesn't matter anymore," I reply as Marcus' rented

SUV comes around the drive, the lights flashing as it turns. "What's done is done. It can't be taken back."

"Rori—" I leave him behind even as he calls for me and descend the stairs. The valet gets out of the car and leaves the driver's side door open. Marcus' footsteps pound against the stairs behind me as I round the front of the vehicle. I have no intention of waiting for him. "Hey! Rori!"

I get into the driver's side and hit the lock button just as he slams into the door, gripping the handle and trying to rip it open before I drive off. I'm calm—probably far too calm for the riot of emotions cascading through me. My seatbelt clicks into place and I slap the button on the driver's side door to roll the window on the passenger side down. It's just enough to see and hear Marcus cursing, but not enough for him to reach inside and unlock the door.

"Catch a ride with Aunt Carmen," I say. "Or call a car, I don't care."

"You can't run away from this, Rori," he snaps. "We need to talk about this. I'm not saying she doesn't need to leave that bastard, but you should've told me before you decided to do anything."

"Like you told me you were moving to Eastpoint in advance?" I retort.

"I did tell you," he argues.

"With very little notice," I remind him, "after knowing that I was coming to Hazelwood for months."

He slaps his palm on the window and the car shudders under the violent onslaught. I don't even blink. Behind him, the valet that brought the car and his partner glance at each other. I'm sure they've seen rich people cause a lot more issues than this. This is nothing.

"Rori, open this fucking door. We need to talk."

I hit the button again and the window rolls up. My heeled foot slips over the gas and I unlock the parking brake, easing forward as Marcus scrambles along the side of the SUV. No. I'm tired of talking around in circles. With him. With Isaac. I did what I thought needed to be done.

I press down harder and Marcus' form is left behind me rather than along the side of the car as I circle the drive and head back up towards the gates. He stands in the center of the rearview mirror, his hands raised up as he holds his head, no doubt cursing up a storm as I drive away.

I've started the process of ending my mother's recent mistake and hopefully, in the light of day, she'll finally come to her senses. Hopefully, they all will.

45
ISAAC

"Is it done?" Even as I shoot the question at Shep, I watch Emilia Summers being led from the room by her sister. Whispers are already starting. She did it. I wasn't sure if she would, and I certainly didn't expect her to do it like this—but she's somehow managed to drive a wedge between our parents.

Relief is light in my chest but it's not alone. It's accompanied by a heavy sense of anxiety.

"Yeah," Shep answers, slipping his phone back into his pocket. "Paris is on his way back. He put tracking bugs in each of the crates. You can give your agent the info and he can find them."

At least we managed to accomplish something tonight even if the rest of the evening has been an absolute shit show. From Eric Wood's arrival to Aurora's and my little rendezvous to the girls in the crates upstairs.

"Good."

My father moves forward in the absence of Emilia, right up to Aurora. My heart drops into my stomach.

"Isaac." Shep's hand snaps out and latches onto my

arm, but I'm already moving. The second Damien's hand closes on Aurora's arm, I jolt forward. "Don't!" His voice is more whisper than shout, but I hear it pierce through my skull. It does nothing to halt the blaring unease in my head. He has to physically drag me back. I clench my hand into a fist, half tempted to reach back and punch him. "Not here," he tells me.

Here. There. It doesn't fucking matter where. He has his hands on her. My fucking father is touching what's mine and he's not being fucking gentle about it.

"She—"

"Will be fine," Shep interrupts me. "He wouldn't do anything in a room full of people. You know that."

He's right. I know he is, but my mind can't seem to catch up with that fact. All it can process is that the girl that I claim as mine—the one I want above all others for some ungodly reason is standing in front of the most dangerous man I know and I'm not between them. The only protection she currently has is the thinly veiled expectations of public interaction. That isn't enough. Hell, bulletproof glass wouldn't be enough. My insides churn with untapped anxiety. It rolls through me.

Aurora's face twists lightly, but she represses her pain and only anger shows through. I can't hear the two of them from where I am, but I know that he's saying something to her. Something threatening. She responds and then, finally, her pain shows through. Her lips tighten and she winces.

"*Fuck.*" I shove Shep away from me, and he all but tackles me as he yanks me back, pinning my arms against my sides as I try to fight back. He spins me away from the sight of Aurora and my father. Luck, unfortunately, is not on my side tonight because as I rear back, ready to slam my head into his to get him to release me, Paris appears.

"Help me, asshole!" Shep hisses, trying not to draw attention to our little fight. Considering that most of the ballroom is wholly focused on Aurora and my father, it's not hard for them to do.

"This way." Paris gestures to a side door and Shep bodily lifts me off my feet.

"Goddamn it, you fucker!" I anchor a foot against the door, but Paris moves forward and punches me right in the leg and then again in the side of the head without restraint.

"Don't be stupid," he growls, getting in my face. "If you want to make it through tonight, don't be a fucking baby, asshole."

I don't even get a chance to respond as Shep shoves me out into a back hallway. I slam into the opposite wall. An employee coming up one side of the corridor takes one look at us and turns right around, skittering off.

"He fucking touched her!" I growl, rounding on the two of them as Shep and Paris each cross their arms over their chests and stand in front of the door we just came through.

"Don't lose your fucking head, man," Paris barks. "Stay calm. He can't do anything to her out there."

"I need to make sure she's okay," I argue, marching forward.

Shep puts out a hand, stopping me. "No."

I turn away from the two of them, rage pouring through me as I shove my hands up through my hair, grabbing onto chunks of it and yanking hard even as my breath saws in and out of my chest. Paris drops his arms and steps forward.

"Go contact your agent friend," he suggests. "We'll go back in and make sure that she gets away safely."

Several beats pass. I breathe hard—in and out. In and out. "Yeah..." I release a breath. "You're right." I straighten. "Follow her, though," I snap. "I want you to make sure she gets home and in her dorm. Both of you."

Paris and Shep exchange a look. Paris is the first to speak, pointing at me with a scowl. "Don't do anything reckless," he orders. "I swear to fuck, man, don't mess this up. Too much is riding on it now. We'll go take care of the girl, but do not, under any circumstances, lose it on Damien."

I release a slow hiss through my teeth. "I got it."

Each of them looks me over, narrowing their eyes as if they're trying to sense a lie. "Fine, we'll meet you later," Shep finally agrees. "Remember, you still have access to the cameras we set up. You can check on her when you get home."

I blow out a breath, holding my body absolutely still as they gingerly step back and then turn and walk away. I don't move, not even a muscle as I listen to their footsteps recede. Only once I'm sure they're gone do I turn back to the door and shove it open. The room is louder now, people not even bothering to whisper as their combined conversations grow into a dull roar.

Cheating? I never would have guessed...
—surprised? No. How many marriages does this make?
The daughter obviously doesn't get along with Icari...
—like this are always dramatic. I never expected...

Ignoring the swirling comments that cascade around the room, I focus my intentions on looking for Aurora. I look and look, but Aurora is nowhere to be found. Neither is her brother, aunt, or mother.

My father, however, is still very much present. His expression is a barely restrained mask of civility as he stomps through the crowd. A short, suited man hurriedly follows at his side with a notebook as my father snaps orders at him. His head lifts and he meets my gaze—fury sparking in his eyes.

Fuck me. I already know—it's going to be a while before I see the guys again. Before I see Aurora again. This is going to fucking hurt.

EPILOGUE: ISAAC

Hours later…

Blood drips steadily from my temple. The soft *drip* is what wakes me out of my stupor. The movies all make it seem like one second you're unconscious and the next, you're wide awake. That's not how it actually goes. I've been beaten into unconsciousness enough to know that it's like wading in deep waters and trying to drag yourself up to the surface to wake up. Sometimes, you don't want to. It's just easier to let your attacker keep going at it while you remain blissfully unaware. I don't have that luxury. Not now.

I press my lips together to keep the groan of pain in my chest from escaping. When I do finally manage to crack my eyes open, one is so swollen that there's nothing but a slit of bare light that penetrates it. Even that small amount of light makes the inside of my skull throb. Thankfully, my other eye is still at least mostly functioning.

I scan the room, carefully seeking out the figure I

know is standing there in the dark. And as if he senses my awareness, he steps into the ring of light that illuminates the place where I hang from a heavy chain slung over the rafter's beams.

When I was a child, I was so frightened of this man. Where other children feared some imaginary monster under their beds or in their closets, I had the unfortunate circumstance of knowing mine face to face. His arrogance. His cruelty. His expectations—the ones I've never quite met.

My father places a thick rolled cigar between his lips and sighs as he leans to the side. A flame ignites in the darkness and I watch as one of his men steps forward with a lighter and burns the end until it glows cherry red. Bastard can't even light his own fucking smokes. Pathetic.

I don't know when I stopped being afraid of Damien Icari and became angrier and more resentful, but the switch was a healthy one. I can't imagine what it would have been like to live the rest of my life constantly freezing over every little thing he does. The day I stopped being scared of him was the day I'd given up on ever making him happy. It was the day he lost most of his power over me.

He's hated it ever since.

"You disappoint me, Isaac." *Shocker.* I'd roll my eyes if I had the energy. "You were supposed to watch the girl, *control her.* We had a deal—you and I."

"A deal?" I cough out the words, spitting a wad of blood directly at his feet. His gaze slides down to the congealed dark mess before it moves back to me. "Deals are only made when both parties have something to gain."

"You think you had nothing to gain?" Damien pulls the cigar from his mouth and blows out a cloud of smoke before taking a careful step over the blood I've spat on the floor. He doesn't stop until he's standing right in front of me, so close I can smell the tobacco and feel the heat of the ashy end as he pushes it right in my face. He holds the end of the cigar right over my swollen eye. A threat. A promise.

I bare my teeth at him. "Don't fucking tease me with it old man," I growl. "If you're gonna do it, then do it."

He chuckles darkly and the heat of the cigar leaves my face. "You're like a wild animal," he says. "So full of spite and anger. I thought I'd raised you better."

"Is that what you called it? Raising?" I hiss through my teeth as he reaches down and clamps a hand over my shoulder. With my knees on the cold concrete floor, even through the ripped jeans I'm wearing, it hurts.

"Pavlov had the right idea," Damien says absently. "Training and raising, it's all the same thing. Perhaps that's why you've become this way. Only, I expected a bit more loyalty. Was it the reward system?" I tilt my head up as he cocks his own to the side, contemplating his own words.

"Fuck you," I spit again. My mouth is flooded with saliva and the rusty taste of my own blood.

Damien looks down at me once more. His hand snaps out and latches onto my chin as he tilts me up further, craning my neck to force my eyes to meet his. He doesn't bend or offer to make it any easier on me. Of course not. Damien is a man that expects the world to fight for his service. To do whatever it takes to grant him his desires.

Wooing Emilia Summers is probably the most work he's ever had to put into anything and Aurora has damaged those efforts of his. As the one responsible for her, it's my duty to take this torture. Just the mere thought of Aurora in my current circumstances—her own hands bound above her head, her body beaten black and bloody, her humanity stripped bare—is enough to make me feel grateful that it's me instead.

How our relationship has changed this much, I doubt I'll ever truly understand. It was so quick, the shift. Like a light switch had been turned on and I never even knew I'd been in the dark. I am the beast and she is the sun. *My sun.*

"Aurora Summers will convince her mother to come back to me," Damien says.

I can't withhold my snort. "You can't get her to do what you want like you do everyone else." She's not controllable. Not to anyone—not even me. Despite all my asking, I know she'd only done what she did tonight because she *wanted* to. Because she saw a good reason to. Not because I'd told her to do it.

Damien's fingers grip tighter until my mouth pops open with the threat of breaking my fucking jaw. "While I respect your pride, my son, I would advise you to quell that rebellious streak of yours now and in the future."

I'd respond if I could, but he's holding me so tight that any words I might speak are a chance that I'd be spending the next few months with a jaw that's wired shut. I love talking too much—and more so, I love what my mouth can do to a certain blonde brat too much to risk that. So, for one of the few times in my life, I restrain myself.

"I don't care what you do to fix this situation I've been put in, Isaac," he states. "I don't care if you continue to fuck her, but you will do whatever is necessary to make sure I get what I want from Emilia Summers. The institution of marriage is abhorrent, I agree, but in this, our goals need to be mutual. Do I make myself clear?"

His hand releases me and allows me to speak. "Why does it even matter?" I snap. "You're just using her. You could use anyone else for what you want."

Damien tilts his head down at me. "What exactly is it that you think I want, Son?" His gaze narrows and I realize my mistake. I clamp my lips shut, but it's far too late for that. His grip slides into my hair and yanks my head back so I'm forced to stare up at him. The burning in my scalp is nothing compared to the pit of rage in my stomach, though.

"Have you been peeking where you shouldn't have been, Isaac?"

While some believe that the truth will set you free, when it comes to my father, I know better. Half-truths are safer. Deflections and distractions. "You've never hidden your dark side from me," I remind him. "I know what kind of *businesses* you run. You wouldn't marry Emilia Summers if you weren't using her for something. You told me as much yourself."

"Yes, I did, but I never told you the specifics," Damien responds. "You're starting to make me think I've allowed you too much freedom. I don't mind a little curiosity—it's natural in a young man. What I don't tolerate, however, is my own son looking into *my* private affairs on his own."

"I—" The slap comes before I can complete a sentence. The back of his hand slams into my face so hard that it whips my head to the side and sends a bolt of pain through my skull. He releases my hair and my jaw drops down as I spit out another wad of blood onto the floor at his feet. My tongue is coated in the nasty taste of rust.

"This conversation is over, Isaac," he states. Damien takes a step away from me, his pristine, Italian leather shoes making soft sounds on the concrete floor as he goes.

"Have Emilia return to me before the end of the week, or the next person to find themselves here will be someone you actually care about. Paris or Shepherd seem like good choices."

My body tightens all over and I look up as one of my father's men moves around to my back. The chains holding me up loosen as they're unlocked. My father takes one look back and smiles. "Or Emilia's daughter," he says. "If I can't have Emilia, then there's no point in saving her anymore."

No! The scream echoes in my head, but thankfully doesn't come out. I force it down, biting down on my tongue until fresh blood fills my mouth. He means it—I know he does. I can see the truth in his cold, greed-filled gaze. And he sees it, too, I realize. The truth I've tried so hard to hide.

"I warned you, Son," he says. "Women are and always will be the downfall of man."

ABOUT THE AUTHOR

Lucy Smoke, also known as Lucinda Dark for her fantasy works, has a master's degree in English and is a self-proclaimed creative chihuahua. She enjoys feeding her wanderlust, cover addiction, as well as her face, and truly hopes people will stop giving her bath bombs as gifts. Bath's get cold too fast and it's just not as wonderful as the commercials make it out to be when the tub isn't a jacuzzi.

When she's not on a never-ending quest to find the perfect milkshake, she lives and works in the southern United States with her beloved fur-baby, Hiro, and her family and friends.

Want to be kept up to date? Think about joining the author's group or signing up for their newsletter below.

Facebook Group
Newsletter
TikTok

ALSO BY LUCY SMOKE

Contemporary Series:

Sick Boys Series

Forbidden Deviant Games (prequel)

Pretty Little Savage

Stone Cold Queen

Natural Born Killers

Wicked Dark Heathens

Bloody Cruel Psycho

Bloody Cruel Monster

Vengeful Rotten Casualties

Iris Boys Series (completed)

Now or Never

Power & Choice

Leap of Faith

Cross my Heart

Forever & Always

Iris Boys Series Boxset

The *Break* Series (completed)

Break Volume 1

Break Volume 2

Break Series Collection

Contemporary Standalones:

Poisoned Paradise

Expressionate

Wildest Dreams

Criminal Underground Series (Shared Universe Standalones)

Sweet Possession

Scarlett Thief

Fantasy Series:

Twisted Fae Series (completed)

Court of Crimson

Court of Frost

Court of Midnight

Twisted Fae: Completed Series Boxset

Barbie: The Vampire Hunter Series (completed)

Rest in Pieces

Dead Girl Walking

Ashes to Ashes

Blood & Vengeance (Boxset)

Dark Maji Series (completed)

Fortune Favors the Cruel

Blessed Be the Wicked

Twisted is the Crown

For King and Corruption

Long Live the Soulless

Nerys Newblood Series (completed)

Daimon

Necrosis

Resurrection

Sky Cities Series (Dystopian)

Heart of Tartarus

Shadow of Deception

Sword of Damage

Dogs of War (coming soon)

Printed in Great Britain
by Amazon